THE DAISY CHAIN

Liz Cornforth has just turned thirty. Comfortable with her partner, Don, she can't see why everyone's suddenly putting pressure on her to marry and have children. When she discovers a photograph of a mysterious ancestor — Daisy — modelling a corset, Liz sees in the pose a wry defiance of convention, to which she is instantly drawn. Liz begins to uncover the chain of events, people and places that made up Daisy's life. Desperately striving for autonomy in her own life, Liz identifies herself with Daisy's determination to be an independent career woman in the 1920s.

Books by Sue Sully
Published by The House of Ulverscroft:

THE BLUEBELL POOL

SUE SULLY

THE DAISY CHAIN

Complete and Unabridged

ULVERSCROFT
Leicester

First published in Great Britain in 1996 by
Headline Book Publishing, London

First Large Print Edition
published 1997
by arrangement with
Headline Book Publishing, a division of
Hodder Headline Plc, London

Jacket Design by Gary Blythe

British Library CIP Data

20012046

Sully, Sue
The Daisy chain.—Large print ed.—
Ulverscroft large print series: romance
1. Women—Social conditions—History
—20th century—Fiction
2. Love stories
3. Large type books
I. Title
823.9′14 [F]

ISBN 0–7089–3819–1

F

Published by
F. A. Thorpe (Publishing) Ltd.
Anstey, Leicestershire

Set by Words & Graphics Ltd.
Anstey, Leicestershire
Printed and bound in Great Britain by
T. J. International Ltd., Padstow, Cornwall

This book is printed on acid-free paper

1

THE girl in the photograph stared back at Liz with a challenging self-assurance. She was dressed in a petticoat and corset, her hair piled high in the heavy, exuberant style of an Edwardian beauty. There was nothing overtly sexual about the image, yet there was no denying its appeal: the figure-hugging corset emphasised the girl's hips and narrow waist; her breasts were thrust forward, her bottom stuck out in the exaggerated S-shape of the day.

Liz took a mug of coffee into her office and propped the photo on the mantelshelf where she could see it. Switching on the computer and sorting through her file of corset photographs and handwritten notes, she sipped her coffee and scrolled back through the text to familiarise herself with her material before beginning the day's work. Delaying tactics. She needed time to think, but not about corsets.

Last night, prompted by the mood of

a family party, Don had suggested they get married. "It's not a sudden thing with me," he had insisted. "I love you. I want to care for you, and for us to spend the rest of our lives together and have children."

"But I'm not ready for all that yet," Liz had protested. "How could I hang around museums, take photographs, or sit for hours in libraries with a baby in my arms, or with a baby and a toddler in tow, or with children at home from school during the holidays? How does anyone even *think* with children around?"

Liz's glance took in her desk, the collection of research notes, letters and cuttings piled in a wicker in-tray, and a number of folders labelled variously: 'Manufacture', 'Injuries', 'Eroticism', 'Dress-reform', 'Subjection/Emancipation of women'. On the shelves were box-files, marked chronologically: 'Origins and Early Examples', 'The Stuarts', '17th Century — 1860', 'Late Victorian', 'Edwardian', 'The Twenties' . . . Below them were the tapes: interviews with museum curators, with women who

2

had designed and made corsets in the thirties and forties, with women who had worn corsets themselves, fitted corsets on others, or remembered their mothers' and grandmothers' corsets.

The published works on the shelves stood as testimony to her previous marathons. In the early days it had been patchwork and embroidery, a follow-on from her university research: *Embroidery for the Bedchamber*, her first; then *Quilts and Pillows, Fashions in Petticoats* . . .

The grey plastic, electronics-age word processor hummed away on the desk. That and the hiss of the fire, and the light rattle of the keyboard under her fingers were the only sounds, except for the occasional heavy rumble of a lorry passing by on the A39.

It wasn't as if she had a particular aversion to children, Don had persisted. She loved her sister Prue's kids. Even Jennifer's boys, when they were home from their respective boarding schools, had their good points. It wasn't as if she couldn't carry on with her work if they married. There were plenty of options open to them. He had enumerated them, nannies, nurseries, a joint commitment to sharing the childcare. And, because in his own mind it was so simple, he believed that he had convinced her.

She supposed she should have understood the way his mind was working, that after a period of 'personal growth', people settled down. Underneath all his easygoing amiability Don was deeply conventional.

She had misled him. She had let him think she was simply postponing the idea. But right now, it was not an aversion to babies but his words, "I want to care for you . . . the rest of our lives," that kept coming back to trouble her.

Liz's glance fell on the picture of the girl in the corset. "What did you feel about it all?" she said aloud. "Did you let yourself be bullied by convention or did you want to rebel?"

Daisy certainly looked as if she might have rebelled, dark and vivacious, with a square jaw, firm mouth and nose; there was no disputing her femininity. Her eyes were humorous, with an ironic gaze that was striking in its modernity. A smile hovered at the edges of the girl's mouth, as if she might at any moment dissolve into laughter.

The picture was mounted on grey card, and the back had been stamped with the name of a photographer and bore a pencilled inscription: 'For Wilfred, from your loving sister Daisy, July 1908'.

★ ★ ★

They had arrived at the party as her father was handing round the drinks.

Don had apologised for being late, saying with a laugh that Liz had been immersed in her research.

"That reminds me. I've got something to show you later," her father had said. "Something I found when I was going through a box of your grandfather's papers."

"Let her open her presents, Ralph," her mother had protested.

"Poor girl. It's her birthday. She doesn't want to be bothered with ancient history tonight."

"You'd never have guessed it half an hour ago. She was lost to the world," said Don. "Nothing existed except the

5

plight of the nineteenth-century woman strapped into her corsets."

Remembering, Liz wished he had not said it quite like that, throwing her a wry smile to apologise for the minor betrayal, as if he were indulging her, as if *she* had been self-indulgent by losing herself in her work. There had been a note of condescension, of proprietorship almost. She had noticed it creep in more often lately, the sort of attitude husbands took with wives, and which she had seen in her sisters' marriages.

"I should like to propose a toast," Jennifer's husband Mark had said suddenly and rather loudly as Liz struggled with a present from Prue and Peter's children, on which four-year-old Ben had been given a free hand with the Sellotape. "I should like to wish Liz a very happy birthday. And to respectfully inquire, now that you've reached the grand old age of thirty, when you and Don are going to name the wedding day and start making babies?"

It was a crass speech to have made, even for her brother-in-law, who was getting *very* drunk by the time Liz was seated next to him later at dinner. Don had passed it off with a joke, something about 'her books being her babies', and she had been grateful. After the questionable toast, Jennifer had withdrawn into a smiling impenetrability whenever her husband opened his mouth to speak. Liz felt sympathy for her, but she wished by then that the family had not planned a party. It seemed to have occurred to no one that on her thirtieth birthday — obviously judged by everyone to be a special occasion — she might have preferred to celebrate privately with her lover.

She hoped she was not now going to be regarded as a problematic 'thirty-something'. Why did everyone seem to regard this birthday as such a milestone? She did not feel any different.

Ralph had brought out the box of photographs after dinner. The pictures were mostly dog-eared and faded: women in thick dresses with frigid expressions and greasy hair, studio shots of frightened-looking children in their best clothes, men in buttoned waistcoats, unsmiling and with an air of their own importance.

Looking at portraits from another era was like entering a world of fiction. Occasionally, one came upon a character who conveyed more than a remote image; something made a connection, struck a chord of recognition. The photograph of the girl in the corset had produced an almost physical shock of understanding. Some intelligence, or sense of personality, or whatever it was that was transmitted through a person's eyes, made a link with Liz's imagination.

"She's lovely. She has such an animated expression."

"I thought you might like to keep it. A family link with your research."

"Who is she?" Turning the photograph over, Liz had read the inscription on the back. "Granddad's sister?"

Ralph said that he knew very little about his father's family and he certainly hadn't heard of a Daisy. There had been a sister called Minnie who died in the seventies, and a brother who was killed in the war; there was a cousin, who had attended his father's funeral, Liz had met him, and his wife; but he too had died recently.

Ralph began to gather up the photographs and glanced at the picture in Liz's hand. "Dad had cut himself off from the rest of his family, which makes it all the more intriguing that he should have kept that photo."

★ ★ ★

Liz stretched with her hands behind her head, pushing her hair behind her ears. She loved everything about the room where she worked: the worn green carpet; the sumptuous, red velvet curtains; the gas fire glowing in the hearth of rich, green-glazed tiles, topped by an overmantel bought for its ugliness and its glorious, cluttered overdecoration; the fake oil lamp on the vast antique desk that in the evenings cast a soft warm glow over her papers from its milky white globe. She loved the solid wall of books next to the window, the crowded pictures, the old-fashioned wicker wastepaper basket, the vases and knick-knacks, the whole phoney Victorian-Edwardian atmosphere.

She scanned the text on the screen:

9

In the nineteenth and earlier centuries marriage limited a woman to a particular role . . .

Was it fate had decreed that she should at this precise moment be working on the chapter on marriage and pregnancy? With a wry smile Liz turned to the advertisements for nineteenth-century maternity wear: sturdy support garments with broad, abdominal panels and rows of belts and buckles designed to accommodate a pregnant figure, looking more like instruments of torture.

She made a note of the illustrations she wanted to put with the text and wrote a reference for each in her notebook under the heading 'gestation stays'. The very name was off-putting.

Oh, hell, Liz thought. Everything had been fine before her birthday. Why couldn't she still be twenty-nine, instead of thirty? Why did Don suddenly have to pick up on the idea of getting married?

She realised she had read through three pages of text on the screen without understanding a word of it.

She turned again to her notes but could not concentrate.

Rejecting the idea of ringing her editor, Liz made another mug of coffee. Moira would make her feel guilty because the work was progressing so slowly. Other people chose not to understand how long it took to gather data before a book could even begin; the frustration of telephone calls channelled from one museum department to another, the weeks of correspondence, trips to museum archives, and then worrying that there was some gem of information that she had overlooked. When Liz had gone off for three weeks to take photographs, Moira had assumed she was taking a holiday, that research trips were perks. "Good idea. You have a little break," she had said reassuringly.

After a further two hours Liz still had not written anything worth saving. She walked up and down the garden in the cold to clear her head. Then, because it was almost lunchtime, she washed up the cluster of coffee mugs on the kitchen counter, cleaned round the sink and put some washing in the machine on a half-load.

A feeling of panic swept over her as she sat at the dining table chewing on a bacon sandwich and watching a robin hop about on the frosted lawn. She could not afford to get a 'block' at this stage, when there was nothing much to do except organise her information into a coherent text.

She would cancel work for the day, get on with something else, and start tomorrow in a really good frame of mind.

Going to her office she switched off the computer.

Daisy smiled challengingly from the mantelpiece. What *do* you want, if not marriage to Don and making babies?

Who are you? Liz wondered. Why did Granddad never talk about you?

Her grandfather's cousin might have been able to tell her something about the photograph if he had not, inconveniently, died. His widow had written to Ralph at Christmas from an old people's home somewhere near Wells. Liz remembered her vaguely, French, elegant even in her seventies, and with an accent in spite of her years in England; she had laid claim to a peculiarly bucolic and English name — Willow White.

* * *

Meadowfields Residential Home was a large, Victorian building with several annexes, and picture windows over-looking the road. Liz could see people sitting around in armchairs.

What on earth was she doing? she asked herself as she drove through the gates. She knew nothing at all about places that cared for the elderly, except for the occasional news report about abuses of authority, and daffy TV shows in which the residents were portrayed either as spunky rebels, or half mad. Why go to visit an old lady she had met only once at a funeral? Willow would probably not even remember her.

She gave her name at the reception desk. "I'm a relative."

"We didn't think Mrs White had any family."

The woman smiled at Liz as if she

13

was very pleased, even relieved, to see her. She dropped her voice confidentially. "Willow can be difficult. She was very close to her husband. I should guess they were one of those couples who lived for one another and nobody else. It makes it all the harder when something happens."

"I suppose it does," said Liz, thinking of Don, trying to imagine a lifetime of living for nobody else.

The phone rang on the reception desk. "She'll be pleased to see you. Go on down to the day room." The woman smiled again and answered the telephone.

Feeling abandoned, Liz went along the corridor towards a sunlit area at its far end. The photograph of Daisy was in her shoulder bag. If nothing else, it would serve as a conversation piece. She carried a gift of a potted primula. Did they allow plants in the residents' rooms? Did Mrs White even have a room to herself?

There was a smell of disinfectant and polish, an airless hush and a muffled sound of voices as Liz neared the day room. The pictures on the corridor walls, of pastel-coloured flowers in large

14

glass frames — anemones, sweet peas and faded daisies on pale, washed-out backgrounds — added to a sense of having been thrust under warm water.

The brown, rubberised floor squeaked beneath her shoes. Surely such a high gloss was dangerous? Didn't old people fall down rather a lot? No wonder there were wheelchairs parked at intervals along the walls.

She recognised the day room as the one she had seen from the road. There were more washed-out flowers behind glass. Plastic-padded armchairs with high backs were ranged against the walls so that their occupants faced one another, yet had a view of the world outside the window. If the aim had been to stimulate an interest in the outside world and one another, the experiment seemed to have failed, thought Liz, or else she had arrived on a bad day. Except for two women chatting garrulously in a corner, and a large television set with the sound turned down issuing gardening tips to anyone who could lip-read, no one in the room communicated with anyone else. A few were reading newspapers or

15

magazines; the rest stared at the floor, at the television, at their fingers. It was like being in a hospital waiting room.

One or two of the occupants moved their heads to regard Liz as she turned the corner; then, because she clearly had not come to see them, they lost interest.

A woman seated closer to the corridor than the rest gave Liz an encouraging smile. "That's a nice plant."

She had white hair. Liz searched the lined face for traces of the person she had met at her grandfather's funeral, but she could not remember exactly what Willow looked like.

"I'm looking for Mrs White."

The woman nodded. "She'll be in her room."

★ ★ ★

"The names are on the doors," the woman had called after her.

Nobody challenged her, nor offered to help her find her way as she went up the stairs. Really, thought Liz, the organisation seemed very slack. What if

16

she had been a burglar or had come to do someone in? What if Willow did not want visitors today and was not as pleased to see her as the receptionist had supposed? Shouldn't someone have asked her opinion first?

Liz found the name printed on a card in a little frame on the door. A surprisingly authoritative voice called out immediately in answer to her knock: "Go away. I'm busy."

Liz hesitated. Should she simply walk away and admit that her expedition had been a mistake?

She tapped on the door again. "Mrs White. It's Liz — Wilfred Cornforth's granddaughter. We met at my grand-father's funeral."

Silence.

Liz cursed herself for bringing up the subject of funerals almost in the very first breath. How long was it — three, four months — since the woman's husband had died? She strained her ears for sounds of movement or indications of distress.

The door opened very suddenly and Liz took a step back. The woman in

17

the doorway was dressed in a short, pink quilted housecoat and fur-trimmed slippers. Her arms and legs were thin, and her legs in particular were mottled with blue patches that showed through her stockings. She had a relatively unlined face, devoid of make-up, with pale blue eyes, and lips that were a bluish pink. Her fine, silver-grey hair was cut short and permed in the tight curls and waves that were the trademark of the over-seventies, a style that seemed to have been designed deliberately to age rather than flatter women. Nothing about her reminded Liz of the woman she had met.

"I'm sorry to arrive unannounced like this. Perhaps you won't want to see me — especially if you're busy." Liz looked at the primula in her hand. "I brought you a present. Please, will you have it anyway — for your windowsill?"

Willow frowned suspiciously at the proffered pot plant. "I don't like flowers indoors. I prefer to see them growing in the garden." She spoke with the marked French accent Liz remembered.

"Well — " Liz continued doggedly. "Perhaps I could ask the staff to plant

18

it in the garden for you. I noticed there are some beds and borders at the back of the house."

"In February? The frost would kill it."

"Perhaps not right now. But another day. I could leave it with them and — look, if the plant's going to be a problem, I can simply take it away again."

They stared at one another with shades of mutual exasperation.

"Wilfred Cornforth's granddaughter, you said."

"Yes. We've met. But only once."

"I don't remember."

"No. Well, it was fairly brief."

The room, like the figure in the housecoat, was pink and grey: striped curtains, a pink and grey carpet. There were clothes strewn everywhere, over the chairs, on the bed, on the floor.

Willow saw Liz's attention focus on the room.

"I was deciding what to put on for tea," she said with dignity. "I like to change in the afternoon."

Liz nodded as if she understood. "I'll

go away. I can see I've come at a bad time."

"No. You can help me choose something."

Leaving the door wide open, Willow walked away from her and sat on the edge of the bed, surveying the tide of clothes with a touching and unexpected air of helplessness.

Liz followed her and closed the door. "I can't decide whether it should be the rust and gold, or the green. Rust is so depressing at this time of year."

"The green is very pretty. And spring-like," Liz suggested.

"But unlucky. Green's unlucky."

"You can't have minded that when you bought it."

"No, I don't suppose I did. But that was a long time ago, when good luck and bad luck seemed to be something for other people to worry about."

There was an awkward silence.

Liz put the primula on the window ledge. She hesitated, then picked up one of the dresses from the pile of clothes on the floor and slipped it on to a hanger.

"I'm very sorry — that you lost your husband."

"You've no idea, you young people — "

Liz picked up another dress. "In the wardrobe?"

Willow nodded.

Liz continued to clear the clothes from the floor and the bed and hang them on the rail inside the large, old-fashioned wardrobe. She could see that Willow was watching her in the mirror.

"Are you married? You seem to be doing that with a certain housewifely skill."

"I live with someone. Not married exactly."

Willow looked at her with fresh interest. "I suppose that means you're living in sin."

Liz smiled. "It doesn't feel very sinful."

She put the last of the dresses in the wardrobe and closed the door, leaving the pale green dress on the bed.

Willow fingered the crêpe fabric of the skirt. "I'm not always like this. I have good days and bad days. I wasn't really choosing what to wear. I — got carried away. It's strange, you know,

21

the way clothes can be associated with memories. People, places, things people have said and done. I can even remember the clothes I wore as a child."

"Is the green OK?"

"The green's good. Nothing to hurt there. Nothing that I can remember." She sighed, and there was an element of theatricality about it. "That's another thing, you know. There are the very strong memories on the one hand. And yet, I can forget the silliest things."

"People say bereavement does that."

Willow shook her head. "I may look gone to seed and past it, but I know there's more to what's going on in here than missing Albert." She tapped the side of her forehead. "The brain's going. Alzheimer's."

Liz felt a pulse of fear and shame. She realised she had begun by humouring Willow, feeling sorry for the poor old thing in her housecoat and slippers. It occurred to her that Willow was perfectly sensible of how she must look to a woman of thirty.

"You could be wrong," she began. "Everyone becomes a bit forgetful as they grow older. I'm always forgetting things — "

"No. It began while my husband was still alive. I was doing things like leaving the gas on." Willow laughed unexpectedly. "*Dangerous* things. We weren't short of money, so I put my name down early for this place. I always knew Albert would be the first to go. He was a lot older than me. And then — when he left me on my own I thought, why wait until it gets to the point where I don't even know my own name? So, here I am."

"I can't believe you could be so rational about it."

"I'm not. Not always. I have a good cry and get very nasty and bitter sometimes. But it isn't half as bad in here as people outside think it is. I'm still mobile, and I've got my eyes and ears. With a bit of luck, I should be dead before the nest egg runs out. Meanwhile, I don't have to worry about cooking and cleaning and leaving the gas on, or getting sick. And they're very good here. I've seen. When — you know, when things do get worse."

Liz felt chastened into silence.

"I'm going to put this dress on," Willow said. "No, you needn't go. You can turn your back if you wouldn't mind, while I'm dressing."

Liz went to the window overlooking a large garden of lawns and benches, rockeries and borders. It was all very pleasant, but she could not bear to imagine living in such a narrow, prison-like world.

She could hear rustling and a shuffling and bumping going on behind her as Willow dressed.

"You can leave the plant. I'm sorry I was so rude to you after you have come all this way to see me. Where is it you live? You're one of Ralph's girls, aren't you? Ah, I do remember some things, you see. There is hope for me still."

"I live with Don, who's the headteacher of a primary school near Bath. We have a lodge in North Middleton, next to a country estate. Various owners have been selling it off over the years in bits and pieces. There's not much left any more."

"It happens. Either that, or some historic Trust takes over . . . There.

24

You can look now."

Liz turned to face her. "That's very nice."

She meant it. The green dress complemented Willow's silvery hair, which she had brushed out over her ears. She had put on lipstick and looked several years younger.

"It suits you. And the green matches your name. Willow. It's very unusual. Where did it come from?"

"I really don't know how it happened. We all had artistic names at Maison Clem." Willow smiled at Liz's look of confusion. "A couture house. I modelled gowns. Oh, that surprises you even more, doesn't it? I have lived a little, you see. I was stylish then. Quite a pretty girl. I had all the men after me."

"Was that where you met your husband?"

Willow's gaze faltered. "No. That was later. When I was living in England." She put on a pair of low-heeled brogues from under the bed and took a camel jacket from the back of the door. "Come along. They'll be serving tea."

★ ★ ★

Willow led the way into a conservatory filled with plants and garden chairs, with green blinds at the windows and doors that opened on to the garden. They were firmly shut. The garden looked uninviting close to, and the room smelled of greenhouse mould. It was very cold.

"It's the only place that's private," Willow said, clearing a space for their tea cups on a white plastic table littered with plant ties and dead flies.

"They don't seem to worry much about looking after the residents. Apart from the tea, which looks nice and hot," Liz added, not wanting to sound too disapproving. After all, Willow had chosen to live there.

"It's not an asylum," Willow said drily, wiping the dust from one of the wicker chairs with a paper handkerchief. "We're all mobile and mostly *compos mentis* in this wing. It's more like a hotel. We come and go as we please." She sat down, sticking out her feet in front of her. "Never mind all that. Now — tell me why you came to see me."

Liz considered all the possible answers. Should she admit to feeling sorry for

Willow because she was alone, or that she had wanted to know what it was like to be old and to lose one's partner?

"I was curious about you. Your name came up at a family party last night. And — " Liz fished for the photo in her bag. "We were wondering if you could shed some light on this picture."

Willow caught her breath and gave a little cry as she looked at the girl in the corset. "Where did you get it?"

"My father found it among my grandfather's papers. It seems she gave it to him. Read the inscription."

"But she would have nothing to do with any of them. I knew that Wilfred was her favourite when he was little, but — "

Liz felt a growing excitement at Willow's strong reaction to the picture. "Do you know why she fell out with her family? It seems as if my grandfather never talked about her. My father didn't even know there was a Daisy in the family."

"Your grandfather turned into a snob when he grew up. I never met him. I only know what Albert told me about his cousins. Wilfred was ashamed of his background. As for her — " She looked at the photograph again. "I had no idea she was so beautiful when she was a girl."

"So you did know her," Liz persisted. "Apart from the fact that she was your husband's cousin?"

"Yes — " Willow seemed about to add something, then her expression hardened. "But she was older then."

"Did she ever marry? Are there more branches of the family? Is she still alive? No, of course not. That's silly. She would be over a hundred by now."

"What a lot of questions," Willow said irritably. "What does it matter who she was, or how I knew her, or how she got on with her brother and the rest of them?"

"I'm sorry. There's something about her picture. It's in her eyes. As if she has a story to tell."

"Oh, yes. You're right about that." Willow handed back the photograph, and her hand trembled slightly. "And to answer one of your questions — no, she never married." She gave an odd laugh. "She had better things to do with her life."

"How did you know her?"

"In Paris. And she wasn't calling herself Daisy then. She told people her name was Marguerite. It had been her life's ambition to work in Paris. We came to England together during the German Occupation. You're right, she would have been over a hundred if she was still alive. She died — was killed — in a road accident soon after the war."

"Did Daisy — Marguerite — work at Maison Clem too? She looks like a model."

"She was in her late forties by the time I was modelling couture clothes." Willow finished her tea and set down the cup. She looked at Liz directly, almost challengingly. "Daisy *was* Maison Clem. And now, I really think I've answered enough of your questions."

* * *

"It was so exasperating. She knew all about her and had worked with her in France, was starting to talk about her, and then she seemed to clam up altogether. She became almost emotional when I showed her Daisy's picture."

Big and blond, with a face that looked as if it had been pushed around in a rugby scrum, Don was piling garden rubbish into a heap at the end of the garden.

"I told Willow I would go back to see her," Liz said, helping him to pick up leaves. "I thought it was because I was curious about Daisy, but it's not just that. I feel — oh, it must be so awful for her."

Don tried to muster an interest in the woman in the nursing home. Seeing Liz's ingenuous air of involvement with her new preoccupation, her fair straight hair pushed behind her ears like a child, he felt an affectionate and mild irritation.

He had been shaken by her resistance to the idea of getting married. On the face of it, Liz was the last person he would have expected to run away from making the commitment; she had Sally and Ralph as such superb role models, whereas he had none. The death of an older brother had driven his own parents apart: his mother towards an increasingly alcoholic and nebulous grief, his father into icy rages. They had finally divorced when he was in his early teens. He had been sent, for convenience's sake, to a school in Norfolk, and for holidays to an aunt and uncle who lived nearby. It had been a large, affectionate, farming household, idyllic for a child, as he remembered it, but he had always been conscious of being an outsider, and that his parents' lives were proscribed by bitterness.

Now he was thirty-four it all seemed a long time ago, and he knew the time had come to put down roots of his own.

"She doesn't seem miserable," Liz continued. "The place is very definitely an old people's home, but it seems to have brought out the fight in her. *Why* was she so reluctant to talk about Daisy? The photograph obviously brought back memories of their life in Paris. She was surprised at how lovely Daisy was when she was a girl. There's something she knows about her, something she didn't want to say."

"Liz — is there any point in this?"

"Why has Dad never known his father had another sister?" Liz persisted. "He knew the names of the others: Minnie, and Sidney, and their cousin Albert. Sidney died years ago during the war, but Daisy was in England during the forties, while Dad was a boy. You'd think she would have got in touch with her family. Why did my grandfather never even tell his wife he had an older sister?"

"Perhaps she was gay," Don said in exasperation. Liz stared at him, amazed by this bland assumption. "Willow would be — what, probably in her twenties at the start of the war? And you say Daisy, Marguerite, was in her forties and head of a fashion house. It's the classic gay partnership: a young girl and an older woman."

"But Willow is grieving for Albert," Liz said indignantly.

"That doesn't mean that when she was young and impressionable she might not have been susceptible to an older woman. If Daisy's family knew, wouldn't that have estranged her from them?"

Reluctant to pursue the argument, feeling angry, Liz went indoors.

The turn-of-the-century lodge they had shared for the past five years was wedged at the junction between two roads on the outskirts of North Middleton. They had agreed to keep its Edwardian features — the tiled floors, fireplaces, and the quaint front door with its minuscule classical portico, which in the end they never used, coming and going instead by the garden door downstairs. They had planned an extension to the Lodge together: a room with French windows, to let in the light and the scent of flowers in the summer — Liz's idea. Above it, Liz's office on a level with the road, and a bedroom away from the dust and dirt of the traffic.

The bedroom was warmed by the sun streaming in through the windows at the back of the house. White predominated in a decor inspired by Liz's various lace and embroidery periods. There were crocheted curtains at the windows, a cotton bedspread scattered with patch-work cushions, and lace mats and pretty white china jugs on the pine dressing table.

Liz occasionally felt embarrassed by

the room's femininity. Don seemed larger and clumsier than ever here in the bedroom — except when he was in bed: he was adroit enough there. Was that why they stayed together? Because the sex was good?

Liz drew herself up short, realising that it was the first time she had begun to question the fact that simply being with him was enough.

She sat on the white coverlet, and glancing at her reflection in the dressing-table mirror appraised the fine blonde hair and widespaced, grey-blue eyes. A nice enough nose with a scattering of freckles. Soft features, and a rounded, well-defined figure with maternal breasts and hips. Mark — with his doctor's hat on and sober this time — had once told her she possessed a 'good pair of child-bearing hips'.

She thought of her mother, remembered watching her put food in the fridge after the family dinner party, wrapping dishes noisily in cling-film. The backs of Sally's hands were ageing, Liz had noticed. The skin was slack and creased, the veins more prominent than they used to be.

Her arms, like her figure, were thickening with middle age.

Was that how she too would look one day? The fair hair coarsening, still enthusiastic about making the best of herself perhaps, but no longer slim.

Sally had closed the fridge door and leant against it, saying, "Darling, I know Mark put it very badly, but nothing would make us happier than to see you and Don settled down."

Liz had wanted at once to get away from the conversation, aware that her mother was expecting confidences.

"I like my work," she had said lightly.

"Would you need to give it up? People don't these days. And after five years you must be sure — "

Her sisters had married without much pause for thought. Why should she be any different? After five years, everyone agreed that she and Don were made for one another. They had been together for so long now that people who knew them only slightly assumed they were already married. They shared a car, a mortgage, and the cooking, at which Don, rather than Liz, excelled. There were several shared jokes and catchphrases, which had turned into comfortable rituals: "Hi, honey, I'm home," copied from American soap culture, "What's up, Doc?" if she was feeling low. Their needs rarely conflicted; they hardly ever fought about anything.

Liz took the picture of Daisy from her shoulder bag and looked from her own image in the mirror to that of the girl in the corset. There had not been much discussion in Daisy's day about marriage and children being a woman's true destiny. A woman would have been thought peculiar indeed if she had said thank you, but she would rather not marry and breed just yet, not now, not ever.

Had Don inadvertently hit on the truth about Daisy and Willow? She tried to picture Willow as a young woman, a lesbian woman. All tweed and cigars in the thirties and forties? It was difficult to picture Willow at all, except as she was now, with permed hair and a faded, outdated kind of chic.

She looked out of the window at Don, searching for signs that time was running short, that his waist had begun to thicken, or his hairline to recede. His dense fair hair was tousled by the wind, and he looked bruisingly robust as he raked up dead twigs and leaves. There was a large hole in his jumper, which was one she had bought him a few years ago. The memory touched a chord of lustful tenderness in her, and she went downstairs and into the garden and, putting her arms round his waist, pressed her hands into the flat of his back and kissed his cold mouth.

"What's that for?" he said.

"I felt like it."

They did not talk about Willow any more, but discussed their plans for the garden. Nor did they mention marriage, but stepped lightly over and around their deeper thoughts, and Don let that particular subject sink back where it had come from: a no-go area, dangerous ground.

★ ★ ★

Liz rang this time before she went to see Willow again. It was March, and work on the book had progressed hardly at all. She was glad to escape for the afternoon, and found herself looking forward to the visit to Meadowfields.

Willow was in the day room reading a women's magazine held in front of her face to screen herself from the other people in the room. Liz recognised her shoes, and a gold-flowered dress that had been one of those strewn across the bed on her previous visit. She found a vacant chair, moving a tea cup and saucer, which she guessed Willow had put on the seat to deter intruders, and waited until Willow grew curious enough to move her screen a fraction.

"Oh, it's you."

"Yes, it's me. I've brought you something."

"Not more flowers?"

Willow shifted the magazine a few inches and contemplated the box of chocolates.

"They're bad for my figure."

"Bad for mine too. But I can't resist them."

"Neither can I." Willow took the box and placed it very neatly on top of the magazine on her lap, adding grudgingly, "Thank you. I didn't think you would come."

"I said I would. I try never to break promises."

"So do I."

"Good," Liz said. "That means we've got something in common besides liking chocolates."

Willow narrowed her eyes with a look of mistrust. "Young woman — what do you want from me? If you're going to start asking questions again — "

"No," Liz interrupted gently. "I simply came to see you. I admit, I was curious about your friend, my great-aunt Daisy. But, honestly, I came to see you. And," she added briskly, "I needed an excuse to get away from work for a few hours."

"It's a funny place to escape to."

Liz had to agree with her. She looked at the collection of people in the high-backed, hospital-style chairs: men and women in various stages of old age; some slumped, legs swollen over shoes; some food-stained and uncombed, with their clothes anyhow; some pink and white and baby-clean; others shrivelled, with legs like sticks inside their baggy trousers, or legs akimbo, revealing too much thigh and knicker; a lot of crimplene, and cardigans, indistinguishable from the knitting growing to the click of needles in women's laps.

"What kind of work do you do? How is it they let you take an afternoon off whenever you feel like it?" Willow said.

"There is no 'they' — unless you count my publishers. I'm writing a book about corsets. Stays. Foundation garments."

Willow looked at her sharply. "You've worked in the fashion industry?"

"I'm a historian. An art historian originally. I started writing while I was researching a project on American patchwork quilts soon after I left university. And I've done a little — still do a little — university teaching from time to time to bring in more money."

"For you and Don."

"You remembered."

"I'm not quite senile yet."

"You're not senile at all if you ask me."

Willow did not answer. She began to undo the cellophane on the box

40

of chocolates. Others in the day room watched her with an interest mixed with envy and a not very confident hope of sharing her booty. Willow did not open the box. She sat with it in her lap and stared at the lid.

"Daisy knew all about corsets."

"I have her picture — "

"Yes, I know. But corsets have a lot more to do with it than you think."

"She was very lovely," Liz prompted cautiously.

"She told me she had a twenty-inch waist when she was a girl. I don't remember her being *that* thin — she was nearly as broad round the waist as thingy over there by the time she was fifty."

Liz glanced in alarm at the woman Willow had indicated, spreading to fill her chair in a pleated frock and cardigan.

"She was never too particular about telling the truth," Willow continued. "So I expect she was exaggerating about the twenty inches, don't you?"

"Daisy has a small waist in the photograph, but that could have been the tight corseting," Liz said. "There was a saying, a long time ago, that a girl's waist had to measure the same in inches as her age in years."

"I've heard it."

"One reason to feel good about being thirty, I suppose."

Willow looked at Liz. "Daisy went to France when she was thirty. Left them all behind. She was like that. She took people up while it suited her and then dropped them."

Liz detected a bitterness in her voice. "You sound as if you're speaking from experience," she said gently.

"I am, believe me." Willow flashed her a look of anger. "Albert knew a lot about the early years and her family. She had her own dress business only a few streets from where she was born, but she was as cut off from her family as if she was on the other side of the world."

"Why was that?"

"They disowned her." Willow shifted in her chair and lowered her voice, as if delivering secret information. "I can't tell you about it here. People are listening. We'll go up to my room."

Liz was pleased to see that the primula was in bloom, a deep, violet blue. Someone had moved it from the window ledge to a table where it got the light without the full force of the sun.

"Did you see how the others had their eyes on my chocolates?" Willow said. "Old age makes you greedy. There are not many enjoyments left except food." She opened the box and selected one, then passed them to Liz and sat in one of the easy chairs in the room, sticking out her feet and wriggling them and her shoulders with exaggerated pleasure.

Liz chose a chocolate, noticing a photograph of Albert, a neatly handsome man, by the bed, as well as an alarm clock, books, and various personal things she had not noticed on her first visit. There was a portable television on a trolley in one corner, a pile of library books next to it, and, underneath on a shelf, a row of paperbacks with dark green spines.

Willow chewed on the sweet. "You get some funny people in here. Last week, Mrs Thingy from downstairs came knocking on my door and accused me of stealing her keys. Keys to what? I asked her. The safe? The house? The car? Keys to the Crown Jewels? None of us needs keys any more. I told her what she could do with her keys." She laughed again and subsided. "Oh, you don't know how much I've been thinking about the old days since your visit. I never supposed I would, but I've thought of her a lot since you showed me the picture. I miss Albert, of course. But now he's gone — I never *realised*, before now, how much I missed — "

"Were you very close?"

Willow looked at Liz, and without warning her eyes filled with tears. She seemed to be about to say something, then to think better of it. At last she murmured, "These things pass." She took another chocolate without offering one to Liz. "Why are you so interested in her? She's been dead for years."

"Perhaps it's because Daisy seems so unusual for her time. It must have been really hard for a woman to fend for herself and build up a business in those days. I wonder how much of a struggle it was, how many sacrifices she had to make."

"Not very many. She wasn't the self-sacrificing type."

Liz waited, realising that for all her show of reluctance Willow wanted to talk.

"Daisy was as ruthless about business as she was about everything else," Willow reflected. "It was the only way she knew of going about things. She had built up a reputation at Maison Clem and she made damned sure nobody ever got the better of her. Of course, things must have been hard for her in the beginning, in her home town. She was ashamed of all that in the end, hated Kirby Langton and everything she had come from." Willow reached for another chocolate. "I suppose she had reason. Her father was one of the old school. Strict. Cruel, people would say these days. Albert remembered him taking his belt to Wilfred and the younger Cornforth children. He had been a gardener at Noonby Hall near Leicester, and their mother, your *great*-grandmother, was a

45

lady's maid. They lost their jobs in the eighteen nineties, and he found work in the open-cast mines while his wife went to work in a shoe factory. Daisy was put into a factory too as soon as she was old enough to use a sewing machine. Stitching corsets for Jerrett's Corset Company." Willow looked at Liz with a twist of a smile. "A bit different from being a couturière in Paris."

2

IN 1908, Jerrett's corset factory took up the whole of one side of Dray Street in the industrial town of Kirby Langton.

There were rooms for seaming, rooms for cutting and cording, rooms for busking, trimming and binding, for starching, blocking, and boxing for despatch. And in every room could be heard the hum and whirr and thump and rattle of machines.

In the cutting room the cloth was spread on long tables and stencilled for the band-knives to slice like wedges of cheese. Men sorted the various shapes and sizes into bundles for the factory women and outworkers. Cloth lay on and under shelves and benches, littered corners, and filled deep wicker skips to be trundled up and down the wooden ramps from one department level to another. Feet clattered on stairways and in corridors as corsets and sections of corset were conveyed from cutter to sewer, to starcher, to packer.

In the machining rooms the women had to shout if they wanted to make themselves heard. Mostly, they concentrated on the work of their fingers, their faces expressing an introspective blankness. They sat in rows, at long benches that housed the machines, and manipulated the sections of cloth under the rapid punching of the needles. The women in Daisy's room were joining sections of corset, binding the seams with strips of cloth. They were quick and skilful and proud of their stamina.

Daisy mentally counted her money as she sewed, deducting her weekly outgoings — most of her wage — for her share of the rent and housekeeping. She was debating whether she could get away for another week with not letting her father know that she had been given a raise back in April. Five weeks, with the extra shilling a week, still only brought her three-quarters of the way to her goal. A sweat broke out across her shoulders as she contemplated her father's fury if he found out her wages had gone up to twelve shillings at Easter.

Daisy concentrated instead on a mental picture of the ready-to-wear dress she had seen in the window of Robertson Callow's department store, its price tag of three guineas, and the delicate flounces at the hem. 'Ideal for summer wear.' She knew passionately that it was hers by rights, it might have been created especially for her. Narrow-sleeved and narrow-waisted, with a bodice that was a perfect sea of lace and ribbon, and a gored skirt that *flowed* from the hips; it was all froth and whispering romance.

The factory siren went for the midday break, and the machinists ran their sewing machines to a halt and eased their backs, flexing shoulders and arms, and turning to pick up conversations broken off hours earlier.

Daisy put her hands behind her head, stretched, and hunched her neck and arms to free them of tension. She closed her eyes and could see herself walking by the river, in a carriage . . . at a garden party, smiling and nodding at acquaintances. There was her friend Mrs Brackenborough, whose clothes came from Paris, so fashionable, such exquisite taste, inviting her to luncheon tomorrow, "Do you like cucumber sandwiches . . . ?"

Daisy heard laughter and, opening her eyes, saw that a group of women and girls stood round her.

"Where were you, Daisy Cornforth?"

"Somewhere you'll never be," Daisy responded quickly.

"Late for your dinner, that's what," someone said.

The machining room was emptying as the workers deserted their benches and headed for the sunshine of the street.

★ ★ ★

The wall on the waste ground over the road from the factory yards was crammed with women, shifting and jostling like a flock of birds. Daisy wriggled into a space saved for her by her friend Mary Digby.

"I thought twelve o'clock was never going to come," Mary said, pushing bread and cheese into her mouth. She watched Daisy ease back her blouse sleeves and unwrap her sandwiches from their paper.

"What have you got today?"

Daisy studied the wedges of bread and dripping thoughtfully. "Asparagus with Camembert cheese and — " She was getting hungrier. "Cucumber."

"You had cheese and cucumber yesterday."

Daisy chewed on the bread before answering. The dripping was good. It was best near the bottom of the dish — if Wilfred and Minnie didn't get there first.

"Asparagus with Camembert cheese and Dijon mustard," she corrected. "Dijon's better than English mustard. More for your connoisseur."

Some of the women close by were listening, poised between mockery and admiration. Daisy knew all about the ways of the gentry; she had a natural gift for mimicry and could talk posh whenever she wanted. She was a born liar too, if it came down to it; you couldn't believe half her stories — her great-grandmother being a Russian princess, one of her uncles knowing Caruso? Pull the other one.

"I don't know where you get it from, Daisy," said one of the women. "*Dijon* mustard! Where in the world did you learn that from?"

"It's made in France. Mother said so. And she learned it from the Brackenboroughs at Noonby Hall."

Daisy was fond of talking about the Brackenboroughs. She mentioned them as if she were dropping the name of casual acquaintances. When my parents knew the Brackenboroughs. When my father was at Noonby Hall.

Daisy could only imagine what it must be like at the Hall. She had been as far as the gates on her half-day Saturday to gaze at the long drive running through the park land, and the red-brick mansion with its hipped roof and the cupola clock tower in the middle. She had seen the gardens where her father used to work among the flowerbeds, and she had tried to picture his heavy iron-ore worker's hands tending delicate blooms and planting seeds. She knew by heart the layout of the rooms inside the Hall; her mother had described the great oak staircase, down which the ladies floated in their wonderful dresses on grand occasions. "We saw such sights, Daisy. Carriages coming and going. Important people in the area might speak to you, a few words, a smile." Daisy could remember sitting on her mother's lap as a child, curling into her warmth, and hearing her voice, flat and comforting as she lovingly recalled the scenes at Noonby. She could imagine the cut glass, the silver, and heavy table linen, the flowers in all the rooms, the laughter and conversation when the Brackenboroughs had company. But imagining was not the same as being there.

Conversation! They never had conversation in their house, only her father giving monologues about the menace of the unions, or the decline of respect and standards, or telling her to keep her mouth shut and her ideas to herself.

The siren sounded the end of the half-hour dinner break. The women slid from the wall and moved across the road. Daisy glanced across the street at the three-storey factory building, with its brown-painted double gates; she was reluctant to return to the din of machines, the smells of oil, and cotton canvas, and starch drifting up from the ground floor where the finished corsets sat, inanimate on the steam forms, like so many hundreds of headless torsos.

She had been at her machine for some hours when a boy from the packing department came looking for her.

"I'm to tell you to go to the top floor," he shouted above the noise of the machines when Daisy had finished her seam and condescended to give him her attention.

"And why might that be, young man?"

The boy, not knowing Daisy's reputation, was unsure whether he should be overawed by her look of hauteur. He fidgeted with a piece of cotton thread on her bench and struggled with a cheeky response. "Don't know," he said at last. "But Mrs Allen says, if it's Mr Jerrett himself wants you, you're to go straight away."

Daisy saw the overseer watching them from across the room. The woman gave her the nod to say she was allowed to leave her work.

She followed the boy, pausing as she passed Mary Digby's bench to shout in her ear that she was 'off to take tea with the gaffers'.

The managers' offices were at the top end of the street, along floor-boarded corridors, up echoing stairs and half landings. Daisy went ahead, the metal rail of the banister cold under hand, glad of the chance to stretch her back and legs. She began to run, causing her messenger guide to call plaintively that she was going too quickly for him as, lifting her skirt and petticoat, she went at the stairs two at a time and banged through the swing doors at the top. Only here did Daisy pause, impressed by the relative silence; the sound of machines was reduced to a muffled hum by the carpeted corridor.

Walking slowly, refusing to allow her curiosity about why she had been summoned to the top floor to hurry her passage, she turned to the boy who trailed reluctantly after her.

"I can find my own way. I'm not helpless. Go on back to your boxes, young man."

The boy hovered on one foot and muttered something about Daisy not being right in the head. She made a threatening move towards him and he dived through the swing doors. There was a stillness when they came to rest, broken only by the sound of his boots clattering on the stairs.

Daisy pulled down her blouse cuffs to cover her wrists, checked with one hand that her hair was secure in its heavy chignon, and walked with a stiff back and regal swing of the hips, looking to right and left as if inspecting a guard of honour as she passed each heavily panelled door.

She halted to examine the framed prints on the cream-coloured walls: advertisements for corset models. Lovely corsets, Daisy acknowledged. The 'Evangeline', with its silk ribbons, lace edgings and fancy machine embroidery was really beautiful. Her own corsets in beige coutil, handed down to her by her mother, were poor things in comparison, though she had mended the eyelets, embroidered over the worn casings and trimmed them up with fresh ribbon.

Reaching Mr Jerrett's door, she contemplated its polished surface, her heart beating a fraction more rapidly, the set of her shoulders more determined as she raised one hand and knocked.

★ ★ ★

"Do come in, my dear. Don't be shy."

A trio of men stood by one of the windows overlooking the street: two from the upstairs design offices, and Mr Jerrett. Daisy remembered him as a kindly gentleman who had once paused by her workbench when she was new there to call her a 'pretty child'.

Seated near the desk with a notebook and pencil on her lap, a middle-aged woman in a striped skirt and high-necked white blouse looked Daisy up and down and gave her a smile of encouragement.

Interrupting their discussion, the men also subjected Daisy to their appraisal.

"Miss Cornforth — Daisy, isn't it?" Mr Jerrett said. "Daisy, these gentlemen are our corset designers. And this is Miss Ware, my secretary." He smiled, rubbing his hands together. "Well, Daisy. You've been recommended to us by Mrs Allen downstairs as a suitable young lady for modelling one of our new designs. What do you think of that?"

Daisy stared. "You want me — "

"One of these gentlemen will instruct a photographer to take your photograph, and then the design department will produce lifelike sketches for our catalogue. You must have seen that sort of thing?"

Daisy nodded.

"Miss Ware will be with you, so there's no need to be anxious about anything. She'll help you with arranging your hair, fitting, and so on. I have a letter here for you to take home for your father to sign, to say that he agrees. And if you would like your mother to be present, as well as Miss Ware, I'm sure that can be arranged. The photographer will be here at ten-thirty tomorrow. What do you say? Would you like to model the latest corsets for us? You will receive a guinea, Daisy, for your trouble."

Daisy's heart gave a leap as she thought of being able to afford right away the dress in Robertson Callow's, but she managed to say quite calmly, "Thank you. That sounds — very agreeable. May I see it?"

"See it?"

"Yes. Is the corset like the 'Evangeline'?" One of the younger men spoke.

"The 'Evangeline' is one of last year's designs. The new corset is one of a slightly longer range, more in line with current fashion."

His colleague went into the adjoining room and returned cradling a bust-stand that bore a white silk corset with lace ruffles.

Daisy studied the elongated front panels and sinuous lines, with suspenders attached halfway down the thigh.

"Do you approve?" said the man, amused that one of the factory-floor girls had asked to inspect his design before agreeing to model it.

"Oh, yes. It's very elegant." Daisy tried to sound unmoved as she pretended to consider Mr Jerrett's proposition. They were offering her a chance to wear that beautiful creation? Not only to wear it, but to have her photograph taken in it for the factory's advertisements! She felt dizzy even imagining it.

"Would your parents allow it? Would you like me to talk to them?" Mr Jerrett prompted gently.

"That won't be necessary," Daisy said in her best Noonby Hall manner. "If you would simply give me the letter, I'm sure my father will sign it this evening."

★ ★ ★

Would he, heck! Daisy thought as she ran down the stairs with the letter in her pocket. She could imagine what her father would have to say about her dressing up to stand in front of a man with a camera, Miss Ware or no Miss Ware standing by. As for her mother being present . . .

"They won't have to know about it, that's all," she said to Mary Digby on their way home that evening. "At least, not until afterwards."

Mary looked at her with awe. "But how will you do that? Daisy — the letter. You said your dad has to sign a letter."

Daisy shook her head pityingly over her friend's naivety.

All the same, her heart was pounding violently as she took the bottle of ink and the nib pen from the dresser and went to her bedroom. She barricaded the door with a chair under the handle to prevent Wilfred or Minnie coming in.

"Is that you, Daisy?" Her mother called up from the yard. Daisy could hear Minnie protesting about having her face and hands scrubbed under the tap in the scullery. She opened the window, feeling hot with excitement and the closeness of the room.

Her bedroom looked out over a narrow garden consisting of two strips of earth either side of a brick path, where her father grew vegetables all the year round and chrysanthemums in a brick frame in the summer. Beyond the garden an alley connected the backs of the houses, running between high red-brick walls. Daisy hated it. Brick walls. Brick houses and chimneys, as far as the eye could see.

Her mother had their cousin Albert in her arms; she was looking after him while her sister, Auntie Ivy, was in the hospital, bad with her legs again. Minnie clung to her skirt; she was always sullen and clinging when their mother had finished at the shoe factory for the day and had collected her from her nan's.

Daisy's mother, Letty, had been lady's maid to Mrs Brackenborough, and was proud of having worked at Noonby. She spoke with reverence and a deep nostalgia about the family she had worked for; lovely people whom it had been a privilege to serve; everyone looked up to you when they knew you worked there, you were proud to do it, proud to let people know you were one of the upper servants.

Letty sounded her aitches, never gossiped with the other women in Morton Street, nor hung her washing across the parlour. It was Letty who had taught Daisy how to sew fine fabrics without damaging them, how to put a finish on linen with a bit of candlewax and a hot iron, and how to mend stockings with invisible stitches.

Knowing that she had come down in the world, Letty strove to maintain standards; her doorstep was scrubbed daily and chalked at the edges; her children never played in the street, went without shoes, or wore their clothes unmended. She hated working in a factory where the women were noisy and disorderly; and they, not knowing how much the noise and dirt hurt Letty's sensibilities, thought she was stuck-up, and said she gave herself airs.

"Be a love — do the tea while I get the little ones ready for bed? Your father will be home before I know it, and if his tea's not on the table — "

"Where's Wilf?" Daisy had half expected to meet her brother on her way home, or to have him come knocking at her door the minute she got in. He generally hung around to talk to her as soon as she came home from the factory.

Her mother shrugged, and pulled a face, as if to say, how could she be expected to know the whereabouts of a nine-year-old when she had the two little ones to worry about?

Daisy made to move away from the window.

"Did you hear me, Daisy — "

"Yes. Father's tea."

Why shouldn't he wait for his tea like everyone else? What made her father so special that they all had to run around after him when he got home — as if she and her mother hadn't had a hard day of it as well?

Daisy turned back to the room. The red, rough curtains gave it a rosy tinge in the evenings. The iron bedstead stood in a pool of light in the middle of the floor, with its striped bolster, like a giant's bulky stocking, and the patchwork-squared coverlet, blue and red and ivory, which she loved because it had come from Noonby; Lady Brackenborough had given it to Letty when she was a girl.

A white jerry stood under the bed. There were pictures on the walls, a Scottish glen, and Derwentwater in the Lake District; and a washstand near the window, with a bowl with a blue rim set into the stand's surface of white tiles, one with a crack across it where she always stood the water jug.

Daisy felt a fleeting pity for her mother, who had once lived in a house where even the attics looked out over acres of garden and green paddocks, and who now had to live in Morton Street. Daisy was going to escape one day, but her mother, pregnant again, was trapped.

Once, when they were alone and Letty

was reminiscing about Noonby over a bottle of stout left over from Christmas, Daisy had asked her why she had left.

In a moment of weakness, beginning to weep as she remembered the shame of being sent away, of having to live in constant fear of the neighbours discovering why seventeen years earlier she had been dismissed, Letty had told her.

"It wasn't your father's fault," she had protested, defending him, sorry for him, because he too had been dismissed from Noonby's gardens. "Not really. He's never been the same since." Meaning, Daisy supposed, that her father's bouts of bad temper and drinking, staying late at the Three Feathers pub on a Friday night, could be attributed to being deprived of his greenhouses and herbaceous borders.

It was then Daisy realised that her mother blamed her for what had happened; Letty could never forgive her, not deep down, for being born. Letty had been horrified after telling her, terrified that Daisy might say something outside the house. But Daisy would never say a word. It would be social suicide round there to admit that her parents had been forced to get married.

Marriage was a poor bargain for women, decided Daisy, taking Mr Jerrett's letter from her pocket. She pictured her mother sleeping next to her father night after night, listening to him snoring at close quarters, letting him do those things to her that husbands did to wives, like he had done all that time ago.

Daisy spread the letter on the bare boards next to the threadbare square of blue and red carpet. She lay on her stomach and opened the ink bottle beside it. Dipping the pen in the ink, with swift bold strokes, she wrote on the bottom of the letter where there was a space for her father's signature:

I, John Cornforth, agree to my daughter being photographed for the company's advertisements. No need for my wife to attend.

Daisy eased back her head to admire her handiwork. Her corset was digging into her ribs from lying on the hard floor, and she sat up and wriggled to get rid of the

66

pain. She screwed the top back on the bottle and blew on the ink to hurry the drying process.

Then, slipping the ink bottle and pen into her pocket and the letter under her mattress for safekeeping, Daisy freed the chair from behind the door.

The pen and ink were in the dresser, the table was set with knives and forks, and the bubble and squeak on the stove by the time her father came in through the back door.

★ ★ ★

"You've a good figure on you, Daisy," enthused Miss Ware, threading up the corset over Daisy's camisole. "Such a trim waist. It's a shame the artist will go over it for the advertisements. I'm sure there's no need."

She accompanied each of her sentences with a sharp pull of the lace. Daisy faced the long mirror in the showroom next to Mr Jerrett's office, where the two women were alone except for a number of corset models on stands, a selection of petticoats for them to choose from and the photographer's equipment. The founder's portrait gazed down from the wall.

Daisy stood with her hands spanning her waist to hold the corset in place. She hardly heard Miss Ware's twittering comments, so intent was she on relishing each second of being dressed like a lady.

If she ignored her surroundings, concentrated on her image in the mirror and the bobbing head of Miss Ware, Daisy could almost imagine they were standing in one of the bedrooms of Noonby Hall. She was preparing for a luncheon party. A light summer dress, and the daintiest pairs of shoes and stockings would be lying nearby, for her maid Ware to help her into when she had finished lacing the corset.

She liked the way Ware had pinned her hair this morning, piled high above her ears and from the nape of her neck, and forward, with all the weight well to the front, dropping into a natural 'Regent Dip' on her forehead.

Ware had helped her choose the petticoat, in white satin, with accordion-pleated flounces that rustled every time she moved. Daisy turned from side to side, letting the flounces whisper and slither, 'frou-frou, frou-frou'.

"Stand still, will you!" Miss Ware panted, giving the lace a final tug, and fastening it before Daisy could breathe out again. "Now! Let me have a look at you."

Daisy twirled round to face her.

"A picture."

"It's beautiful." Daisy swung her head round to look over her shoulder at the back-lacing reflected in the mirror.

"It's true what they say about clothes making a woman. You wouldn't look out of place in society, Daisy."

"Do you *really* think so?" Daisy said earnestly.

"I'm sure of it. I went with the company's fitter to help measure up young Miss Brackenborough at Noonby when she was ordering her new season's corsets the other week. I know it's disrespectful to say so, but Alice Brackenborough doesn't fit a corset half so well as you do, my dear." Miss Ware lowered her voice. "Miss Alice is a good five years older than you, but she simply hasn't got the figure. And she stands like a horse, though don't tell anyone I say so."

"But they say all the Brackenboroughs are very stylish," Daisy protested, remembering her mother's stories and not wanting to be disillusioned.

Miss Ware shrugged, to indicate that what people *said* did not always fall in with her own opinion. "*Mrs* Brackenborough has always had style, right enough. A proper lady. But this new generation falls short, if you ask me. Young gentlemen going about in motor cars and soft collars. Young women smoking cigarettes like young gentlemen, striding about with their friends arm in arm. Times have changed. Standards are slipping." Miss Ware sighed, for she had grown up in an era when men had been men, and women had known their place.

"Nonsense." Daisy gave a final twirl and, holding her ribs, came to rest against the edge of a table. "All the smart set have style. They know how to make the most of all their advantages."

"If you mean, they know how to spend money, that's true. Are we ready?" Miss

Ware gathered up a pool of hairgrips from the table and tipped them into their box. "Do you want me to loosen the lace a little?"

Daisy shook her head. The pain in her ribs was outweighed by the pleasure of being bound so expensively at the waist and abdomen by silk broché and ribbon. "It feels *frightfully* good." She tipped back her head, feeling ready to face an army of photographers, exhilarated further by the thought that she was escaping half a morning's work at her sewing bench, *and* being paid for the pleasure. If only Mary and the others could see her now.

★ ★ ★

The odd thing about being photographed was that the man with the camera so obviously thought he was in charge of the affair. Placing her, first here by the table, then against the wall under the founder's portrait, instructing her to raise one arm, then to drape a scarf from her shoulders, or to stand with both arms above her head as if pinning her hair.

71

"Look towards me, dear. Now, look away."

The man clearly believed he was directing the finished picture. And yet, Daisy knew, the photographer could do nothing except stand behind his box on its tripod. His words meant nothing unless she responded to them; the photographs could convey nothing unless she revealed the corset's elegance and style.

It was to the camera, not the man, that Daisy responded. She flirted, arched her head, turned with a half smile that seemed, teasingly, to say, "Here am I, Daisy Cornforth, wearing Jerrett's latest design. Do you really think it could look any better on a duchess?" She was conscious only of the camera's unblinking eye, and when the photographer, after some dozen poses, said he thought he had taken enough, she felt a profound disappointment because the fun and excitement were over.

Miss Ware, who all this time had been standing against the door as if to guard it from intruders, wrapped a shawl across Daisy's shoulders and fussed round her, asking if she was tired, saying what a pretty mannequin she had made.

"What are they going to call the corset?" Miss Ware asked the photographer.

"I don't believe they've thought of a name," he said, packing up his camera.

"I shall mention to Mr Jerrett that they might think of calling it the 'Daisy'. Wouldn't that be nice?" Miss Ware had adopted a proprietary air over Daisy, as if she had decided to take her under her personal wing.

But Daisy was scornful of the name. She said that it was too commonplace. 'Marguerite' meant the same and it had more of an artistic sound.

Miss Ware, annoyed that Daisy had bettered her idea, made the amended suggestion anyway, and the corset went into the firm's catalogue:

La Marguerite. Ideal for summer or evening wear, price twenty-one shillings.

It was the amount Daisy had received for her morning's work.

★ ★ ★

73

Daisy thought she had got away with it, and dreamed of escaping to Leicester one Saturday, as she helped her mother wash down the dining chairs with vinegar and water in the yard.

Letty was talking about the old days, when Mrs Brackenborough was at the height of her reign as a society hostess in the area. The Brackenboroughs had been manufacturers back in the eighteen sixties, but when Letty had started work as a girl the family had already retired on the bulk of their fortune and had turned to farming and breeding horses.

"There were ever so many more servants in those days. A life of service wasn't what people think today," Letty's voice lectured comfortably. "The work was hard, the master and mistress expected a lot, but there was the companionship of the other servants as well. Some of them were really clever, not at all the type you get today. There was always plenty of food, and a nice uniform. Your father was such a smart fellow in those days, Daisy. Handsomer than any of the other men. The family thought a lot of him, they talked to him

74

with real respect about his gardens. They called him by his own name, John. I was always called Lily because, when I was nursemaid to Mr Austen and Miss Alice, there had been a Lily there before me, and Mrs Brackenborough reckoned she'd get mixed up if she started to call me by my proper name."

"But you're not Lily, you're Letty," Daisy protested.

"I didn't mind. What's a name?"

"If I'd been born into the gentry, I'd not have been called Daisy. I'd have been called something like — " She thought of Jerrett's latest corset. "Marguerite."

"That sounds French," Letty said, standing back to admire one of the chairs stripped of its polish.

"It is French." Daisy scrubbed harder at a chair leg. "I'm going to Paris one day."

"You'll do no such thing. Paris is a wicked, sinful place."

Daisy laughed. "Did you learn that at Noonby too?"

Her mother's stories about Noonby had convinced Daisy that there was nothing in the world more desirable than living in beautiful surroundings and owning fine things; but her mother's own life held drudgery, unwanted pregnancies, and thwarted longings. Letty's ideas of what was decent involved re-polishing the 'dining-room' furniture, even though she would never own a dining room. Her expectation of happiness lay in cooking a good meal, a few kind words from her husband, an outing with him to Leicester once in a while, and living on her memories as a lady's maid. Daisy wanted none of it.

"One day I shall be rich."

"You'll be doing like me," said Letty flatly. "Worrying about your children and keeping the place clean."

"No, I won't," Daisy said under her breath.

She thought of the extra guineas to be earned from modelling more corsets for Mr Jerrett. She began to plan how to get to Leicester unnoticed. Daisy was beginning to realise that keeping a new dress concealed from her family was going to be a problem.

★ ★ ★

The chairs were round the table again, smelling of polish, and Daisy was setting out the knives and forks for supper, singing softly to herself, *"I've a penny in my pocket . . . "*

Wilfred, leaning against the wall to catch the evening light from the front window as he read his book — he always had his head in some book — joined in with each chorus of " . . . *La-di-da*".

The young ones were out in the yard. A good thing too, thought Daisy, seeing her father's face when he came in from the Three Feathers. He stood blocking the short passage between the front room and the kitchen, where Letty was draining potatoes over the sink.

A thickset, hard-faced man in his mid-forties, John Cornforth cocked his head with a truculent air of contemplation, one arm raised against the doorframe to steady himself. Daisy's heart missed a beat as she realised he had been drinking.

"Now then, my girl. What's this I've been hearing?" He spoke quietly, with a dangerous calm that Daisy knew always heralded the breaking of a storm.

77

She continued setting the table and, though she knew it drove him to a deeper fury, affected a careless, mocking tone. She could not help herself; it was instinctive with her, to push him to the edge, because her mother never would and someone had to stand up to him. Besides, it helped steel her nerves.

"Now, how do I know, Father, what you've been hearing, unless you tell me? The price of beer is going up half a penny? Something's been at your pea sticks in the garden?" She heard her brother's wincing intake of breath.

"Don't bandy words with me, girl! You know damn well what I'm talking about. It's all round the town what you've been up to."

"Well, it hasn't reached me, and that's for sure."

"You minx!" John Cornforth took a step forward, and Daisy, with a yelp of fright, ducked behind a chair.

Before he could reach her, Wilfred had jumped up from his place by the window and, putting up his fists, stood between them. "Don't hurt her. You mustn't hurt her. She's a girl."

Thin and fragile for his age, Wilfred cut a brave but pathetic figure that not even his father had the heart to crush.

John Cornforth chose instead to squash his son's challenge with sarcasm. "Oh, yes? And what sort of girl is it, goes taking off her clothes for the managers and bosses when they ask her? Is that what you'd defend, eh? A sister who's not got the decency, nor the self-respect, to know right from wrong? Oh, there's a fine, upstanding young man you're likely to turn out to be."

Letty, coming to see what was happening, stood in the passage, wringing her hands in her apron. "Oh, Daisy — you never."

"It wasn't like that," Daisy said sulkily.

Wilfred put down his fists. He looked at her, wide-eyed, as if she had betrayed him.

"It wasn't like that," Daisy repeated, talking to Wilfred this time, not caring what her father thought, but desperate that the brother who thought the world of her should not have his innocence shattered. "It was an honour to be picked out. The latest corset design, and so beautiful. The best silk, and really good lace. It was for the firm's advertisements. It was no more indecent than when ladies in society sit for their portraits dressed in their evening gowns."

"And half of *them* have peculiar ideas about how to behave," said her father. "You don't have to tell me about ladies in society." He threw a look of bitterness at Letty. "Nor any woman, for that matter. You're all the same when it comes down to it — flaunting yourselves, stirring men up."

"Daisy, what happened?" Her mother's voice was frightened.

"Nothing *happened*. Mr Jerrett was really nice. Everyone was nice." Daisy felt close to tears. "Miss Ware — that's Mr Jerrett's secretary, who's a really respectable, proper lady — she was with me all the time."

Relief smoothed out the anxiety on her mother's face. She turned to her husband. "There you are, John. Miss Ware was with her. Mr Jerrett's secretary wouldn't go along with anything indecent."

Daisy took strength from her father's brief indecision. "I don't know why

I'm explaining about it. If you want to think — "

"It's not what we think. It's what others will think." He jerked his head to indicate the world outside their front door.

"Oh, you are so — " Daisy put her hands on her hips. Her scorn included her father's beery truculence, her mother's pregnant figure, and the shabby pretensions of the house in Morton Street, with its door leading straight on to the street and a chenille curtain to hide it; she saw the worn sofa with its stiff back and narrow arms, the crockery cupboard with the 'best' china from the local market, the oil-cloth under the embroidered tablecloth, and the overmantel with pitted mirror and photos and toby jugs on the shelves. Family portraits. Family heirlooms.

"You are so — *small-minded*. And what's more — you're a damned hypocrite."

This time her father hit her.

Wilfred was too slow or too awestruck to intervene, and the blow, deflected by Daisy's arm as she raised it to protect herself, caught her on the side of the head. She staggered and fell against the table.

"Get upstairs! Get out of my sight before I take my belt to you!"

Giddy, and with a ringing in her head that made her feel sick, Daisy reached the door to the stairs. She slammed it behind her, could not see where she was going in the darkness of the staircase, and stumbled over her skirt hem as she scrambled on hands and knees.

She was terrified that he would come after her, remembering childhood games when he had pretended to be a giant or a wild animal coming to eat her. Then the terror had been savoured — this time it was for real.

Daisy lay across the top of the stairs, her head resting against the foot of the ladder that led up to Wilfred's bed in the attic. She realised after a while that no one was following, and waited for the turmoil in her to settle down.

The door to her parents' room stood open. She could see the huge round feet of the wardrobe, and the edge of the rug curling under them, and — if she moved her head sideways a little, though that made her feel sick again — the dark bedstead with its brown shiny counterpane, a jerry underneath it, and her father's boots that he wore for church on Sundays.

I hate him, she told herself. I'm not staying in this house a moment longer.

She sat up and pressed her fingers against the side of her head, feeling for a bruise.

★ ★ ★

Daisy lay on her bed for a long time before lighting the oil lamp. Realising she had missed supper, she indulged in a mild form of self-pity; someone ought to come up and find out how she was; she could be dying up here and no one would care. They would find her body in the morning, cold and white, with a bruise staining her temple. The police would come to take her father away, and the judge would sentence him to be hanged.

The latch on the door at the foot of the stairs clicked. After a few seconds

Wilfred appeared in the doorway looking scared.

"Does it hurt very much?"

"Not really." Daisy raised herself on one arm. "Don't worry. He can beat me black and blue but he can't hurt me." She rested her hand dramatically against her breast. "He can't get at what's in here."

She patted the edge of the bed for him to sit down. "Where is he?"

"Gone out. Mother says to see if you're all right, and she'll let me bring you some tea later."

"I know I was right to do the photographs, Wilf. That's important," Daisy said earnestly. "It doesn't matter what other people say or think when you know you're right about something."

"Was it a very pretty corset?"

"The best." She lowered her voice to a whisper. "Do you want to see it? They gave me one of the photographs."

Wilfred stared in admiration as she reached under the mattress and pulled out a picture of herself, mounted on card.

Mr Jerrett, summoning her to his

office, had handed her the photograph with an air of ceremony. "A souvenir for you to keep, Daisy." He had said they were very pleased with the finished advertisement. One of the best they had ever done. He wanted her to pose for more.

"Look, Wilf — see how beautiful it is. See the cut and the lines. Only a very ignorant person could call that indecent. Miss Ware says I look ten times better in a corset than Alice Brackenborough at Noonby Hall who can have the pick of any clothes she chooses."

Wilfred cradled the picture between his fingers, as if afraid he might spoil it. "It's lovely. I reckon it looks better than the Queen of England's photograph."

"I shall be rich like Queen Alexandra one day, Wilf. I'll not get married, but I'm going to be rich, a real lady, and get out of this house and this street, and away from *him* throwing his weight about."

Daisy saw the reverential way Wilfred was holding the photograph.

"You can have it, if you like."

"But, you can't — "

"No. I mean it. I want you to have it. But you mustn't let *them* know you've got it. Promise me you won't let on?"

Wilfred nodded, and gazed at the image of his sister, so ladylike and glamorous, so beautiful. "I've got a box in the attic. I keep things in it."

Daisy thought for a moment, then she got up from the bed and searched in the dressing table for a stub of pencil.

She wrote on the back of the photograph: '*For Wilfred, from your loving sister Daisy, July 1908*'.

"You're to keep it. Always."

3

"DO you suppose it was all so very innocent? They were peculiar times," said Liz. "You can just imagine the managers and undermanagers handing Daisy's picture round with their grubby little fingers."

"All good fun," said Ralph. "Where was the harm?"

"Apparently Daisy was paid on several occasions. She became a regular model for the firm's adverts."

"So that's not why the family disowned her?"

"According to Willow, it was." Liz put Daisy's photograph back in her bag. "But I get a feeling she's holding something back and that there was more to it."

"Coffee?"

She nodded.

Liz had decided to call on her father while her mother was at work. Curiosity about the long-dead Daisy was all a bit too sentimental, too bound up with romantic speculation for Sally, and Liz had detected an irritation with Ralph's interest in a family 'mystery'.

She glanced round the spotless kitchen; all signs of breakfast were cleared away, and there was no evidence that her father had been occupied with anything before she arrived. What did he do all day now that he had taken early retirement?

"Have I interrupted anything?"

"I might have a round of golf later."

Of course — there was golf. And gardening through the summer. And the local amateur dramatics in the autumn. But after a lifetime of dealing with problems in a large industrial company it hardly seemed enough.

"Thank you for coming over," Ralph said, filling two mugs and sitting at the breakfast counter.

"I thought you'd want to know about Daisy." Liz sipped her coffee. "Willow's very odd about all this. She seems to want to talk one moment, and the next she goes all coy on me and won't say another word."

"Perhaps she has something to hide."

Liz hesitated about telling him Don's

theory that the two women were lovers.

"I think they were — very close friends."

"Ah — a couple of dykes."

She had been right. Her father was embarrassed, despite his attempt to sound trendy.

"They lived together for a long time, stayed together in England even after the war."

"And you say Daisy had her own couture business in Paris?"

"For some years."

"Quite a girl." Ralph shook his head, pleased at least by this idea. "And how's the book coming along?"

"Slowly. It's too easy to get sidetracked."

"You mean, by visiting elderly ladies and your old dad?"

"I wanted to see you," Liz protested, feeling guilty, aware that she only ever visited when summoned to a family event, or when she was at a loose end. "It's Daisy who's the real distraction. Something about her has really got to me."

"And what about — other things? Are you happy?"

"Yes, of course," Liz said brightly. Too brightly, and too quickly.

"Only asking." Her father drummed his fingers on the table.

They drank their coffee.

"Hang on a minute," said Ralph. "I'll get Dad's box down from upstairs. We'll see if we can uncover anything else about Daisy."

★ ★ ★

A smell of mould and damp spots rose as they sorted through army discharge papers from 1919, yellowed news cuttings and Liz's grandfather's early sermons, handwritten on sheets of foolscap and tied with a faded piece of black tape. Had there been a hint of pride in keeping them? Ralph was amused by the idea of his father being touched by vanity.

They moved to the photographs, several taken in the forties: bony knees, baggy shorts, grinning faces. Degree day. And the wedding photos, Ralph and Sally — looking far too young, Ralph said.

His mother had not wanted the photographs when his father died — had not even looked at them. "Take them away," she had said wearily. "What use is all that to me? I never looked at any of it when he was alive. Why should I want to now?" Odd how one could feel upset by such indifference even at the age of fifty-eight, and with his mother nearly ninety.

He would stick the photos in one of the albums, he told Liz. For posterity. Was that what the box was all about? Had his father saved all these mementoes from his life with the same thoughts on mortality and sense of continuity as when he collected photos of his own children and grandchildren?

"I've been through these roughly." Ralph turned over letters and envelopes. "Those postmarked London seem to be from Dad's younger sister Minnie. She never married, and it's fairly dull stuff except for some of the later ones written during the Second World War. I don't think she had any contact with her sister. If she did, there's nothing about it in her letters. In any case, these were mostly written in the twenties and early thirties, when you say Daisy was living in France.

I'd have noticed any foreign postmarks. I haven't read any of the others. There could be references to Daisy."

"Or even a letter *from* Daisy," Liz said, aware of the quiet, extraordinary thrill she always felt when handling old papers.

They began unfolding the documents and reading, dividing the pile of letters between them, the bulk of them from Minnie and the others with a variety of handwritings that seemed to promise something more intriguing.

They proved less than absorbing reading: most of the letters were from fellow clergymen or from parishioners, on parochial matters: local politics, finance, parish teas.

They had been occupied for half an hour, when Liz opened a letter with a Kirby Langton postmark.

"This one's from a Major Brackenborough, written not long after the First World War."

"Dad's old army commander?" Ralph suggested. "He was just old enough to get caught up in all that. I know he was in the trenches."

Liz scanned the handwriting, brown and faded, but in a broad, rounded script that was easy to read. A burst of excitement ran through her as she picked out the name 'Daisy' at intervals down the page.

Noting the heading, 'Noonby', and with a reluctance to share the discovery — a historian's paranoia that someone else might muscle in on one's research material — Liz pushed the letter to a position where her father could read it with her.

"It could be from his army commander — but it's got nothing to do with the war."

Noonby Hall,
Kirby Langton
21 January 1920

Dear Mr Cornforth,

I have given some thought to your request. To be truthful, your inquiries about Daisy have been so much on my mind lately that I have begun this letter on and off several times. Who can say what made me refuse you until now? Thoughts of how you might receive

93

news of your sister perhaps? What you might do — bearing in mind the revealing tone of your first letter to me and the bitterness you and your family feel.

However, your last letter moved me, and I am sending the address Daisy is now known at. As you will see, she was never so far away as you believed, and certainly not 'gone to the bad in London'. She has established a very respectable dressmaking business in Leicester. If you decide to visit her, take care. She too has been hurt by the long separation. I hope this now concludes the correspondence between us. I am glad you have resolved the question of your future, and I wish you well in your theological training. I am sure that, for you, this is the right course.

Yours sincerely,
Major Clement Brackenborough.

"It seems a bit brusque towards the end," mused Liz. "Supposing it's not from his army commander. What connection could anyone from Noonby

Hall have had with Daisy?"

"Something to do with your great-grandparents once working there?" Ralph searched through the letters for the rest of the correspondence. But there were no earlier letters from the Major, nor was there the address in Leicester, and, after reading through all the papers in the box, they found no further references to Daisy.

"It's odd to think that a person's whole life can simply disappear like that," said Liz.

"Perhaps if Daisy had had children — " Ralph packed the letters and envelopes back into the box, adding carefully, "Your sister Prue's pregnant again — she didn't want to announce it at the party the other night."

"But little Josie is still a baby! How can they even contemplate having another one?" Was that really what her sister wanted? thought Liz. Spooning baby food into ever-open mouths? It occurred to her that by the time Prue had her baby, her mother and both her sisters would each have borne three children before they were thirty. Even though she had no wish to join them, the thought made her uncomfortable, as if she was being left behind.

"Your mother says you and Don aren't very interested in the idea," Ralph continued.

Liz was aware of a deeper sense of oppression. She had thought she could trust her father to steer clear of the subject. She took it for granted that conversations with her mother were mostly limited to 'family' or 'female' subjects, but Liz had always believed she shared something less determinedly domestic with Ralph.

"It seems as if Prue is looking after the interests of grandchildren quite nicely for you at the moment," she said defensively.

"But not you, Liz. Are you sure you really know what you want?"

Liz remembered the many times she had been asked that question, and had not known the answer. Through school and university; in and out of several disastrous relationships; when she threw up a 'safe' job at the university to head, briefly, for America in the late eighties. She had got it wrong, it was true, more times than she cared to remember.

And then she had met Don. She had not known, of course, that it would last five years, but she had hoped, sensed even, that this time would be different.

Her father stood with the box under his arm, a look of concern making him frown, and she was at once back in the days when she had been subjected to well-meaning parental advice.

"I don't want my life to change, Dad. Things are fine just the way they are."

★ ★ ★

Don had come to teaching relatively late. His memories of a childhood split between various schools and warring parents had made him determined to create a 'happy' school under his jurisdiction.

He stood at the window of his office and watched mothers with pushchairs turn and head for home with their offspring in tow as the last of the children left the playground. Almost all were in their twenties. They made him feel old.

Eve Benson, on 'home' duty, came

slowly towards the school building to check the cloakrooms and lavatories for stragglers. She looked tired and, though he had not been aware of it before that morning, noticeably pregnant.

Why did everyone seem to be conspiring to remind him that other people were getting on with the business of enriching their lives with a family?

Eve knocked on his open door. "Something I didn't have the courage to remind you about this morning, Don. The French trip."

She was genuinely upset, knowing how difficult it was to fill a post at short notice, and how much he disliked resorting to supply teachers who did not know the children.

Don nodded. "Don't worry. We'll manage. You go on home right now. Put your feet up."

Don went to the wall-charts when she had gone and studied the roster duties for the rest of the term. He would have to change them around a little, give Eve less to do. And as for next term . . .

He tried not to think about the summer trip. Eve had always been the inspiration and mainstay behind the whole scheme. He relied on her to make it work. What was more, she was the only member of the staff who spoke fluent French.

He went into the corridor and saw his deputy by the assembly hall. "The Paris outing. Eve won't be able to come."

Cliff put his hands in his pockets and pulled a wry face. "What will you do? Call it off?"

"We can't. The kids are looking forward to it. Some of the parents have already started paying. We'll have to rope someone else in."

★ ★ ★

Liz looked up from the computer screen with an expression of horror. "Paris. With thirty ten-and eleven-year-olds. For a whole week! You must be joking." For a moment she wondered if he *was* joking.

"I wouldn't ask if it wasn't so desperate."

Don had explained the situation: Eve's untimely pregnancy, the importance of the trip for the older children, who had been learning French in preparation for their secondary schools, the necessity of having an adult on board the team who spoke half-decent French, and who knew the other members of staff well enough for the trip to go off without too many hitches.

So, Eve Benson was pregnant, thought Liz. She who had sworn that wild horses would never drag her from her career. Liz remembered, two or three years earlier, feeling an affinity with the recently married Eve, who had declared her goals in life with such certainty.

"You wouldn't have much to do," Don promised. "Eve always makes up project sheets for the class, and Cliff and I can work through those with them. You would simply be our interpreter where we needed it. It could be fun."

She looked at him disbelievingly.

"I promise you won't need to do much supervision."

For a moment, Liz saw a distinct irony in the fact that Don was asking her to step into the breach.

"Shouldn't we be acknowledging here that there are certain advantages to

100

my being unencumbered by my own offspring?"

"What about *my* pupils while I'm away — and all my other work? I might not want to take a week off from the book at that stage?"

"Your university classes will have finished by June. And it isn't as though you have absolute commitments with the book. You can surely take a holiday?"

"You don't seem to be taking the book very seriously."

"I am. Yes, I am. I do. But you have to admit that corsets *are* a bit ephemeral."

Liz felt profoundly shocked and hurt. "You mean compared with a school trip to Paris?"

"Compared with all sorts of things."

"Such as?"

"Such as settling down, getting married, raising a family — " He had not meant to say it. He would not have said it if it hadn't been for Eve, if he hadn't felt so damned empty that afternoon.

"If you ask me," Liz said with a sudden ferocity, "the subject of corsets is very relevant to all of this. It's all about women being fastened into a straitjacket, being forced into doing what's expected of us: turning ourselves into someone's wife, or someone's mother — "

"You know what you're turning into? One of those earnest feminist types we men used to come up against in the eighties."

"Oh!" Liz said, affronted. "Oh, that's so sexist. The whole thesis underlying my book — "

"You know what? You're no fun any more."

In the end, Liz gave in over the Paris trip. She could never sustain an argument with him for very long. In any case, they so rarely disagreed over anything more important than who should do the washing up, or whose turn it was to buy the weekend wine. To provoke conflict felt dangerous. Besides, she did not want to quarrel. She wanted to get on with the book.

"All right. I'll come," she said that evening.

"You will? Liz — sometimes you're amazing."

Yes. Sometimes I amaze myself, Liz thought, driving to see Willow the next day. After all, she did not *want* to go to Paris with thirty school children.

"So why agree to it?" asked Willow when she told her.

"To prove I *can* make sacrifices for his sake? Because sometimes a few compromises are necessary to make life run smoothly?"

"Perhaps you're making this relatively small sacrifice in order to avoid more important compromises?"

Willow, dressed in the housecoat and slippers she had worn on Liz's first visit, had been slow to answer the door, and a look of alarm, almost of pain, had crossed her face when she saw her.

"Go away."

"Very well. If you really don't want to see me."

"Poking and prying. Stirring things up with all your questions."

"We don't have to talk about Daisy."

"No, we don't. We certainly don't."

103

Liz had not attempted to enter the room, but neither had she moved away. "I've brought you a book. You may have read it. I took the risk."

Willow, trying to sustain her hostility, had been too curious about the contents of the bag in Liz's hand, and ultimately pleased with the volume of feminist short stories.

Liz had looked round for the primula. "I've planted it in the garden," Willow said. "It should flower again next year. Not that you'll see it. You'll have stopped coming to visit me by then. You'll have married your lover, and be raising a family, and you'll forget all about visiting a senile old woman."

"Stop it." Liz had turned on her sharply. "If this is what being in here does to you — "

She had been in time to see a spark of surprise, and then something close to enjoyment strike a glint in Willow's eyes. They had looked at one another with an air of challenge, as if waiting to see who would back down first.

"I *shall* come to see you. And I shan't forget about you. And I certainly won't be having babies. I thought at least I could escape that subject while I'm here." And Liz had told her all about it, Don's recent urge to make their relationship permanent, and the row over the trip to Paris.

"I'm glad you came," Willow said when she had finished. "Shall we go out in the garden? I'll show you where I planted the primula."

Looking determined, with her hands thrust into the pockets of her camel coat, Willow led the way along the paths through the garden. She paused by various clumps of bushes, saying each time, "Now — was it here, do you think? Can you see anything?"

"It really doesn't matter," Liz said, after the third attempt at peering among leaves and scrabbling through the undergrowth. "After all, we shall see it when it flowers again."

"I suppose so."

Willow waited for Liz to rejoin her on the path. They walked on, their feet crunching on gravel.

"I never wanted babies," Willow confessed after a while. "Some people don't.

There's nothing mystical about mother-hood in the way a lot of women try to make out. They do that to make you feel guilty, you know, because they've realised for themselves that it's not all it's made out to be, but of course, for them it's too late."

"My sister Jennifer's not really cut out for it," Liz said. "Nor was my mother," she added, thinking aloud as she remembered her own childhood. "Though she would deny it, and would call herself a good mother."

Liz remembered Sally's style of mothering: interested in her daughters' progress and achievements, generous with praise — but loving? Of course I love my children, she would have bridled convincingly, and Liz, with hindsight, saw that it was true; but there had been no sense of nurturing, no natural maternalism.

"There is no such thing as a good mother," said Willow. "And I, for one, would have made a *very bad* one."

"Didn't Albert want children?"

"He already had a child. His wife ran off with a GI and took the boy to America after the war. So he was disillusioned about the whole business. We had each other. That was all either of us wanted."

"The trouble is," Liz confessed, "I don't know what I want. I thought it was Don. I was head-over-heels when I first met him."

"And now?"

"The trouble is — " Liz repeated, frowning with concentration. "Things always seem to get claustrophobic. On the one hand, I quite like feelings of security, on the other — it's as if I can't quite make that final commitment. It was the same with everything once. Jobs, as well as relationships. I met someone at university. We were going to get married. He had the future all planned out: I would take teaching jobs to fit in with his work. Him leading. Me following. The classic little woman. Then I realised I didn't love him."

"How did he take it?" said Willow.

"Badly. Afterwards I started going out with a disc jockey called Ray. Crazy. Totally unsuitable. But we were together for nearly a year. Then I found out he was sleeping with someone else."

107

Willow gave one of her unexpected laughs. It was infectious, and Liz laughed as well.

"I'd been offered six months' research in America. The offer was still open, so I took it. Everyone thought I was mad — or else pining over Ray." She remembered the sheer relief of being a free agent again. "And then," she said levelly, "I met someone who was working at the same museum. He wanted me to stay there and marry him. I suppose I must have thought I loved him at the time, but when he too started talking about marriage I felt trapped. I bolted. Never even said I was leaving or why. Isn't that dreadful? Wasn't that a terrible thing to do to someone?" Liz went hot and cold as she thought about it.

Willow did not answer, except to say, "And then you met Don?"

"I was back in England. He was nice and kind and decent, with a distinct touch of heroism about him."

Liz described how they had first met; running for a train on Paddington Station he had, literally, crashed into her. She had dropped a badly wrapped jar of liqueur-soaked peaches that she was taking home for a family Christmas, and he had helped her to clear up the mess.

"We seemed to like the same things, to want the same things out of life. We were happy simply being with one another . . . "

"Until now," finished Willow. "Now you're wondering if you've got *this* one right . . . even, that you might, conceivably, be better off without him?"

Liz shook her head and did not answer. After a while she glanced at Willow, who was chewing on her lower lip as if deep in thought.

"Oh, well, at least I've managed to show commitment in one area," Liz said. "I feel as if I know what I want when I'm writing. The books are the only things I *am* sure of."

"*She* was like that."

"Who?" Liz said in surprise, and then, half afraid that Willow would change the subject, feeling as if she were creeping up on a butterfly that might be gone in a flicker of colour: "Like what, Willow? What was Daisy like?"

"She only felt secure when she was working. She knew she wanted to make money. But she was no good with relationships. She couldn't stay the course — a corset maybe, but she had no staying power with men."

Liz smiled. "Willow — that's a terrible pun."

"I've still got my wits."

"Nobody said you hadn't."

"Then why can't I remember where I put that damned plant?" Willow stared helplessly around the garden.

"It's easy to forget a patch of bushes. There are quite a few shrubs that look alike."

They walked up and down the paths for a while, but without much expectation of discovering the missing primula.

"It's so awful — not being able to remember things. The wrong words come. Thoughts fly away from you before they quite reach — " Willow's voice trembled, and she shifted her eyes away from Liz's too open compassion.

Liz caught hold of her hand. "I *shall* keep on coming here. I promise. I shall see it through with you, whatever *it is*."

They walked back towards the building, Willow's hand on Liz's arm, as if unconsciously drawing comfort from it.

Liz hoped she would be able to keep her promise. What about later? What if Willow was right about Alzheimer's, and the time came when she couldn't remember who she was? What if food slopped out of her mouth, or she became rambling, or incontinent? Could she 'see it through' with her then? Fear gripped her — a general fear of old age, for herself as much as for Willow. For her parents' future, for her sisters, for Don.

They went indoors, and Willow seemed to have forgotten her confusion over the primula. Her attention lighted on the afternoon trolley, and she concentrated on furnishing them both with cups of tea and a plate of biscuits, which she insisted they take into the conservatory.

Someone had tidied up the room for the spring and summer. Plants had been moved to a bench near one of the windows. The tables were clean, and the floor freshly painted with red tile paint.

Willow munched on a custard cream

and pushed the plate towards Liz. "Let's forget our waistlines, shall we? Go on. Make the most of a free biscuit."

Remembering their earlier conversation, Liz prompted her. "You suggested Daisy was bad at relationships."

"Did I?"

"Yes. You know you did."

"No man was ever good enough for her," Willow said quietly. "Not after Clem."

"You mean her commitment to the couture business — Maison Clem."

"Perhaps I do."

Clem? . . . Clement Brackenborough? Liz felt a thrill of discovery run through her, sending out ripples of deepening excitement. The implications of a link between Daisy and the writer of the letter in her grandfather's box spread in her imagination.

"Are you saying Daisy was romantically linked with Major Brackenborough?"

"You've heard of him?" For a moment Willow looked uncertain.

"My father has a letter written by him."

Willow listened with a closed expression

112

and apparent lack of interest while Liz told her about the Major's response to Wilfred's inquiry concerning his sister. Then she took another biscuit.

"He wasn't a major when she first knew him."

"What did you mean about her not getting over him?"

"Did I say that? I say all sorts of silly things these days and then I forget what I'm talking about."

"There's nothing wrong with your brain right now. You know exactly what you're saying."

Liz was beginning to understand Willow a little. She saw that the aggression and indifference and apparent forgetfulness masked more than a need to talk; more even than the pain of long-buried memories. Willow was enjoying holding back details. The revelation hit Liz with considerable force that Willow's reluctance was manipulative; she was feeding her enough titbits about Daisy to keep her interested each time she visited. To ensure that she would come back to see her?

Willow looked evasive. "It will come to

you too one day, young woman. Don't imagine your sharp little inquiring mind will last for ever."

"Did Daisy have a love affair with Major Brackenborough?"

"She tried to deny it." Willow's mouth took the shape of a sneer. "The fact is, Daisy never really loved anyone but herself."

4

DAISY had little time or sympathy for women crusaders, so when a mob of ladies wearing fancy hats and carrying banners invaded the yards outside the factory one afternoon, she enjoyed the diversion as much as the rest of the workers who had crowded to the windows to see what was going on.

The banners were painted with slogans: *Support the Female Health and Emancipation League*, *Women of Kirby Langton Unite!* and, more inflammatory, *Abolish Corsets!*

The top lights of the windows were open to let in as much air as possible in the July heat, and the women workers could hear clearly as well as see what was going on.

"Tight-lacing causes disfigurement of the natural female form," called one of the protesters. "Corsets are unhealthy."

The leader was about Daisy's own age, fair-skinned with very pale, frizzy hair. All were dressed in loose-fitting, sack-like dresses and jackets in shades of mauve, green and white, the colours currently being worn by the votes-for-women campaigners.

Their hats gave them away as members of a distinct class, thought Daisy. Hats like that, large and elaborate, were not worn simply for decency's sake nor to keep off the weather.

"Silly tart. Corsets never did us any harm," said one of the machinists.

"Come and join us," urged the fair-haired girl. "Tell your bosses you will not tolerate making garments that force women to pull themselves into unnatural, crippling shapes."

The women machinists laughed and jeered from the windows. There were shouts of, "What shall we tell them to make instead?"

"Health garments," cried the protest leader with great earnestness. "Rational clothes that allow freedom of movement. I have some pamphlets here."

She pulled a handful of papers from a satchel and began posting pamphlets where she could reach through the gaps in the windows.

"Call that healthy?" said Mary Digby heatedly. "They look like bags. A lot of sad, horrible bags."

This was not entirely true, thought Daisy, who coveted the hats, the good shoes and gloves, and the whole demeanour of the women; but Mary's comment had drawn a cheer from those machinists who had heard her, and the protestors retaliated at once by waving their banners more vigorously.

"Ho ho — we shall see some sparks fly now," said one of the women overseers, as some of the men from the packing and cutting rooms emerged from the doors at the lower end of the building and began to barrack the demonstration, provoking a series of boos and cries of "Shame" from the anti-corset campaigners. The factory women responded at once in support of their male colleagues.

Daisy stood on a chair and shouted through the window, "Why not come and join *us* there's room for a few more on our bench." She was enjoying the fun, but she felt a sneaking admiration for the way the girl spoke back to the works manager when he asked her to "Move away from the building, my dear, and take your female companions with you."

"We believe it's our duty to warn your women workers — to point out to them the dangers of wearing corsets. Women have subjected themselves to the wishes of men for far too long."

"Well, that's true at least," said Daisy. She thought of her mother, who only that morning had gone into labour. Daisy had run all the way to the bottom of town to fetch the midwife, Wilfred had taken Minnie to their nan's, and all the while her father had calmly eaten his breakfast before going off to work, saying he expected all the fuss would soon be over, which was supposed to pass for encouragement. By midday the baby had been in its cradle, and her mother already fretting about their father's supper and who would pick up the fish from the fishmonger. Daisy had made Letty go back to bed, promising to fetch the fish and to collect Minnie on her way home that evening. If anyone had ever thoroughly subjected herself to the wishes of a man it was her mother, Daisy told herself. But what had any of that got to do with corsets?

The works manager had begun on a different ploy from wheedling and flattery, gradually easing the protesters away from the windows by force, sweating under the glare of attention and the unusual nature of his task.

Mrs Allen, remembering her duties, told the machinists to get back to work.

"Women of Kirby unite! Off with your corsets!" cried Daisy, in perfect mimicry of the fair-haired girl at the head of the demonstration, and, laughing, the women left the windows.

Picking up a leaflet on her return to her bench, Daisy stuffed it into her pocket. She discovered it there on the way to the fishmonger's that evening and read as she walked along that the wearing of corsets caused a whole list of physical ailments, but also, more importantly it seemed, that the corset was a symbol of female frailty and male domination. There followed a selection of approved undergarments which supporters of the League might choose to wear instead: healthy bust bodies, woollen and silk drawers; and the names of the few stockists and mail-order companies who manufactured 'hygienic' corsets with fewer bones.

Too much time on their hands, thought Daisy pushing the pamphlet back in her pocket. It was all very well for some. She doubted that any one of those women, with their banners and fancy hats knew what real slavery was about.

* * *

Her mother had developed a fever when Daisy got home that evening, and could not eat the fish she cooked for her.

Daisy put Minnie to bed and sat by Letty's side until it got dark, when her father came in from the pub. He told her she could go off to bed, he would take over, and she left him crooning sentimentally over the cradle, whilst her mother slept heavily, her breath coming in harsh gasps in the hot bedroom.

Wilfred waited in the yard for Daisy when she came out of the water closet. "Is Mother going to die?"

"No. Of course not." Daisy was quick to reassure him, but the thought had not been far from her own mind; she had never seen her mother willing to stay in bed for so many hours, not even when Minnie was born, and that had been a hard birth. There had been other births, babies that had died, a boy-child that survived nearly a whole year; but Letty had never taken to her bed in this way.

Daisy changed the subject. "Are you glad it's a girl, or did you want a brother?"

He shrugged. "Don't mind. I just don't want her to die."

"She had a bad time, that's all. Sometimes it's like that when women have babies. She'll be all right. You'll see."

Daisy sat with him on the back doorstep and put her arm round his bony shoulders. "Still got the picture I gave you?"

He nodded.

"I get a guinea every time, Wilf. Even with Father pocketing five bob a time I shall be rich."

Her father had got used to her being photographed, after he had found out she was getting paid and he could insist on her handing over half the money — which she had told him was ten shillings. He even expressed pride these days about her being chosen, and supported her against their nan's disapproval.

"What will you do with the money?" said Wilfred.

Daisy did not need to think about an answer. "I shall buy clothes. Lovely clothes. Hats — " She recalled the protest women outside the factory. "Hats with feathers and flowers and ribbons, like ladies in society wear. And *silk* underclothes. And pretty shoes — and lots of dresses, one for every day of the week."

She told him about the dress in Robertson Callow's. With so much to do lately on Saturdays, there had been no time for tripping off to Leicester to look at it in the window, let alone going there to buy it.

"Father will kill you if he finds out," Wilfred said.

"But he's not going to find out, is he?" Daisy spoke with more confidence than she felt. "I shall hide it once I've bought it. Anyway, it's my money. I've earned it. Why should he care?"

"But if Mother can't work now. If — "

"That's different," Daisy said, and fell silent, contemplating the future if her mother should die, alone with her father, and with the care of the younger ones on her hands, too bleak and awful even to think about.

Daisy squeezed her brother's arm and gave him a push. "It's time you were in bed. You'll be falling asleep over your school books tomorrow."

Daisy was proud of Wilfred's ability at school. She had been no scholar, glad to leave at fourteen. But Wilf was clever. He would make something of himself one day, through his learning rather than his wits.

"Are you going to the factory in the morning?" Wilfred said.

Daisy studied his foxy, worried face in the semi-darkness. "I'll fetch Nan over to look after Mother. It'll be all right, Wilf. I promise. When have I ever been wrong about anything?"

All the same, it was a near thing. Their mother going into the hospital the next day was the only thing that saved her, the doctor said afterwards.

"She was a hair's breadth from the end," Daisy told the women at work. "If I hadn't run all the way, at midnight, *two miles* for the doctor, and if the fever hadn't broken when it did — " For once, she was telling the truth.

Besides all the worry, they had their father's moods to contend with during the weeks that followed, prowling the house like a caged animal, and, when he was not at home, drinking away his misery at the pub.

There was a sadness over the baby dying, even though they had half expected it, and though none of them had time to grow too fond. Minnie cried the most. She had been looking forward to having a baby sister, to pat and pet and make a doll out of.

Poor little scrap, Daisy thought, when she saw the baby laid out, and the size of the box for the funeral; the infant looked every bit like a wax version of the doll Minnie had wanted.

But in a way, the worst of it all had been having their grandmother come to stay.

There was nothing much to worry about once everyone knew Letty was going to recover, except for the fact of their grandmother being there morning and night, sleeping on a mattress downstairs and fussing over their father as if it was he who had suffered some terrible martyrdom.

If Daisy was as much as ten minutes late home from work, Nan was asking questions about where she had been, and who she had been with. If she went over to Mary Digby's house, or to the bathhouse to do the washing, or even up to the hospital to visit her mother, Nan wanted to know every detail of her journey.

Nan thought she was hanging around with boys. That was probably what *she* had done at eighteen, Daisy thought scathingly, in Easden Street where young men and women congregated after work at the weekends to flirt and eye one another up and down. The women giggling, gossiping, parading in gangs of two and three in the middle of the street; the men grouped for protection against a wall, slouching and feigning bravado, cat-calling, or moving along the pavement from time to time, with sidelong glances. Daisy would not have been seen dead there.

* * *

The day came at last when their grandmother went back home, and Letty was re-established in her own kitchen.

One Saturday lunchtime Daisy came home from work and found Minnie sitting up at the dining table polishing the knives and forks.

"Is that you, Daisy?" Letty was halfway up the ladder to Wilfred's attic, hanging on to one of the cradle rockers with one hand; she had been determined to move the crib out of the bedroom, but she lacked the strength to lift it above her head.

"Here — let me do that." Daisy took her place and hoisted the cradle up and through the hole in the ceiling, while her mother pushed from behind to stop her toppling off the ladder.

Letty climbed up after her into the attic.

They stared down at the cradle. Heavy and ugly and stained almost black, it looked like a miniature open coffin on rockers.

"Do you wish very much the baby had lived?" Daisy asked, curious that her mother should have welcomed another mouth to feed when she had Wilfred and Minnie still dependent on her, and their cousin Albert to look after half the time as well since his own mother was so sickly.

"I'd have loved her," Letty said, pushing a strand of fine hair behind her ear. "You can't help but love your own. But I can get back to work sooner this way, and it's one less to worry over. I know that. I'm not daft." She leaned against one of the roof timbers, holding her side after all the exertion, tipping back her head and closing her eyes briefly. Daisy realised that she must once have been more than pretty, alluring enough to catch the eye of others besides John Cornforth at the servants' parties and socials at Noonby Hall. She was thin though after her recent illness, and looked much older than thirty-seven.

Letty opened her eyes again. "Better hope we don't have to fetch it down for a while," she said with a little laugh.

"I should burn it," Daisy said fiercely.

"Don't be silly, girl. It will be yours one day — for you to rock your own children in."

Daisy bit back the retort that she would never be so foolish as to have babies unless she found a decent husband to share them with, who could afford a decent crib to put them in. She thought of the nurseries at Noonby, where her mother had started as a nurserymaid making up babies' feeds at thirteen years of age; she pictured the white walls and Dutch tiles, the washstands and big bright Turkey mats, miniature tables and chairs, books and pictures, a fort full of soldiers, a musical box that played 'Polly Put the Kettle On', and a rocking horse with a leather saddle and real horsehair for its mane. Did Letty never resent the contrast with the way she had brought up her own children?

"Daisy! Will you come over and give me a hand?"

They pushed the cradle into a corner.

No one but Wilfred usually came up here; the steep ladder was too much of an obstacle. The room was bare, except for Wilfred's mattress and the blankets over it. Daisy glanced about her, curious as to where he kept his box with the photo she had given him, and she saw it, tucked into an angle between the rafters.

Daisy went down to the bedroom and handed up a stack of baby clothes and cradle blankets.

"And that's that," said her mother, brushing her hands together, dusting off the whole episode. But her mouth was trembling, Daisy noticed, and when Letty came down the ladder to the landing she was trying not to cry.

"You should have burned it," Daisy said again. "I mean it. Don't have any more. Not if it's going to make you ill. Tell him."

Her mother looked away, her glance falling on the quilted counterpane of her marriage bed. "It's not as easy as that. You'll find out for yourself one day."

Letty saw that Daisy was still in her working clothes. "This has all been a bit

129

hard on you — never getting out to enjoy yourself as you ought."

"You mean Easden Street," Daisy said sarcastically.

"I mean a girl your age should be meeting people, going out with your friends. I know there's more to life than finding a decent young man, but that will come, I'm sure, now that you've been noticed by the management."

Daisy knew her mother was hoping she might find a husband from among the factory foremen, might even manage to catch one of the under-managers or designers if she was lucky. In Letty's eyes, Daisy should be looking out for a decent man who was kind and steady, drank only moderately, and was conscientious about his work.

"Tell you what — I can manage for this afternoon," Letty said. "Your father's at the football. Wilfred's taken Albert out for the afternoon, so there's only Minnie, and she can help me with the baking when she's finished on the cutlery. Go call on some of your friends. Get on out for the afternoon."

Daisy's spirits lifted. "I could catch the

train into Leicester. I'll ask Mary to go with me."

"That's the idea. Put your nice print dress on. The one Mrs Brackenborough gave me."

★ ★ ★

Daisy walked towards Granby Street and the centre of town from the railway station, savouring the moment when she would see the plate-glass windows of Robertson Callow's department store. She wore a green and mauve dress with small white daisies scattered over it. The style was old-fashioned, but she had altered the fullness of the skirt at the back, changing the line with skilful seaming; and the fabric was as good as it had been when it was handed down from mistress to maidservant.

Daisy told herself that it was the sort of dress a lady might wear even today: the embroidered voile was delicate and very tasteful. The flowers reminded her of the first corset they had named after her at Jerrett's. The Marguerite.

There had been several even classier

corsets to model since then; Mr Jerrett had shown her the finished pictures in the catalogues, saying that she got better and better. "You ought to have been an actress, my dear." He thought it was a compliment to imply that a factory girl might aspire to being an actress. He would say things like, "You could have the pick of anyone you choose, Daisy. Do you know that? You could have kings and princes kneeling before you." He meant she could be some man's mistress, if he were honest about it. What king or prince would want to *marry* a corsetmaker?

Mr Jerrett fancied her a bit himself. She could tell by the way he complimented her, and when his hand lingered over her shoulder in a fatherly gesture of reassurance, and by the way he looked at the advertisements, as if he didn't really want anyone else to touch them. Daisy was beginning to understand that she had power. But she was not going to waste it on old men and corset designers, and she was not going to get the most out of it either in a print dress handed down from her mother's past employer and twenty years out of date. She did not want her mother's ambitions for her: a decent husband, children of her own to clothe and feed, a nice little house away from Morton Street, with a bathroom perhaps and electricity.

She felt a rising excitement as she saw the department store ahead of her, and was glad she was alone. She had never intended asking anyone to come with her; Mary would only have spoiled everything by showing her up, twittering on about how 'lovely' all the dresses were, and commenting in her broad, uninhibited way on everything in the store, as if it was all foreign to her and out of her experience to enter the portals of Robertson Callow's.

Two windows along. The right-hand side. Daisy hoped the dress would be as sophisticated as she remembered, as lacy and full of romance. What if the price had gone up? What if it no longer worked its magic for her. What if — "

It was not there.

Daisy told herself she had the wrong window, walking the length of the shop front until she had persuaded herself that the dress no longer existed. Perhaps it had been a figment of her imagination from the very beginning. But of course, she told herself, the store wouldn't keep the same window display for two whole months running. She hurried inside, hopes reviving that she would find the dress somewhere on a stand in all its remembered glory.

But, though she described the afternoon dress in detail to the assistant in the dress department, she was told that it had been sold.

"We did have that model," said the assistant. "I remember. It *was* very lovely. Perhaps Madam would like to see something similar? This one is very like the ladies are wearing to garden parties this season."

But Daisy did not want her aspirations spelled out for her by a shop girl, nor did she want a poor substitute for the dress of her dreams.

"No, thank you. I shall leave it for today," she said, and swept away.

She wandered on soft carpet among the glass counters and dress stands, not seeing the displays, biting back the threat of tears. The dress had been more than a dream, it had begun to symbolise her eventual escape from Morton Street; and for that reason if no other, a different dress would not do.

Approaching the millinery displays, a defiant impulse took hold of her. She would buy a hat. Not any old hat. Not a boater like the one she was wearing, nor a dull, serviceable hat for work, but a glorious, frivolous hat of the kind worn by women of wealth and leisure. One that would have suited the afternoon dress, a hat someone might wear to a garden party.

Daisy examined each model and its price tag, imagining the occasions where one might wear them. There were straws of all colours; soft, low-crowned hats with lace-covered brims; hats trimmed with feathers and ribbons and roses made of pink fabric.

Straw was too reminiscent of her plain boater. She tried on a voile hat with an enormous brim, and then a toque covered in ribbons. "Always buy the best you can afford," Mrs Brackenborough had told her mother, who had passed the advice on to Daisy. "You can make clothes look good by wearing clean shoes and gloves and a smart hat. People look at your feet, and they look at your hands, and they notice if you're wearing a cheap hat."

"May I help Madam to select a style?"

A stony-faced assistant in a black dress, with black hair that looked like polished straw, had appeared by Daisy's side; her hands were raised, as if she would snatch the toque from her, and in a moment she did exactly that.

Daisy was about to protest that her money was as good as anyone's. But, instead of putting the hat back on its stand, the woman turned the toque in her hands and pressed it very firmly over Daisy's hair, saying, "If I might suggest — you were wearing it too far to the back, Madam. *This* is how this particular model is meant to be worn."

It was very stylish, thought Daisy surveying her reflection in the mirror. The very hat for a *best* dress, but not for the dress of her dreams. Nor did it suit the cotton voile she was wearing, and she said so.

"You're right. I think Madam needs a lighter touch. Perhaps a larger brim?"

The assistant seemed to be taking the whole business very seriously. With a feeling of delight, Daisy saw that the woman had mistaken her for someone whose money was, indeed, as good as anyone else's.

Daisy put on her Noonby voice: "It is for rather a special occasion. A garden party."

"Of course. I couldn't help noticing Madam is wearing the Suffrage colours. We have a special display of hats in support of the suffragette rally in London. They've been very popular."

Daisy glanced at her hand-me-down frock, realising only now that the pattern consisted of the purple, white and green of the votes-for-women supporters. She was on the point of saying that she certainly had nothing to do with *that* crowd, when the woman added, "All the ladies have been buying them for the garden party."

Putting the toque back on its stand, Daisy followed the assistant to a group of hats of all sizes, in shades of purple,

137

white and green. She began trying them on, saying how much she liked this one and that, and how suitable they were for the garden party — no longer a figment of her imagination, but to be held at Noonby Hall, she learned from the woman's chatter. By judicious twists and turns of the conversation Daisy discovered that the party was to take place the following week; Miss Brackenborough of the Hall had organised the event to raise funds for the Kirby Langton League, a branch of the women's Social and Political Union. Daisy said that she knew Miss Alice well.

"Noonby parties are always such fun in the open air," she added, quoting Letty. "You should see the little tables with their posies of flowers in the sunshine — purple, white and green, I expect — the big marquee will be on the lawn, and bunting in all the trees. And the carriages! Such a lot of arriving and departing, and everyone in light and lovely dresses, and a band playing and — oh, it will be so elegant."

She chose a hat trimmed with green velvet ribbon around the crown, with a large, sweeping brim decorated with bunches of violets and white roses. The assistant packed it into a round hatbox and Daisy handed over a guinea to pay for it.

"Thank you, Madam." The woman looked up with a smile. "And where shall I say it's to be delivered?"

"Delivered?" Daisy's heart missed a beat. She imagined the store's wagon arriving at her front door, the neighbours peering out from behind their curtains, the story of a hatbox delivered to Morton Street, told over and over with scorn and amusement by the shop assistants and by her parents' neighbours.

"Delivered?" she repeated. "Oh, no. There's no need. Since I need the hat very shortly I shall be taking it with me."

Daisy left with the hatbox string hooked over her arm and swung along the street as if she were still treading on carpet. She had bought a hat, a garden-party hat, and nobody had guessed she was not really a lady.

She spent an hour looking in all the shop windows, the hatbox banging reassuringly against her hip; she hoped people would notice, and admire its quality, and, reading the name 'Robertson Callow', would know at once that it contained a very elegant, very expensive hat that had cost her a guinea.

Idling away the time before catching her train, she went into a shop and bought a new pair of gloves — green to match the hat ribbon. The purchase necessitated lifting the lid of the hatbox to check the colour with the salesgirl, and explaining that the gloves must be an *exact* match with the ribbon because they were for a garden party at Noonby Hall.

"What a lovely hat, Madam," said the girl. "Just the thing for a summer occasion."

* * *

Daisy walked with a swing of her hips in her flowered dress, singing softly to herself, glad that the sun was shining. Every so often she raised her arms and spread her fingers to admire the green gloves, and checked the brim of her hat with both hands to make sure its dimensions were as grand as she remembered.

She had not meant to go beyond the gates of Noonby Hall. She had told herself that she would walk up the hill and pretend a little in passing, eager to catch a glimpse of the prettied-up gardens, the bunting and tables, and signs of people enjoying themselves; she would imagine she was attending the garden party. But, in a flurry of dust and sound, a motor car drove up alongside her at the very moment she reached Noonby's gates. Its driver was rigged out in tweeds and a motoring hat and goggles. The passenger, a young woman, leaned her arm on the passenger door. Daisy recognised her at once as the anti-corset campaigner who had led the demonstration outside Jerrett's factory.

"Are you on foot?" the girl called. "Hop in." With hardly a pause to think what she was doing, stepping forward with a murmur of thanks, Daisy climbed up into the rear-facing seat of the runabout as if it was second nature to her.

"I'm Beatty Knighton," the girl

volunteered. "And this is Clem."

They all shook hands over the seat rest.

"I'm — Marguerite." Daisy glanced about her for inspiration, seeing only the leather upholstery, shining chrome and bodywork of the motor car. "Marguerite Car-r."

Daisy was beginning to enjoy herself, putting up a delicate hand to hold on to her hat, and congratulating herself on the way she had slipped out of the house with Wilfred keeping cave. They bowled along the drive to the house and she watched the gates to the world outside Noonby's acres grow smaller and smaller behind her.

The man spoke for the first time since Daisy had joined them, tossing the remark over his shoulder. "Are you one of Beatty's merry band, Miss Carr?"

"Miss Brackenborough invited me," Daisy shouted above the noise of the motor.

"Do you know that it was Beatty who talked Alice into all this votes-for-women stuff in the first place?" Clem said. "And now Alice is preaching the word like billy-ho, as if it were all her own idea."

"It makes one feel almost superfluous," Beatty confessed to her with a laugh.

"You'll never get my sister to leave off her corsets though, Bea. You can bang on about some things to Alice until you're blue in the face. She has grown very attached to them. As is my mama."

His sister? His mama? With a mixture of horror and delight, Daisy realised that she was about to arrive at the Hall in the Brackenboroughs' own private motor!

Beatty turned to Daisy again. "Where are you from, Miss Carr? Do your family live locally?"

They had reached the front of the house, and a fortuitous spurt of noise from the engine drowned out any reply Daisy might have made.

Clem took off his hat and goggles to help the women from the car, and Daisy was able to get a good look at him. She knew very little about the youngest of the Brackenboroughs from Letty's stories; her mother had been promoted to lady's maid before he was born, and had left in disgrace soon after.

Daisy liked what she saw; he was

not very tall, but slender, with brown curly hair, nice eyes and a humorous mouth. She did not miss his discreet, but interested glance to see if she were corseted as he asked, "Are you anti corsets, Miss Carr?"

"Not me."

"Very wise. Don't mix campaigns. Beatty is a great mixer. If it's not one new cause, then it's another."

"Better than having no convictions at all, like some." Beatty flicked his ear with one of her gloves.

They seemed very familiar with one another, thought Daisy, as Clem's arm drifted to Beatty's shoulders and the girl smiled adoringly into his face.

"I don't hold with causes." Daisy had spoken before she could stop herself.

They looked at her in surprise.

"There's a frightful lot of nonsense talked about what's important in the world and what isn't, if you ask me," Daisy added, falling into her Noonby manner.

A blush spread over Beatty's pale neck and cheeks, and Clem regarded Daisy with a faintly approving amusement.

144

He let his arm drop from Beatty's shoulders. "I think I had better bow out at this point and leave you ladies to argue about what's at stake. Beatty, darling, would you mind if I restrict my appearance to later on? You know what it's like — one man cast adrift among a sea of ladies. Apologise for me to Mama."

"Just make sure you do put in an appearance," Beatty warned, as, stripping off his gloves, and with a bow to Daisy, he crossed the front of the house and made for the stables.

Beatty seemed willing to forgive Daisy's comment about causes as they approached the front steps. Hearing laughter and raised voices from the far side of the house, Daisy's heart pounded at the enormity of what she was doing — here she was, on the point of entering Noonby Hall; a situation which, minutes before, she could only have dreamed about.

Beatty greeted the butler, Warboys, as if he were an old friend, and Daisy, feeling she knew him too from her mother's descriptions, restrained herself with difficulty from doing the same. The man led them through the gloom of the entrance hall; there was an impression of dark furniture, paintings of dogs and horses, red marble pillars, vast areas of carpet and a carved staircase leading loftily upwards. They passed through a dining room with a red and blue richly decorated rug, more pictures of horses, a large tapestry screen at one end, and a heavy oak table that would have seated fifty. And then, before Daisy could draw fresh breath, they were outside again, through French doors and a conservatory leading to a grass terrace. She could not suppress a gasp of pleasure as, after the sombre darkness of the house, a blaze of colour met her eyes.

More than a hundred women of all ages milled about on the lawns among the flowerbeds, their dresses frothing with lace; some in white and ivory and cream, some in sweet-pea tones, with hats like plates of confectionery; many of them wore the colours of the suffragette movement.

Daisy thought she had never seen anything more glamorous. The flower borders, dotted with urns and topiary in front of a yew hedge, formed a backdrop to the graceful, undulating parade of colour; the vast lawn was a stage of green baize.

"Do you already know Alice's mother?" asked Beatty.

Unable to speak, Daisy shook her head.

"I'll introduce you."

They crossed the lawn to where Mrs Brackenborough, looking extremely regal and dressed in magenta, was dispensing tea from a number of silver teapots with a posse of maidservants in black dresses and caps standing behind her, waiting to replenish the pots with hot water.

Daisy was sure she was about to be found out, suddenly terrified of meeting her mother's one-time employer, the most beautiful woman in Kirby Langton, whose parties in Victoria's reign had been the talk of the area, and whose clothes were made in France. Her hand shook, as a maid handed her a china cup and saucer and Mrs Brackenborough poured a pale stream of tea, smiling a vague welcome, saying that friends of her daughter were always welcome at Noonby.

147

Daisy looked at the quartet of maid-servants, recognising Mrs Peaches the cook from Letty's stories, realising that twenty years ago her mother might have stood there too, equally patient and deferential, scurrying to the house at top speed if sent on some errand, doing exactly as she was bid. Daisy felt a pulse of humiliation for her.

Beatty was leading her away from the teapot ceremony. Furnished with tea and dainty sandwiches they paused by a bed of nicotiana and catmint, and Daisy, wondering if her father would have approved of the planting, listened without much interest to Beatty explaining her position on corsets. "I think, if you took time to examine the issues — "

Daisy let her companion talk about her campaign before saying after a few minutes, "Have you thought how many women you'd put out of work if you had your way, and corsets were abolished?"

Beatty opened her mouth to answer.

"Besides — " Daisy continued. "Most women I know *like* wearing corsets."

"Only because they have been trained to think that way. It's too bad. Men have been dictating what we should or shouldn't do for centuries, even down to how we should dress."

"Rubbish," said Daisy energetically. "Is that really what you think? I'll agree with you, men have had it all their own way in most things for far too long. But are we women too weak-minded to say, I'll wear what I jolly well like?"

"I think women have been persuaded to conform. To wear what *men* want them to wear."

"We want to be admired. But that's because we enjoy it. What's wrong with that?"

"We shouldn't pander to men's ideas of what's pleasing."

"No? I noticed you're dressed to the nines for the afternoon with your best hat on. Don't you go telling me you didn't want your Clem to admire you when you sat next to him in his motor?"

Beatty was looking at her with a startled expression, and Daisy realised that she had allowed her 'Noonby Hall' manner to slip and had begun arguing as she might do with Mary, or any of the other women at Jerrett's.

"Where did you say your people are from, Miss Carr?" Beatty prompted.

"I didn't."

Daisy gave a mental prayer of thanks as a young woman approached, diverting Beatty's attention. The newcomer, tall and angular, with an abundance of glossy fair hair pinned high on her head, held out her arms in greeting and the two women embraced, their lips brushing the air with affectionate enthusiasm.

Beatty turned to introduce Daisy.

"This is Miss Carr. But — I forgot, you already know one another."

"Do we?" Alice Brackenborough smiled at Daisy expectantly. "I'm so sorry. Remind me of where we have met."

"We haven't." Daisy felt herself growing hotter.

Beatty looked at her with growing suspicion. "I thought you said Alice invited you."

"I didn't actually say that we had met." Daisy clutched for ideas. "Actually, I shouldn't be here at all. I'm from Kirby. I'm — " she grasped for inspiration, "a sort of spy."

"A spy?" said Alice with amusement.

"Yes. My family is in the corset trade."

"I see," Beatty said coldly. "No wonder you attacked me so roundly. Which company?"

"Jerrett's. Mr Jerrett is — my uncle."

"And I suppose he sent you here after our demonstration at his factory?"

"Yes." Daisy was beginning to warm to the idea of being on a mission. "Well — no, actually. He doesn't know I'm here."

"So — " Alice said. "Are you one of us or not? You're wearing the colours."

"That depends what you mean," said Daisy quickly. "I'm not anti-corsets. But I believe in women's rights and in standing up for ourselves."

"So do I," said Alice. "But lose sight of my *waist*? Good Lord, what an idea! Beatty gets such *fads*. Don't you, Bea?"

Still regarding Daisy with suspicion, Beatty did not answer. But Alice linked her arm through Daisy's in a companionable way.

"I think you *are* one of us, Miss Carr. I admire your spirit, even if it was rather naughty of you to spy on Bea's contingent. We are all going to be photographed to mark the Suffrage League's fund-raising event. You and I shall stand in the front row, secure in our corsets, and wave the banner for women's more general emancipation."

★ ★ ★

Was it simply bad luck? Or was there such a thing as fate? Having escaped once, Daisy could only assume that the devil had decided to take a mischievous hand in the afternoon. How else could anyone explain why the only photographer in Kirby Langton who might recognise her had been appointed to photograph the garden party.

She pulled the brim of her hat down to one side to shield her face as she passed him, but Alice was intent on placing Daisy in a prominent position, steering her towards the front row, chatting all the while in a loud voice as she greeted friends, tossed fragments of conversation to one or another and, in between, asked Daisy about her 'uncle' and his factory, remarking that she believed she had ordered her latest corsets from Jerrett's. "Wouldn't it be fun if Brackenborough's Machine Companies had supplied Jerrett's factory in the old days — I must ask my father if he knows."

Daisy gave up trying to hide from the photographer, deciding that, since she was going to be found out sooner or later, she might as well enjoy what was left of her adventure.

Alice said that with Kirby Langton being such a close community, it was surprising their paths had not crossed before. She was sure her father must know Mr Jerrett. What did Daisy's father do? Was he a manufacturer too? Had she been to any of the Percival family's 'at homes'? Did she know the Lefevres? Or the Moulds?

Daisy was vague, saying that her father had a financial interest in quarrying. She said she found the Moulds depressing, and the Lefevres too 'foreign', and as for the Percivals — were they ever *at* home? Seizing one end of the League's banner, flanked by Alice and Beatty, she faced the camera with a broad smile. She prayed the man would be so dazzled by the crowd of females that he would not notice her, and completed the rallying call for the women of Kirby Langton by unfurling the word 'Unite'.

* * *

Daisy watched distractedly as the crowd of women dispersed, drifting in twos and threes across the lawn when the photographer had finished. The scene seemed to have slowed down, as if everyone were moving through a dream from which she could not wake. She felt strangely lightheaded, as if she were going to faint, but was rooted to the spot as she saw the photographer making a determined path towards her. At the same time, Clem Brackenborough was walking across the lawn. If she made a run for it, made a dash between them for the conservatory and out through the house . . .

"Daisy? Daisy Cornforth from Jerrett's? Fancy seeing you here."

Daisy threw the photographer a look, half threatening, half pleading. Perhaps he would take the hint and go away.

But the silly man, who hardly said a civil word to her when she was modelling for him, stood there, smiling, wanting to be sociable.

"I beg your pardon?" said Daisy. "You've made a mistake."

"Come on, Daisy. I'd know that face anywhere. I spotted you as soon as I looked through the camera. What's going on?"

"I'm sure you *are* mistaken," Alice said. "This lady is Mr Jerrett's niece."

It was probably quite an insult, thought Daisy, to imply that a photographer's eyesight was at fault. He began to look annoyed, insisting she was a model for Jerrett's corsets, and that he had the plates to prove it.

"Are you saying Mr Jerrett's *niece* has modelled corsets?" Alice was still confused.

"She's Daisy Cornforth from the machining room. If you've been passing yourself off as Jerrett's niece, Daisy, I think Mr Jerrett himself ought to hear about it."

Clem Brackenborough spoke lazily, deciding to intervene. "Is that really necessary? I'm sure this was all some harmless joke."

"Thank you," Daisy said quickly.

"I'm sure," said Beatty, "there was no criminal intent."

"Criminal? Now look here. If any of you think I came to pinch the silver — "

"I should keep quiet, if I were you," said Clem in quite a different tone. "You're in rather a tricky position."

"You came here under a false name!" Alice grew indignant as she realised that the girl she had been chatting with and had taken under her wing was an imposter, a member of the working classes; she had been made to look a fool. A thought struck her. "Have you paid your five shillings?"

"Five shillings! For a thimbleful of tea and a sandwich?"

"It's for the League," said Beatty drily. Now that Daisy had been exposed, she, unlike Alice, seemed amused rather than angered by the situation.

Daisy took the money from her purse, handing it to Alice with the air of handing over a tip.

"Here's five shillings for your silly

League. Don't let anyone ever say I don't pay my way."

* * *

Daisy's sense of pride faded as she marched along the drive. She had handed over five precious shillings for the satisfaction of being humiliated. She dared not think of all the things she might have bought with the money, nor how many hours she would have to work to earn as much again. She felt dangerously close to tears.

Not for an instant did she believe they had been in their rights to turn her out after she had *paid*. Not that she would have wanted to stay. She remembered the way everyone had stared, some had even sniggered, as the red-faced Warboys escorted her round the side of the house and through the kitchen gardens; she told herself it was the last time she would envy or admire people like the Brackenboroughs.

Daisy consoled herself with the thought that at least there had been nobody else there who knew her at Jerrett's and

157

so might spread the story among her friends; the photographer had agreed to forget the incident. But she had reckoned without the photograph itself, exhorting the women of Kirby to unite, attracting attention in the photographer's window, as well as in the League's magazine.

A week after the garden party, Daisy was summoned from her workbench to go to Mr Jerrett's office. Anticipating another modelling assignment, she sped up the stairs with a light heart.

Mr Jerrett was alone, a magazine open on the desk in front of him. He greeted her coldly instead of coming to meet her as usual and putting an arm round her shoulders or telling her how nice she looked.

He said it had been brought to his attention by 'various people' that Daisy had aided an organisation that sought to bring about the abolition of corsets. What did she have to say for herself?

Plenty, thought Daisy. But he had the photograph in front of him; she could see the banner, urging women to unite, and herself standing behind it.

"It isn't how it looks."

"You were there. Heaven knows how or why you were at Noonby Hall. But you were there, amongst all these — *protesters!*"

"My mother knows Mrs Peaches, their cook. I was invited. Former staff and their families."

"There's a story that you were pretending to be my niece."

Daisy's heart sank. So much for her trust in the photographer's discretion.

"I went in disguise," she began. "On behalf of the factory. Some of these women are saboteurs, you never know what they could be planning. I couldn't have told them who I *really* was, could I?"

"I'm afraid, Daisy, I don't believe you."

Daisy did not blame him. But his disappointment in her was harder to bear than his anger. He said how he was hurt by the escapade; he had thought she was honest, a good girl, loyal to the company. He had thought of her almost as a daughter.

Not quite true, thought Daisy, but never mind.

She heard him explain how, because of the damning evidence of the photograph, he was going to have to 'let her go'.

Daisy stopped thinking up stories. If that was how it was going to be, after all she had done for them, she no longer cared, she washed her hands of the lot of them.

* * *

"Is that you, Daisy?"

The full force of her position hit Daisy as she reached the house in Morton Street. She was out of work with no references.

Her mother came into the front room, wiping her hands on her apron.

"I've got the sack." For once Daisy was too shocked to think up a lie. "I was told to collect my money and leave right away."

Letty's expression of concern froze into one of panic. "No. How will we manage? I'm not back to work yet."

"I'll get another job," Daisy said brightly, but without conviction.

"What did you do? What happened?"

"Nothing — "

"You don't get the sack for nothing!" Her mother began to cry.

Daisy told her. Some of it. She said she had been seen with a few Women's Suffrage supporters, that she had got carried away, had waved a banner.

"But that's not fair."

"Life isn't fair, Mother," Daisy said gravely. "Mr Jerrett simply wouldn't listen to me."

Letty set her mouth and reached for her coat. When it came to protecting her family from outsiders . . .

"I'll go and see him. I'll have it out with him."

"No — " Daisy said in alarm. "No, Mother. It's too late for all that."

They looked at one another, and Letty began to weep again. "How are we going to tell your father?"

★ ★ ★

Beatty and Alice had been friends since childhood. Their parents moved in the same circles, though the Poplars, a large house on the outskirts of Kirby Langton,

161

was far less grand than Noonby Hall.

The girls were discussing the 'opposite sex' with lighthearted candour in the garden at Noonby, analysing the merits and failings of the various young men they knew.

Algie Mould had pots of money, but an irritating laugh. Monty Percival was a bore, there was nothing in his favour except for his delectable looks. Richard Lefevre would inherit a glamorous title, and was very, very amusing, but he spent money like water, and all on horses — a fact which troubled Alice more than Beatty; she was twenty-three, and was going to have to make a choice some time in the not too distant future.

The discussion returned frequently to Alice's brothers, Austen, who was already married, and Clem, whom Alice thought absolutely perfect as a brother. In Alice's mind, he and Beatty, her very best friend, were already halfway to the altar, and she could think of no more perfect arrangement. But in Beatty's opinion, Clem could do with a few hints about paying a girl more attention whenever he was home from university.

"He absolutely adores you, Bea," Alice protested, irritated by the insecurity that made Beatty need such reassurances. Alice had a way of seeing things in clear-cut terms; she could not be bothered with nuances of feeling, or complications of character. Besides, her brother Clem wasn't complicated. Not in the least. She only wished she could feel as enthusiastic about a match between herself and Algie, or Richard Lefevre, or Monty Percival.

They were laughing about Algie Mould's way of pronouncing '*s-spiff*licated', when one of the grooms came out from the house and towards where they were sitting.

"Excuse me, Miss Alice. There's a *person* here to see you. She's very insistent that she won't leave a message, but she says you know her. Says she's a supporter of the Women's Suffrage League."

"No name, Freddie?" said Alice.

"She wouldn't say, Miss. She's quite irregular. A proper termagant."

"Is she, indeed? Well. We approve of 'irregular' persons, do we not, Bea?" They laughed, a little unkindly at the young man's inexperience and embarrassment over the situation. "Show the termagant into the garden."

The groom returned to the house and, blushing deeply, returned with Daisy.

"Good Lord." Tipping back her head, Beatty regarded Daisy with detached amusement. "Who are you today? Miss Carr or the corsetmaker? You've got a nerve. I'll say that much for you."

Daisy had put on her workclothes and boater for her expedition to the Hall: a grey serge coat and skirt which were too hot for July and mended over and over from the times when, walking too quickly, she had caught her heel in the hem. But she had worn them to make a point — that she had no time for people like the Brackenboroughs. Now she wished she had put on her best dress and the new hat. She would have felt less exposed.

"I've come for my five shillings."

"You really think — " began Alice.

"I've lost my job. Because of appearing in your photograph for the League I lost my job at Jerrett's. So, I think you owe me my money back. That's the least the league can do."

"She means it." Beatty shook her head in exaggerated amazement.

Daisy was determined not to leave without the money, but Alice had noticed something.

"How did you get that bruise?"

Instinctively Daisy's hand flew to cover the mark on her jaw where her father had let fly when he learnt she was out of work.

"I fainted in the factory when I heard I'd been dismissed. It was the shock, knowing how short money is at home, and how much they rely on me. They say I went down with such a crack, I was lucky not to knock out my teeth as well."

Alice curled her mouth in distaste. "Really, this is too bad. You come here demanding money — "

"*My* money. You owe it to me. I paid it towards the League. And it's because of the League I've got no job."

"Oh, I'll give her the five shillings," said Beatty, searching in her purse.

"No." Alice had her own sense of justice. "Young woman, you talk as if it's *our* fault you were trespassing at the garden party, pretending to be who you were not."

"I didn't trespass. *She* invited me."

Alice looked at Beatty in surprise.

"Her and your brother. 'Hop in the car,' she said. I never asked to come here."

"You *looked* as if you were coming to the party. This is ridiculous. You allowed us to think that was where you were bound. Good Lord. We didn't exactly kidnap you." Beatty was defensive, beginning to feel a degree of responsibility for the situation; after all, she and Clem had driven the girl to Noonby without any questions.

"I was out for a walk."

"Dressed like that?"

"I like to look nice on my days off. Do you think a corsetmaker shouldn't wear nice things?"

"I didn't mean — "

"I don't see how you can afford to wear expensive clothes," said Alice. "After all, you say your family's short of money."

"We weren't short then. Only now. With me being out of a job, and you owing me five shillings."

Beatty counted out the money. "You ought to join the League. You said you believed in women standing up for themselves."

Daisy could hardly believe she had won back her five shillings; she knew she would be a fool to push her luck further, but something made her press on with an idea that had been brewing since she had left Jerrett's.

"Will you listen to me for five minutes?"

"We already have," said Alice ironically, glancing at her watch. "At least that."

"I've read your leaflet about you and your band telling everyone to wear loose-fitting clothes, and the kind of corset that doesn't damage a lady's insides. I've been thinking about how I'm good at making things. I can make up dresses as well as corsets. I can make the kind of clothes you want. I've got no references from my last place of work. It's going to be hard to find another job. But I could make these clothes for you and your friends — tailor-mades, woollen underwear. I would charge half the price you'd pay in a shop, and the money you all save by coming to me could go towards the League."

"But you don't believe in the League," said Beatty.

Daisy did not see what any of what she had said had to do with believing in something. This was a business proposition.

"I told you. I think women ought to do what they want. And if what your people want is to wear woollen bust-bodices and vote for parliament, and what I want is not to get thrown out of a job because of getting my face in some photograph, that's good enough for me."

"Where would you make the clothes?" Beatty asked. "At home?"

Daisy was beginning to see that there were drawbacks to her plan. There had not been enough time yet to think about it.

"You'd have to find me somewhere to work. And a machine, and flat irons and all the rest of it. But I know where the suppliers are. I'd need money to start off. I could pay it back to you, bit by bit."

Alice stared at Beatty. "You're surely not considering the idea, Bea?"

168

"Why not?"

"Because it's preposterous."

Alice was prepared to feel a little sympathy for Daisy because she had lost her job — she was not totally without feeling — but she was not prepared to take someone as cheeky as Daisy seriously. The girl came from a different background, one that repelled her when she thought of the way some people lived. Daisy had little or no education; they and she had absolutely nothing in common except the fact that they were female.

"The girl can't be trusted."

"Yes, I can."

"I believe her," Beatty said. "It seems to me that her idea could benefit all of us. She could set up a workroom here."

"At Noonby!" Alice's voice came out as a squeak. "My parents would never allow it."

"At the Poplars then. My parents are very encouraging towards free enterprise, Daisy. My father is extremely forward-thinking."

"I wouldn't need much room. Somewhere dry to store the fabrics. Enough space for

169

a sewing bench and a cutting table."

"The coach house. Perfect."

Alice shook her head with frank scepticism.

Beatty smiled confidently, and Daisy returned the smile with a growing sense of excitement. She could not believe it, was still not sure it was happening, but she thanked God for bored wealthy women.

★ ★ ★

"How do you know she won't cheat you? She's proved she's a liar," said Clem, when Beatty explained why the room over her father's coach house was being turned into a workshop.

"I trust her. I *like* her. There's something very refreshing about her nerve. Don't be an old sourpuss."

"We Brackenboroughs believe in being more careful with our investments."

"You Brackenboroughs were tradesmen once, like Daisy. That's why you only enthuse about a scheme when you're sure there's a profit in it. Well, I'm telling you, this has profit in it for the League. And for Daisy. And if my parents are keen to go along with the enterprise, so can you, Clem. You and Alice are outvoted."

"Your father would do anything that you asked him," Clem said, watching Beatty unpack the straw from around a newly delivered sewing machine. The loft, where the Knightons' stable hands had slept in the days when the household kept more than one carriage, had been scrubbed out and painted in green and white, with mauve curtains at the windows; militant colours, a domestic touch that amused him.

"This could make Daisy quite comfortably off, and she knows it," Beatty said. "I'm going to help her. I shall teach her how to behave. Refine her a little."

Clem looked at her sceptically. Beatty's enthusiams were notoriously draining on those around her. Inherently lazy, he sensed he was in danger of being dragged into her scheme. "Does she know? Should someone warn her?"

"You can help too." Beatty stepped back to admire the machine in its place on the bench. "I thought we might start by taking her to a restaurant for

171

dinner, to celebrate the arrival of the equipment."

"If she's going to eat her peas with her knife, I think I'll give it a miss."

"No, Clem. You will not give it a miss. You'll escort me and Daisy, and you'll be nice to her."

Beatty put on a determined pout, an expression she thought was appealing. Clem, who liked Beatty because she was generally free of affectation, hoped this was not an example of what she meant by refining Daisy. He felt instinctively that the girl should not be meddled with, and that teaching her how to put on the charm could ruin her; she had a natural audacity that was, he had to admit, appealing.

"Very well, we shall go to a restaurant, and anywhere else you please." He put his hands in his pockets and rocked back on his heels. "It will be interesting to see whether she resists your attempts to improve her."

5

"WHAT I want to know is whether Daisy and Clement Brackenborough had an *affair*," Liz said to Don. "Willow can't, or won't, say."

The idea of a love affair disturbed as well as intrigued her. Liz had never quite believed Don's lesbian theory, but she had enjoyed the image of Daisy as a woman who had gone against all the conventions in order to pursue her career.

"It's so difficult to sort out how much Willow really knows. She falls back on talking about Paris, but it's a bit over the top. You know? All that stuff about the twenties and thirties when young people were uninhibited and very glamorous."

"Perhaps she doesn't know as much about Daisy as she makes out. After all, she didn't meet her before Paris."

"That's true. She could only have known what Daisy, as Marguerite, wanted

173

to tell her, and Daisy apparently told lies. So, what have we got so far? Daisy made corsets and modelled them for a firm in Kirby Langton, hence the photograph. Her father found out and there was a row, but that's not actually why her family disowned her, although, at first, Willow said it was. Daisy sets up in business in Kirby Langton, and then in Leicester according to Clement Brackenborough's letter. But we still don't know why she really fell out with her family . . . "

Don was watching her with an air of barely contained impatience as she pondered the enigma, her elbows on her desk, her fingers twisting her hair.

"Is any of this relevant to your research?"

Liz looked at him in surprise. "Does it matter?"

"It's only a little while since you were telling me how difficult it would be for you to take time off to come with me to France. How come you can afford to spend hours every week with some half gaga old lady you hardly know, chatting about the sex life of a dim and distant relative who died ages ago? Do you think

174

we might discuss something else, instead of whether your feisty ancestor did or did not have it off with Major whatsit of the manor?"

Sarcasm was so rarely a part of Don's armoury that Liz was jolted out of her mood of reflection. Logging off, she followed him downstairs where he had begun slicing courgettes and onions in the kitchen, banging the knife about vigorously with a heavy hand.

"What is it?"

"Stir fry — "

"Not the dinner. What's bothering you?"

He halted his attack on the vegetables. "I don't understand why you've got so much time to go off to this nursing home to visit this woman Willow — nor why you've developed such a thing about Daisy."

"It's a *residential* home. And, while we're on the subject, Willow is far from gaga."

She watched Don, feeling angry with him over Willow, and defensive about identifying with Daisy. "I like Willow. I'm probably the only friend she has at the moment, if you must know."

"How very nice for her."

"Don't be childish."

Torn between the habit of conciliation and a much stronger desire to retaliate, Liz remembered what Willow had said. *Was* she unsure of her feelings, beginning to wonder if she might be better off without him?

Daisy had been like that, incapable of sustaining a relationship. Hugging her arms round her, Liz suddenly felt cold. Oh, why couldn't everything simply be as it was? They had loved one another for half a decade without having to think too deeply about it.

Don watched the onions turn translucent in the pan as he stirred them. "There's a headship going at Yarnest next year. I heard about it from Cliff. I think he might apply."

"The school in Norfolk?"

It was a post Don had coveted since she had known him. He had talked about it in the way people muse about dream situations in the future, if they could choose their favourite place to live. Norfolk, reminiscent of childhood

176

holidays spent with hordes of cousins and his aunt and uncle, had always been a romantic idyll.

Not sharing his enthusiasm for the eastern counties, Liz had been casually confident that Yarnest, a model school, would never be more than a dream. She began cutting mushrooms into thin slices. "There'll be competition for it, besides Cliff."

"I expect so. But I stand far more chance than he does." He hesitated. "There are things that could make a difference."

"Things?" For a moment she genuinely did not understand.

"I mean, if I were married — "

Suddenly Liz was really angry. "You want to marry me as a career move now?"

"No. Of course not. It came out badly."

"It sounded clear enough to me. You're trying to blackmail me! I won't have this. You're not being fair."

They did not resolve the matter during supper; weighted by the news of the headship, they ate in silence, whilst Liz brooded. They would have to move, she thought, sell the Lodge, start afresh. Logically, a fresh start meant marriage. What was the alternative?

"I can't marry you for all the wrong reasons," she said at last.

"I know. It doesn't matter. It's only a school, only a job after all."

"But you've always wanted to go back there." Liz tried to imagine how she would feel if something she wanted as much was in her reach and then about to be snatched away again. She knew instinctively that she could not have said she would give it up for his sake.

★ ★ ★

Jennifer called the next day after Liz returned home from her classes at the university. Mark, it seemed, had embarked on a sordid — and not his first — affair with a new receptionist at the group practice.

"The trouble is, I love him, the *pig*," Jennifer sobbed, mopping at her nose.

Liz handed her a box of tissues, marvelling that the sister she had once looked up to — of the three sisters, Jennifer had been blessed with the most striking looks, a wedge of glossy dark hair, and aggressive, confident features — the sister she had followed slavishly, envied and tried to imitate, should now be such a stranger, and that she envied her not at all.

"I ought to leave him. I know I ought. But what can I do? I can't live without him." Jennifer began to weep afresh.

Liz made them both coffee, sat her at the kitchen table, and told her it was probably not as bad as it seemed; if the rumours were true — and privately Liz had no doubts that they were — the affair would fizzle out like all the others had in the past. Mark loved her. He was simply one of those men stuck in a permanent adolescence, who needed the excitement of the sexual chase.

"You're so lucky," Jennifer sniffed, calming down, sipping her coffee with both hands locked round the mug. "Don would never so much as *look* at another woman. And you're not even married to him."

"I suppose so."

"I *ought* to leave. All my friends tell me I should. But I'm thirty-four, Liz. I've got an insecure job and three kids." Jennifer worked as a production assistant for a struggling TV film company. "Where am I going to find anyone else? It's not like being in your twenties. Men in their thirties and forties are either married, divorced, or gay."

Liz was beginning to feel depressed. She had been oddly unsettled by the university students that afternoon; seeing couples with their arms wound round one another as they walked along, so naively young, she had found herself envying them because their lives and loves were only just beginning.

Jennifer noticed her mood. "Am I interrupting you? I suppose you were working."

"It's all right, I've only this minute got in. It's my day for teaching."

"Oh, Liz — I'm sorry. You'll be tired. I only came round to borrow some ideas for the next production. Really, I never meant to tell you all my troubles."

"What sort of ideas?" Liz was happy to change the subject.

180

"Oh — about the Stuarts. Stays, stomachers, farthingales. You know the sort of thing. If I could look through some pictures?"

They went upstairs to the office, where Liz had already switched on her computer.

"How's the book coming along?" Jennifer glanced at the screen, on which was displayed the next chapter, 'The Corset and the Fantasy Female'.

"OK. Very well, in fact. I thought I might go back to the Midlands museum before Easter and confirm a few details."

"That's a good idea. Have a break."

Jennifer read aloud from the text on the screen while, pretending not to mind, Liz photocopied pictures for her.

"The ideal female shape has altered over the decades and centuries, according to whether breasts, hips, or waists have been in fashion. Thus the bum rolls and panniers of the seventeenth century, and crinolines and bustles of the nineteenth were as important in creating a sexual image as was the corset. The discarding of the corset at certain periods in history has often in itself been a fashion statement. In the early 1800s the ideal shape was quasi-Grecian; androgenous in the 1920s; wafer-slender in more modern times. Never has the feminine ideal allowed for the natural variations in individual figure types. All must strive towards the image of the fantasy female."

"When would I have been in fashion?" asked Jennifer with typical and disarming self-centredness.

Liz regarded her sister's tall, pear-shaped figure. Good 'child-bearing hips', she thought, remembering Mark's commendation. But Jennifer's hips had already done their duty in bearing her husband three sons. Would Don's interest begin to roam too once he had what he wanted?

No. That was ungenerous of her; she knew him better than to believe that.

"Liz — ?" Jennifer said plaintively. "What about me?"

"You'd have looked gorgeous in any era," Liz said, turning off the copier. "And, if you ask me, your husband needs a good shaking up."

Jennifer frowned. "I don't know what to do. I'm tired of forgiving him and then being trodden on all over again. Now that the children are older I could leave him. It's tempting to start over again."

Her words brought Liz's thoughts back to Don. She told Jennifer about the headship in Norfolk. It was a bigger, better school. It would be a good career move.

"But that's marvellous — " Jennifer hesitated. "Isn't it? You'd go with him of course?"

"Why should I want to go all that way across the country? I like it *here*. And there's my university teaching to think of."

"But you could do that somewhere else. And your books are the main thing, Liz. You'd still be able to write. It's not a million miles. Only to Norfolk."

"He wants us to get married. He feels it's time to settle down."

"That's what the rest of us have been saying for ages. You and Don are made for each other."

"How can you stand there and say that? How can you possibly think you know something like that? People change."

Liz thought of the women she knew who had once sworn with feminist certainty that a career was the most important thing in their lives. That afternoon after her classes, Sarah Kendrick, a fellow lecturer, had confided that she was undergoing IVF treatment; Liz had been shocked to learn that Sarah and her partner had been trying to have a child for six years.

"It's hopeless, Liz," she had said. "They tell us there's not much point in trying again. What's the point of anything, if I can't have children?"

"You've got your work — " Liz had protested.

"Where's the satisfaction in that! I've had enough of pretending it's all so very fulfilling, and how much I really love the job. There's more to life than being a career woman. Women *need* motherhood."

"It's pretty terrifying, the way people change," Liz said gloomily. "What if I do marry? What if we had a family? How do I know I would still want to carry on with my work?"

Jennifer laughed, puzzled. "But, if you didn't want to do it — " She did not understand. "It wouldn't matter."

"Of course it matters," Liz said passionately. "It matters terribly. This — " She waved a hand to indicate the files and papers and muddle. "This is what I am. I don't want to be anyone different."

"Well then. You can carry on being you *and* have a family. It's easy. If I can do it — "

"Why should everyone assume that marriage and family is what I want, when I feel perfectly contented with the way things are now?"

"Because it's what every woman wants deep down."

"Willow didn't. Daisy didn't," Liz said desperately.

"Who?"

Liz reminded her of the photograph of Daisy, and told her about her visits to Meadowfields.

"So, the girl in the corset was cut off by Granddad's family because she had an affair with this man Clement Brackenborough?"

"I don't know whether she did or she

didn't have an affair. Perhaps there were other reasons, nothing to do with him. Willow's being enigmatic about it. But the family certainly turned against her. It looks as though Wilfred — Granddad — tried to get in touch with her again after the First World War. Dad and I found a letter — "

Jennifer glanced at her watch. "This all sounds *really* interesting, Liz, but I must dash. Thanks for the pictures." She picked up the pile of photocopied illustrations. "And thanks for the chat. I feel heaps better. What you said about being contented as you are has made me see things in perspective again. I've got my job, got my kids — what could be more important?"

★ ★ ★

Willow sat, cutting a cream cake contentedly into pieces.

They had driven to a café in Wells after Willow had said she was bored with staring at the garden every time Liz came to visit. Willow had also said that she remembered now *exactly* where she had planted the primula, and she took Liz to see it before they left Meadowfields.

Looking up dementia in a medical book, Liz had been reassured to read that victims " . . . *do not necessarily progress from mild dementia, failure to remember recent events and disorientation regarding time and place, to the more severe forms of disability . . . "*

But which sort was Willow's? How did one know?

They had stood looking at the yellowing leaves of the pot plant. The place was marked with a long stick broken from an ash tree. "Next year," Willow said. "Married to your young man or not. You're to come and see it flowering."

Liz had told her about Sarah at the university, about Mark's transgressions, and Jennifer's and Sarah's opinions that every woman wanted marriage and a family. She said nothing about the possible move to Norfolk.

"Is there really only one way for a woman to succeed?" she said. "If you don't fit the ideal you've failed? Even Jennifer, whose rating as the perfect wife and mother isn't very high, thinks there's

187

such a thing as a norm to which every woman should aspire."

"Perhaps, in your case, it has nothing to do with whether you should or should not settle down and have babies."

Liz glanced at her, knowing her too well by now to challenge the statement; more would come, and it did, making her wince.

"Perhaps I'm right in thinking your Don's simply not *the* man."

"But — "

"You've told me how you've always seemed to back out of commitments."

"But I didn't *love* those men."

"Perhaps you don't really love Don."

Willow wiped cream off her cheek and licked cream from her fingers, looking pleased with her deductions.

Liz said with a sinking feeling, "How do you know whether you really love someone?"

"One just does. I did. There had been others before Albert, but when I met him it was different, like nothing I had ever experienced. He was such a darling of a man. And it was the same for him as it was for me."

188

"What about Daisy?" asked Liz. "Do you think it was like that for her and Clem?"

Willow did not answer. She pretended to ignore the question. "Sometimes, of course, it's all one-sided. And then there's not much either party can do about it. We saw that rather a lot at the couture house — men hanging around the doors carrying big bunches of flowers. Poor things. I had my admirers. And so did the other girls."

"And Daisy?" Liz ventured again.

To her surprise Willow took up the question this time. "There were a few. One in particular, an Englishman in Paris, but she was not really interested by then."

Willow drank the last of her tea. "She ought to have married Clem, she could probably have had him if she had really wanted him. She could have carried it off. She had the 'grand manner' for Noonby Hall. It came naturally to her."

"Perhaps he never asked her."

Willow glanced at Liz swiftly, then looked down. "Perhaps he never did . . . Shall we go?"

189

They walked along the narrow streets near the cathedral. "Do you remember the letter I found from Clem to my grandfather?" Liz asked after a while.

"Did you?" said Willow noncommittally.

"He wrote after the First World War. Wilfred was trying to trace Daisy. Did Albert say whether Wilfred found her in the end?"

"I don't remember. I wasn't all that interested."

They walked on slowly across the Cathedral Green.

After a while Willow said, "Wilfred had seen her *before* the war. Albert went with him and Daisy's mother to the dress shop in Kirby Langton, one Christmas. Albert was only a little boy, but he never forgot it. He always said he wasn't surprised about Daisy going to Paris and making money. He didn't know about the other business, the one in Leicester."

"Do you know where any of these places were?" Liz prompted.

Willow frowned. "No. Not really. Oh — I've seen them. But it was a long time ago."

"I thought I might try to unearth Daisy's past. I'm visiting a museum in the area. I might go to Noonby Hall, look for Jerrett's factory, and try to find out where else Daisy lived and worked while I'm there."

"Why?"

"Because Daisy was my great-aunt and because I'm curious about her. I'd love to have met her. I wish you would tell me more about what you know of her."

"I've told you all I know. And it's no good expecting to find out anything about her at Noonby Hall. It's owned by a trust now."

"I want to go all the same."

Willow was hostile. "I don't suppose I can stop you."

"Why should you want to?" Liz asked gently. "Willow — you've not said much about when you first came to England. Did Daisy go back to the place where she'd been born? Is that when you met Albert? And did Daisy ever meet Clem Brackenborough again?"

Willow said nothing. She shivered suddenly and, pulling her coat round

191

her more closely, turned away from the front of the cathedral. "I can't bear churches. All that towering ostentation. I'd like to go back now if you don't mind."

6

DAISY had no intention of objecting to any of the advantages that came from being befriended by Beatty Knighton. Eager to learn all she could about the ways of the wealthy, she asked endless questions: which cutlery and glasses to use at table? Would Beatty teach her to speak French? If she was going to Paris one day she would need to speak the language. She wanted to know how to use a telephone and to write a business letter. Daisy told herself she would have to pick up whatever Beatty did not know about dealing with customers and accounts as she went along.

Beatty spread the word among her friends that she had taken on a dressmaker who could make up garments to the specifications of the Kirby Langton League: simple clothes that had something special about them. Daisy was a sewing genius, and she understood their cause.

The venture was an instant success; members of the League were eager to take part in Beatty's latest project. They were playing, thought Daisy; most of them sat secure on family money, or were married to some swell, with a background that indulged, or mildly disapproved of, their little rebellions. They probably never gave a thought to the fact that, for her, earning a living was a matter of survival. All the same, she relished the accumulating orders that pushed her to spend more and more time at the Poplars. She was discovering that she had talent as a designer as well as a machinist, adapting what she knew about corset patterns to make a League-approved corset, with elastic gussets and fewer bones. She had a natural flair for tailoring. Although she had never learned the skills of a cutter, she seemed to know instinctively how to make a garment suit a particular figure; and as she grew more confident she eased the women away from the lumpish, frumpish styles favoured by the League, and insisted on flowing lines, on 'style' and elegance, saying that they ought not to hold themselves up to ridicule by dressing badly.

Best of all, Daisy reflected, was the fact that Beatty, who had begun by patronising her, amusing herself with teaching her how to hold a fork correctly, enter a room effectively, or behave well in company, no longer checked her at every turn, nor acted as if she were surprised at how quick she was to learn. But Daisy had no illusions about the situation; she knew that Beatty would one day grow bored with the League. Alice Brackenborough, thawing a little, perhaps even trying to warn her, had hinted at her friend's reputation for never sticking at any one thing for very long. When that happened, Daisy would be ready. Her ambitions were modest to start with: she would move all her stock out of the Poplars and rent a little dress shop in Kirby Langton. One had to look out for oneself in this world, stay one move ahead, she told herself.

Clem was annoyed to find himself almost ignored during all this activity. He had come home for the summer vacation expecting to spend time with Beatty, but whenever he called at the Poplars he was told that Miss Knighton and Miss Cornforth were in the workroom. Clem was a young man of considerable personal charm, but he was not without vanity; he liked to be the centre of attention, and he was used to having his own way.

He would walk moodily across the old overgrown stableyard and up the outside stairs of the coach house, to find the women immersed in fabrics, patterns, and sewing jargon, or engaged with a client, one of Beatty's intimates, so that he was obliged to sit in a corner, feeling foolish, and listen to wearisome discussions about the cut of a dress. Or, worse, he would be shut out altogether because the women were involved in fitting a 'health corset', or some other unmentionable item of underclothing.

On these occasions Clem would pace the yard smoking cigarettes, hearing laughter ripple out from the upstairs windows, and Daisy's voice, in charge of the fitting. If Beatty had thought herself mistress of the situation, she could not have been more mistaken, Clem reflected, oddly pleased that Daisy, while selecting what she needed from Beatty — a place to work, ready-made clients — was not in any fundamental way letting herself be taken over.

After some weeks of being a visitor to the workroom, Clem was aware that Daisy was watching him. He would glance across the room after remarking on something to Beatty, and Daisy's gaze would be fixed on him in an unsmiling observation that was discomforting, and made him feel as if he had been caught out in some act of insincerity.

Once, after an afternoon drive to collect a special order of fabric from the wholesalers, Beatty had gone to the house to call one of the servants to help them unload and, as he waited by the car, Daisy said in a low voice, "Do you disapprove of me *very* much, Clem?"

"I don't disapprove of you at all," he said, disconcerted by the extent to which she had misunderstood him.

"Then why do you always look so severe when I'm around?"

"I don't. See? I approve. I love everything to do with rational dress." He pushed his mouth into a grin with his fingers, making her smile a little.

It was then that it happened, like a kick in the stomach. The force of her smile! It was gentle enough, slightly patronising, with a serious, almost worldly-wise look in her eyes, but it had stripped Clem of all his defences.

"I'm glad you're not hostile," she said, "because the League and its members have saved me. If it hadn't been for Beatty — " She threw him a more practical look. "Well. Let's simply say, I owe her a lot. I do realise that she has been very good to me, and I don't want you to assume I'm taking advantage."

Beatty reappeared at that point, and Daisy gave her attention to the parcels in the car, leaving him with a clear view of her back. He found himself staring at the set of her shoulders and the nape of her neck, where the hair swept up in a soft cushion, crammed under her straw boater. She had adopted the style of dress worn by Beatty's friends: dark sturdy skirts and jackets, white shirts and floppy cravats. The effect was mannish on tall, angular women like his sister Alice, and looked outlandish on anyone as pale and deceptively fragile as Beatty; but it was seductive and strangely confusing on a girl like Daisy.

Clem stared for several seconds, mesmerised by the grace of her figure as she raised one arm and counted for the manservant — one, two, three, four — the bales of jersey cloth. Angry with himself, he deliberately broke the spell and went to assist with the unloading.

* * *

Daisy lay on her bed in Morton Street, watching the dawn stain the curtains a deeper red, listening to Minnie's snuffling snores beside her and mentally counting her earnings since meeting Beatty.

In less than two months she had made enough money to draw a wage and begin paying back what she owed on equipment and materials. She had not told anyone in the family, not even Wilfred, about setting up in business for the League. They thought she was working as a sewing maid at the Poplars, and that the money she brought home — or the proportion of it that she let them see — came from mending the Knightons' household linen, darning stockings, or running up uniforms for the rest of the staff.

She liked the feeling that she could walk in and out of a place like the Poplars, with its large, airy rooms, heraldic stained glass in all the windows, and a bust of Beatty's grandfather, who had been a member of Disraeli's parliament, in the hall. The Knightons were unusual in that they did not treat her as 'trade', but were kind to her because she was Beatty's little experiment; they expected her to make use of the Poplars' tennis courts and gardens, and to 'drop in whenever she felt like it'.

She would tell her family one day, Daisy promised. She would tell Wilf first, when the time was right and she had paid back what she owed and saved what she needed from the profits. And then . . . Daisy allowed herself to dream with her hands behind her head and staring at a crack in the bedroom ceiling.

Beatty had agreed to give her French lessons.

Voilà! Daisy practised silently: *Bonjour,*

madame, mademoiselle. Au revoir. De trop, de luxe. En route, entre nous. Savoir faire.

"Why are you doing this?" Beatty had asked her one day. "What do you want from life, Daisy?"

"Everything. I want never to have to live like my mother has lived all these years, scrimping and saving and wishing everything was different."

"Well then, we shall have to marry you off to a rich husband."

"Marriage is a trap for women."

"What if you fall in love?"

"I don't believe in it. Men are no good to women. Ask my mother."

Beatty had laughed, thinking Daisy was joking. Then, when she saw that she was not, she had said, "You're a funny girl. You don't believe in love. You don't believe in the League. What *do* you believe in?"

"Myself. *Je suis fidèle à moi-même.* I believe in doing what I *feel* at the right moment."

"You're as bad as Clem."

"Is that being bad?" Daisy was secretly pleased at the idea of being like Clem, for she was attracted to his air of arrogance, and his light mockery of the League. He seemed interested too in what she was doing, in fact openly admiring since the day he had denied that he disapproved of her.

"Clem is a cynic," Beatty had said. "As a matter of fact, on second thoughts, I don't think he even believes in himself very much. This will be his final year at Cambridge. Then what? He couldn't bear to work under Austen in managing the estate. Clem will be seriously at a loose end."

"I hadn't thought."

"The younger son has to do *something*."

Daisy got out of bed and washed by the window, quietly, so as not to wake Minnie, then buttoned her corset over her camisole; she had adopted neither the League's 'health corset', nor the bust bodices and all the rest. Daisy was proud of her tiny waist; if she had her way, she would not be making sack dresses and plain suits, but glamorous evening gowns, garments that were rich and romantic; she had seen enough of make-do-and-mend to last her a lifetime.

The air was cool outside in the street, the sun had not warmed the pavements and brick walls, but Daisy was hot from hurrying by the time she reached the Poplars.

The gravel crunched under her feet, and dogs barked frantically somewhere at the back of the house, then fell silent as she made her way to the old stableyard and up the outside stair to the workroom.

Unpinning her boater, Daisy opened the windows to air the room and turned to survey her work space.

There was something very satisfying about the clutter of materials on the shelves: the dress fabrics, some already cut out for stitching; a few bales of chiffon and silk; crêpe and wool for underclothes; the canvas and webbing for corsets; the rolls of ribbon, elastic, lace inserts and trimmings; and, best of all, by one of the windows, her own sewing machine — or it soon would be, she reminded herself, when she had paid it off — the latest Singer.

The room had all the familiar elements of her life at Jerrett's, but it was all so much *nicer* and more *refined*. She was surprised how little she missed the old days, even the company of the other women.

The large cutting table was clean and empty, waiting for the satisfying thump of a bale, the swish of fabric, the crunch of scissors and the whispering sigh of silk.

Beatty had helped her to make a toile, a muslin version of the dress she had planned. She had four days until Saturday, when Clem had promised to take her and Beatty to the races. If she came out here an hour earlier every morning and left late, she could work on a gown for herself; a beautiful, elegant creation, as near as she could remember to the dress she had once coveted in the window of Robertson Callow's. She wanted so much to look the part, so that nobody seeing her with Beatty and Clem would be able to tell she was not a lady.

Pushing up her sleeves, Daisy lifted down the fabric she had chosen, a sea-green silk organza, machine-embroidered with red roses.

Daisy had cut out the dress pieces and was running up the first seam when she heard the dogs barking again and the noise of a car engine. She ignored it, continuing to sew, until she was interrupted by the sound of someone on the stair.

Clem stood in the low doorway, stooping slightly, his hat in one hand, the other hand against the door jamb as if to protect his head.

"What — no Bea? They said at the house they thought she was up here."

Daisy turned back to the machine, anxious not to waste time. "It's a bit early for you, Clem."

"Got an eight-thirty start. We're driving up to London today to stay with Bea's cousins. Didn't she tell you?"

Daisy had been so concerned to get on with the dress that she had quite forgotten Beatty would be away for a few days. Come and go as you please, Beatty had told her. Treat the place as your own.

"You could have come with us," Clem

said, walking into the room.

"I don't know what Beatty's cousins would have said to that. Anyway, I have to work."

"They're very broadminded. Open house."

He sat on the edge of the cutting table, watching her run the machine expertly down a seam. "What are you making this time?"

Daisy felt at ease with him. No longer in awe of his connection with Noonby, she treated him with the sort of affection she usually reserved for Wilfred and Minnie.

"A dress."

"For one of Bea's friends?"

"No." Suddenly she was embarrassed. "For me."

He was silent, continuing to watch her. He picked up a piece of fabric and draped it experimentally against her shoulder.

"I like it. The colour suits your dark hair. Looks delightful."

"Thank you." She did not halt her sewing.

Clem watched her head bent over the

machine, his gaze drawn to the nape of her neck. He still held the piece of silk, warm and light in his hands, and had a sudden, almost uncontrollable urge to run his fingers along the bone at the top of Daisy's spine and push his hand into the wealth of hair that was looped into a chignon. Beatty's hair was light and wiry, curiously non-sensual, but Daisy's would fall heavily over his hands, thick, extravagant . . .

He put down the piece of dress fabric and his hands trembled slightly. He reached for his cigarette case, then remembered that smoking was forbidden in the workroom, and that, anyway, it was bad form to smoke in the presence of a lady.

It was difficult to think of Daisy in those terms. And yet, she fascinated him. More than that, more than the business of finding her sexually intriguing, he admired her. She seemed so untouched by the superficialities he generally associated with females. She was so — singleminded, a quality he would normally attribute to a man.

Daisy glanced at the clock on the

wall and, finishing a seam, cut the thread briskly. She began collecting up the sections of fabric.

"Don't let me put you off."

"You aren't. My time's up. I have to start work for the day. You can stay and watch, or you can go to look for Beatty."

He realised he had been dismissed, but he felt a curious reluctance to leave and go trailing round the Poplars in search of Beatty.

"What do you *really* think of the League?" he said. "All this business of health corsets and rational dress."

"It's providing me with a living for the time being. So I suppose I'm all for it."

"I find it beastly tiresome, to be honest. Bea never talks of anything else. I suppose she'll get over it."

"Well — when she does, I shall be out of a job."

"What will happen to you then?"

Daisy stopped folding the dress pieces. "That depends how long it takes. If it wears off too quickly, before I've made enough profit, I shall be back where I started."

208

"I should be rather sorry about that."

"Would you? I think you'd get over it pretty well, Clem." She remembered that her parents had been fired from Noonby without any qualms from his family.

Curiously, Clem was thinking the same thing. He had learned almost by accident, after mentioning her name, that her parents had once been servants at Noonby. 'A small world,' his mother had said. But he could tell she had disapproved of him associating in any way with Daisy.

He felt a vague guilt on behalf of his family, making him say earnestly, "I mean it, Daisy. I would worry about what was going to happen to you."

"You'd think of me while you were at Cambridge, would you?" She was mocking him a little. She smiled, that devastating, *kindly*, slightly patronising expression that was beginning to exasperate him. "You're very sweet, Clem. But now — I really must get on."

"See you on Saturday then — at the races?"

Daisy went to the window after he had gone, sidetracked from her resolution to get on with some work.

Clem's car stood in front of the house; Beatty came running across the drive, and met him beside it.

Daisy watched them kiss. Beatty was holding a bunch of carnations; she must have been in the garden cutting them to take with her to the cousins in London. She held them to Clem's face for him to smell.

Two of the servants came out from the house carrying cases and boxes, and loaded them on to the back of the car.

It occurred to Daisy that, for all her protestations about not wanting marriage, it would be very pleasant to have someone like Clem as a husband, to be driven around in a motor car and be waited on by servants. Of course, Clem was 'in love' with Beatty and one day they would marry. Beatty would perhaps ask her to create a wedding dress for her, and they might even invite her to the ceremony.

Daisy turned away from the scene outside with a sense of being unable to watch any more.

★ ★ ★

The noise and colour of the race course billowed towards them, and Daisy felt as well as heard the hum of excitement from the crowds, like an electric charge, as they joined the queues of traffic heading off the road.

The rumble of carriage wheels and sounds of jingling harnesses joined that of the car's motor, as they moved between the mass of people wandering towards the stands and white rails of the track.

Eventually they abandoned the lumbering security of the car and plunged into the crush on foot. Everywhere across the green field, groups of people pushed their way apparently aimlessly: gents in gaiters, bowler hats and checked tweeds; top-hatted horse owners; women of all classes and ages, in pastel colours with matching parasols; women in dark shawls, with brown faces, selling oranges; tipsters dressed like music-hall acts; fortune tellers; and over all, a smell of tobacco, horses and people, and the harsh, hot sunlight.

Clem led the way, the women following, mixing with the owners and breeders in the paddocks, watching the jockeys in their silk shirts carrying the saddles to the weighing scales. Clem chatted with several men who knew his father, whilst Beatty and Daisy walked in silence, each of them remembering an incident when Clem had picked them up at the Poplars.

Daisy had changed in the workroom into her new dress and hat, stripped of its suffrage colours and re-trimmed with feathers and lace. "You look divine," Beatty had said, sensible enough to know that she was eclipsed by Daisy's more vibrant colouring and the air of intense energy that radiated from her.

And then Clem had arrived, pretending to be dazed with astonishment. "Is it? Can it really be? Is this really Daisy Cornforth? No. It has to be royalty."

Daisy had volunteered the information that her great-grandmother had been a princess.

"This accounts for it. You're the Princess Agabaga-Bellino my father met at Cowes."

Delighted, Daisy had responded by flirting as he helped her step into the car. She had tapped his cheek with her glove. "You must visit my yacht next time

212

you're in Cowes, Mr Brackenborough. Bring your young friend Beatty with you."

The touch of her hand against his face had seemed to startle him at the time. A blush stained the tips of his ears and the back of his neck as they drove out on to the Leicester road.

Beatty had smiled, but she had looked cross and had watched him closely after that, though Clem had behaved impeccably, his usual lightweight, charming self.

They reached the grandstand and mounted the steps to find their places.

"Made it." Clem turned to them both. "Fancy a flutter?"

Daisy responded that she did not know which were the good runners.

With an air of male superiority, Clem said that he would pick out a horse for her, he knew the owner. "She likes the going here and beat a massive field at Doncaster." He told her the name, 'Rosy Future', and Daisy said it sounded promising.

"You shouldn't encourage Daisy to gamble," Beatty said, arranging herself comfortably, fiddling with her gloves and bag and craning her neck to make sure that she could see.

Daisy, turning to Clem, said, "I'll lay a bet on Rosy Future if you do."

She had five pounds in her purse, and told him to put half the money on the horse and bring half back with him.

Beatty, with an air of obstinate niggardliness, chose a horse called 'Some Spirit', and told Clem to place a shilling bet for her.

A burst of certainty that Rosy Future was going to be lucky made Daisy call after him, "No. Put all of it on. Five pounds, Clem."

The two women fell silent, awkward with one another as Clem slipped through the crowd.

Daisy was beginning to have misgivings about such a large bet. She felt hot, then cold with fright at the way she had let herself get carried away. She turned to Beatty. "Perhaps he'll be too late to place the stake."

Beatty did not answer, remembering still the blush that had suffused Clem's face when Daisy touched him.

She felt disappointed in him, refusing to blame Daisy, who would do nothing so foolish as to set her sights on someone from Noonby. In any case, Daisy had made her opinion of the male sex very clear: she wanted nothing more from life than to work for her living and make a lot of money; in that sense, Daisy was probably more of a genuine feminist than any of Beatty's friends.

So, the fault lay with Clem, Beatty decided. She had hoped, after their visit to London, that he might have asked her father about getting engaged; she had supposed, wrongly she saw now, that he had been keen to visit her cousins to involve himself more thoroughly with her family. What other reason could he have for going with her when the season was almost at an end, and when neither of them was drawn anyway, either by position or inclination, to the more exclusive of the season's social events?

The trouble with Clem, thought Beatty, pushed by the incident with Daisy to regard him in a more than usually critical light, was that he was so *unreliable*. One never really knew what he was thinking or what he felt about things, nor when he was being entirely serious. Were all men so *unsatisfactory*?

The runners were cantering out from the paddock and, as the noise of the crowd fell, the air of excitement grew more intense. People watched their chosen favourites when the runners moved off towards the start, a shifting line of dark horses and brightly coloured riders. Clem returned, squeezing through the crowds in the stand to join Beatty and Daisy at the precise moment the cry went up in an explosion of anticipation: "They're off!"

The crowd began to yell louder, until the distant line of riders was lost round the curve of the track, hidden by the crowd of people massed at the centre of the race course. The spectators in the stand turned in one movement, watching for the moment when horses and riders would appear at the opposite curve.

"There they are!"

They seemed almost mad with excitement as the line of runners entered the straight.

Daisy heard Clem shouting, a blast of encouragement, with none of his usual

216

urbane charm: "Come *on*! Rosy Future!" And then, with the thought of her five pounds in her head, Daisy heard her own voice, as harsh as Clem's, over and over: "Rosy Future, Rosy Future . . . "

Beatty was not shouting at all. She simply leaned forward a little with the crowd as the crouching riders scudded past them amid a thunder of hooves and flying earth. The noise rose to a crescendo, until in an instant it was over.

"Who won? Who won?" Daisy danced up and down.

Clem was hugging her, swinging her round in his arms. "Ten to one! A hundred pounds!"

"That means I've won fifty!" Daisy gasped. Had it really been that easy? Fifty pounds! She turned to Beatty. "What a turn up!" She saw Beatty's expression. "Oh, but you didn't win anything. I'm so sorry."

"It doesn't matter." Beatty did not seem to mind about losing as she gathered up her gloves and parasol, murmuring that she had seen a friend on the other side of the stand and would be back shortly; and she slipped away with a reserved smile.

Clem still had his arm round Daisy's waist, his elbow resting casually against her hip; she could feel the weight of it through her dress. The sensation of being connected to him was very strong; the pressure of his hand on her arm made her flesh tingle.

They stood watching the track, as if it might magically produce more in the way of thrilling spectacle; but the horses were being led away and the excitement of the crowd was fading; people shook hands and congratulated one another, or else smiled wryly.

Clem said something about it all being over until the next race.

"Was your grandmother really a princess?" he said lightly.

"No. But she could have been. Nobody knows where she came from."

He glanced down at her and, for a second, Daisy's heart seemed to rise into her mouth. Slowly, he removed his arm from her waist.

Beatty returned, and the two women stood in the stand making small talk while Clem went to fetch the winnings, neither of them acknowledging their private turmoil. What was there to say? After all, nothing had happened.

The glow of Daisy's win remained, but she felt oddly empty. What did it all *mean*? she asked herself again. Beatty was subdued as they drove back to Kirby Langton, and all three felt disinclined towards conversation. Confused, Daisy tried to concentrate on thoughts of the bundle of notes in her purse. There was so much one could do with fifty pounds.

She could tell from Beatty's silence that she was still angry with Clem. Daisy began to feel angry too at the situation. What if Clem *had* been playing up to her a little. It was not worth making a fuss about.

"It's Sunday tomorrow," Clem said when they reached the Poplars. "Time for you to get over all the excitement and decide how to spend your money, Daisy."

"Oh, that's easy enough. I owe most of it to Beatty for the equipment in the workroom."

"I didn't expect you to pay it back

so soon. Spend some of it on yourself,"
Beatty said generously. She spoke normally,
and even smiled; but there was a reserve
between her and Clem.

Daisy went up to the workroom and
changed out of her clothes into her
blouse and skirt, wanting for once to
get away, to leave them to quarrel if
that was what Beatty wanted.

Clem was waiting for her when she
came outside again. Beatty was nowhere
to be seen.

"Shall I drive you home?"

Daisy shook her head. "I wouldn't
want anyone in Morton Street to see
me arrive in a motor car."

"Would they be so very outraged?"

He was teasing again, had recovered
his old manner with her; but Daisy
still felt unsettled, knowing exactly what
people in Morton Street would assume
if she were seen getting out of Clem
Brackenborough's car.

★ ★ ★

Daisy's father did not come in that
teatime, and her mother was glancing

anxiously at the clock by half past eight.

She inspected a plate of meat and gravy put to warm in the oven. "All dried up. And who will get the blame? Not him. Oh, no. It will be all my fault he can't eat it."

"He'll probably be too drunk to eat it anyway," commented Daisy, leaning against the sink with her arms folded.

Wrapping her arms round Daisy's legs, Minnie banged her chin against her skirts, and Daisy lifted her on to her hip, tickling her, and making her yell to be put down again. "Time for bed, you. I'll come and tell you a story if you're quick."

"You're good with her," Letty said, watching Minnie scuttle out of the kitchen and make for the stairs. "You'll have some of your own one day."

Daisy ignored the remark, not wanting to get involved in the kind of discussion that was becoming more frequent. Her mother was hoping to discover where she went in her time off, assuming she was 'walking out' with someone. She was always asking questions. Was Mrs Knighton a decent employer? Were

221

the upper servants nice to her? Was she happy working at the Poplars?

"Are there any nice fellows working at the Knightons' place?"

"They're all very nice people. Can we stop talking about them? It's my day off tomorrow."

"But you weren't working this afternoon."

"No. I was out."

"I saw Mary the other day. She said she hasn't seen you for a long time."

"I've finished with the people at Jerrett's," Daisy said dismissively.

"Oh, very nice for them. So, who do you go about with now? Anyone in particular?"

"Mother!"

"You can't blame me for asking, Daisy. You've been that secretive lately." She paused. "If you've been up to anything — "

"You mean with some man? Well, I haven't. I promise. Here comes Wilf."

Daisy could have hugged him. He had been to choir practice, looking very shiny and holy in his good trousers and jacket and with his hair slicked down.

"Father not back yet?" Wilfred said,

sounding relieved.

"Where's he been today, anyway?" Daisy asked her mother.

"He thinks I don't know about it, but he went to the races at Leicester. Mrs Roberts told me her husband was going with him. If they've spent all their winnings in the Three Feathers — " Letty did not finish the threat, knowing that whatever she felt about it, she would do and say very little.

She noticed Daisy's expression — exposed at the mention of her father being at the races — and she caught hold of her arm when Wilfred had gone upstairs to change out of his good clothes.

"What's the matter?"

"Nothing."

"You don't look like that for nothing." Letty gave Daisy's arm a shake. "It's a man, isn't it? *Have* you been doing something you didn't ought to?"

"Don't you think, Mother, that I might have more pride than that?"

Daisy pulled her arm from her mother's grasp and left the kitchen.

She should not have said that to her mother, Daisy thought, remembering

Letty's dismissal from Noonby. But why did everyone always assume that getting involved with some man was the first thing on a woman's mind?

She felt uneasy, thinking about her father being at the races, and was telling Minnie a story when she heard the slam of the front door and her father's voice downstairs.

Minnie's eyelids were drooping. Daisy brought the tale to a swift close, kissed her sister and, because it was a hot evening, pulled the counterpane to the foot of the bed. By the time she looked back, Minnie was already asleep.

★ ★ ★

"Daisy — is it true?" Her mother's face was white in the darkening parlour. "You told me. You gave me your word."

Daisy's father sat at the table, his dinner untouched, his head bowed as if he were contemplating the ring of congealed mince and gravy round the rim of the plate and the mounds of vegetables.

Letty's voice rose in a frightened

whine. "Daisy! Tell me you haven't been misbehaving."

Her father raised his head, speaking through the blur of remembered images of his day at the races. "You're a bloody disgrace."

He had seen her — or one of his cronies had told him. Out of all those hundreds of people at the racecourse that afternoon, someone her father knew must have seen her with Clem and Beatty.

"You've made a laughing stock of me. You know that?"

Surprised by how little fear she felt, Daisy responded quickly, "You do that well enough for yourself."

He raised a threatening fist, and let it fall back on the table. "You'll not give me any more of your cheek. I want you out of here. You can pack a bag and get out."

"I want to know first what I'm supposed to have done?"

"He saw you," her mother said in a half whisper. "At the races with some fellow — a toff." She gave a little moan, hugging her arms round her ribs. "Oh, Daisy! Whatever have you been up to?"

"Acting up to him, looking like a trollop," shouted her father. "I saw you going off in his car. Who is he? I'll bloody kill him."

"He's a friend," Daisy said, grateful at least that Clem had not been identified.

"I bet he is. Pays you well, does he? Buys you nice clothes?"

Daisy turned away. "You're disgusting."

"Oh, Daisy — " Her mother's whisper of anguish was cut short by the sound of the plate of food hitting the wall close to Daisy's head. The women stared at the mince sliding down the wall, and the plate lying in pieces on the carpet among a splatter of dinner.

Letty began sobbing, and Daisy moved quickly, putting an arm round her. "It doesn't matter. We'll clean it up."

Her father reared up from the table and let out a roar of incoherent fury. "Leave it!" He made a snatch at Daisy as she stooped to pick up the pieces of plate.

"Do as he says, Daisy. I'll clear it — "

"I want you out." Her father clung to the edge of the table as if he was about to upend it. "I'm *disowning* you. I'm sick of the sight of you. Out. Get out. Go to your fancy man."

Letty pleaded. "At least let her stay till the morning."

"I'm going." Daisy went to the stair. "I'm not staying here a minute longer. I want nothing more to do with him."

★ ★ ★

Minnie was still asleep.

Daisy collected her few clothes together — undergarments, nightclothes, and skirts and blouses — and threw them on to the bedspread, bundling it up and knotting it like a traveller's pack.

Wilfred was watching her from the bedroom doorway as she turned to go.

"Don't leave. You know what he's like. He'll talk different in the morning, when he's sober again."

"I've got to get out one day. It might as well be now. Better than waiting at home until some man asks me to marry him."

"I don't know what you did — " Wilfred's mouth faltered and he wiped a hand across his face.

227

"I haven't done *anything*." Taking hold of his chins she made him look her in the eye. "Do you hear? Nothing to be ashamed of. You remember that when he starts saying bad things about me."

He nodded.

"I'll try to get to see you, Wilf, but you've got to be brave. You're a big lad now." She took out her handkerchief and dried his eyes.

"You look after Mother and Minnie."

"Where'll you go?"

"I've got somewhere. And it's not like he thinks. You're not to worry."

She hugged him fiercely, and the hurt of leaving him tightened her chest and pricked at her throat and eyes.

"Wait." He went to the attic ladder and came down with the hat box. "You forgot this."

★ ★ ★

Standing by the window of the workroom the next morning, Daisy saw Beatty's family and a few of the servants leave for church. She felt confident that no one would come near the old stable on

228

a Sunday. She had a breathing space for a day.

All the same, the Poplars was no more than a temporary refuge. When Beatty asked why she had been thrown out, Daisy's explanations would involve Clem. One way or another, it was time her friendship with Beatty and Clem came to an end.

She had supposed, after a night's sleep, that everything would seem clear; but it was all a hopeless muddle. Although she did not know what she would do, or where she could go, Daisy rejected thoughts of appealing to her grandmother for help. Nan would take her father's side once she heard what he had to say.

She flexed her shoulders, stiff from sleeping on the cutting-room table, and tried to push down the feelings of terror that had risen in the night and lurked still, ready to confuse her further. The dress she had worn to the races hung behind the door. Daisy took it down and folded it lovingly, and was untying her bundle of clothes to accommodate it when she heard a car outside.

Clem stood on the doorstep after

ringing the house doorbell, tapping his hat against his hand. Daisy watched as he turned to the house to speak to the servant, handing something over, an envelope. The door closed and he walked back to the car.

Daisy let her breath out slowly, then froze.

Clem had changed his mind and was coming over to the coach house.

Picking up her bundle, Daisy ran to the door and flattened herself to the wall behind it. Her heart beat hard against her ribs as she held on tightly to the door-handle, hearing his feet on the staircase.

He was whistling. A smell of cigarettes and eau de Cologne drifted towards her, making her feel faint as he paused in the open doorway. Daisy could hear him walking about on the wooden boards. Then silence.

Curious, she eased the door forward.

He was standing with his back to her, one hand resting on the drive wheel of the sewing machine. In the other he held a piece of fabric from the dress she had worn at the races. As Daisy watched, he raised the scrap of fabric to his lips and held it there for a moment, before tucking it inside his coat pocket. Suddenly, as if sensing he was not alone, he swung round and saw her.

"Good God! Daisy! What are you hiding there for?"

She moved away from the wall. "I had work to do."

"Behind the door? Why skulk there like a burglar?"

"I heard someone coming. I thought you were a burglar too."

"Does Beatty know you're here?"

"Does she know you are?" she countered.

He looked uncomfortable, and she guessed he was wondering if she had witnessed his extraordinary behaviour with the scrap of dress fabric.

"Bea is at church. I thought I'd better make sure everything was secure up here." He ran his hand along the top of the machine. "Don't your family go to church?"

Daisy thought of Wilf singing in the choir that morning, her mother cooking Sunday dinner, Minnie waking to find the bed empty beside her. Tears filled her eyes without warning and, as she stared at Clem, they spilled over. Sitting down hard on a stool beside the cutting table, Daisy gave herself up to her misery in a fit of sobbing.

Clem could never have imagined this side to her. Nor to any woman for that matter. People he knew and had grown up with had been taught to smother their emotions, girls as well as boys. It was not the done thing to cry, and certainly not with such noisy abandon.

Sob by sob he learned that Daisy's father had thrown her out of the house, after she had been seen yesterday at the races, that her father had assumed — here, Daisy could not go on. She refused to say what her father had assumed, but with a leap of relief that it was nothing worse, Clem could guess.

"We'll explain," he coaxed. "Come on, Daisy." She always seemed so strong; the sight of her weeping made him feel inadequate and helpless. "It's not so terrible. I'll write to him. I'll go to see him," he added rashly, hoping it would not come to that. He told her that he knew all about family misunderstandings — they blew over after a few days and everyone was as charming as anything to one another again.

"My father's never charming." Daisy blew her nose and scrubbed at her face with her handkerchief. "And nobody's explaining anything, if he's going to be so stupid. I'm never going back."

He tried to humour her. "You've got to talk to him. Be reasonable. What will you do? Where will you go?"

"I don't know." She looked at him with an air of defeat. "But I'm not kidding, Clem. I can't go back there." The tears began to flow again.

Clem watched them slide down her cheeks as Daisy bit the edge of her handkerchief, trying to stop, with gulping sobs. She was distraught. She was beautiful. He was falling in love with her. What could he do, but take her in his arms and promise to help her?

7

LIZ enjoyed driving when she was alone. She liked the sense of space in the car: a feeling of being cocooned and yet free as the vehicle sped along the motorway.

Vivaldi's 'Four Seasons' was on the radio; and the passing countryside was appropriately spring-like, with fields of pale early wheat and acid-yellow rape breaking out in patches.

April, a time of rebirth, new beginnings. An appropriate time to consider marriage, added her conscience. "Will you do some thinking while you're away?" Don had said to her. And then, hesitantly, ominously even, "We both ought to give some thought to where we are heading."

He had been so tender the last few days, so grateful about Paris, so funny and comfortable — the old Don — that the idea of parting now seemed crazy.

And, at this moment, the sense of

spring in the air was too exhilarating to spoil with prolonged introspection.

Liz began singing. Softly at first, then more loudly, without words, to the Vivaldi. She had promised to do some serious thinking, but not yet.

★ ★ ★

Liz would be there by now, thought Don, coming out of school and anticipating a night alone at the empty Lodge — several nights alone, he reflected. Perhaps he should follow Liz's example and take off somewhere for Easter.

Cycling hard along the A39, a top-heavy figure on two wheels, he tried to make sense of her resistance to the idea of marriage.

There had been various girlfriends before Liz; he had even been in love once or twice, though nothing had come of it.

He had taken the post of assistant head at a school near Bristol, and for a year had been celibate and dedicated to his work. He became 'too serious' according to his Aunt Poll, who had wanted him to go back to Norfolk, complaining that they saw hardly anything of him any more. So he had gone to stay for the summer, nostalgic for the idyllic farm holidays of his childhood, and had become involved with a former girlfriend, who was on the rebound from an affair with a married man. The second time around, their relationship had been very intense, Don remembered: he had spent weekends at Pamela's flat in London, she had come to Bristol when she could get away, and they had visited Norfolk together to see their respective relatives. That intensity had frightened Don and he had broken off the relationship. One Christmas, visiting Poll and Bill and learning that Pamela would be at home, he had been unable to face seeing her, and had headed back for the West Country. Liz, in a hurry to get home from London for the traditional Cornforth family Christmas, had bumped into him on the platform, and they had missed the train.

He had paid for coffee. They had taken a later train, discovered her parents lived near the school where he was working, and, on one of Liz's impulses — the kind

236

that he was later to find both endearing and maddening — she had invited him to join her family for Christmas, insisting no one would mind.

He had been overwhelmed by the family's welcome, unaware that for weeks they had been urging Liz to bring home the 'boyfriend' she had invented to keep them from pestering her about her love life; she had apologised to him afterwards for the deception, but by then it was too late, he was in love with her.

And still was, Don told himself, parking his bike in the garage. Had he the strength of will to go for the Yarnest headship without her?

There was a message from Liz's sister Prue on the answerphone:

"Thought you might be feeling a bit low without Liz, Don. Peter and I would love you to come over for a meal. The day after tomorrow? You can help Peter celebrate the end of term. Nothing very grand — and no matter if you can't make it, or if you'd rather be on your own. Didn't want you to be lonely. Lots of love."

Trust Prue to make Liz's trip to the Midlands sound like a bereavement. All the same, the house was full of thoughts and memories, and there was an air of melancholy about Liz's office, the door left open, papers strewn about the desk.

He stood in the doorway, feeling sentimental about her chair, her books on the shelves, and her muddle of papers and files. She had pinned up postcards from her friends in publishing and the university: the skyline of Hong Kong; a smiling Nepalese child, round-cheeked, sloe-eyed.

Turning away, his glance fell on the picture her father had given her on her birthday of the girl in the corset, propped against a vase on the mantelshelf.

Liz's interest in Daisy and the woman, Willow, had become an obsession lately. One that seemed to have imposed a barrier between them.

Confident of her attractions, the girl engaged his attention with a look of mocking arrogance. Don felt an irrational, but unequivocal flow of hostility towards her. Had finding the picture got anything to do with Liz's reluctance to confront their future? he wondered with a sudden and uncharacteristic stab of superstition. He would have been glad to find a scapegoat.

★ ★ ★

Liz had arranged to visit a corset collection on the second afternoon of her stay in the Midlands. She went through her notebook list of the points she wanted to check with the museum's curator, looking at the corsets they had selected from the archives.

On these occasions, in close contact with the fabric and steel, the rigid tramlines of machine-stitching, laces, and 'Hercules' metal clasps, Liz could only marvel at the sense of duty that must have been necessary, daily, to fasten oneself into such a contraption.

Liz owned a corset. It was Victorian. She had bought it from an antiques market in Bath. Made of ivory-coloured coutil, with a front-fastening and lacing at the back, it had pink ribbon threaded through the top edge. There were sweat rings under the arms, evocative of unladylike exertions, nights dancing the Lancers, tight dresses on hot summer days. Don had once persuaded her to wear it to indulge some erotic impulse, and for a while at least she had been in touch with other, distant women's lives as she felt the laces tighten and the corset close on her waist. For a while too the experience had been erotic — intensely pleasurable, as she recalled — though she preferred now, in the interests of feminism, not to acknowledge that there was anything pleasurable in the sensation of being trussed.

There were recorded accounts of the pleasures of tight-lacing that teetered on the edge of sado-masochism; Liz had come across them and used them in her research; but these apart, why had women supported the corset habit for so long?

She said as much to the curator. "How on earth did such a cult of respectability grow up around corsets? To the extent that women stuck with them right through the forties and fifties.

My grandmother wore one, a salmon-pink thing. I remember being fascinated by it as a child."

He did not attempt to offer an answer. "How's the book coming along? Nearly there?"

"I thought I might take a look at some more of the old factories. Ever heard of Jerrett's at Kirby Langton?"

He said that it had closed down, like so many others, in the sixties. They had some of the sales catalogues if she was interested.

With a flicker of excitement Liz said that she was, and she told him a little about Daisy.

But the catalogues, when she saw them, dated from the twenties.

"If Daisy worked for Jerrett's earlier than that, the museum at Kirby might still have something of interest," the man suggested.

Liz set up her camera, took a few photographs and left, knowing that as far as the book was concerned the visit had not been necessary. She drove to the county record office with a sense of having freed herself from an obligation and spent an hour searching through the manufacturing and commercial directories from the early 1900s, not sure what she was looking for, until she came across an advertisement for 'Maison Clem: costumes, gowns and original modes'.

So, Daisy had called her business after Clem even in Leicester, Liz thought with a sense of satisfaction.

She walked around the city shopping centre, finding little to stir her imagination and evoke Daisy's presence. Instead she found new office blocks, fifties glass and concrete, streets of boutiques, pubs and tea rooms, and dress shops, some with a genuine sense of history, one even with corsets and brassières, Lycra step-ins and girdles in the window. Halting briefly to take a photograph, she retraced her steps to the multi-storey car park.

She had hardly expected more; nevertheless, Liz was disappointed. Her journey was beginning to look like a time-consuming piece of self-indulgence. Joining the commuter traffic out of the city centre, she drove to her hotel.

Having missed out altogether on lunch, Liz ate hungrily in the hotel restaurant, compensating for the day's disappointments with a bottle of wine and a calorie-laden pudding that made her think of Willow, who would have enjoyed it, smacking her lips and wiggling her toes.

Back in her room, feeling tipsy and slightly ill, her sense of conscience reawakened by thoughts of ringing Don, Liz kicked off her shoes and lay on the bed, waiting for the room to steady. When it did, she picked up the phone.

Don did not answer. She heard her own recorded voice on the answerphone and left a message, then, deciding it sounded hostile, rang again.

"Hope you're having a nice time somewhere, darling. I'll talk to you tomorrow."

She went to bed early.

* * *

The guide at the Kirby Langton museum, a man in his sixties, with a mottled scalp and the air of a retired non-commissioned officer, was eager to help. It was a long time since an outsider had shown more than a passing interest in the museum.

243

He found archive film about the local industries, and Liz watched faded black and white footage of men and women making boots and shoes in the thirties, of farm labourers, dairy-workers, and women machining corsets and streaming out from factory gates, offering swift shy smiles to the camera. But it was all too recent to induce strong impressions of Daisy's life in the first decade of the century.

The film over, the guide took great pains to recall firsthand the scenes Liz had just witnessed. Trying to ward off a flood of nostalgic, boyhood tales that had little bearing on her search for Daisy, Liz said, "What can you tell me about Clem Brackenborough at Noonby Hall?"

The man's face brightened. "Oh, now, the Brackenboroughs have been an important family around here for years. The estate passed to the London branch of the family through Clement Brackenborough's son Howard. He was there until the Trust took over. What a pity — the house isn't open to the public today." He fetched a leaflet from the reception desk. "The house, gardens and tea shop don't open until Easter Monday."

"It doesn't matter," Liz said, but she was disappointed, annoyed with herself for not realising that the Hall would be closed for the winter. "I simply thought, if I had a spare afternoon . . . "She paused. "Do you have any archive material about the Brackenboroughs?"

"Yes. But it's got nothing to do with corsets."

"I'd be interested. Two of my ancestors worked at the Hall in the nineteenth century."

"Well then — you'll be wanting to see the Brackenborough Gallery."

The man explained as they climbed the stairs: "The people of Kirby have a lot of fond memories of Mr *Howard* Brackenborough's years at Noonby. He was one of Kirby's great benefactors. We owe the Memorial Gardens and the benches in the Borough to him, and he served with distinction in North Africa in the last war. Most of the Brackenborough Gallery is devoted to Howard's war exploits and those of his regiment. The family was kind enough to donate them to the museum when he died."

Liz's interest faded as they stepped into a room, some fifteen foot square, the walls lined with cases of military photographs, medals, and pieces of weaponry and uniforms.

She toured the exhibition, trying not to appear impatient as her guide hovered, eager to assist with explanations for each showcase.

"This picture must have been taken at the Hall." Liz halted in front of a photograph tucked into a corner: a group of Victorian country-house servants carrying the implements of their trade: spades, handsaws, horse-brushes, dust-pans, rolling pins and pastry boards. She scanned the unsmiling faces. Were her great-grandparents among them — that hesitant maidservant, the gardener with his hat set at a jaunty angle?

"Most of the pictures to do with Noonby, the family paintings, are in the house itself."

"Where does the family live now?"

"When Howard Brackenborough inherited, he managed to keep the estate going in spite of heavy death duties, but his children had no wish to live at the Hall after he died. A pity, but there you are, it's the upkeep as much as anything. His nephew Lewis takes an interest these days and sometimes stays at Noonby if he's advising on exhibitions. They've got some of his pictures at the Hall. I'm told they're very good."

"He's an artist?"

"A photographer."

"So — who did *Clement* Brackenborough marry?"

"That I don't remember. I don't know all the names going back to the Great War. Howard had a sister. That's her." He pointed out a photo of a young woman in a WRAC uniform. "She was called — "He read from the label. "*Viola*. Pretty girl. And there was Hugo. Lewis Brackenborough is his son."

"Clem's grandson," Liz murmured, and asked the guide, "I suppose Clement Brackenborough would have been too old for the last war?"

"Oh, I don't think so. It would have been a desk job, of course. But he was

247

in it — I'm almost sure of that." He went to a central island of glass-topped showcases. "I think there's something here."

Leaning over the showcase, Liz saw a photograph of a man in his fifties, dressed in the uniform of a World War Two army officer. The inscription read: *Major C. L. Brackenborough, DSO, MC*.

He was squarely built and grizzled, with a military moustache; there was nothing in his face to suggest why Daisy might have fallen in love with him when he was a young man.

"He died during the war."

"How sad," Liz said. "He probably had only a little longer to live when this was taken." Daisy too. According to Willow, Daisy had been in her fifties when, crossing the road, she was hit by a car. So neither of them had survived into old age. Daisy's end, in particular, seemed to Liz to be poignant and unnecessarily undignified.

She returned her interest to the corset factory in Kirby Langton.

"It's still there in Dray Street," the guide said. "It houses smaller companies

248

these days: computer firms, printing, that sort of thing."

"The Leicester museum thought you might have some advertising material."

The man searched through a cupboard in an upstairs store room, pulling out box-files while Liz stood back, restraining an urge to leap to interfere.

"Jerrett's catalogues. I thought so. We decided they were of no special interest and they weren't in good enough condition — "

Liz took the box from him reverentially. Inside were a handful of trade catalogues dating between 1901 and 1912. Picking out a catalogue for the year 1908, she turned the pages slowly until she found what she was looking for.

The illustration was almost identical to the photograph her father had given her, except that Daisy's hair and the seams and boning of the corset had been enhanced with ink, and her figure was narrowed to an implausible 'wasp' waist. But Daisy's self-assurance, her challenging gaze were there.

La Marguerite. Liz smiled. So that was how the name in Paris came about.

"Is there something special about this one?" the man asked, waiting for her to turn the page.

"I have the original photograph. She was my grandfather's sister. I only discovered her existence fairly recently."

"Did she work at Noonby? You said your ancestors — "

"My great-grandparents were servants at the Hall. There's a rumour though — " Excitement had made Liz rash about sharing confidences. "I think my great-aunt may have had an affair with Clem Brackenborough." She turned to him. "Do you think that's a possibility?"

He looked affronted, as if his own character had been challenged. "As far as I know, the Brackenboroughs have always behaved very well in that respect. I'm sure Mr Howard's father was a good family man and very happily married."

Liz saw that she had misjudged her audience. "Of course, there's no proof," she added, feeling as if she had betrayed Daisy by speaking too freely.

"If you don't have proof, may I suggest it's best forgotten. You don't want to go round upsetting people. There are some who remember *Howard* Brackenborough very well — and wouldn't like to hear things said about his father."

Liz turned the frayed and torn pages of the catalogue. There were two further illustrations that featured Daisy. Each seemed to give a fresh glimpse into her personality. The first was in profile, and had a look of haughty disdain; the second, full face, revealed a trace of wistfulness that suggested Daisy was more vulnerable than she at first appeared.

Liz asked if she might have copies of the illustrations. Taking the catalogue from her, as if not quite trusting her since her imputation against Clem, the guide ran off copies.

★ ★ ★

Liz walked up the hill, past blank windows and high double gates, which bore a notice to the effect that a security patrol was in operation. The factory was derelict here, at the lower end of the street, but at the top end, by the main entrance, various signs read: 'Quickprint Design & Organisation', 'Kirby Langton

Developments', 'Connect Marketing', and 'Office space to let'. The lobby was painted cream and brown, with doors on either side.

Liz could hear voices, and the sound of a printer, and shapes moved in a blur of colour through the opaque-glass panels on the doors. Ignoring them, she climbed the stairs, until, reaching the top floor, she entered a corridor that was silent, with glass-fronted doors opening on to offices stacked with desks and filing cabinets, glass-panelled shells. Walking to the end, Liz found herself at the top of a staircase well, which, she realised, connected the main building with the various floor levels at the lower end of the street. The swing doors closed behind her, and she entered the abandoned section of the factory.

Thoughts about the safety of old buildings, laws of trespass and, not least, the outside warning of a 'security patrol', halted Liz only briefly. The temptation to step into the past was stronger.

Daisy walked these corridors, she told herself, as she went from floor to floor, and entered what she guessed would have been the old cutting rooms, empty, with ramps for trundling the skips loaded with cloth. She pictured the long tables, the band-knives, the bales of coutil cloth, and a gang of men in waistcoats and aprons, and took pictures, making a note of each one, guessing at the purpose of the workrooms from their position in the building and scribbling text:

The manufacturing processes worked downwards from the arrival of raw materials on the top floor — canvas, cane, wool, twine, quillbone, steel, horn, jean and coutil, lace and ribbon — to the boxing up and despatch of the finished corsets in the basement . . .

In the main workroom, where the women machinists would have sewed corsets at their long benches, barred light from the windows made patterns on the floor, iron pillars held up a lattice of girders from which hung ropes of electric wiring from more recent times. The sound of Liz's skirt brushing her legs made whispers, and her feet echoed on the floor. The sunlight caught the dust stirred by her passage, and made shadows behind the pillars, so that she fancied shapes and images of the women at their machines.

Had Daisy sat *here*, near the window, looked out at the sky dreaming of an escape? Liz wiped a clear patch in the grime on the glass, and could see an area of derelict yard, rising steeply to meet the wall below the windows. Grass and weeds grew among rusting boilers and pieces of machinery.

Retracing her steps, Liz returned to the main entrance, and left the factory without being challenged.

★ ★ ★

A draughty shopping mall dominated the town centre. The shop windows in the new mall were full of consumer goods and badly made clothes.

She bought a pack of plastic-wrapped sandwiches from a supermarket and ate them in the car, watching people wheel trolleys full of shopping to their car boots and unload the groceries.

Remembering that Don's term had

finished, she went to a call box and rang the Lodge.

"Hi. I just remembered, you're home this afternoon."

"Hi. Wish you were here." His voice sounded close and comfortable and cheerful. "What's up, Doc?"

"I've been walking round Kirby Langton's town centre, feeling depressed about twentieth-century consumerism."

"An hour here in the garden, helping me spread compost, would soon cure you of that."

"It sounds great."

"Everything all right? I didn't expect you to ring in the middle of the day, but I'm glad you have." He told her about Prue asking him to dinner.

"That's nice."

"You'd have spoken to the answerphone again. I got your message, by the way."

"Where were you?"

"At an end-of-term pub crawl with Cliff and the others."

"I forgot. I mean, I only remembered today that term had finished."

"You haven't said why you rang."

"I was missing you. Do I need a reason?"

"No. Of course not. Liz, I'm — "

"I've been to see the factory where Daisy used to work," Liz said quickly. "It's a bit spooky. Full of echoes."

"So, when are you coming home?" There was an edge to his voice that made her feel defensive.

"Oh — soon. No reason to stay much longer really — the old town centre is gutted, no sign of Daisy's little shop. The day after tomorrow, I expect."

She could hear, in the silence, his unspoken question. Why another day? Why not tomorrow? Liz closed her eyes. Not over the telephone. Please, don't ask me over the phone whether I've thought about our future?

"Liz — I thought I might take off for Norfolk for a couple of days over Easter. I thought I might go to see Poll and Bill."

"Good idea. They'd love to see you."

"I mean — " He had expected her to understand the sub-text. "I shall go and have a look at Yarnest."

The school. Of course, and he would

check estate agents' windows for property prices, and get the general feel of areas where they might want to live; but he would not say so. Not yet. He would not force the issue in so many words.

"That will be nice," Liz said, deliberately being obtuse. "I think I'll go now. I thought I might have a look at Noonby Hall this afternoon. I might as well have a drive around."

"See how the other half live."

"Something like that. Have a good time at Prue's. Give them my love. Kiss Josie and Ben for me."

She put down the phone.

★ ★ ★

Prue had made a special effort with the dinner.

Some women succumbed utterly to marriage and motherhood, thought Don. Prue, for instance, had devoted her life to domestic and child-orientated activities: Ben's playgroup, baby-sitting circles, home-cooking. Somewhere along the way, the sister that Liz spoke of from their girlhood had disappeared.

Jennifer, on the other hand, was happy to rely on nannies and boarding schools, and on the hired help, Renate, who ruled with *cordon bleu* flair in the kitchen. Why shouldn't Liz jiggle her life into some kind of compromise halfway between the two?

Don felt unhappy. Liz was not behaving as she should. The last few weeks seemed to have challenged his understanding of her as sweet, muddled, utterly maddening, but for the most part uncomplicated. It was all very well being involved in her books and hooked on the research, he was used to her excitement over uncovering research details, trails of linked facts. But this obsession with the girl in the corset had become more personally threatening.

Ben pushed his dinner around his plate and complained that he did not like mushrooms.

"I hate them," he concluded. "They taste like bits of slugs."

Don pretended to take his statement seriously. "No, they don't. They *look* like bits of slugs, but they don't taste like them."

"How do you know? You've never eaten a slug."

"Well now, I've eaten snails. And slugs and snails are both gastropods, so I should guess they taste very similar."

"U-ugh!" Ben made an elaborate pretence of being sick.

Prue apologised. "I'm sorry, Don. He's in a funny mood today. I only said he could stay up to have dinner with the grown-ups if he behaved like one. I can see now that I should have sent him to bed with Josie."

The child picked sullenly at his dinner for a few minutes, then said, "If I've got to behave like a grown-up I ought to be allowed some wine."

"You're too young for wine," his father said.

"No, I'm not."

"Yes, you — oh, for goodness' sake, Ben. Go to bed."

"I haven't finished my dinner."

"You're not eating it anyway. You're simply pushing it about."

Ben pushed a heap of rice experimentally, and some of it fell on the tablecloth.

"Right, that's it!" His father pointed

commandingly towards the door.

Following the child from the room, Prue flashed Don a smile and shut the door firmly on the boy's wails, which grew more distant and then stopped altogether.

"Kids! Who'd have them, eh?" Peter poured more wine. "We must be mad."

Don tried to imagine what Liz would look like if she were expecting a child, but could not visualise it. Some men found pregnant women sexy, but to him they simply looked worn out and misshapen. Prue was no exception. He tried to imagine Liz surrounded by children instead of her books and papers — and abandoned the attempt. Liz did not fit any purely domestic scenario he could think of.

★ ★ ★

Liz parked the car in the long lay-by that flanked the entrance to Noonby Hall and walked to the gates with her camera slung round her neck, her hands in the pockets of her waxed jacket, frustrated by the screen of ornate cast iron. The house was symmetrical, imposing and vaguely Dutch in style. It was framed by an avenue of mature trees. To one side was a large stable block, on the other a car-parking area. A notice attached to the gate gave information about opening times. It was all very austere and grand.

As she surveyed the estate, wondering about attempting a photograph, a dark green sports car drove off the road and pulled up in front of the gates.

"The house is closed," she called, as the driver opened the car door.

Climbing out, he took a bunch of keys from the pocket of his sports jacket.

"I know."

He proceeded to unfasten the padlock and unwind the chain that held the leading edges of both gates. Pushing them open, he paused.

"Can I help you? Noonby's closed to the public, but if there's anything you want to know — "

She supposed him to be some kind of curator, one of the estate staff. He was in his late twenties or early thirties, dark-haired, pleasant.

"I was hoping to take some photographs."

261

"I'm sorry. If you come back on Monday — "

"I shall be gone from the area by then. It doesn't really matter."

He glanced at the heavy camera round her neck. "Are you working for someone? Ought I to know about you?"

"I shouldn't think so."

He propped open the gate, and, since she did not move, seemed to feel constrained to continue the conversation.

"I recognise the camera. I had one just like it a year or two ago. I wish I'd kept it."

"Are you a photographer?"

"I do it for a living."

"You're Lewis," Liz said, with a feeling of surprise.

He smiled a little uncertainly and tipped his head on one side. "Is that significant? Do we know one another?"

"I almost feel as if we should do. I mean, there are all these links; my great-grandparents were servants here in the last century, and my father has a letter from your grandfather addressed to mine."

He tried to look interested, obviously

262

deciding she was an over-enthusiastic tourist with 'roots' in the house's domestic history. "Really? Did your grandfather work here too?"

"The letter was about a woman."

"And your grandfather was — ?"

"The woman's brother." She paused. "I'm sorry. You must think I'm a bit crazy. This is something that has caught my imagination lately. The woman was my great-aunt. She was quite lovely. Her life seems so intriguing."

"Go on. I'm interested."

"I don't know what they were to one another. I only know that Daisy — "

"Daisy," he repeated. "Your great-aunt was called Daisy?"

Liz's heart quickened. "You've heard of her?"

He held out his hand. "Mrs — "

"I'm Liz Cornforth."

"Lewis Brackenborough." He smiled. "Liz, I do believe you may have the answer to something that has been intriguing me for a long time."

8

MRS BRACKENBOROUGH studied Alice's guest list with a frown. She was in favour of the League for female health and emancipation, and she and her husband had made it a point that their children might invite whom they liked to Noonby — believing themselves, as Victorians, to have become rather liberal in their attitude compared with many of their contemporaries — but this girl her offspring had taken up with was another matter; Daisy was a daughter of the servant class.

"In my day, one did not invite one's dressmaker to luncheon."

"This is quite, quite different from trade. Daisy is Beatty's friend and very stylish," said Alice, who in the months since Beatty had adopted Daisy had become more egalitarian in her way of thinking.

"Is it true she lives alone in Kirby

Langton?" For Mrs Brackenborough, a young woman 'living alone' indicated low morals.

"There's a shop assistant for company."

Her mother shuddered.

"Clem thinks Daisy's a terrific girl."

"That is no recommendation whatsoever. Young men are notoriously bad at making distinctions."

"You're forgetting one thing."

Her mother waited, wanting to be convinced since it was too late now to withdraw her permission. A vivid memory came to mind of the girl's mother, a decent, likeable maidservant, she could picture her drawing the curtains and helping her dress for dinner. It had not been very liberal to dismiss her from service, she remembered with a stab of uncertainty; all the same, she regretted the passing of an era that had supported stricter mores.

"You're forgetting that Grandpapa was 'trade',' was Alice's parting shot, whisking the guest list from her mother's hands.

"*My* father wasn't," Mrs Brackenborough called after her indignantly. "My family were members of the baronetcy in the days before titles were being handed out by the government two a penny."

It was all very irregular. She must be getting old.

★ ★ ★

Beatty sat on a chair by the counter watching Daisy's assistant shut up the shop at midday.

"This was *such* a good move." She looked about with approval, smiling at the shop-girl, who, with silent deference, slipped into the back room; after a few seconds the sound of a sewing machine started up.

The shop was arranged sparsely. No more than three dress models stood in the bay window, separated from the rest of the shop by discreet 'café' curtains on a heavy brass rail. The woodtiled floor was polished to a high shine, and there was a seating area furnished with a rug and chairs. This 'showing space' at one end of the long shop counter, with its shelves of parcels and bales of fabric behind, displayed a single model of a chiffon dress on a dark, polished stand; Daisy had added a mirror and a potted palm.

"I want everyone to know about it — your hard work, your sheer cleverness."

"It's not very clever closing the shop for an afternoon," Daisy remarked.

Frowning over a ledger, she was dressed, like Beatty, in a tailored costume; but where Beatty's outfit was long and loose-fitting, Daisy's jacket of quilted linen was nipped in at the waist and had a collar shaped like butterfly wings.

"Alice wants you to be there, to meet people over luncheon. And so do I. As it's so near to Christmas, everyone will be starting to think of their spring wardrobes."

Daisy's had been a token protest, she knew that an invitation to lunch at Noonby, among women with a strong interest in clothes, and money to spend on them, was an opportunity not to be missed.

Daisy's shop made dresses to order. Her better clients rarely came to her for a fitting, she visited them in their homes; but she had, in opening near the centre of Kirby Langton, captured a wide range of customers for whom she stocked sewing needs and bought in scarves, blouses, collars, and occasionally complete outfits from wholesalers.

"I miss the Poplars sometimes." Daisy closed the ledger, thinking of Clem, and his enthusiasm in helping her to plan what could be done by pooling their winnings from the races. She had not seen him since September; and during the shop's early weeks she had been so busy with stock-buying and supervising workmen that she had barely had time for him.

"Oh yes, I miss the fun we used to have in the workroom," said Beatty. "But even I could see that the advantages of the Poplars were almost used up, Daisy. Your fifty pounds at the races, and the windfall from your cousin came at exactly the right time. You were right to expand when you did."

Daisy bent her head at the mention of the non-existent 'cousin', and tucked the ledger under the counter. "So — shall we go? We mustn't be late at Noonby."

"By the way, Clem's coming home,"

Beatty said, as they caught the tram from the town centre.

"Today?"

"He telephoned Alice. No more lectures, and he's sprained his knee playing rugger, so he'll be home for Christmas early."

"That will be lovely for you," Daisy said generously.

"Yes," Beatty admitted. "I've missed him like anything."

★ ★ ★

Daisy had been determined not to be excited by the invitation to the Noonby luncheon party. "The usual League crowd and a few new friends," Alice had said. Customers.

Dressing with great confidence and careful attention to the importance of first impressions, Daisy had chosen a large hat trimmed with three pheasant's feathers and a band of fur. Now, as she moved towards the throng of laughing, chattering women in Noonby's drawing room, panic seized her, and she wanted to turn and run.

A log fire burned in the hearth. That

and the crowd of women made the room very hot in one's day clothes. The room seemed over-stuffed with chintzy sofas and chairs in various rose patterns with a worn, polished look to them. There were several small tables to fall over, littered with silver snuffboxes, ivory figurines, and little oriental pots and dishes.

Daisy greeted Alice and allowed herself to be steered towards Mrs Brackenborough who was standing by one of the windows. Her mouth dried as they came face to face. Why subject herself to this? she asked, and reminded herself that it was essential to make new contacts and reclaim established customers. Besides, how could she have turned down a legitimate invitation to Noonby?

"Miss Cornforth?"

Daisy met her hostess's gaze with a half smile, without flinching under the critical, indomitable scrutiny.

"I remember a certain garden party," Mrs Brackenborough said with raised eyebrows. "Well, my dear, you have come far since then. Alice has been persuading me that you are a very good *modiste*, and that I should think of patronising your establishment. She insists you have an eye for the latest fashions." She glanced at her daughter, dressed in a 'sweet-pea' mauve and navy costume. Mrs Brackenborough was wearing a richly brocaded and beaded *fin-de-siècle* dress. "Not that Alice is fashionable."

"I think Alice could wear some of my more adventurous creations," said Daisy. "I have been trying to persuade her into stronger colours."

"And what would you persuade *me* into?"

"I think you have developed your own sense of style through experience, and have absolutely no need of my advice," Daisy said with a smile.

A man's voice behind her laughed. "Well said. I like it. Stop trying to unsettle her, Mama."

"Nothing of the kind, Clem," protested Mrs Brackenborough. "I was interested in Miss Cornforth's opinions."

Daisy added without turning round, "Well, my considered opinion is that you would be well advised to try me, Mrs Brackenborough, because my workmanship is very good."

"She's absolutely right," Beatty told them.

Mrs Brackenborough smiled and moved away to greet one of the other guests.

"Clem — you're home already," Beatty exclaimed, pink with excitement. "How's your knee? Did you have a beastly journey? Are you coming in to lunch?"

"Lunch with all these ladies?" Clem pretended as usual to quail at the thought.

"Austen is around somewhere. He's here with Sylvia."

"Well, then, that's all right."

"You don't need protection, Clem. You've got me," Beatty said firmly.

Glancing his way at last, Daisy saw him brush Beatty's shoulder with a gesture of affection.

"I hear you've been injured, Clem," Daisy said.

"Only a sprain." His glance met hers. "How's business?"

"Doing well."

One of the servants rang the gong for lunch, and the guests began to drift towards the dining room.

Alice drew Beatty away momentarily,

and Daisy and Clem were left together.

"You look disgustingly well for someone with a sprained knee," she told him.

"So do you. You look sensational."

Offering her his arm, they went in to lunch.

★ ★ ★

At some time in the previous century, Noonby's owners had drawn up plans to remodel the house to suit Victorian taste, ripping out various seventeenth- and eighteenth-century features. Not all these plans had been completed, leaving a peculiar mix of decor. The service end of the house had been modernised, as had the dining room, a long, dark and draughty room decorated in Morris style with William de Morgan tiles round the fireplace, and a huge rustic refectory table and sideboard.

The women kept their hats on during lunch, giving the effect of large, sumptuously laden dinner plates hovering over the more modest portions of meat and vegetables which they were attacking with their knives and forks. The conversation moved from clothes to League gossip, mainly concerning who was hosting the next luncheon, and covering the more serious business of politics, as well as details about forthcoming rallies.

Daisy's gift for mimicry made it easy to affect the manners of the women, so much so that she began to fear they would think she was mocking them. It was all in the hang of a garment, she said, when asked how on earth did one make a dress fit?

"It must first of all sit correctly on the shoulders, and then move with the body, the back of a dress being roomy enough to allow one to bend." She wriggled her shoulders to demonstrate.

She caught Clem looking at her from time to time with laughter in his eyes, and felt a flip of happiness. It was good to see him again.

"Daisy's fashions are beautiful, so wonderfully detailed. Not pretty, mind you. *Beautiful*," said Alice.

"Daisy ought to be employing you as a saleswoman," laughed Beatty.

As the discussion turned to the League and the campaign for votes,

Daisy's interest waned. Listening to their talk about equality and rights, she felt alienated from their world.

Clem too was bored by League talk. Daisy was an emancipated woman, he thought, and none of them could see it, not even Daisy herself. In a real, practical way she was making her own destiny.

He went to the shop a few days later, knowing that the girl assistant would not be there on a Sunday.

Sitting on the edge of the cutting table and watching Daisy work, Clem tried to convince himself that this final year at Cambridge would cure him of his infatuation. But Daisy seemed more dazzling than ever. Her smile lit up the room. He felt himself trembling like a helpless idiot whenever he was near her.

"I'll pay you back, Clem," Daisy had said seriously. "I don't want to be owing you anything. I won't be kept."

"You're hardly that," he had said with mocking regret.

"Nor ever will be."

"Does anyone know?" he asked, picking

up a spent cotton bobbin and playing with it.

"That you advanced the money?"

"I don't mean my people, obviously — but your family."

"I don't speak to them. I have hardly seen them since that day at the races."

"What do you want, Daisy?" he said. "What's your ambition?"

"To expand the business. To be rich," Daisy answered quickly without looking up from her sewing.

"There are other ways of becoming rich."

She looked at him swiftly. "None that I want."

"Will you stay in Kirby Langton?"

"No. Of course not. Kirby's too limiting."

He laughed, not believing that she was serious. "I shall come and help you then, in your grand couture house, wherever it is."

"You mean you'll sit on the table making improper suggestions and trying to stop me working?"

She did not tell him that her dream was Paris. She thought he might laugh,

276

and, in any case, she saw Paris as a private aspiration, an escape route.

"I'll be your business partner."

"No, you won't." She snapped off a thread and spun round to face him.

"Daisy, I have to be a part of it somehow. I've been here from the beginning. Promise me there'll always be room for me and that you won't forget me."

"You'll have married Beatty by then."

"So?"

"She wouldn't like it."

She searched his face, pretending to consider deeply. "Perhaps I should call the business after you, *Maison Clem*."

"Now that really would upset everyone," he laughed.

She turned back to the machine. "They would think I was your mistress."

"I wish you were."

"Keep on wishing, Clem."

"Why? Is it such a terrible idea?"

"I'd never do that."

He thought she was responding to a deep-seated, working-class morality, and that this time he had perhaps offended her; but Daisy knew that being someone's mistress would drain her. A love affair would be no less disastrous than marriage; she would become dependent on him, wasting her energies on fitting into his way of life.

* * *

It snowed that Christmas. Letty, Wilfred, and two-year-old Albert, wrapped in coats and scarves and carrying parcels, came to the shop after Daisy had let the assistant go home on Christmas Eve.

"I thought, with it being the season of goodwill, it was time . . . " Letty said nervously; her glance flicked round the shop, taking in the models on the dress-stands, the balls of wrapping string, and boxes of buttons and threads on the counter. "Everyone says how well you're doing." She paused, gathering courage to say, "How has all this been paid for, Daisy?"

Daisy told her about Beatty helping her find customers after she lost her job at Jerrett's. Lying, she said that Beatty had gone into partnership with her in September after she heard that Daisy's

278

family had thrown her out.

"Miss Knighton? The people you were in service with."

"I never was in service," Daisy said contemptuously. "Beatty is my friend."

"Oh, my word!"

Her mother sat down with her hand to her mouth, not knowing whether to laugh or to cry. Albert hung on to her skirt as if overawed by his surroundings, whilst Wilfred stood by awkward and silent.

"I'd have told you if you'd given me a chance," Daisy said. "I was with *Beatty*, not a man, that day at the races."

"It wasn't my doing, Daisy," Letty protested.

"No, but you believed what *he* said."

"He won't believe this when I tell him." Letty indicated the shop and the dress models. "Your father won't come near, goes all round the houses to avoid this bit of town."

"I don't care if he does or not."

Letty looked down at the parcel in her lap.

"I didn't bring Minnie, for fear she'd cry too much, but I've made you a Dundee cake."

Daisy swallowed hard as the poignancy of the moment got the better of her. In the end they both cried, embracing awkwardly.

Reminded that he too had a present to give her, Albert handed over a little enamelled brooch from her Auntie Ivy. Wilfred was like a stranger, thin and hard-edged, his hair slicked down, and his cap rolled tightly in his hand; he was trying not to cry.

Letty nudged him. "Go on, Wilf. Show Daisy what you made for her."

He had copied several Christmas carols into an exercise book and decorated the cover with Sunday School cut-out pictures. The verses were written in a neat and very beautiful script, with drawings at the head of each carol: the three kings in colourful, oriental robes, a shepherd tending his flock in a snowy landscape beneath a night sky.

"It's lovely, Wilf. I'll sing every one of them to myself tonight."

He smiled then, and thawed a little, and Daisy took them into the back room and cut the cake and made everyone eat a slice. She showed them the workroom with its cutting table and the sewing machines and the half-finished garments, and found presents for them all: for Wilfred, a wooden bobbin that Clem in a fit of boredom had carved into a totem pole; and for her mother, a half-opened rose, made of a deep pink, stiffened fabric that had been destined for a customer's corsage.

"You can wear it on your hat," Wilfred said, touching the softly crimped petals.

Letty shook her head. "It's too good to wear. But I'll always keep it, Daisy. It's a beautiful present."

★ ★ ★

A few days later, Daisy learned that her father had found out about her mother's visit; Letty sent a note saying that, to keep the peace, it was best if she did not come to the shop again.

★ ★ ★

After going back to Cambridge, Clem did not return home until the Easter vacation. Beatty had gone with her family to London for Easter, and Clem tried to rid himself of boredom and a longing to visit Daisy by riding and hunting around Noonby.

One afternoon, driven indoors by pouring rain and obliged to suffer feminine company in the shape of his sister and Austen's wife Sylvia, the conversation turned to Daisy.

"She makes such romantic, colourful clothes," Sylvia said.

"The whole thing has grown astonishingly since Christmas," Alice told Clem. "It's amazing. Beatty's friends have passed the word on to other friends. We have yet to persuade Mama, but you never know — "

"Ask her to tea," said Clem.

Sylvia said, "What a splendid idea." But Alice looked at him oddly; and he was afraid he had been too eager.

★ ★ ★

Daisy hesitated over the invitation, but the thought of an afternoon at Noonby was tempting. Besides, she needed to talk to Clem. She had written to him at his college a few weeks earlier, puzzled by the bank's readiness in allowing her credit on her business account, and she was shocked to discover, when he replied, that the bank's amenability was due to his depositing securities with them.

They made small talk at first in the drawing room, until Clem, craving to be alone with Daisy, suggested she went with him to the stables to look at a new yearling they had acquired.

"Does your father know what you're doing?" Daisy said, starting straight in about the bank's offer of credit.

"Of course not. He doesn't ask about money. And, in any case, it's got nothing to do with my allowance." He grinned. "I've had some luck lately."

"You mean gambling," Daisy said contemptuously.

"Don't pretend to disapprove. After all, it was our winnings on the horses that started you off."

"You should have told me about the bank," she fretted.

"You shouldn't be so proud. Why can't I help you when I'm in love with you?"

"Because I have to do this by myself!

Anyway," she added, "you're not in love with me. You're in love with Beatty. You and I have a purely business arrangement."

"I've thought about you constantly this term."

"Don't talk such rot," Daisy said more sharply, detecting a note of seriousness in his voice.

"Daisy, Daisy. What have you done to me?" he said, swinging round in the stableyard. The horses, recognising him, scraped their hooves and bumped against the doors of their stalls. "I want to shout your name from the roof of Noonby, write it in huge letters across the sky. I want to tell everyone I love you."

"Oh — Clem," Daisy said in exasperation. "One day, I shall tell Bea, and then you'll be sorry."

"It's true. My college notebooks are full of your name, scrawled over and over, entries in the margins of all my essays."

Clem led the way into a loose box, where a couple of horses were tethered. Pausing, he rubbed one of the horses' noses, and the animal shook its head and mane vigorously as he moved to the next.

The Brackenboroughs bred hunters: big, dependable animals with strong personalities. The new yearling wrinkled its nose and curled back its lips over its teeth, but it was quiet when Daisy stroked its head, and pushed its face against her sociably, making her take a step backwards.

Clem told her how to tell the age and condition of a horse by looking at its mouth. Putting his hand in his pocket, he gave each animal a sugar lump. He showed Daisy how to do it, with her hand quite flat so as not to get bitten accidentally, and the horse took the sugar in its soft, dry lips, very gently. The smell was sweet and grassy, and its breath was warm.

Clem watched her for a while, fascinated by her absorption with the horses.

"You have a lovely neck," he said. "At the nape here. So tender. And here." He traced his hand from the vertebrae of her neck along the line of her shoulder to the collar bone. "So aristocratic."

He could not have said anything more

flattering to her. She did not need to be told that she was lovely, but — 'aristocratic': it was the essence of her fantasies.

"Clem — "

He put his arms round her and kissed her. He would not easily forget the expression in her eyes, nor the fact that she held him closely before finally pushing him away. She said he was behaving like a cad, which was true, and looked at him in that serious way she had, as if seeing through to the bones of a situation.

"What do you want, Clem?"

Marry me.

What would she have done if he had said it? He wanted to, but the words stuck fast. Instead he apologised for kissing her and promised it would not happen again.

"Don't even see me again if we can't be friends like we always have been," Daisy said angrily.

But the rebuke had little to do with the look she gave him.

She said — so low he almost did not hear her, "You are not being fair to me, Clem. Don't make me think badly of you."

★ ★ ★

Daisy was in love with Clem. She did not know how or when it had happened, perhaps it had started all that time ago at the Leicester races, but she would not let it get in the way of her ambition, and she was glad when he went back for his final term and they could both concentrate on work. She dreaded the summer when she knew he would be at home and bored for weeks at a time.

They met one day by accident in the town and, going in the same direction, fell into step together.

"You and Bea are still strong pals?" he asked. "She's said very little about you since I've been home."

"She's unhappy with the suffrage movement now they've started going round smashing things. But Bea falling out with her friends means my losing some of my customers."

Daisy did not mind unduly. The League customers had been limiting, with their preference for rational dress.

"I'm thinking of moving on, opening a proper workroom and employing more staff."

"Where will you go?"

"Leicester. I said I wouldn't stay in Kirby and I shan't. For one thing, it's difficult being so close to home as this, afraid that if my mother or brother sneak visits and my father finds out he'll knock them about. Perhaps I should just go somewhere without telling them." Anywhere, she thought, where the chance of meeting Clem was more remote.

"I shall miss you."

"No, you won't. You've managed very well all this year."

They were sheltered briefly from prying eyes by a clump of trees, and she avoided his arm as he tried to pull her against him.

"You haven't improved much since passing your finals," Daisy said.

"Marry me."

This time he had said it. Shocked by his declaration, he stared at her, half afraid, half hopeful of what she would say.

"If you don't stop this I shall go away altogether. Not to Leicester. Somewhere you won't ever find me. You and I both know you have to marry Beatty. Anything else is unthinkable."

For a second, and no more, Daisy weakened before walking away from him quickly.

★ ★ ★

Wilfred persisted in coming to see Daisy. She did not tell him she was planning to leave Kirby. He showed her he had kept the bobbin she gave him, wanting to know who the initials 'C.B.' belonged to, carved into one end.

"A friend," Daisy said. "The same friend who carved the bobbin."

"A man?" Wilfred asked suspiciously, a frown of concentration wrinkling his brow.

"Yes, a man." Daisy laughed. "And you needn't look like that."

"Father says you're a bad lot."

"He doesn't know what he's talking about."

"Promise you told the truth when you

said you hadn't done nothing to be ashamed of."

"*Anything* to be ashamed of," Daisy corrected. "And you're to trust me. I wouldn't lie to you, Wilf."

* * *

The summer passed. Daisy, suspecting that Clem was really serious about wanting to marry her, tried to avoid him. When he heard that she was leaving Kirby, it was Beatty, not Daisy, who told him.

"Can't you persuade her to stay?"

"Whatever for?" Beatty seemed at last to be growing bored with Daisy's enterprise. "She's doing well and has big ideas. Daisy is a born business woman, Clem. She has her sights on something far grander than a little shop in Kirby."

Clem felt desperate when he thought of the future; a position was being prepared for him, a desk job linked to the Brackenboroughs' financial interests in London, and Beatty was steering him skilfully towards marriage, saying she would not mind at all living in London, that she was tired of housekeeping for her family at the Poplars.

The Brackenboroughs held tennis parties through the summer, hunts and shooting weekends in the autumn and, in November, a ball, for which Daisy had created several of the dresses but had declined an invitation to attend herself. Beatty wanted Clem to announce their engagement, and he stalled, but, miserable with confusion, could give no logical reason for waiting. Beatty was a terrific girl, and would make a terrific wife. What could he say? That he thought he was in love with a dressmaker from the back streets of Kirby Langton, whose parents had once been in service at Noonby? Daisy was right, it was unthinkable.

★ ★ ★

Telling himself he wanted only to say goodbye and wish her well before she left for Leicester, Clem went to see Daisy one evening.

She was angry about his coming there at night, saying he should have had more consideration for her reputation. The workroom at the back of the building was stacked with boxes and parcels ready for the removal wagon the next day.

"It all looks very impressive."

"It's hard to think I've been here for over a year, but it's done well for me. It's served its purpose."

"And have I?"

She looked at him with her head on one side. "That's not fair, Clem, and you know it. It's you who have used me, pretending some great romance when you should have been paying attention to Beatty, stirring me up, when I've got better things to do than wonder what it all means."

"Then you admit it could mean something?" he said, and suddenly he reminded her of Wilfred when he was trying not to cry.

"Oh, Clem." Daisy sighed, and adopting a mood of sisterly affection, she put her arms round him to comfort him.

They stood wrapped together for warmth.

"Poor Clem. You'll get over it, I promise you. You have to forget these . . . feelings about me."

"You said I stirred you up."

"Well, of course you do. I'm very fond of you. You're like a brother to me."

She let him kiss her, although, remembering the last time he had kissed her, she knew that she should not be doing it again. She felt reckless on this, her last day in Kirby, and his mouth on hers made her feel giddy.

"I want to marry you," he murmured.

Breaking away from his kiss, she said, "No, you don't. You want to go to bed with me, which is quite a different thing."

"Do you always have to be so knowing? You're not any older than I am. In fact, not even as old."

"But I've seen more of life. I know what men are like."

"But not me, Daisy. It's not like that for me."

"I expect your set are no better. Your father probably has his mistresses."

She made him leave, saying she still had work to do.

* * *

293

Christmas drew closer, and Alice, visiting Daisy's new premises in Leicester, had persuaded her to accept an invitation to the Noonby Christmas Eve party.

As if to add a suitable picturesqueness to the scene, it was snowing as guests started to arrive at the Hall. Noonby was ablaze with lights at almost every window. The carriages, rumbling towards the house through the whiteness, their occupants wrapped in furs and velvet, were reminiscent of a more romantic era than the first decade of the twentieth century. The guests, seeing the lights of Noonby through a veil of softly drifting snowflakes, hearing the voices and laughter of those who had arrived before them, were enchanted by its atmosphere.

"Don't you just love Christmas?" Alice linked her hands through her brothers' arms. "It always takes me back to when we were little, when Mother and Father let us watch everyone arrive from up here on the staircase." She gave Clem's arm a little shake. "You're not paying attention to me."

Clem was studying the tide of incoming

guests in the hall as if searching for someone.

"He's looking for Beatty," drawled Austen. "Bea always looks divine at parties."

"Like the fairy on the Christmas tree," murmured Alice with a trace of envy; she did not look her best in evening dress, and was self-conscious, having been persuaded into a bright blue taffeta bodice by Daisy.

"Isn't it time we joined the parents?" Austen suggested, seeing Sylvia come towards them along the upstairs corridor, darkly pretty with her olive skin and thin features; he brushed his wife's forehead with his lips. "My darling, you look absolutely adorable."

Uneasy about Clem's jittery concentration on the scene below them, Alice waited for the others to go ahead. She took her brother's arm as they descended the staircase, hoping her gown would go unnoticed. She disliked parties unless they were jolly, sporting affairs to celebrate a hunt or shoot.

A servant carrying baggage from one of the carriages squeezed past them.

"Do wake up, Clem," Alice murmured. "Anyone would think you had been drinking."

"Me?"

"You've hardly said a word all day, and you were quite rude to Algie Mould on the telephone this afternoon. Whatever you do, be nice to Bea when she gets here."

"Of course I'll be nice to her. Why shouldn't I be?"

"I don't know. Clem — is there something wrong between you two? Beatty's my best friend. I feel responsible for her."

"And I do too." He squeezed her hand. "Stop being so earnest. Happy Christmas."

But Alice's anxieties refused to be stifled, and they deepened when the Knightons arrived. Beatty looked beautiful in a slender white dress that Daisy had made for her with a cummerbund trimmed with pearls; her hair shimmered like gold wire in the haze of candlelight from the chandeliers; yet, as soon as they had greeted one another and moved into the drawing room, Clem's attention wandered again, searching beyond the door to the vestibule and the lighted entrance, where Daisy was stepping out of a cab.

* * *

She wore a black evening cloak over a gown in the new Empire style, high in the waist and clinging to the hips. It was a deep, wine red.

Daisy was conscious of several eyes upon her as she walked in through the doors, aware of the effect her appearance had on those who saw her: the contrast of black and red against the thickly falling snow, the colour of her cheeks, heightened by the cold, and the sparkle of snowflakes melting in her hair.

A servant took her cloak. The fact that Daisy had arrived unescorted seemed to have caused a minor stir; she could hear people asking one another who she was.

"Daisy! You look stunning." Sylvia took her husband by the arm. "Austen — Clem, doesn't she look wonderful?"

Daisy had not seen Clem until this moment. She met his gaze, and was shocked by the nakedness of his expression.

Clem, for pity's sake, don't look at me like that, she thought tenderly. Everyone will guess.

Did Beatty know? And, supposing she did, did she feel so secure about him that it no longer mattered to her? Beatty embraced her; and there was an element in her smile that said, I know he is attracted to you, but, you see, you don't stand a chance. I am the one he will marry.

I could never take a man on those terms, thought Daisy. I could never want a man, knowing that he was in love with someone else.

She avoided Clem, and moved away towards Alice and a group of her friends. As she chatted, she began to feel more at home in Noonby's drawing room, where there was a Christmas tree smelling of pine needles, a log fire blazed and crackled, the lamps illuminated people's faces with a golden glow, and curtains at the windows shut out the cold and darkness outside.

Someone said that it was snowing harder. By mid-evening it had covered up all the tracks made by the cars and carriage wheels. Those who had not been invited to stay overnight began to joke about having to struggle home through snowdrifts.

Daisy, seated between Austen and one of the Moulds at dinner, far away from Beatty and Clem, put her energies into convincing Basil Mould's wife Ettie that she should hire her to design a spring wardrobe.

"Daisy, it isn't really *done*," Beatty murmured to her afterwards, finding her alone in the hall.

"What isn't?"

Daisy had been admiring the Italianate effect of the walls and pillars. She loved the incongruous, isolated patches of decorative richness at Noonby, the Morris dining-room wallpaper, the cloisonné vases in the drawing room, remnants of seventeenth-and eighteenth-century mouldings here and there, and a stained-glass panel in the study door across the hall. She paused before a mirror with a fretwork of Art Nouveau tulips round its edge, and caught a glimpse of her reflection next to Beatty's. Her own image was dark and richly textured, vibrantly coloured; Beatty's was ghostly pale, ethereal.

The gipsy and the princess, Daisy thought. The contrast was a trick of the light, but it seemed to represent a more significant difference between them. It's true, I shall never be able to compete with Beatty. Do I want to? she wondered. Noonby had once been an icon for her, and the people who moved in its ambience were a closed circle, but she realised now that she was no longer in awe, nor even envious of them. Nor did she want the distraction of Clem as a lover, she told herself. She knew what men like Clem wanted. If she gave in to him, he would believe he was happy for a while, but then he would go back to the comfort, the manners, the familiarity of someone like Beatty.

All the same, when she saw the look in his eyes tonight, there had been a part of her that wanted him, and for a while she had questioned her motive for coming here.

"I mean," continued Beatty, "one doesn't tout for custom at one's hosts' table unless one is invited to do so — as, for instance, at our ladies' luncheon party last year."

"Are you telling me how to behave?"

"I suppose I am, but it's not meant unkindly, Daisy. Only for your own good. There are certain things — "

"Things one doesn't do unless asked."

"Yes."

"Thank you for the lecture."

"That isn't all."

Daisy turned to her and saw that Beatty was as pale as she had looked in the mirror; it was not a trick of the light.

"It's about Clem. *You* and Clem."

"There is no *me* and Clem."

"I know he used to come to the shop in Kirby. He's given himself away once or twice — Clem's not all that clever really. He has no natural cunning, whereas, I think perhaps, Daisy, you have plenty."

"You're thinking that I've lured him to me in some way, but you're wrong."

"I don't know. I've seen the way he looks at you, and the way you pretend to be indifferent." Beatty's face was icy with concentration; she hated scenes, she

301

hated having to say these things, but it was necessary. "I've thought about it, and I really don't know what you're up to. I simply want to say that if you care for him, I mean really care for him at all, you'll stop what you're doing. Any liaison with you would do Clem nothing but harm." Beatty fell abruptly silent and walked away.

Daisy folded her arms tightly round her waist and leaned against one of the pillars, needing its support; she was trembling violently, more angry than she had ever been in her life.

She had to go home. She would ask for her cloak and leave at once. She should never have come here, where, for all their pretence at admiration, people thought of her even now as their little seamstress.

It was still snowing, huge flakes fell slowly beyond the windows on either side of the main entrance. Daisy leaned her arms on one of the window ledges and pressed her head against the cold glass. She could see in the light from the house the ghostly pale waves and hummocks of snow deepening by the second.

She turned as Austen came into the hall.

"All on your own? You mustn't feel shy, you know. We're all very friendly. We won't bite."

"I was wondering how I'm going to get home."

"My mother has just been talking about everyone staying overnight. Most people were going to stay anyway, except for Beatty's people, and you and a few others, who were leaving before morning."

"I don't particularly want to stay the night."

"You may have no choice about it, old thing."

"Then I'll walk."

"I say." He looked at her more closely. "Is anything wrong?"

"I simply don't like altering arrangements once they've been made."

"I think it would be rather foolish to insist on sticking to them. The best-laid plans — and all that."

Daisy saw that he was genuinely concerned. He seemed kind. She ought not to have been rude to him.

She left the window and gave in. "Very well then. Thank you. It's very hospitable of your mother."

She returned with Austen to the drawing room, and he told her what fun it was at Noonby on Christmas morning, with all the traditions of opening presents, and snow fights — when the weather obliged, as it seemed to have done this year.

As the guests at Noonby stood around the Christmas tree at midnight, singing carols, Daisy remembered Christmas in Morton Street. Wilfred and her mother would be at the midnight service. Did Minnie still miss her? She was young, and at that age one easily forgot. And Wilfred was nearly eleven now; each time he had come to see her he had been a little more distant. They did not know about her move to Leicester and she had deliberately laid a false trail in Kirby Langton, talking to her neighbours of plans to go to London. Only her wealthier clients knew where she had gone.

Should she go back to Morton Street and face up to her father? "Look," she would say — being very reasonable. "Isn't it time we made it up?"

Sentimental rubbish, Daisy told herself. All that was over. She had come too far for reconciliations.

★ ★ ★

Accepting the sleeping arrangements made for her, and the loan of one of Alice's nightdresses, Daisy slept fitfully that night. Her dreams were disturbing, and she woke more than once in the night, wondering where she was, listening to the darkness. Her heart beat softly, thud, thud, like snow falling inside her.

Christmas morning dawned, crystal bright, with an almost painful stillness clamping the whiteness to the landscape. Daisy sat at the window with the counterpane wrapped round her for warmth. Gazing across the estate, she thought she had never seen anything more beautiful than the expanses of untouched snow.

A team of men and horses were at work in the distance, clearing one of the drives with a snow plough. She could hear the scrape of metal, the ring of hand shovels, and an occasional voice carried on the thin air.

She did not know what was expected of Noonby's guests first thing in the morning. She stretched and let the counterpane fall from her shoulders, looking around at the four-poster bed, the flowers on the writing table, and remembering the jugs of hot water, and the comfort of a fire burning in the grate the previous night; it was as if they had been conjured there by magic, though she knew the servants must have been scurrying around after midnight to get the bedrooms ready for extra guests.

Daisy knew that the custom in society was to rise late. But how late? She would have been up and working by seven if she were at her flat in Leicester. She thought lovingly of her new premises, the nicely furnished sitting room and bedroom and little kitchen upstairs, the showroom, workrooms and store rooms on the ground floor, and a closet outside — no embarrassment about fetching and carrying slops. She wished she was waking up in her own bed instead of wasting time

306

here, wondering if she dared put her head outside the bedroom door.

Someone had laid out a set of day clothes for her on the ottoman near the fireplace. She recognised one of Alice's dresses. They were all very kind, she reminded herself. She should be grateful, but Beatty's accusations still rankled, and it occurred to her that, after today, she must make a clean break.

The room felt too close, and Daisy dressed quickly, deciding to go in search of breakfast. She would thank her hosts and ask the butler Warboys to get someone to drive her to Kirby Langton station.

There seemed to be nobody about downstairs. She walked into the drawing room, where the tall Christmas tree was choked with presents round its base. A housemaid opening the curtains seemed surprised to see her.

"I was wondering about breakfast."

The girl explained that the servants would put out breakfast in the dining room shortly, but that the ladies generally preferred to breakfast in their rooms. It would be brought to her on a tray in due course, though of course if she wanted an early breakfast . . .

She said, no, a tray in her room later would be fine. She asked the girl to fetch her cloak and, if it were possible, a pair of galoshes as she felt like walking in the snow.

* * *

The men had shovelled the snow from the steps at the front of the Hall, leaving the stones dark and wet in the sun.

Daisy hurried along the cleared paths and plunged into an avenue of trees on the east side of the house, where a high hedge put her out of sight of the windows.

The snow was level here, its fall broken by the trees. Daisy crouched down, scooping up a handful of it in her bare hands, and moulding it into a ball, hurled it with all her strength at a stone statue at the end of the walk, then followed it with another, and another. With a satisfying thump each hit its target, a godly hero wearing very little except a laurel wreath. Surprised by the vicious energy behind her actions, Daisy halted.

The avenue of limes met with a farm lane, and here the snow was deeper. Retracing her path, unwilling to return indoors, she crossed the front of the house and wandered among the greenhouses, discovering a walled garden laid out in squares.

The gravel paths, the box hedges, and the rose bushes in the flowerbeds were reduced to rounded upholstered shapes, with dark skeletons of branches showing here and there. It was like entering a dust-sheeted room from which the ceiling had been removed, so that the austere whiteness of the decor was flooded with the blue of the sky.

Daisy followed the paths for a while, making footprints. Spreading her arms, she flung back her head, offering herself to the glittering sunlight.

It was then that she realised she was not alone, and swung round to see Clem leaning against the garden wall.

"What are you doing here?"

He smiled. "I live here. Remember?"

"Were you following me?"

309

"I didn't know you were about until I saw you throwing snow around."

"I was being childish."

"I know. I thought you looked very charming."

"You can keep your flattery. It doesn't impress me."

He came towards her. "Why so angry? What's wrong?"

"Nothing." She kicked at the snow, then made an attempt to pass him, but he caught hold of her arm.

"Please — don't go."

She looked at him, expecting him to become charming and persuasive, which she could have dealt with, she was prepared to rebuff any attempts at seduction. But he was pale, and he said nothing more at first, so that her own emotions were all at once uncertain.

"I don't know what to do, Daisy. It's becoming clearer and clearer to me that I don't love Beatty."

"Of course you do. And Beatty loves you. She's terribly upset about the way you've been neglecting her. She practically accused me of trying to tempt you away from her."

310

"I feel as if I don't care what happens any more. I want to be honest and open about everything. I love you so much, it affects everything I do." He touched her shoulder. "Love me," he murmured.

"I do love you. I love you more than I ought to. But what's love, Clem?" She kissed him experimentally, testing her reactions. "I don't know. Is what I feel for you *love*? Is it enough to sweep me off my feet if I don't hold on to my sanity? And I'm holding on, you can believe it, for all I'm worth. I'm not my mother. I'm not like Beatty. Love isn't what I want. I've got *my* life to lead."

She had spoken so fiercely that she frightened him a little. They stared at one another for a long time, and searching his face Daisy tried to resolve the confusion of her thoughts and feelings. She was trembling, and told herself it was because of the cold. He put his arms round her, and she moved closer for warmth.

Very slowly the embrace altered, moved from a mutual need for warmth and comfort to a sensual clinging, and Daisy, drawn towards feelings that were too powerful for her, did not want to turn back, did not want to listen to herself saying again in cold reason, this isn't what I want.

"I love you," Clem said with a break in his voice.

"Make me believe you," Daisy murmured.

★ ★ ★

Beatty had risen early. She had a Christmas present for Clem, a pair of cuff-links with their initials intertwined, which she wanted to give him in private, before the public handing could of presents from under the tree took place in the drawing room. There must be no distractions when he saw the linked initials, so that he would be sure to understand their meaning.

'Clement Brackenborough — no, Clem and *Beatty*,' he would say in surprise. The moment would be very romantic, and portentous.

He was not among the handful of men already breakfasting. One of the Moulds said they had seen him outside heading off towards the rose garden.

Beatty waited for a few minutes for him

to return, then, because the snow looked inviting in the sunshine, she asked for boots and a coat, deciding to surprise him.

She saw Clem and Daisy as soon as she entered the walled garden, apparently oblivious of the snow, their bodies close, Daisy's arms round Clem's neck. He was kissing her, holding her in a way Beatty had never experienced, their bodies horribly intertwined.

★ ★ ★

Daisy first heard Beatty's cry of anguish. She broke away from Clem and, saying his name, tried to warn him.

Dazed, he reached out as if to pull her back to him, guilt surfacing only slowly as he saw Beatty in the gateway. "Oh, no — " He turned away.

"You said — " Beatty spoke to Daisy, trying to enunciate calmly. "Last night you said to me, 'There is no me and Clem.' After all I've done for you, helping you better yourself, rescuing you — this is how you repay me."

Clem tried to speak and she turned on him.

"You! Don't talk to me. You're despicable!"

Choking back a sob, trembling with humiliation, Beatty hurried from the garden.

Clem paced in the snow furiously without speaking, not looking at Daisy. He halted. "I'll have to go after her. Heaven knows what she might say or do."

Daisy nodded, feeling numb and angry, sure only of one thing: it no longer really mattered what Beatty did or said; Clem was hers, she loved him and she wanted him. She had wanted him all the time and had been too blind to admit it, but if he was prepared to sacrifice everything, so was she — her work, her career, everything.

She called after him. "Clem — I'll marry you. Let's do it. Let's defy them all."

★ ★ ★

Clem had reached Beatty on the front steps and was trying to reason with her when Daisy caught up with him.

Beatty turned on Daisy. "*Now* tell me you had no designs him."

"I hadn't. I never planned — "

"You *planned* it right from the beginning. You had it all planned from the very first time you set foot in this house, ambitions that were laughable when I first met you." She twisted away from Clem's restraining hand. "Well, now you can choose, Clem. Daisy or me."

Mr Brackenborough had come out on to the steps from the main entrance. "What the devil's going on? Do I need to remind you, Clement, that we have guests in the house? That it's Christmas morning?" He noticed Daisy. "Perhaps you can tell me what's happening?"

"I don't know," Daisy was looking at Clem's frightened expression. "That's for Clement to answer."

He did not speak, looking helplessly at Betty and at his father, and then at Daisy, his eyes pleading with her to be discreet.

Daisy's mind grew clearer. She had been right to try to hold on to her sanity.

Beatty was beginning to cry, pounding

Clem's chest with her fists.

"Bea," he pleaded in a low voice. "Bea, don't make a scene."

Why shouldn't she? thought Daisy. Scream and yell all you want, Bea. Her mind hurt with the tension. Choose, Clem. Choose, she willed him.

Looking at him, she said very calmly, "Well, Clem, why don't you tell them how it is?"

"Tell us how what is?" said Mr Brackenborough. "Clement?"

"Daisy — give me time to explain," Clem murmured unhappily. "I'll make it all right."

"Marry Beatty," she answered flatly. "Just — leave me alone."

"Is this young woman your mistress?" Lowering his voice, Mr Brackenborough tried to move them down the steps away from the house. "Do you mean to say, we've entertained your *mistress* here overnight?"

The insult in the suggestion, without reference to her except as baggage for Clem to recognise or deny, transformed Daisy's disenchantment to anger.

"Of course. What else?" she said

bitterly. "I've been his mistress for ages. In and out of his bed all the time."

"Daisy!" Clem protested in an anguished voice.

Beatty sobbed hysterically. "After all I did for you — and then to betray me like this."

"You didn't help me half so much as Clem if the truth be known," Diasy said, becoming pragmatic. "It was Clem who set me up in business." She turned to Mr Backenborough. "Isn't that what men do for their mistresses?"

"Daisy!" Clem protested.

"You see, I think one should be honest and open about these things. After all, poor Beatty ought to know what she's in for if she marries him."

This was too much for Beatty who stumbled indoors.

Fearing a spread of the disturbance through the household, Clem's father hurried after her.

Clem made a conciliatory move towards Daisy.

"Don't you dare touch me. Don't you ever come near me again."

317

"If you had only let me do it my way
I could have explained how we really love
one another. There are ways of doing
things — "

Daisy turned away from the house
without answering.

"Where are you going?"

"Home. Thank Alice for the clothes.
I'll send them on."

She walked down the drive in the snow
towards the distant gates, hearing him
call after her, refusing to look round.

"Daisy — I'm sorry."

"Grow up, Clem," she shouted back.

★ ★ ★

The following week, Daisy's evening dress
was returned from Noonby. A brief note
accompanied the parcel:

I understand that circumstances make
it necessary to terminate our friendship.
I do this with regret. Alice.

Slipped among the folds of the dress was
a letter from Clem.

Daisy tore it up without reading it. She

took a pair of shears from the table and cut systematically into the fabric of the dress she had worn at Noonby, tearing the skirt into long ribbons.

There was a swift pleasure to be had from the sound of threads breaking, a satisfaction in having spoken out freely, but it was all too short-lived. However much Daisy assured herself that Clem was a miserable coward, a liar and a seducer, it was not enough. She wanted to write her anger in large letters where everyone could see.

★ ★ ★

"Maison Clem. The name is in gold letters above the workrooms," confirmed Alice. "And she has sent a card to Noonby and to all Beatty's friends, inviting everyone to an official showing of her next collection."

Clem felt he had died a little when he learned that she had carried out her one-time threat to name the enterprise after him. It was as if Daisy had wanted to reduce his love for her to a joke, though he had no doubt that she had

319

done it too, in a calculated way, to do him the maximum harm. He felt emasculated by the gesture, and yet, for all the hurt, he could not help admiring her revenge.

The Brackenboroughs assumed that Daisy had been after the Noonby fortune, or as much of it as was due to the second son — amounting, now that he was in disgrace, as far as Clem could tell, to no more than a pair of sporting pistols with which he might shoot himself as far as anyone cared.

His mother would not speak to him. Austen was miserably embarrassed by the whole business but stood by him, saying it 'would all blow over'. His father had made it clear that if Clem tried to communicate with Daisy or have anything more to do with her he would renounce him entirely.

A few weeks earlier Clem would have defied them all. Now, Daisy's vengeful gesture had shown him the depths of her anger. Beatty too had surprised him. She was leaving Kirby Langton. In a letter oozing vitriol she had told him what she thought of him and made it clear he had no more claim even to friendship.

In January Beatty went to London, and Clem wrote to Daisy:

I know I deserve nothing, yet, if I could begin all over again, I would lay myself at your feet in front of everyone and offer you my life as well as my heart . . .

For a week he waited, but there was no reply.

Still 'deeply disappointed' in him, his mother re-established communication, but it was decided by family consensus that Clem must be settled in London as soon as was feasible. In the meantime, he roamed about the estate, trying to get Daisy out of his head.

Driving to Leicester one afternoon, he stood outside her workrooms, looking for a long time at the name above the showroom, window. She saw him, locking the door before he could talk to her, and would not come out though he banged on the windows and doors for more than half an hour, exciting and

321

terrifying the girls at their workbenches.

The sound of Clem hammering to be let in stayed in Daisy's head. She shut herself in her flat when he had gone and would not come out for the rest of the day.

He came again, once, in the spring, and, because she had no longer been expecting it, she was not quick enough to bar the door, nor to tell the staff that she was 'out' to callers.

"You can leave us, Norah," Daisy said. "Get on with one of the orders. I shall deal with the gentleman."

They stood in the entrance at the foot of the stairway. He could hear the quiet rattle of machinery in a back room, the murmur of feminine voices, and the sound of traffic passing in the street.

Daisy folded her arms, severe in a plain, fitted dress; two high spots of colour touched her cheeks.

"Go away, Clem. What's the point?"

"You've got to forgive me. I can't go on like this. I feel such a heel."

"You are a heel. And there's nothing to discuss. It all seems very clear to me.

You let me down."

"I've been going crazy."

"Good. I hope they put you away."

"You even called the business Maison — " He broke off, distressed. "How could you? Everyone is highly embarrassed."

"Not here, they're not. No one here could care less. Anyway, you ought to feel flattered. You will live on in my memory. True love is for ever."

"You really hate me so much?"

"I don't hate you." She forced herself to smile. "I feel quite indifferent about you, so you don't have to apologise, or explain, or whatever else your gentlemanly code expects of you. I *forgive* you. Is that what you wanted?"

"No," he said miserably. "Marry me, Daisy. We'll go away somewhere. I'm leaving Noonby. They're finding me something to do in London. You could still run your dressmaking business — "

"Don't be ridiculous."

"Am I?"

"Of course you are. Absolutely ridiculous. Isn't Beatty living in London now? Make it up with her. It will be very convenient for you both."

"I don't care about Beatty. Only you."

He saw that it was hopeless and held out his hand.

"At least wish me good luck?"

Daisy refused his handshake. "I can't wish you luck, Clem. Go to hell."

★ ★ ★

A story had spread in Kirby Langton that Clem had been caught in compromising circumstances with a local girl.

His name could not have been blacker. It only needed Daisy's father to arrive at the Hall and set about him, or Beatty's father to come after him with a horse-whip, for justice to be complete.

One day, before Clem left for London, a small, badly wrapped parcel was handed in at the servants' entrance. There was no message, but Warboys, who delivered it to Clem, said that he thought it had been handed in by a child.

Opening the package, Clem found the little totem pole he had once carved out of one of Daisy's bobbins. He stared at it as he turned it over in his hand for a long time, feeling a twinge of superstitious fear at the way the markings on it had been badly defaced, and his initials, cut into one end, had been hacked at and completely obliterated.

9

"SO, you have been on the Daisy trail as well?" said Lewis Brackenborough as they drove towards the Hall.

"I can't believe you've even heard of her." Liz felt drawn by invisible nerve wires towards Noonby's blank windows, to the imposing flight of shallow steps and double doors at the front of the house.

"I know very little, except from hearsay. You realise that my grandfather was once deeply in love with her."

"Deeply," Liz repeated with a sense of pleasure and satisfaction. "I didn't know — I mean, I wasn't even sure if it had happened at all."

"I guess my grandmother didn't make it up."

"Your grandmother — his wife?"

"Virginia."

"She knew?"

He glanced at her and smiled. "I was

326

very close to her. My grandfather died before I was born, so I never knew him, but *she* told me things. And one of them was that Daisy had him tied up in knots for years even after he had married."

"How very satisfying."

"Not for my grandmother. Nor for him, as far as I can tell. Daisy seems to have been somewhat difficult. My grandparents married in 1913, but it didn't go very well in the early years. It was fine when they were older, but early on he kept drifting back to Daisy."

"They were lovers?"

"Oh, yes. I don't think there's any doubt about it."

They fell silent, aware of something voyeuristic and intrusive about their interest. Liz said so. "It doesn't seem quite fair on them, does it, to want to know about them after all this time?"

"No. But I bet that won't stop you being curious. It didn't stop me. I think my grandmother wanted to talk about it and get it off her mind. She put up with a lot from Clem, all things considered."

"Is she still alive?"

"No." He pulled up in front of the

house. "But that's enough of what I know for now, I want to hear your side of it. Have you come a long way to find out about your family?"

"From Somerset. I'm here on a research trip. Nothing to do with Daisy — at least, only indirectly. I'm a fashion historian." She explained about the book as they went into the house.

"I shall have to look out for it when it's published," he said politely.

The large entrance hall had been restored with plasterwork detail to show how Noonby would have looked in the late seventeenth century. It was full of alabaster statuary and Chinese lacquered cabinets. Liz glimpsed a dining room with a polished table, set out as if for a banquet with a collection of fine porcelain and crystal glass. Chandeliers hung from all the ornate ceilings. Was this how the Brackenboroughs had lived?

"May I take photographs?"

He nodded.

"So, was Daisy really a little gold-digger?" he said as she set up her tripod. "A dressmaker and the daughter of dismissed servants? You can see, can't you, why it was such a scandalous situation? I mean, in those days! A Brackenborough wanting to marry a little seamstress."

"A corsetmaker first of all."

"Really? She sewed corsets? Well, that must have made it even more impossible — although, I can see your interest of course."

"I don't think there was anything very little about her," Liz said, beginning to feel a need to defend both the position of corsets and Daisy, and resenting his epithet 'gold-digger'.

"Daisy modelled for Jerrett's corset factory. The museum in Kirby Langton has a couple of illustrations that feature her. She was very vivacious — generous mouth and figure, extremely good-looking."

"I thought she would be petite and pretty, with a spiteful little face."

"Spiteful?"

"Oh, yes. After what she did. She broke his heart and ditched him completely in the twenties."

"She went to France," Liz said, stooping to look through the viewfinder. "She had a very successful career as a couturière in Paris."

"Really? I don't think my grandfather knew where she had gone when she left him. In fact, I'm sure he didn't. He told my grandmother everything in the end."

"Everything?" said Liz with scepticism. "Does anyone ever tell someone everything?"

They went into the drawing room, furnished in white and gold, with spindly settees and chairs with embroidered upholstery. Liz tried to imagine Clem living there, but faltered at the attempt.

"What did he look like? I've seen a photo in the museum, but what was he like when he was a young man?"

"There's a painting upstairs."

"I'd love to see it."

Liz told him about Willow working for Daisy in Paris as they crossed the hall to explore the rest of the downstairs rooms.

"Willow says Daisy never married, and lived only for her work, calling herself Marguerite. She says Daisy's only interest was in making money."

"She doesn't sound very pleasant, does she? One doesn't really want to like her."

"Willow clearly feels ambivalent. And yet — "

"Exactly. It gets to me as well. That, *and yet*. If Daisy was such a heartless monster, why was my grandfather in love with her — and for such a long time, from well before the First World War until the nineteen twenties?"

"Her brother kept a photo of her," said Liz, "One can only suppose he kept it out of a sense of affection. But he never talked about her. She had quarrelled with her family."

"I suspect even my grandmother admired her."

"She knew her?"

"I think she met her a couple of times. She wouldn't say much about it, except that Daisy was 'the sort of woman men are attracted to' and that she once came to their house in London and behaved outrageously."

They walked along corridors, looking into rooms, sidestepping isolated piles of dust-sheets and painters' ladders.

"The house needs a lot of work each year," Lewis explained. "The Trust went for a complete restoration when they took over. Most of the family furniture had been sold so there was nothing here but a shell. What you see is on loan, except for a few family paintings."

"That explains it," said Liz. "That's why I can't picture him here."

And yet, here and there, she saw glimpses of Noonby's Victorian and Edwardian past: a large, nineteenth-century conservatory at the back of the house, a few de Morgan tiles in the dining room, the family paintings of dogs and horses. Upstairs they entered a room that must once have been a bedroom, but was now furnished as a sitting room, with very worn, chintz-covered sofas and easy chairs. It was crowded with boxes, camera carrying cases and tripods. Windows overlooked the garden at the back of the house, and there was a small, panelled walk-in closet fitted with an oldfashioned washbasin and bath fittings and cluttered with more photographic equipment.

"This is where I keep my gear when I'm at Noonby. This is *not* on general view to the public. The whole business of opening to the public makes me very nervous and embarrassed," Lewis confessed. "I hate the way the place has been turned into a museum. If it wasn't for the exhibitions — " He touched a plan chest lovingly and, folding his arms, smiled at Liz. "It's nice to hide myself away when the hordes come round."

It was not the camera equipment that held Liz's interest. She was staring at an oil painting above the door of a young man in First World War army uniform. It reminded her at once of the photograph she had seen in the Kirby Langton museum, but this must have been painted about thirty years earlier, and here, in the portrait of Clem as a young man, she could understand why Daisy had fallen for him.

"It's uncanny. There's something so alive about it. I felt the same about Daisy's photograph — I wish now I had brought it to show you — something about the mouth and eyes."

"I know what you mean. It's hard to capture. But when you do — "

She glanced at the plan chest. "I should like to see your photographs."

"Later. Are you like her?" Lewis said.

"Your great-aunt Daisy?"

"I'm not at all like Daisy," Liz laughed, feeling oddly flattered. "Although I think I'm beginning to understand her a little. Are there any more pictures of Clem?"

"None of when he was a young man. But there's one of him as a child, and another painted when he was older. They're in the long gallery."

She followed him up a further flight of stairs to a broad corridor carpeted in rush matting and lined on either side with paintings. He flicked a switch, and the walls were immediately bathed in a theatrical glow from strategically placed spotlights in the ceiling.

Leading her from portrait to portrait, Lewis explained each one: William Brackenborough who had bought Noonby Hall in the eighteen fifties, an industrialist, portly and red-cheeked; Clem's father, James, who had retired on the family fortune and investments to manage the estate; James's wife, raven-haired and aristocratic in her youth; their children, Austen, who had inherited the Hall, and Alice, an angular, horsy woman, seated at a piano, who married someone called Algie Mould.

They halted in front of a painting of Clem as a child, a sturdy, serious boy seated on a pony, and another taken in his forties, a few frown lines, but no obvious signs of disappointment in love. His brother Austen's face revealed more dissatisfaction as an older man.

Liz allowed herself to be guided from painting to painting: Austen's wife Sylvia, painted in the twenties, their son, and Clem's children, Howard, the war hero of local museum fame, Viola, and Hugo, Lewis's father.

"This is Clem's wife. My grandmother."

Liz searched the painting, curious to know if Virginia was at all like Daisy. She saw a pretty woman with dark, curling hair, and a china-doll complexion.

"I loved her very much," Lewis said simply. "Perhaps because I was her favourite. She spoiled me like hell. And towards the end she told me my grandfather's secret, about his affair with Daisy lasting all through the First World War — 'Clem's skeleton', she called it."

"My father has a letter that seems to corroborate the affair, at least, it proves Clem knew where Daisy was living in 1920."

For the first time, Liz acknowledged that there were other aspects to Daisy's story, and that people had been hurt; but she did not want to accept a darker side to Daisy, that there might even have been good reasons for Willow's disaffection.

"How unhappy for his wife that she knew about it."

"I think people always know about that sort of thing, even if they're not told, especially if it goes on for a long time. Unless they don't really want to." His glance met hers and flicked away, and she sensed he had been on the brink of a confession.

"Tell me about Daisy in France," he said. "Do you know why she went to Paris?"

"Perhaps she simply got more ambitious? I know very little, except that she had a couture house and was there until the German Occupation. She and Willow came to England. They were friends.

Daisy was killed in a road accident in the end."

"Did Clem ever see her again?"

"I was hoping you might know the answer to that."

"My grandmother didn't say."

"It's possible Virginia might not have known about it."

"What about Daisy's friend Willow?"

"Willow is no help," said Liz.

"Perhaps she doesn't know either."

"Oh, I'm sure she knows something, but she wraps everything up in an air of intrigue. Willow is lonely, and also afraid of going senile. She knows if she holds back elements of Daisy's story I shall want to keep going back to her for more. It works. I've been hooked from the moment I saw Daisy's photograph."

Liz looked round the gallery. "I wish there were more pictures of Clem."

"He kept a diary, mostly infantile stuff from his childhood. Nothing about Daisy. Either he hadn't met her at the time he went to Cambridge, or he was careful not to confide anything even to a diary."

He fetched the books for her and they

returned to his room.

Saying he would bring them some tea, Lewis switched on the electric fire and left her to read in private. Liz curled up on a sofa with the pile of leather-bound diaries, thin and black and softly bowed.

There were family crises, sibling rivalries and squabbles, school heartaches, triumphs, and Clem's early experiments, extremely innocent, in love. And then, at seventeen, his enthusiasm for someone called 'Bea', who was 'a good sport and dashed pretty'.

With his entrance to Cambridge the diary grew more reticent, entries were confined to the vacations at Noonby. References to Bea and her family became more perfunctory: 'Bea came to Noonby', 'Went with Bea to a dinner at the Moulds . . . ' and then Liz came across a brief entry in 1908.

A girl infiltrated Alice and Bea's garden party, a stunner. Some nerve. Turns out she works in a factory.

A few weeks later:

Bea has a project to 'educate' our gate-crasher, says she feels guilty about her losing her position. I shall let her get on with it. But I object strongly. One should never try to improve on nature.

Liz searched greedily through the succeeding entries, finding references that might, or might not, refer to Daisy, but the diaries ended abruptly before Clem's final year at Cambridge.

Lewis returned, carrying a tray of tea things. "I thought it might be thirsty work."

"I feel as if I know all the members of the family after reading the early diaries. I can understand now why Clem didn't simply get on with it and marry Daisy. Their backgrounds *were* light years apart."

"No confessions about her though. I told you there was nothing there."

"Have you seen these?" She showed him the extract about the garden party and the succeeding passages that seemed ambiguous:

Talked to our friend all afternoon at the Poplars before Bea arrived.

D. came with us to the races and won fifty pounds, I won twice that. Cheered her up over the row with her father, and told her not to worry, we will think of something.

"It's her," said Lewis. "How could I have overlooked it? And this — 'Have found the perfect place in Kirby Langton, a prime site. Think I can get up loans from the bank — '"

"He paid for Daisy's first dress shop? He must have done."

Lewis laughed. "Now do you say she wasn't a gold-digger?"

They drank the tea.

Perching on the arm of one of the sofas, Lewis flicked through the later diaries, and studying his features Liz searched for family similarities with the portrait of Clem.

The room was darkening, and it had started to rain, the wind whipping it in gusts against the window. Lewis reached out an arm without looking up from his reading and switched on a standard lamp, throwing his face into shadow. The flex trailed over worn rugs. The clutter of the room and the shabbiness of the furniture was intimate and comfortable. Kidnapped by Noonby, Liz felt detached from the outside world. The sensation was seductive, and she did not want to move from the sofa.

"The light's going." He glanced up at the window. "And the weather's foul. I expect you were hoping to take some photographs outside. Can you come back tomorrow?"

There was absolutely no need for photographs, Liz told herself. There was nothing to be gained from compiling pictures of the Hall, which in its altered state had no bearing at all on Daisy or Clem's lives. In any case, if she had wanted pictures of Noonby there were postcards.

"I should like to come back," Liz said. "I haven't seen your photos yet."

"Tomorrow?"

"I'll try not to get in the way if you're busy."

"You won't be in the way. I'll show

you the grounds."

"You're very kind." She glanced at her watch. "I really ought to be getting back to my hotel."

"Do you have to? I mean, I can offer you dinner after a fashion. The staff will be knocking off for home, but the fridge downstairs is well stocked. I'm a dab hand at the impromptu meal."

★ ★ ★

Why had she refused? Liz wondered as she sat at a single table in the hotel restaurant. She would rather be at Noonby talking about Daisy than here in this dreary hotel.

She scanned the other single tables, where men on business trips ate stolidly, or read newspapers between courses to soften their isolation.

She had refused to let him cook her dinner, Liz told herself, because Don was on his own at the Lodge and her conscience told her she should not be sharing a meal with a stranger in the setting of Noonby Hall when she could so easily be speeding home to her lover.

342

Liz slept fitfully that night, and her dreams were of Clem Brackenborough, erotic, silly, and very vivid. She woke feeling unhappy.

★ ★ ★

"Do you want to start straight away?" Lewis said, indicating her camera.

They left the house, walking through an avenue of pleached limes to the east of the house. The air was balmy after the previous day's fury of wind and rain.

Noonby was beguiling in sunshine. They toured the grounds, eventually entering a walled garden where gravel paths led between low box hedges, and white tulips and blue muscari lined the beds where rose bushes were coming into leaf. The sun warmed the high brick walls; no breezes stirred the air, heavy with the sound of bees.

"How magical." Liz forgot that she had wanted to take photographs and sat on a wooden bench by the wall, letting the warmth soak through her.

He sat beside her, his hands behind his head.

"Do you think Clem used to sit here?" said Liz, pleased by the idea.

"I think they both came here. My grandmother had a story about something that happened here before he married: Clem was found kissing Daisy in the snow one Christmas during a house party. There was a family row, and Clem was given an ultimatum. Give her up, or never darken our doors again."

"So, he gave her up?"

"Wouldn't you — if the alternative was to be cast out penniless? He had been used to a life of some comfort."

"I suppose so. But it makes him rather less of a romantic figure, and Daisy slightly less culpable."

"He waited for a decent period before he married my grandmother."

Liz unfastened her camera. She began taking pictures, wandering along the gravel paths. "I like the idea that Daisy and Clem met here."

"It was winter."

"All the same, you can imagine how it was, secluded, away from the prying eyes of the house party, Clem confused about what he really wanted."

"Sex."

"Don't be so cynical."

He watched her take photos. "Are you married?"

"I live with someone. Don. We've been together for five years."

"And?"

"And nothing. We get along really well."

"What does he think about Daisy?"

"He's bored with the whole business. Don's a headteacher, wondering about changing schools. He's got enough to think about without speculating about my ancestors."

"You sound as if you're a bit cross with him."

"No, I'm not."

Liz stopped taking photographs and came back to sit on the bench. "Are you? Married?"

"I was."

She remembered him saying that people always knew if their partner was having an affair, and speculated a little, wondering who had been unfaithful to whom.

"I wonder how Daisy felt," she mused,

"when she saw Clem again — and obviously they did meet again after the never-darken-our-doors business."

"Not indifferent."

"She would be well into her career by then."

"According to my grandmother, Daisy had called her dressmaking venture 'Maison Clem'; an act of spite after Clem had succumbed to family pressure to give her up. Daisy's customers thought she was a widow — presumably called Clementine."

"Hard to imagine her cultivating an air of widowed fortitude."

"Making a tidy profit," suggested Lewis.

"Was she curious about his wife, I wonder?"

The name Virginia sounded antiseptic, fastidious. Liz felt somewhat disappointed in Clem.

10

DAISY was instructing her new fitting assistant, Gertrude, about the drape of a costume on display. She was dressed in black, as befitted a young widow, in softly draped jersey over a long-line corset. Without corseting, Daisy told her girls, how could anyone expect to achieve a sleek silhouette on a figure with halfway decent hips and a good shaped bust? Maison Clem had been among the first to embrace Poiret's flowing designs and oriental fabrics, but how did Poiret, who advocated abolishing corsets, expect his clothes to hang well without a foundation garment? The man was a fool.

In the showroom the atmosphere was stifling; trade had been sluggish that week, with nothing to account for it except the heat. There were threats of war in the air, and, although ordinary people in Leicester did not take them very seriously, the midsummer heat was overlaid with a peculiar restlessness. The only sound was the intermittent buzzing of a fly against the glass, and the muted rattle of the sewing machines from the workroom, where a team of seamstresses were at work.

Glancing up, Daisy saw a car slow as it passed the building. The vehicle halted. A woman got out from the rear passenger door and, crossing the street, glanced first at the board above the windows, then peeped in over the row of café-style net curtains, looking from Daisy and Gertrude to the models on display.

"I think we have a customer, Mrs Carr," Gertrude said, talking to Daisy between her teeth in a way that she supposed was unobtrusive. "She's very stylish, looks like a 'special'."

Plenty of money, thought Daisy, moving swiftly to meet the woman as she entered the building. Definitely a personal customer rather than a shop buyer.

She was softly pretty, with dark, curling hair under a grey suede hat shaped like a mob cap, and dressed in a chic grey silk costume. The woman pulled off her gloves, looking beyond Daisy into the showroom.

Daisy glanced automatically at the customer's left hand, confirming that she was wearing a wedding ring, already mentally selecting the garments to show her. She counted silently to three as she had trained Norah and Gertie to do, creating a small suspense, before they entered the showroom.

"What kind of costume are you looking for, Madam?" She noted the woman's appreciation of the dress models as she steered her towards one of the little gilt chairs. "Evening wear or afternoon dresses? One of my girls will model our garments for you."

Gertrude was summoned to assist, and Lucile, because she was taller than the other seamstresses, was brought in from the workroom to demonstrate the hang of their afternoon dresses.

Daisy remarked on the various features — a flattering neckline, the trim, the cut of a skirt — and suggested suitable fabrics and colours.

Daisy's designs had flair. Pirating the occasional toile from people in the trade

349

with Paris contacts, she subscribed mostly to fashion magazines, such as *Vogue* or *Harper's Bazaar*, for her information and inspiration. She had taught herself to sketch, as well as to pin and drape a fabric straight on to a dummy, working a lot from instinct.

The woman selected a dress, to be made up in slubbed silk.

"Maison Clem. It has an unusual ring to it," she said. "In fact, it was the name that drew me in."

"Clem was my late husband," Daisy said, writing the details of the sale in the order book.

The woman smiled sympathetically. "My husband is known to everyone as Clem too. That's why I was attracted by the name of the salon. I'm staying with my husband's family at Noonby Hall. Perhaps you would send someone there for the fitting — Mrs Clement Brackenborough."

"Tomorrow, at eleven?" Daisy kept her attention locked firmly to the order book.

"That would be splendid."

Daisy wrote the address and name with a steady hand, but when she glanced up it was with a sharpened perception of her customer's curling hair, dark-fringed blue eyes, and pert nose and petal-pink lips. Sweet, charming, and trusting. Oh, Clem, how very suitable.

★ ★ ★

She might so easily have sent Norah, a competent fitter, or even Gertie to measure for what was, though a 'special', an isolated order. No need for exclusive attention; since the client lived in London, there was little likelihood of gaining a regular customer. No likelihood at all once the client's husband discovered the source of his purchases.

But Daisy was curious. Had marriage altered Clem? Was he happy with his pretty little wife?

It was more than curiosity — Daisy was bored. Life was so very settled, and it was rather dull being a 'widow' at twenty-four. There was the occasional visit with Lucile to show her garments to stores in London, or even as far north as Edinburgh, but as a general rule buyers visited the salon to see her small winter and summer collections and select what they wanted for their limited range of ready-to-wear. Designing was fulfilling, always exciting, but she had almost completed her next winter collection. Daisy wanted something to happen. She was tempted to take a tiny risk, to disturb the status quo a little.

* * *

The footman kept her waiting in the hall as was customary at Noonby with 'trade'. Gone were the days when Daisy might have been invited to tea or to a party as Alice's guest. According to the newspaper gossip pages, Alice too had married and moved away.

It had not been easy, building up a clientele after losing so many customers loyal to Beatty, but these days few people knew of the connection between the widowed proprietress of Maison Clem, and the girl who had once caused a small scandal at Noonby Hall.

What was it about Noonby, thought Daisy, that made her want to exhume the disasters of the past, her ill-judged gate-crashing of the suffragists' garden party, and, worst of all, that Christmas more than four years ago? She told herself she believed in moving on, not looking back. And yet she was drawn by something — nostalgia, envy, a sense of matters being unfinished?

She had dressed carefully, casting off her black, and wearing a jade-green V-necked collarless dress to show off her elegant neck, because Clem had once told her it was aristocratic. Her hair was brushed into fullness and pinned, as in the old days, high on the head to expose the nape of her neck. She wore a little colour on her lips, and had rubbed some into her cheeks. The dress toiles and Daisy's order book and tailoring odds and ends were packed into a cardboard dress box.

She thought of the very first time she had come to Noonby, attracted by the romance created by her mother's stories of being in service. Even now there lingered a sense of belonging to the house's history.

Austen came towards her wearing a black mourning band on his sleeve; he frowned with alarm when he recognised her.

"You? But William announced a 'Mrs Carr'."

"Carr is my business name," Daisy explained. "It's more convenient. I mean, being a widow sometimes helps avoid misunderstandings."

"I must tell my mama," he said drily.

Daisy glanced again at the mourning band. "Your father?"

"He died a few weeks ago."

"I'm sorry. So, Noonby is all yours now."

"Miss Cornforth — " Austen began.

"Please, Mrs Carr's the name. And your sister-in-law is expecting me by the way. Clem's wife."

"Virginia — you mean Clem knows you're here?"

"No. But I'm sure his wife is allowed to hire a *modiste* without his permission. Ah — here she is."

Austen gave way with embarrassment as Virginia came down the stairs.

"I see you've already received Mrs Carr, Austen. The name of her salon caught my eye when I was in Leicester yesterday. Maison Clem. I couldn't resist."

She took his arm, wanting him to share the joke. But her brother-in-law was being obtuse, or slow-witted, and seemed anxious to escape.

"What do you think? Isn't it deevy? Mrs Carr named her salon after her late husband."

Austen made a peculiar choking sound and, throwing Daisy a look of outrage behind Virginia's back, retreated to the dining room.

Daisy chatted conversationally as she followed Virginia up the stairs. "It's funny, your husband being a Clem too."

"He's Mr Austen Brackenborough's brother," Virginia explained. "We live in London — Hampstead. Near the Heath. I have a very good dressmaker at home, but I thought it might be rather fun to surprise my husband with a Maison Clem outfit. Don't you think?"

"Oh, I do. I think surprises are glorious."

Daisy was beginning to enjoy herself; she was even rather hoping to bump into Clem himself as they went along the upstairs corridor, and was disappointed to learn that he would be out all day. She tried to picture him in London, behind an office desk, shuffling papers, and she realised that she could no longer remember clearly what he looked like, so successfully had she turned him into a caricature of a cad.

"It must have been terrible for you. So young, and losing your husband," said Virginia.

"We had only been married a year. It happened on a sales visit to Edinburgh. He was run down by a railway carriage at Waverley Station — helping to rescue a little dog that had strayed on to the track," Daisy invented happily.

"How dreadful!" Virginia's expression registered horror.

"At least I still have my livelihood. So many women have nothing at all to fall back on when their husband is taken from them."

They entered a dressing room, done out in a pretty blue and white Victorian wallpaper with a hanging wardrobe, cane-seated chairs and a long mirror on a stand.

"Make yourself at home," Virginia said, going into an adjoining room. "That's a picture of my husband on the writing table."

Putting her box on the floor, Daisy unpinned her hat and looked around. A marquetry table near the window was set out with various penholders and ink, a leather-bound blotter, and a thick wedge of grey-blue paper.

The photograph came as a shock.

It was one thing, re-inventing Clem in her mind as a seducer, quite another to see him smiling at her disarmingly from a photograph frame. He wore a pullover and was smoking a pipe. His hair was boyishly tousled, his eyes alight with genial amusement. Daisy's heart missed a beat, and she could not trust herself to speak.

Virginia returned wearing a finely embroidered camisole and underslip, and, over them, a long, hip-hugging sky-blue corset.

Daisy's mind instantly filled with images of Clem in intimate familiarity with his wife's corset, helping to unfasten the busk or the laces.

Picking up the photograph, Virginia said, "We've been married nearly a year. Isn't he deevy?"

"My Clem was nothing like that." Daisy bent to unfold one of the toiles from its tissue.

"I'm sorry. How insensitive of me. You must miss him dreadfully."

"No." Straightening, Daisy slung her tape measure round her neck. "I don't miss him at all. He was a womaniser, Mrs Brackenborough. To tell you the truth, I named the salon after him to remind me that I must take care never to make the mistake of falling in love again."

Virginia gave a little gasp of surprise. She put down Clem's picture as if it were hot. "Oh — my dear. You should have told me."

"I don't think so," Daisy said calmly.

★ ★ ★

She had not known she was capable of such jealousy, nor that a photograph and a sky-blue corset could produce such feelings. If she had known, she would

358

have sent Norah or Gertrude instead. How could she have been so stupid as to believe it had all ended that Christmas?

The thought that this pretty, tender-featured woman had a claim on him, that Clem smiled amiably on his Virginia, watched her dress and undress, and touched her intimately, nagged at Daisy until by the end of the fitting she was in a fever of bad temper and ready to stick pins into the living flesh of Clem's wife.

She said the dress would be ready the following week, her chief assistant would bring the garment for the final fitting. Refusing all offers of hospitality — to accept some lunch, to wait at least for someone to call her a cab — Daisy hurried away from the Hall.

It was good to walk quickly along the drive; the exercise gave her a sense of doing something to get rid of the hurt. She had gone there to stir up Clem, to make mischief. "Well, Daisy Cornforth," she told herself, swinging the dress box against her legs. "That just about serves you right. She's a nice woman, is Clem's Virginia. Nicer than you'll ever be. And she doesn't deserve your spite."

Reaching the road, she saw a car come up the hill from Kirby, and watching it draw closer knew instinctively that Clem was at the wheel.

He glanced at her without much interest at first, then drove erratically on to the grass.

"Daisy? Well, I say! I was only this minute thinking about you."

"You always were a one for the flattery," Daisy said when he had turned off the engine.

"You don't seem a day older."

Daisy said nothing, but transferred the heavy dress box to her other hand and tucked it under her arm. She was disappointed; he seemed not at all embarrassed by the coincidence of meeting her.

"Well, I say," he repeated — fatuously, Daisy decided.

"I've been to the Hall to see your wife."

"My wife? Don't tell me she's been buying dresses?" He looked at her uncertainly, glancing at the box under her arm. "I say — can I give you a lift?"

"Yes," Daisy said with a hint of waspishness. "Yes. Why not?"

He turned the car round and they drove in silence for a while.

"Well," Daisy said at last. "You're very cool, for someone who begged me to marry you and swore it wouldn't matter if your father cut off your inheritance."

"Did I really say that?"

"Yes, you did." Daisy sat with her hands folded tightly in her lap.

"What a young fool I was."

"What a — ?" she repeated in amazement.

"Daisy. I was twenty."

"Twenty-one."

"You said yourself I was ridiculous."

"Did I?" Daisy frowned in disbelief.

"You said you had never heard anything more ridiculous than my proposing to you." He laughed. "You were always so much wiser, so much more experienced than I was. I think that's what I fell for."

"You did fall then? I haven't imagined that bit."

"Oh, yes. Quite, quite badly." He looked at her fondly.

"You got over it pretty quickly."

"No. I didn't, to be truthful. But it's a long time ago. And then I met Virginia."

"She's very nice."

"She's a splendid girl."

They fell silent.

"So, how's the fashion business? Doing well? Are you married?" He glanced at her gloved hand for signs of a ring.

"No. I'm not married," she told him. "And never shall be. I've got my salon." She told him about her plans to create space for more stockrooms at Maison Clem.

"You kept the name — ?" He seemed more affected by this than by the rise in Daisy's fortunes.

She ignored the remark, telling him about the girls who worked for her, and who always left to get married the minute they had become dependable, because women were such fools about men. Talking, Daisy did not notice they had passed the railway station until they were well out of town and heading towards Leicester.

"I didn't want you to drive me all the way home."

362

"It's no trouble. They're not expecting me for lunch at Noonby. It gives us a chance to talk about old times. Do you remember the day at Leicester races when we won all that money? What was the name of the horse?"

"Rosy Future," said Daisy. "How could I forget it? I had never had so much money in my life."

She remembered the heady excitement of that afternoon. "It was the same day my father threw me out of the house, and after that you said you'd lend me your winnings for my own business in Kirby."

"Do you remember your very first commissions at the Poplars, when I used to come and talk to you while you worked?"

Flirting with danger, Clem resurrected memories of Daisy as she had once been, ambitious, vulnerable, and distraught in his arms after her father threw her out of the family home; some images were still sharp.

"I'm sorry about your father dying," Daisy said.

He nodded. "I didn't see much of

him, kept away most of the time. I wish I hadn't now." He glanced at her. "Has your father forgiven you, now that you're a successful business woman?

"He doesn't know," Daisy said quietly. "I haven't seen any of them for ages, and I'm sure they didn't know where I went after Kirby. I call myself Mrs Carr these days, so they probably won't ever find out."

"Daisy, that's terrible. I can't believe anyone could be so pigheaded. At least I spoke to my people on the telephone."

"We don't find it so easy to forgive and forget where I come from. Anyway, there aren't any telephones in Morton Street."

They drove in silence, each drawing closer to their memories of what had happened.

"What are you doing these days?" Daisy said after a while. "You have a pretty wife. You live in London. Are you pleased with life?"

"I've got used to working for a living. Though, now my father's gone, I suppose financially that's going to be rather irrelevant and unnecessary. If

364

there's going to be a war I shan't be sorry, at least I shall have something real to do. Austen gets the Hall, of course. He's already moved in with my mother. I suppose you guessed that there are difficulties with Sylvia."

"No, I didn't."

"Sylvia doesn't want to live at Noonby. She'll come round to it, but she's making life hellish difficult, says she won't move the baby to Noonby because my mother would get her hooks into the child and take over. Why does marriage have to be so complicated? I wonder."

"Is it?"

He drove further and was thoughtful, before saying, "Yes. It is."

He sat, when they reached the salon, looking at the double frontage of show-room windows.

Pleased with the artistic and exclusive effect she had created, Daisy followed his gaze to the words in gilt letters.

"Well, Clem. I didn't get over you quite so quickly as you got over me."

"I thought — "

"That I had no heart? That I found you *ridiculous*?" Daisy climbed from the car and shut the door. She leaned on its edge. "I *loved* you. And then I was hurt and disappointed in you. Perhaps, if I'd been as wise as you thought I was, or a bit more experienced, I'd have known how to keep you as well as the business."

She walked away from him and in through the entrance, and did not look back until she heard him drive away.

★ ★ ★

There was something terribly dangerous about a letter, thought Clem, listening to Virginia and Austen playing tennis in the garden, hearing the regular 'bop, bop' of the ball against the racquet strings. And it was so deceptively easy to write, seeing emotions he had imagined were withered up and dead flow from the pen into words on paper, like something living, organic on the page.

But then, sealed and in his hand, the letter had taken on a potent force of its own. There was that heart-stopping moment of slipping it into the box in the hall and letting go. And the further terror when the postman came to collect the mail, the realisation that there was no going back, no way of wiping clean the words that had been written, as he watched the van drive away from Noonby.

My Dear Daisy,
   Meeting you seems to have brought everything back so vividly. I *have* to see you. We are not twenty-one and nineteen any more, but, believe me, if I could turn back the clock I would do it without a second thought. I go over and over how much you meant to me, and am nearly out of my mind when I contemplate what an idiot I was. I shall drive by Maison Clem on Wednesday, at midday, and I shall wait half an hour at the end of the street. If you don't give me a sign, I shall understand that I have left it far, far too late.
   Clem.

Daisy did not go straight up to her flat that evening after everyone had gone home.
She walked into the showroom, where

367

the stands, with the dress models on them were covered in dust-sheets, and a hush had fallen over everything. She paced restlessly, picking things up, pairs of gloves, a scarf, and putting them down, aware suddenly of how lonely it could be, dividing her time between the business and the basic practicalities of her daily life. There was little else. She had narrowed her opportunities either for romance or friendship for the sake of concentrating on her work.

Pulling back the cover from one of the stands, she ran a hand lovingly down the sleeve of the garment, seeking reassurance in the luxury of the fabric that this, and only this, was what she wanted.

Maison Clem was a success. Her models were stylish, colourful, romantic. Her department-store trade included Robertson Callow's, for Daisy the biggest coup of them all. Her private customers came to her mainly by recommendation. The salon did business with only the best silk and cloth-house representatives; she employed expert seamstresses, who could execute fine needlework and were scrupulous about cleanliness in the workroom. She had a reputation for being arrogant but fair, she was sometimes explosive with her staff, but she was liked by them.

Why then, did she feel so empty, and why had meeting Clem again made her feel as if she were poised on the brink of some danger?

★ ★ ★

Opening the post the next morning, Daisy was glad that she was alone. Panic flooded through her, a mixture of terror and excitement.

Her first thought was to tear up the sheet of heavy grey-blue writing paper. Her next, as she pictured him seated at the marquetry table — with Virginia in the next room? — was that she should never have let him know her true feelings; it had been an open invitation, one any womaniser worthy of the name would have lost no time in picking up.

She put the letter in her pocket, and when Norah and the rest of the girls arrived, they were moved to remark to one another that Mrs Carr seemed rather edgy that day.

Daisy remained edgy all that week, until, at ten minutes past twelve on the Wednesday, she announced that she was going out and did not know when she would be back.

Norah and Gertrude noted that she had changed from her usual shop dress into a salon-made outfit of cream, slubbed linen.

"It's too hot for black," Daisy said, seeing Norah's attention fasten on the square-cut neck.

They watched her leave the salon, then retreated into a giggling speculation, convinced that behind it all there lurked a man.

Clem was not so much lurking as pacing the pavement, nervously smoking his third cigarette when he saw Daisy come down the street towards him. He ground the cigarette into the paving with his heel and hurried to meet her.

"Not here. Don't say anything here," Daisy said furiously. "Where's your car?"

"Round the corner."

"At least you had that much sense."

They walked side by side, quickly, without speaking, until they were out of sight of the salon.

"I thought you weren't coming."

"I wasn't going to. I shouldn't be here."

Daisy saw the car, parked in the gateway of a hotel yard.

"I have no idea where we are going," Daisy exclaimed.

"Neither have I." He turned the car on to a road out of the city. "Do you mind?"

"No. Just drive."

"I brought a picnic." A travelling rug and a hamper lay on the back seat.

"Anything. Anywhere. It doesn't matter."

"I told so many lies the other day. All that about being too young to know what I was doing, and about being married to a splendid girl."

"Some of it has to be true."

"Virginia *is* splendid. Everyone says so." He banged the flat of his hand against the steering wheel. "Then why is it that I know I've made the biggest mistake of my life?"

"You must have thought differently at the time."

"She was, is, very pretty, and agreeable. She's a good hostess, and she gets on well with my mother and Austen and Sylvia." He looked at Daisy with an expression of despair. "And that is all, absolutely all. She's a splendid girl. But I don't love her."

"I hear echoes of Beatty. Poor Virginia."

"I know. She deserves better."

"Yes, I'm sure she does."

He pulled the car off the road and parked it under some trees.

"One thing I said was true — if there's going to be a war, I'll be in on it. I feel stifled by my life, Daisy. I want to take risks, it doesn't matter how disastrous."

"And is that all this is? Am I to be an adventure?"

"I don't know what you are to me, Daisy. I never have done. But what if we don't seize this moment? Are we going to look back with nothing but regrets?"

She did not know whether she could trust him. He had let her down before. But she understood utterly what he meant about needing to take risks and seizing the moment.

"I shall be back in London next week," he said. "The last thing I want is to hurt you, but I don't want to lose you again either. I can't offer you anything. We shan't be able to meet very often — "

"You mean, I deserve better too."

"Oh, you do." He looked at her with an anguished expression. "Yes, you do, so much more than a shabby affair with a married man."

"And the grubby scandal if we're found out?"

"Don't — " He reached for her and touched the back of her neck.

Shivering, Daisy traced her fingers over his mouth. She had been drawn to him when she was younger by a need for his solidity, and the confidence of his class. If that was still true now, there were other needs as well.

"You're forgetting something," she told him. "I've already been through it once. My father threw me out of the house. 'A bloody disgrace.'" She mimicked her father's accent. "He called you my fancy man." Daisy threw away her last remnants of conscience; let his wife take care of herself. "I want you, Clem. It doesn't matter how it works out. I might not see you again for weeks, months, perhaps never — but I keep thinking how good things were between us."

A wood bordered the road; the hedge enclosing it was broken in places, and the ditch was deep but narrow enough to cross. Beyond these tenuous barriers, a green dappled light offered temptation from the sun's glare. Mossy banks, the smell of leaf mould and of cool vegetation added enchantment.

Clem took her hand, and they crossed the ditch.

He spread the rug, still warm from the sun, in a clearing far from the road. Old beech masts crackled under them as they lay side by side.

Daisy turned her face to the rug's smothering softness. Even the birds, here in the deep, secret heart of the wood, were silent. High above them, through the leaf canopy, she could see a pattern of eggshell-blue sky.

"I know what I'm doing, and I feel perfectly happy," she breathed. "I never knew I could feel so happy." And guiltless, she thought. How could anyone, doing what she was doing, feel so free?

She closed her eyes as he moved closer to kiss her, responding immediately. His fingers fumbled over the buttons of her dress, and she helped him.

Suddenly shy, Daisy placed her hand over his.

"There's never been anyone else."

"I know." He pressed his forehead against hers, and Daisy forgot her anxiety in her ache to hold on to the moment. Opening herself to him, mind and body, warming to the sensations he drew from her, sensations she had only half understood before now, she was dreamy, then clutching and self-absorbed.

Conscious of her virginity and of a need for caution, Clem burned with reawakened longing. His passion was gentle, though he trembled with a need to possess her, and with a fear that this first time could also be the last.

11

LIZ felt as though she were taking Noonby's atmosphere with her. Remembering the walled garden, the house with its portraits and the diaries, she was glad she had stayed another day. Gone was the sense of aimlessness, of wasting time; she felt stimulated, inspired by the Midlands trip.

Lewis's photos had been very beautiful. The stables at Noonby had been turned into an exhibition gallery and cafeteria, with the cobbled floors and some of the old stalls still intact, and framed black and white photographs spotlit on all the walls; they were atmospheric and haunting pictures of the exterior of the Hall and the local countryside.

"I prefer landscapes," he had explained. "Nature in all its moods. And Noonby of course. Noonby has moods as well."

"What is Noonby's mood today?" Liz had asked.

"Sunny, benevolent, cheerful about opening its doors next week."

"The house likes visitors?"

"Oh, I think the house likes nothing better than having people around — whoever they are. Noonby isn't too choosy — she's a bit of a tart. It's I who feel invaded when I'm here. My family were forced out by death duties. I can't help resenting what Noonby has had to become."

"People need access to the past," said Liz, contrasting the house, steeped in its history, with her own poor attempts to recreate an atmosphere of Edwardiana at the Lodge; she thought of Jennifer's ideas of gracious living, her parents' mock-Elizabethan, modern estate house, and Prue and Peter's shabby semi, a mix of styles and patterns that hurt the eye: flowered curtains, and bright blue melamine kitchen fittings; there were usually clothes airing, and, always, the smell of washing and cooking.

In his sitting room again, Liz had been drawn once more to the painting of Clem.

"Do you do portraits?"

"Sometimes." He followed her gaze.

377

"You seem fascinated by him."

"I think I may have fallen a little in love with him. And I feel so sorry for them both. I've been wondering why they split up."

"It's my grandmother you should be feeling sorry for. She knew what was going on all through the war; she knew that when Clem came home he would rather be with Daisy than her."

"Do you think Daisy was lonely after she gave him up? Did she spend the rest of her life regretting it?"

"She had her career, and you say Willow was a particularly close friend."

"But there was a big age difference. And besides, Willow married Albert."

Lewis wanted to know about Willow. What was she like? Without many details he seemed to understand Liz's need to visit her.

"You really have begun to care about her, haven't you?"

"Yes," Liz said in surprise. "She's obstructive. Obstinate. Ambivalent about her memories of Daisy, but I've grown very fond of her. She's not really typically French," Liz went on. "A slight accent still, but that's all."

"And you met her husband — once?"

She nodded. "I didn't know any of my grandfather's relatives, but I think I would have liked his cousin Albert. Willow was obviously very much in love with him."

"She had no French lovers?"

"Oh, I think so. She's told me very little about her own life — except how *avant-garde* they all were in the thirties. I get the feeling Willow and Daisy fell out over something when they came to England, and now Willow regrets it."

"Do you think they could have quarrelled over Willow's marriage?"

"Perhaps. Albert was Daisy's cousin, a bit too close if Daisy didn't want to be reminded about the past."

"Was she perhaps possessive about Willow? Too much so — obsessively so?"

"Daisy had her work. She wanted to preserve her independence. A woman can make friendships with other women without it meaning she's possessive in any sinister way."

"Nowadays, perhaps."

"Why not then? Why must we always think of other eras as being somehow foreign? I don't believe people really change that much from generation to generation. Women must have wanted autonomy over their lives then as much as now, been just as frustrated by circumstances, and irritated by conventions that said they *had* to marry to be fulfilled, *had* to look for happiness through a man, *had* to be contented with a woman's role, woman's work, woman's subordinate place in the scheme of things."

She had expected him to challenge her, to mock her a little perhaps. Instead he had said, seriously, "Isn't that how *you* feel, rather than Daisy?"

"I understand her driving force, her ambition. I admire her for knowing what she wanted, for not letting a man become the centre of her life, as so many women in her situation must have done at the time. I even admire her for leaving Clem in the end, if that's what was necessary for her to concentrate on her career."

He fell silent.

"You don't agree that Daisy should

have concentrated on her career?" Liz had said, when he was still reticent.

"I think you were right before, to wonder whether she was lonely."

"Without a man."

"You've just said more or less the same thing yourself."

"Only because of Clem. I was thinking about her love affair with Clem. Whereas, *you* mean, in general terms, Daisy needed a man in order to be fulfilled."

"Men and women need one another. Unless they're gay, and then, men need men, and women need women."

"Are you? Gay?"

"No — and I assume you're not either, so you know what I'm talking about. Men and women need one another."

"Why must it be at the heart of everything?" Liz said wearily.

"Sex."

"That doesn't answer *why*. You're simply agreeing that it *is*. Why are we so primitive?"

"You said it yourself — we haven't changed much."

He had offered her lunch, and this time she had accepted. He said as they went downstairs to the kitchens, "I suspect Daisy must have been lonely, because my own marriage broke up for precisely the reasons we are assuming Daisy gave up Clem. Work always came first."

Liz was quick to rise to the bait. "Don't you think your wife had every right to a career?"

"Yes," he said calmly. "I would have loved her to have outside interests, but I meant me, not her. I withdrew more and more into my work, tried to pretend everything was fine, until in the end my wife went off with someone with a steadier job, a man who wanted nothing more than to come home every night at six o'clock to a woman who doted on him."

"I've got you all wrong, haven't I?" Liz said.

"Yes." They paused, and he smiled at Liz's rueful expression. "But I'll forgive you. It doesn't matter as much as it once did. We weren't suited. There's no magic formula to relationships."

Eating lunch with Lewis and the skeleton staff who were preparing Noonby for its opening at the weekend — genteel

382

conservative men and women, steeped in the house's history — Liz thought about his comment on relationships, and wondered again how anyone ever found it possible to make the necessary compromises. She studied their lunchtime companions: nice, married women with pleasant lives. Did they have a formula, or were their marriages a mesh of frustrations and triumphs, sacrifices, concessions and regrets?

The women were all enthusiastic about Clem's son, Howard, and talked about him to the exclusion of all the other family members. Lewis, sharing Liz's impatience, had winked at her across the table, and, afterwards, as he walked with her to her car, he had told her what he knew about Clem's army service in the First World War: he had seen action on the Somme, risen from captain to major, had a reputation for headstrong bravery and a disregard for danger, and won the Distinguished Service Order to prove it. "My uncle Howard did not have a monopoly on heroism."

But what about Daisy? Liz wanted to know as she drove south alone on the motorway. Had Daisy resented Clem's role as a hero, knowing that courage was not a simple matter of sticking one's head over a parapet. Did she live for his visits, write long love letters to the Front, torture herself with thoughts of his being killed or wounded? Did she brood, yearning for him in the months of his absence, ignorant about his movements, resenting the wife who had first claim to letters and visits? Or did she simply get on with her life, pragmatic, detached, tolerating Clem's intrusion on those occasions when he came to her on leave?

12

DAISY watched the sky, superstitiously willing a cloud to break the monotony of blue to challenge the decision she had made; when it did she turned her face to the pillow, twisting the edge of the patchwork spread that always reminded her, like a comfort blanket, of when she was a child.

Fool! Fool! How could she so readily have let herself be seduced by a warm afternoon and soft memories of the time when she first knew Clem? Seduced, not once, but every afternoon, with a mad kind of hunger, before he had gone back to London. She, who had promised herself she would never be like her mother and had her own life to lead. I don't believe in love, she had said, and still didn't. Love was all self-delusion.

The change had been noticeable from the very beginning, she realised now, looking back. There had been no point in waiting all this time, no need to count days and weeks.

Sunday wore on to the evening, and still Daisy lay there, watching the sky, knowing she had let herself down in the worst way possible, by proving that she was like all the rest, her mother, her Auntie Ivy. No better, no different after all.

* * *

"I'm closing the salon early. I've decided to go to London to try and drum up some trade," Daisy told the girls when Norah arrived the next morning. "I shan't be opening again for a few days. War or no war, it's time we all had a holiday."

"She's got a man friend," Norah told Gertrude in private. "I knew it." And they spent an entertaining half hour speculating on which of the fabric suppliers or department-store managers Daisy's suitor might be.

* * *

"The bleeding will last for a few days," the physician told her, washing his fastidious hands. "It's good you were swift in coming to me. So many ladies take fright and simply hope these things will go away of their own accord."

He was kind after a fashion, and talkative without asking questions, accepting her money with a business-like air, and chatting all the while he poked inside her with a cold metal instrument, telling her of the tortures she might have suffered had she put herself in the hands of a cheaper or less scrupulous doctor.

She remembered little of what he had said while she drifted in and out of consciousness; she recalled afterwards only that he apologised for causing her pain and, giving her a towel with which to pad herself, called a cab for her.

There was so much blood. Far more than for her monthly time, too bad to get up and dress or think of venturing outside the door of her hotel room. Knowing a little of what to expect after seeing her mother's lyings-in, she had brought towels and sheets from her flat, but she was afraid she might run out of padding if the bleeding did not ease soon, or that the housekeeper of the hotel would grow suspicious about her staying in bed all day.

The blankets on the bed made her sweat, and yet her body felt ice cold. She had not slept, trying to control the pain by smoothing her hands over her lower abdomen. She had guessed about the bleeding, but she had not supposed there would be so much pain.

Daisy lay all the next day, leaving the bed only to use the chamber pot and change the towelling napkins. The sun moved round towards the late afternoon, making her head ache and intensifying the fierce pains in her back and abdomen. Dragging herself to the foot of the bed and pulling a fresh napkin from her valise, she thought that if she could only get to the window, if she could prevent the sun from beating through the crack in the curtains, she might begin to feel a little better.

Swinging her legs from the mattress and clinging to the bedpost, Daisy reached with her hand to close the gap. The sun flashed across her eyes briefly. In the same moment a stab of pain brought her crashing to the floor.

★ ★ ★

"Ah. She's awake."

A man sat at the end of her bed, and she recognised the woman standing behind him as the housekeeper who had first shown her to her hotel room.

The man leaned forward. "Do you feel able to talk? Can you tell me what happened?"

"I fell down. It's the time of the month when I'm unwell."

"This is no ordinary bleeding," he said severely. "I have made a brief examination. I know what you have been up to, young woman, and I must say, you have been extremely foolish. You are lucky I was called to attend you."

Daisy said feebly, "I don't want to be any trouble. I'll go just as soon as —"

"This lady understands the reason for your indisposition. She has agreed you may stay here until you are well enough to travel."

"Against my better judgement," muttered the woman.

"You must rest. Do you understand?" said the doctor. "It's very important. You've been damaged. I don't know who did this to you, but I suspect he has made a thorough job of it. In fact, I should say you'll be lucky if you ever bear children again. I shall be back in a day or two. Can you pay?"

Daisy nodded.

"Just as well."

"You have been very wicked," said the housekeeper.

"I had no choice."

"You had a choice when you went with the fellow," the woman responded. But she brought Daisy a bowl of soup later, and tended her all the next day with a mixture of grudging sympathy, disapproval and prurience, wanting to know about Daisy's background and the 'scoundrel' who had got her into trouble.

Daisy was uncommunicative. "He's not a scoundrel," was all she would say.

★ ★ ★

390

"Go away," Daisy called through the window, reaching up to pull down the blind and seeing a uniformed figure in the December darkness beyond the showroom, supposing him to be one of Gertrude's young men — Gertie was dazzled by the glamour of khaki. "The girls aren't here."

The figure came closer, and with a sense of unease she saw first of all that the man was an officer, and then, with a lurch of the heart, that it was Clem.

"What kind of a welcome is that?" he said when she opened the door.

"None. You're not welcome here."

"I'm going abroad. I've been commissioned."

"Go away, Clem. You can't just turn up whenever you feel like it or get a bit bored with Virginia."

"You know that's not how it was."

"It's how it seems now." By now she would have been heavy with his child, Daisy thought. What a shock for him that would have been, to have found her in an embarrassing condition.

It had been hard not to blame Clem. Nor had it been as easy as she had imagined to forget what she had done. Daisy had not been prepared for the guilt and sense of mourning — and certainly not the longings that attacked her when she thought about the life that might have been.

"Why didn't you get in touch?" she demanded.

"I couldn't get away from training. And Virginia's needed me."

"Of course. She's your wife. Wives need their husbands in times of war."

"Daisy — I've thought about you. I tried to imagine what you would be doing, whether you were thinking of me."

"You couldn't begin to imagine! I can do without this. It's not what I planned. You disrupt my life, Clem, and the minute I am getting over it, you turn up again."

"I'd been to see my mother. I couldn't come to Noonby and not see you before I go. Our regiment's being sent to France."

"And I'm supposed to feel sorry for you? Is that it — you want me to treat you like a hero, in case you die?"

"I don't know what I was thinking,"

he said, bewildered, a little angered by her petulance — he had never thought of Daisy as petulant; the memory of her vitality had sustained him all through the recent tedious months of training.

"You never thought that I might have died?" Daisy said angrily.

He repeated her last words stupidly. "Might have — " He shut the street door behind him and followed her along the corridor. "I don't understand."

"It doesn't matter. Tea? Or brandy?"

"Brandy," he said automatically. Had Daisy taken to drinking?

The sewing room they passed was in a state of disarray, but the disorder seemed organised, with dresses on hangers and half-made garments strewn over the tables and sewing machines.

"How's the business going?"

"Very well." The initial panic of the war over, Daisy's customers had decided they must have their clothes. She had sent out fliers bearing the slogan, 'Business as Usual', urging them to support the industry and dress well in defiance of the Kaiser.

She started up the stairs.

Until now Daisy had guarded fiercely the privacy of her flat above the salon. No one, not even Norah or Gertrude, had been invited through the doors that separated her personal domain from that of her business. Daisy felt secure here, among treasured pieces of furniture, a collection of ornaments on the overmantel, rugs and pictures and books — an impressive and growing collection on art, on fabrics and costumes, on cultures and traditions in other countries.

She pulled the curtains across the window and bent to light the gas fire before turning to face Clem.

"Well, you're going to need that brandy."

"Am I?" he said uncertainly.

"If you're off at last to fight for King and country."

"I'm looking forward to it, after all the waiting. It should be quite a show . . . Why did you say you might have died?"

Daisy did not answer; she sat on the sofa and took a swig of brandy, her knees together under a full, ankle-length skirt of soft green jersey. "This damned war. Everyone's gone mad. I can't even remember how it all began."

But she could remember how it had felt, she thought, her mind going back to the excitement on the streets in August. Everyone had been in a fever of eager anticipation, while she had been aware of the first doubts, the first intimations, that for her things were not as they should be.

Seeing him by the fireplace, so handsome in his uniform, so complacent about his little adventure in France, she wanted to hurt him for putting her through all that.

"Daisy?" he repeated. "Why did you say you might have died?"

She lit a cigarette without offering him one and put the packet back on the table before saying quickly, "Getting rid of it. I had to get rid of your child."

The colour left his face.

"It does happen — when people do what we did, it does sometimes happen that a woman ends up pregnant." She spoke in a flat, pragmatic tone.

"Why didn't you let me know?"

"What would you have done?"

He shook his head, unable to give an answer. "It must have been terrible for you," he said at last.

"Yes," she acknowledged, holding herself in tightly, trembling with the effort of not revealing any emotion. "But I got over it. I got over doing that. And I had got over you coming back into my life last summer. And now — " She was shaking violently. "Now — here you are again."

"Daisy — " He made a sound of protest, and sat beside her, pulling her to him.

Daisy began to weep, silently at first, then with noisy, tearing sobs, beating her hands against his uniform jacket. "Why did you have to come back? I hate you. I hate you for what you did."

He held her, rocking her against him and murmuring words of comfort and remorse into her hair until she was quiet.

"I wish you'd stayed away," she said after a while. "I wish I'd never met you again."

"I can't stay away. I love you. I tell myself, if only I hadn't married Virginia, if only I hadn't been such a kid, so *stupid* all that time ago. Such a coward," he added.

She sat up and moved away from him, retrieving her cigarette from the ashtray. Aware that he watched her anxiously, Daisy began gradually to talk, becoming pragmatic again. The room was warming to the gas fire, and softened by the effects of the brandy Daisy wondered, now that she had told him about the abortion, why she had needed so badly to wound him. Quits, she thought. They were even again.

She talked about the business, saying she thought she would be able to keep going now that the girls were so keen to ignore all the changes caused by the war; it was not like having a workforce of men who might have volunteered.

"What's it like, Clem — doing something at last?"

"Boring." He smiled. "Very boring." He drained his glass. "Still — we should get on with it now. France will be different."

She leaned her head against the sofa, watching his profile as he nursed the empty glass in his hands, his head bowed.

"Do something now, Clem. Love me. Make me *feel* again."

He turned to her with an anguished look. "I didn't come here for that. Not now — "

"Yes, you did. Don't lie to me. I know you. And if I'm honest it's what I wanted the minute I saw you in the street."

Their eyes met, searching.

"It's all right," said Daisy. "I'm damaged — it's all right. The doctor said it can't ever happen again."

* * *

Norah was talking about an item she had read in the newspaper.

"Do you remember?" She turned to Daisy. "The lady who was staying at Noonby Hall that time. We made a dress for her. Ever so pretty."

"What about her?" Daisy had picked up late on Norah and Gertie's conversation.

"It says in the paper her husband is in France fighting for his country. They're to call it Howard."

"They're to call what Howard?" Daisy

said slowly, understanding even as Gertrude spoke.

"It said she was 'delivered safely of a baby boy'. Isn't that lovely? They ought to have called it Noel."

"What?"

"Because of it being Christmas. They should have — "

"For goodness' sake! Get on with your work."

The girls stared at Daisy, and Gertrude flashed Norah a look.

His wife must have been pregnant when he made love to me last summer, thought Daisy. And when I told him I had got rid of his child, she was about to give birth.

Did it matter? Did it really make any difference? If Clem walked in the door that minute, wouldn't she want him as much as ever?

Not that it was going to happen. His regiment was in France, probably in the front line; he might be killed, and that would be the end of that. The war would soon be over, victory declared, and everybody could get on with their lives.

Daisy was alone in the showroom when Clem arrived one summer morning carrying a bunch of roses.

With a cry of alarm Daisy ran to shut the workroom door on the girls at their sewing machines.

"My God, Clem. What if there had been someone with me!"

She leaned against the staircase wall, taut with anger.

"I'm on leave." He thrust the flowers at her. "For you. From Noonby's rose garden."

"I don't want them," Daisy said fiercely. "I heard about the child." She lashed out with one arm in a weak attempt to hit him. "You should have told me about your wife being pregnant."

"I couldn't. Not after what you had gone through. How could I?"

Daisy glanced at the workroom door separating them from the dull murmur of voices and machines. Outside a horse and cart rumbled past along the street. Along the corridor someone in the packing department was whistling.

"Go away, Clem. I've got nothing to say to you. It's all over."

"You don't mean that."

Anger at his complacency boiled up inside her and, moving away from him with a twist of her body, Daisy ran up the stairs. Taking the stairs two at a time, Clem followed her. He reached her flat and was inside the sitting room before she could slam the door on him.

She turned her head in a swift movement and bit his hand between his thumb and forefinger until with a yelp of pain he let go of her arm.

They were struggling then, Daisy scratching at him, hitting out with her fists and elbows and kicking until, imprisoned in his arms, she continued to fight and they fell on to the settee.

"Clem, I hate you! I hate you so much, I wish you were dead."

Her body slackened, and Clem's arms came round her more gently.

"You know that Virginia is my wife."

"But what am I? There's no place for me in your life."

"If it wasn't for the war — "

"It wouldn't make any difference. You'd still have other duties, other people."

He had no answer, kissing her hair, rescuing the flowers from the carpet where they had scattered; he put them in the sink in the kitchen.

Daisy sat on the sofa, hugging a cushion against her.

"It's no good, Clem," she said when she was calm. "You must see that. It isn't fair on me. And I've a business to run. I wish you'd stay away."

"I had to see you."

"No, you didn't."

"I had to."

He stood in the kitchen doorway, and she looked at him properly for the first time. He had altered since going to France. The war was not going well. The glamour that had seduced so many people was fading and the action in Europe was dragging on. In spite of his clean uniform, Clem's appearance was grubby, and looked somehow undernourished.

He held out his arms.

"Leave me alone," Daisy said savagely.

Clem shook his head. "Come here."

402

★ ★ ★

They went out to dinner that evening, driving miles until they found a country inn where they were not known, and where they got preferential attention because Clem was in uniform and they were both young and good-looking.

"Is it as bad in France as everyone is saying?" Daisy asked when, in an unguarded moment, a look of fatigue cross his face.

"It's not what anyone expected. You have to abandon all the old ideas about battles being won by manoeuvres. There's a lot of confusion." His finger traced a pattern on the tablecloth. "I was brought up on stories of campaigns and brilliant acts of heroism. Well, there are plenty of heroes — but most of them are dead."

Afterwards, they went back to her flat and he stayed until the early hours of the morning.

It was the same whenever he came to her. She refused to welcome him, fought for her right to be free of him, and afterwards they made love.

"It's so humiliating," she told him

once. "How can anyone be so driven by emotions?"

"It's not only that." He stroked the skin of her inner thigh. "You and I have more than that. We need one another. We'll never lose that sense of belonging together."

"Fine words, Clem," she said derisively, beginning to dress.

He lay on one elbow, watching her. "You don't believe this is special?"

"I do when I'm with you."

"And when you're not?"

She came to him and kissed him firmly. "I have my work."

13

LIZ never liked returning at night to an empty house. The trees, swaying like black giants in the dark, towered and hissed over her as she closed the garage. Inside she drew the curtains and switched on all the lights upstairs as well as down, a habit from when she had lived alone.

Don had put her mail on the desk.

Half expecting him to have stayed on a few more days to wait for her and suggest they go to Norfolk together for Easter, Liz felt vaguely wrong-footed. She had anticipated that he would attempt to put pressure on her, and instead he had behaved better than that.

There was a note with the mail. Liz recognised a studied detachment in the style of his message.

Don't know what time you'll be getting home, but there's a quiche and some cold chicken in the fridge.

Back Tuesday or Wednesday. Phone my Aunt Poll if you need to get in touch. Love you — Don.

He had left a telephone number.

"*If you need to get in touch.*" Nothing to say he would phone. No passionate or sexy postscripts.

Feeling neglected, Liz pressed the message button on the answerphone even though the light did not indicate there had been a call. The machine emitted a trio of empty beeps to emphasise its point. Glancing up, her gaze met Daisy's photograph.

"You want it all, don't you?" said Daisy's smile. "He's left you a quiche and cold meat. Imagine that from an Edwardian lover? You should think yourself lucky."

Eating the quiche, Liz imagined what it might be like to live on her own again. For a start, she would have to do her own cooking and washing up. Putting the plates in the sink, she ran cold water over them; the words of a song went round in her head: 'Love and marriage, love and marriage . . . go together, like a horse and carriage.'

She lay in bed, missing Don's bulk in the space beside her, feeling a perverse need for really good sex, and falling asleep with the tune of the song and its silly refrain, playing itself over and over.

★ ★ ★

Jennifer rang the next morning.

"What! He's left you all on your own for Easter? Have you two quarrelled or something?"

"Of course not. I was in the Midlands, and Don wanted to — "

Jennifer was not interested in what Don wanted to do.

"Listen, Liz," she interrupted. "Why don't you come here for Easter? Come for dinner tonight and stay over. The boys would love to see you, you're their very favourite auntie, and you can keep me company on Sunday when Mark takes the boys fishing."

"I'm not sure — " Liz saw her weekend dwindling away.

"I insist. I have to confess the motive's not entirely unselfish. I need a sympathetic ear right now." Jennifer lowered her voice and it quivered. "He's being such a bastard, Liz."

Damn, thought Liz after putting down the phone. Why had she accepted? She would have to listen to Jennifer listing Mark's failings. She would have to buy Easter eggs for the boys. Why, for once in her life, could she not have said what she meant?

★ ★ ★

Parking on her sister's drive, Liz approached the flight of steps to the porch entrance of the substantial Victorian house, with its strips of coloured glass and black-painted double front doors. The large, unkempt garden, the air of careless neglect in the flaking paintwork, seemed to suggest a household that was far too busy doing things to waste time on repairs or mowing lawns.

The hallway was bursting with shoes and sports gear, there was even a bicycle parked against the banisters, to signal that the boys were home for the holidays and everyone was having fun. Muddy footprints on the tiles and a threadbare

Axminster on the stairs advertised the wear and tear of children's feet.

There was a strong smell of cooking, a rich, garlicky scent drifting from the basement stair as Mark took Liz's coat.

"Renate's busy?" commented Liz.

Mark nodded. "Isn't she fantastic? To tell the truth, we only asked her to stay on because of her cooking."

"She's very useful during the boys' holidays," added Jennifer in a tone of contradiction. "She's what people used to call a 'treasure'."

"Face like the back end of a cow, but can she cook! Drink, Liz?" said Mark.

Liz nodded, picturing Renate in the kitchen, being a 'treasure'. Perhaps she enjoyed it. Some women loved to cook, even lived to cook. She went to the top of the stairs and called out, "Hi, Renate," hearing the German woman's cheerful shout in return.

"Hallo, Elizabeth. How are you?"

"I'm fine. Whatever I can smell cooking is making me hungry."

There came a delighted, unintelligible response.

"The boys are watching TV in their

rooms. They'll be down for dinner," said Jennifer, edging Liz away from the basement stair, jealous of her rapport with the hired help.

"I brought Easter eggs for the boys. Is that all right?" Too late, seeing her sister's strained smile, Liz remembered the family ban on sweets.

"Well — just this once, perhaps," Jennifer said. "It's harder to control that sort of thing, anyway, now that they're off our hands in term time."

Going into a room furnished with vast sofas, heavy coffee tables, and prominently displayed gardening books, Liz accepted a whisky.

Mark was in an amiable, hospitable mood.

Remembering that he was having an affair with Sandra — Sally? Susie? — at the group practice, Liz watched him pour himself a drink with long-fingered hands. She had to acknowledge that he was attractive, with bony features and a high complexion. Rather like a TV doctor, or the pictures of TV idols she, Jennifer and Prue had once pinned on their bedroom walls. They had sent away for autographed photographs and nursed dreams of working in television one day, and what else? Marriage? Liz supposed that she had once dreamed of love and marriage.

Mark downed his whisky and poured himself another.

"Good trip, Liz? All in search of corsets?"

"Not entirely." Liz told them what she had discovered about Daisy and Clem.

"I'm glad Daisy left the cheating bastard," said Jennifer with a heavily significant glance at Mark. "His poor wife. She knew all about it? Virginia ought to have left him as well."

Mark poured himself another drink, avoiding looking at his wife. "So, Liz, when is Don planning to get back?"

"The bastard," Jennifer muttered, without apparent reference to anyone.

★ ★ ★

Renate had cooked until she was red-faced and shining, presenting each course with a flourish. A fragrant herb and wild mushroom soup was followed by

411

medallions of lamb in a rich sauce and dumplings.

"Renate — you've out-banqueted all past banquets!" said Liz, as the *au pair* brought in a walnut tart and pushed up her sleeves to cut it into slices.

"The children miss my cooking at school. Eh, boys?" Renate laughed.

"No, I don't," Henry said rudely. "It always tastes funny."

"They'd rather have burgers and chips these days, I'm afraid," said Jennifer.

Were children always a product of their parents' combined awfulness? Liz found herself wondering whenever she was presented with Jennifer's three boys. The eldest, Jeremy, precocious and opinionated, argued all through the meal with his father. Henry competed for Mark's attention, with a look-at-me kind of silliness, defended by Jennifer simply to annoy Mark. And Nigel, sulking about something, resisted Liz's half-hearted attempts to draw him out.

Jennifer clearly thought she was cheering Liz up, that no one could possibly want to be on their own over a public holiday when everyone else was enjoying themselves, Easter was like Christmas — a family occasion.

And wasn't it true, thought Liz, that twenty-four hours ago she had been missing Don and wondering what she was going to do for three whole days at the Lodge without him. As she wandered the supermarket aisles, shopping for Easter eggs and washing-up liquid, she had found herself observing that Don would have known instinctively whether Jeremy, Henry and Nigel would prefer rocket booster-style eggs or chocolate cuddly bunnies. Had she really become so dependent on her man that she no longer functioned without him?

The next day, a bottle of sherry between them, Jennifer poured out her heartache over Mark's infidelities. Murmuring words of sympathy and support, Liz handed her a box of tissues.

"He even flirts with Renate," gulped Jennifer. "Honestly, I'd leave him tomorrow if I didn't think it would be so destabilising for the boys. One has a duty to one's children, to one's marriage — "

413

"Leave him anyway," said Liz, her judgement influenced only slightly by the sherry. "Branch out on your own. Take it in turns to have the kids during the holidays."

Jennifer looked shocked. "I'm sorry," she said coldly, "I can see you don't want to hear any of this."

And Liz, longing to be back at the Lodge, realised that she didn't. She had overheard Henry saying that his Easter egg was 'naff' that morning. Mark had talked to her about the eroticism of suspender belts all through breakfast; and she was tired of Jennifer's traumas. When she had brought up the subject of Noonby this morning, her sister, drawing irritating and irrelevant parallels between Mark's behaviour and Clem's, had taken offence when Liz said there must have been reasons why Clem preferred Daisy's company to his wife's.

The fact was, Liz realised, putting up her feet on her desk that evening and looking at Daisy's picture, that it was not love and marriage she rejected, but all the examples she had seen of it so far. She did not want Jennifer's version

414

of family life, nor Prue's pregnancies and maternal cosiness. She did not even want her parents' successful version of married bliss: mutual interests, walks on Sundays, holidays in the Algarve.

"We are too hard to please, you and I," she told Daisy's picture.

Perhaps Daisy had found the answer. Fall out with one's family, launch oneself into a creative and satisfying career, and take a lover to combat the loneliness, but only until one no longer needed him.

Had the time come when Daisy had felt ready to let go — a confrontation? A growing sense of futility? What if the only reason for keeping a relationship going was a fear of being alone?

Sorting through her notes, Liz transferred them from her notepad to her computer files before going to bed.

She thought of Noonby as she went to sleep. The Hall would open its doors to the public tomorrow, Easter Monday. Unless he had gone back to London, Lewis Brackenborough would probably stand around chatting to visitors, and they would admire his photographs. Or perhaps he would hide in his photography

415

room while those nice, genteel women showed the visitors round the house, issued tickets, and told anecdotes about Clem's son, Howard Brackenborough, 'quite a character in his time' and a hero. They would say very little about Clem himself: the quiet, family man, who had achieved nothing out of the ordinary, except doing his bit in the Great War and fathering three children. Liz drifted to sleep with the memory of Clem's portrait and the alien, gracious atmosphere of Noonby in her head.

* * *

Hearing a sound, Liz stopped writing.

She had lost all sense of time, enjoying the sense of being cut off and immersed in her work, with no reason to think of anything else. But the bang of the door had startled her, and now she noticed that the sun was low in the sky.

"Don?"

His figure filled the darkness of the hallway below; his face loomed, phantom-pale, very still and unsmiling.

"Hi, hon. Surprised?"

She had been engrossed, happy in her isolation.

"I'd done and seen all I wanted," he said. "So I thought I'd come home a day early."

"That's marvellous." Going downstairs to meet him, Liz decided that it was. He looked tired, slightly anxious.

"It's been strange without you," she acknowledged, wrapping her arms round his waist. "Hard to believe it's only been a week."

"You had a good few days in Leicester?"

"Mmm. Very. Lots of notes. Lots of photos." She hesitated. "And you?"

"I saw the school. I'll tell you about it when I've unpacked."

They went out to eat, as if they needed to be on neutral ground before they could talk about anything of importance. They chose the informal, noisy atmosphere of a local pub offering home-cooked food.

He took her hand across the table. "I love you, Liz. And if loving you means forgetting the job, I'm prepared to do that."

"But — ?" Liz said. There had to be a 'but' with that kind of sacrifice.

417

"But — more than anything I want you to come with me. I promise it can be on your own terms. No strings. No marriage plans. Just — carry on as we are now. Is that blackmail?"

"I don't think so," Liz said uncertainly.

"I know, I haven't even got the job yet — "

He told her about the school; he had been extremely impressed with what he saw; it had lived up to the reputation he remembered.

"Do you think you *might* get it — even without the bonus of a wife?"

"Just say you'll come. And — if being married makes that much difference to them — well, they can stuff the job."

But it's you for whom it makes a difference, thought Liz. You who first made that stipulation.

She felt something was required of her. "Thank you."

"What for?"

The waitress brought their food and he began eating.

"For taking the pressure off."

"It's not a gambit, Liz. No strings — "

"I know." She knew he believed he was

418

telling the truth. "You're being nice and decent, like you always are."

"Will you think about coming with me?"

"It will be a wrench, leaving the Lodge after all the work we've put into it, and there are all the memories." Could they let go of those and still be as strong together?

"I don't want to lose you, Liz."

★ ★ ★

Liz lay that night, after they had made love, knowing that sex was the factor that had swayed her decision.

It was difficult to imagine being without the touch and comfort of Don's body, or wanting that sort of comfort from someone else, after five years of shared intimacy.

Having more or less promised to go with him to Norfolk, Liz had persuaded Don to go with her to visit Willow, a conscious attempt at sealing the bargain. Each acknowledged that it was important to get closer to one another's preoccupying interests. They talked about Liz's trip to the Midlands, about the school trip to Paris and, with enthusiasm, about Norfolk. Where would they live? Don had visited several estate agents, scouting out the possibilities while he was there.

Could they really have resolved things so easily? Liz wondered, amazed by how quickly the move had become a certainty, limited only by the possibility that Don would not get the job.

"Don't tell Willow about Norfolk," Liz told him as they parked the car outside Meadowfields.

"You'll have to tell her something if I get the job."

"I know — but she's only just got used to my coming here."

Willow was sitting on a bench in the garden, wrapped in a cloak and wearing a black hat with a theatrical brim and a jade-green band. She greeted Don with suspicion.

"Who are you?"

"Liz's friend," Don said, holding out his hand.

"You mean, you're the live-in lover."

"I suppose so." He glanced at Liz with

an expression of half-amused inquiry.

"He won't come again, Willow, if you're going to be rude to him."

"Good. I didn't ask either of you to come."

Don dug his elbow into Liz's ribs in silent protest.

Willow looked at Liz, her eyes sharpening with interest. "Did you go to Noonby Hall?"

"I did. And I saw the town where Daisy grew up, the factory where she worked — I have some photos to show you."

Liz took a packet of prints out of her bag. Don, who had not seen them before, leaned over her shoulder as she handed them to Willow, explaining: "These are mainly pictures to do with my research. Corsets, liberty bodices — and here is the factory where Daisy worked. Guess what — I found more pictures of her when she was a girl, adverts for Jerrett's corsets in the local museum."

"Never mind all that. You said you went to Noonby."

"It's a beautiful old house."

Liz showed her the photographs she

had taken. "It has changed, I think, from Clem Brackenborough's day. I couldn't imagine his family living there. Except — look, this is the rose garden where he and Daisy were found together. Did you know about that? Did she tell you?"

Repeating the story Lewis had told her about the scandal, Liz tried, and failed, to understand what Willow was thinking behind her blank expression.

"Do you remember, you once said Daisy could have had Clem if she had really wanted him? Did she tell you that? Did he really ask her to marry him? I really fell for Clem." Liz turned to Don, as if making a confession. "He looks such a charmer in his portrait."

But Willow refused to be drawn. She sat in silence as Liz repeated Lewis's story about Clem having served in two wars and being decorated for bravery.

"He died during the Second World War," Liz said. "Did you ever meet him?"

"No." Willow stared at her feet, pointing the toes of her shoes as if examining them for scuff marks. "No. I never knew him."

"Lewis — that's Clem's grandson — is as intrigued about Daisy and Clem as I am. I suppose their love affair seems very much more romantic to anyone who is distanced from it all."

"Romantic!" Willow turned down her mouth with derision.

Don said softly, "I'm with Willow on this one."

"But that's because you haven't seen Noonby or the portrait," Liz said. "Or got so caught up by their story that you want to know whether she got in touch with him again. What happened after she came back from France, Willow? You came back to England with her. You *must* know."

"Well, I don't," Willow said obstinately.

Don gave Liz a warning nudge; she was too persistent, the subject was becoming strained. There was a ruthlessness about her when she was in pursuit of something; it surfaced from time to time, shifting his perception of her a fraction. He tried to steer the conversation in another direction, but succeeded only in sounding patronising.

"And where did you live after the war,

Willow? Were you able to continue with your work as a model?"

Willow glanced at him suspiciously. "Has she put you up to this? Why don't you both leave me alone? Questions all the time. Was I with Daisy? Did I meet Clem? It was all a long time ago. I don't want to talk about it."

Don apologised, embarrassed.

"I don't even know you. At least with *her* — " She looked balefully at Liz. "I know what to expect by now."

"I think," said Don, "I shall go for a walk and leave you two to chat."

He was angry, thought Liz. He resented being brought here to visit a hostile old woman, and he was irritated by the obsession with Daisy; he saw absolutely no mystery in the love affair.

Was he right to debunk it? Was Daisy and Clem's relationship like any other extra-marital affair — sordid, commonplace, and best forgotten?

Willow watched Don stride away with his hands in his pockets. "Why did you bring him?"

"He was interested in meeting you."

"That's not it. You wanted me to have

a look at him. You want to know what I think."

Liz gasped, realising that Willow was absolutely right. More gradually, it occurred to her that much of Willow's hostility had been an act.

"You are wicked, pretending to be so rude to him."

"I was rude. No pretending."

"Well, then, I suppose you had better tell me. What *do* you think?"

"Very nice. But don't marry him."

"Do you have a reason?"

"Yes. But I'm not going to tell you. And, anyway, you know it already."

"I see. Well," said Liz, unsettled by the exchange, "no one's talking of marriage at the moment."

"You were, a few weeks ago."

"And now we're not."

"Because of a trip to the Midlands?"

"We've been doing some thinking."

Willow began to sing softly to herself in French, rudely, and very irritatingly.

Liz said, "I talked to Clem's grandson, Lewis. He had diaries Clem wrote when he was a boy, going right through to adulthood. School, Cambridge — "

Willow sang more loudly, ignoring her.

"There was a girl called Bea, and mention of Daisy at a garden party, and then at the races. Clem lent her money."

Willow stopped singing.

"To start her dress shop, do you think?" said Liz.

"I wouldn't put it past her."

They sat in silence.

"I should have liked to have seen his portrait," said Willow unexpectedly.

"You would have understood why Daisy fell for him if you saw it. There were other portraits of his sister and brother, and the rest of the family. I felt as if I was getting to know him through seeing them all. And then, reading his diaries — "

Willow pushed her hands into the arms of her cloak. "Oh — I should like to have come with you. I would love to have seen the portrait."

Surprised by this apparent sentimentality — or was it a signal that Willow's mind was wandering? — Liz prompted her warily. "What happened, Willow? Did

426

she ever talk about why she went to Paris? Did she give up on him? If they were so much in love — "

Willow's voice sharpened again. "You assume so much, you with your ferrety ways. And yet, the fact is, you know absolutely nothing about them."

"I know his wife was very much aware of the affair, and that when Daisy disappeared Clem was devastated."

"There you go again — devastated!"

"Lewis's grandmother told him all about it. The affair had gone on all through the First World War, until 1920."

Willow stared at her for a long time, and then sighed.

"I'm tired. It was very nice of you to come today, dear, but if you don't mind, I think I should like to rest now."

Don was coming towards them across the garden. He would catch her eye when he drew closer, raise his eyebrows in a question, ready to leave?

"I'll come again." Liz took hold of Willow's hand.

"There's no need. I don't want you to."

427

"All the same — "

"Next time — we won't talk about her. Not one word."

"If that's what you want." Liz put the photos in her bag.

"What I *want* is for it all to have been different."

★ ★ ★

"Well, now. That was a complete waste of time. She didn't even want to see you," Don said as they drove home.

"I think that's just an act. In the same way as not wanting to discuss Daisy in an act. There's something she's not telling me."

Liz puzzled over it. She visited Willow in the next few weeks; but, though she probed, Willow would say nothing more about Daisy.

"I'm off to Paris," Liz said on her last visit before the school trip. "I'm going with Don and a party of children."

Willow stared at her, then gave a cynical laugh. "You don't give up, do you?"

"I'm hardly going to be able to pick

up the Daisy trail in Paris, not after all this time."

"Is that what you call it?"

"It's what Lewis Brackenborough called it."

"Well, then — " Willow hesitated. "Say hello to the Café Bresil in the Rue des Petits Bois for me."

"You used to go there?" Liz asked.

But, if she did, Willow was not going to say.

"I was the star at Maison Clem," she remembered. "I had all the young men after me."

Liz worried about Willow; she seemed to have grown even more frail since the visit with Don some weeks earlier. Liz tried to understand her. Was she still playing games? There was the address in Paris, dropped casually. Another clue. Or was it a red herring, to sustain the element of intrigue?

"I shall look it up," Liz told Don. "I've made a note of the street. You never know. Someone there might still remember Daisy in her heyday."

"Daisy runs off to Paris after a fling with some poor guy, probably having wrecked his marriage in the process, turns into a hardened bitch according to her best friend, and you still insist on seeing her as a feminist role model," Don complained.

"She *managed* her life. She knew where she was going and what she wanted."

He did not answer, not wanting to stir up all the old questions again.

14

AFTER the Somme Clem had been promoted from captain to major, and leave was in short supply. But there were times when he and Daisy could meet. They spent a weekend together on the east coast, and, for a few days one summer, Clem joined Daisy on a selling trip in the North.

Demand for clothes was improving. Women who were earning were also spending, and they wanted the luxury of new dresses and costumes. Clem met her in Edinburgh, where she was showing her collection of costumes, two-pieces and gowns to a collection of buyers.

The War seemed very far away as they toured the cobbled streets. The rain-soaked, blackened stones of the Gothic buildings oozed a sense of doom-laden history, yet nothing could dampen their delight with one another as they climbed, hand in hand, to the castle. Only there did the presence of cannon and soldiers in uniform prompt Clem into talking of the war.

"One wonders if it's worth all the sacrifice," he said, leaning on the castle wall and surveying the mist-veiled city far below them. His feeling of having come through the recent years and months with integrity was confused by increasing doubts about questions of duty and honour and the war's high moral purpose.

Daisy leant on the wall and smiled up at Clem, linking her arm in his, not caring about the rain; she did not want to talk about the war, which — discounting the difficulties over shortages and running a business — had always seemed to her a national problem rather than a personal one.

"You would never have had the chance to be a hero without this war," she said, squeezing his arm.

Clem did not smile. What did Daisy or Virginia know about the horrors of the Front, or the overwhelming blend of elation and misery of being on leave? Due to all this he had a child who hardly knew him, and the past four years were suffused with an overwhelming sense of estrangement from home and family. Clem felt a constant, aching guilt about his marriage, aware that Virginia needed more from him than he could give. Had she guessed about Daisy? She rarely came with him on his visits to the Midlands, saying that the atmosphere at Noonby between Austen and Sylvia was bad for the child.

"Bad for us too," he had joked once. "It's a good thing we don't bicker."

"No," Virginia had said with an odd smile. "No, Clem. That's something we don't do."

The same could not be said for Daisy. Sometimes, if they had not seen one another for a long time, or if he had displeased her, she fought him fiercely. "Go away!" she would scream. "You're no good to me." Often without warning. "Go to hell, Clem. Leave me alone! You only come to see me to tell me how miserable you are."

But the result was always the same. He stayed, and almost always they made love; and when he looked back, the only anchor in the entire mess of the past four years seemed to have been his erratic, unpredictable relationship with Daisy.

"It's you who give me strength," he said, taking her gloved hand and pressing it hard against his lips. "You who offer a refuge, the brightest contrast — "

Horrified, Daisy saw his eyes fill with tears. She took his face in her hands. "Don't, please, Clem, don't." And, kissing his lips, she dried his face with her gloves.

★ ★ ★

Listening to the traffic that night from their hotel room, Daisy lay, drowsy with love, reviewing the occasions when Clem had made love to her; it was the intensity of their relationship when they were together that sustained her during their times apart. She pictured him in the quiet, gracious house he inhabited with his wife, and for an instant Daisy envied all married women and her thoughts turned for the first time in years, and with sadness, to the child whose life she had terminated. Jealously she pictured Virginia and the son Clem had hardly known all through the war, welcoming him home when he returned from France to civilian life.

He stirred in his sleep, and Daisy raised herself on one arm and watched him. He seemed restless, and he was muttering something she could not understand. Her name, his wife's? Perhaps neither — but some reference to that other life, in the trenches. Daisy lay with her arms around him until he was quiet.

That afternoon he had called her his refuge, she remembered. But when the war was over, would it be to her, or to Virginia and his child, that he would turn?

★ ★ ★

Daisy knew precisely where Clem lived. He had felt secure in telling her, unaware that when she went to London on business, she sometimes took the tube train to Hampstead station and walked up the hill to the lane of gracious houses, trying to picture him there, hoping to glimpse something of

435

the life he kept so separate from her.

Daisy was in London when the Armistice was declared. Walking along to Paddington, she heard the boom of maroons being fired from the nearby police stations; they were echoed by others in the distance. People looked at one another questioningly, and soon the news was on everyone's lips: the war was over.

Daisy felt no elation, only a sense of anti-climax and frustration at the waste of it all.

The din and celebrations, when she reached home, depressed her. The women in the workroom had fastened up home-made bunting, fashioned from strips of coloured binding. The evening was punctuated by the sound of hooting motor cars, the piping of police whistles and ringing of bicycle bells, and Union Jacks seemed to have sprung up everywhere like bright flowers in the November drizzle.

* * *

The letters from Wilfred came as a shock.

Clem was picking up the threads of his old life, and having to pretend to Virginia that letters from Daisy's brother were from a soldier in his old battalion made him uneasy.

The first was redirected from Noonby in July of 1919. Its tone was bitter. The writer was looking for his sister, 'the only decent, lovely thing in a corrupt world', whom Clem had seduced and ruined years ago.

Suspecting the man was crazed by the war, Clem was dismayed to receive a second letter a few weeks later. References to the war — the filth of Flanders, the waste of it all — and rantings about God were intermingled with questions about Daisy. Had she gone off to London as everyone supposed? If Clem knew anything it was his duty to reveal it.

Clem wrote back:

In the light of the hectoring tone of your letter, and for Daisy's own safety, I feel I cannot respond to your inquiries about your sister . . .

He said nothing to Daisy about the correspondence, though he had begun to meet her when she came up to London. They went to the theatre, risked being seen together at jazz and dancing clubs and in restaurants in the newly popular area of Soho. Now that they met more often they also quarrelled more frequently, and Clem truly did not know whether Daisy loved him, or whether she was perhaps growing weary of him.

Over the months, the vein of bitterness in the letters from Daisy's brother lessened; there were frequent references to Wilfred's rediscovery of his faith in God; the writing was infused with reflections on his childhood and, shortly before Christmas, he sent the letter that changed Clem's mind about keeping Daisy's whereabouts a secret:

Dear Major Brackenborough,
    I am making one final appeal to your better nature, believing these days that all men possess a capacity for goodness. If again you refuse to help me I shall be bound to give up my attempt to trace my sister. I am leaving

the Midlands in the new year, having decided on a career in the Church, something that has long been on my mind.

I hope you will excuse my persistence in writing to you, but, to be truthful, I was in a desperate frame of mind after coming out of the army.

Perhaps seeing Daisy again might have made all the difference. The fact is, I am at peace now, and wish to meet her and make my peace with her too. I am given to understand, sir, that you are married and have a family. No doubt you have put your past association with Daisy aside, a thing between you and your conscience. But if you can tell me where she was last known I would be much obliged.

Yours sincerely,
Wilfred Cornforth.

Daisy stared at the young man in a cheap striped suit and repeated stupidly, "You are Wilfred? But you can't be. You were such a skinny thing. How old are you?"

"Nearly twenty-one." He stood, smiling foolishly, and at last Daisy recognised, in the hawk-nosed, serious-eyed stranger, the brother who had once adored her.

Fighting back sentimentality, Daisy took him to her flat, made him tea and asked questions about her mother and Minnie. How had they come through the war? Were they well? Was Minnie working, courting, happy? But she felt no deep curiosity about any of them; she had put them behind her a long time ago.

"You could have got in touch, Daisy. It seems very hard, to have changed your name and everything."

"I've moved on."

"But all through the war — "

"I was busy."

"Minnie has ambitions to work in London. She learned to typewrite in the war. Mother's not been well since Sidney was born."

"Another baby?" Daisy exclaimed, her resolve not to give way to sentiment faltering as she recalled moments of affection and intimacy with her mother."

"Sidney's a good boy. Just seven. Cousin Albert is a clever lad too."

"And Father?"

"As contentious as ever. He was too

old for the war, but he talks about it, as if he was there. He won't hear of me going into the Church."

He saw her look of surprise.

"It's what I want, Daisy. It was hard for me to get back into civilian life again. I was so *bitter*. It's little wonder Major Brackenborough refused to tell me where you were at first."

Daisy stared at him. "*Clem* told you I was here?"

"He was the only person I could think of who might know, because of that row at Noonby over you and him. Everyone knew about it, but we all thought you'd gone off to London."

"Clem told you," Daisy repeated, feeling betrayed.

"I'm so glad I've found you, Daisy. I hated you and him at first. Brackenborough most of all for getting you a bad name at home. But I've grown up a bit since the war. I've dreamed of telling you about my plans . . . "

He chatted on, talking about his hopes of becoming a Christian minister, and about the changes that had taken place in Kirby Langton; but all the time, Daisy was fuming that Clem had been writing to Wilf, and told him where she was, without even asking her permission.

"I can't tell you how glad I am you've reformed," Wilfred said. "I can go with an easier heart to do the work of the Lord."

"Did Clem tell you I'd reformed?"

"He wrote that you were running this place alone, a very respectable business."

She smiled wryly. "By all means, go and do the work of the Lord, Wilf. But don't go under the illusion that I've sinned and am somehow forgiven."

Wilfred flushed scarlet. "I thought — "

"I *love* Clem. I've loved him for years."

"I thought — "

"You thought that because he has a wife and child, it makes everything tidy. She's cold, Wilf." Daisy's mouth turned down, expressing her distaste; remembering, and exaggerating, Clem's hints at Virginia's rejection of the physical side of marriage. "She's not a proper wife to him. In the biblical sense," she added, in case he was still in any doubt.

"No — " Wilfred shook his head. "You

won't get me to condone adultery."

"Don't put on your parson's ways with me," Daisy said, wagging a finger at him. "I've done nothing I'm ashamed of."

"But it's wicked. Think what you're doing."

"It feels right. That's what matters."

Wilfred continued to look at her reproachfully. He hesitated. "I had hoped I might come again to see you."

Feeling him recede from her, Daisy said, "It looks as if these years have made quite a difference to us."

"I won't condone adultery," he repeated. "You can't bully me into agreeing with you. Not now. I'm not a kid."

★ ★ ★

"How dare you tell him about me without asking me first."

Sprawled on the sofa, Clem tried not to be intimidated by Daisy's attack. "It seemed for the best. I didn't want to stir you up needlessly beforehand."

"Didn't want to get too involved, you mean. As usual."

443

"Come here, and stop making a fuss about nothing."

"No." Daisy wriggled from his grasp, determined to make a scene. "He's my brother. I hadn't seen him for years and I didn't want to. All that's over." She paced the floor in front of the fire. "You told him I'd *reformed*."

"I didn't," Clem protested indignantly. "I simply — left out a few details."

"You didn't use the word 'reformed'?"

"I wouldn't dare. Will you come here and kiss me?"

Daisy stopped pacing. "You take over my life, Clem."

"I know. Forgive me?"

"I'll be thirty soon," she said, holding out her hands as if examining them for wrinkles.

"And I shall be thirty-two."

"But for me it's worse. Where am I going? What do I want from life?"

"Don't start having doubts. Not now. We've come so far."

"You expect such a lot from me," Daisy said angrily. "You've got all you could want. A wife. A child. An income for life."

"I know it's not fair on you."

"No, you don't. You have no idea what it's like for me, here on the edge. *Outside* your life." Daisy remembered his wife before the war, self-assured in a pale blue corset, confident of her darling Clem. Daisy longed for him to tell her that his marriage to Virginia did not matter to him.

There was a silence, and Daisy sensed some hidden thought before he said, "You're central to my life, Daisy. I couldn't bear to think of being without you."

She did not believe him. She tortured herself with sentimental scenarios: Clem and Virginia discussing domestic matters over dinner, Clem teaching his child to play cricket in the garden, taking him for walks with the dog — she had discovered there was a dog, a King Charles spaniel. Once, during the war, Daisy had watched the house and seen Virginia leave, recognising her slim, dark figure in a tailored outfit; she had followed for several yards before pulling herself up with a start, asking herself what she was doing.

Daisy went to London in the late spring of 1920 without telling Clem she was there or arranging to see him. A compulsion had grown to observe him and his family together, to see how he behaved when he was with them. Perhaps she wanted to frighten him. Only a little. But after the episode with Wilfred she wanted to shake his complacency.

Spring was soft on the air and bulbs were flowering in all the parks and gardens. If she saw his wife she would walk away, Daisy told herself; but if Clem came out from the house alone she would let him see that she was there. Then what? An hour together? A chance to judge how pleased he was to see her, how much he was prepared to risk?

But when Daisy saw them, Clem and Virginia were together, arm in arm as if they had been out for a morning stroll, and on a course that led them directly towards her, the spaniel frisking around Clem's feet.

The fact that Clem had recognised her was evident in his frantic expression.

Daisy did not move, transfixed by the

sight of Clem's arm linked solicitously in his wife's. She wondered whether he was going to walk right past her and pretend to ignore her: the final humiliation, his last act of betrayal. But not the worst, Daisy thought, as she watched Virginia's heavily pregnant figure draw nearer in a long coat with a fur trim bulging before her.

How slowly she moved; how placid and blooming her face, with a pleased, satisfied smile on her lips; how delicately she placed her feet, as if to counterbalance the weight of the unborn child.

Clem's expression of alarm turned to panic when Daisy did not move.

Virginia saw Daisy too then; she frowned, turned a questioning smile on her, obviously trying to place her.

"You rotter, Clem."

Daisy spoke quietly, but with a force that seemed to throw his wife off-balance, as she tightened her grip on her husband's arm.

"Daisy — for God's sake!" Clem looked up and down the street, and his wife's free hand flew protectively to the bump in front of her.

"You liar. You damned liar," Daisy intoned.

In a swift movement Clem moved forward and gripped her by the arm. "Not here. For pity's sake."

His grip tightened as Daisy thrashed at him with her free arm. Glancing round in desperation, he took note of their exposed position and the fact that she was not going to be silenced. He hurried her across the road and bundled her inside the house.

"You weren't going to tell me!" Daisy shouted.

"Be quiet!"

There was a glimpse of a frightened maidservant at the end of the hall, and Virginia, pale, yet determined, climbing the front steps after them.

Clem turned to Daisy. "This time you've gone too far. You've done it now. You've really done it now." He pushed her into a room off the hall and shut the door, leaving her alone.

Daisy heard raised and angry voices, but she did not want to abandon her temporary isolation; she had not really wanted to make a scene in front of his wife, and was even now beginning to feel sorry for her. But not for Clem. She did not care how much she embarrassed Clem.

The room smelled of leather and tobacco, and was obviously his study; one wall was lined entirely with books. There were newspapers and books on the sofa, a gramophone in a rosewood cabinet in one corner, and, by the window, a heavy desk with a telephone and heavy metal lamp on it and an open cigarette box, half empty.

Taking a cigarette, Daisy lit it with hands that shook, and sat on the edge of his desk.

Clem came into the room, closing the door quietly behind him.

"You lied. You told me you never sleep with her."

"Will you keep your voice down? The servants will hear you. What were you thinking of, coming here? Waiting outside!"

"I wanted to see where you lived."

"Why?"

"I needed to know about you and her. And, now I do, I can see why you don't

449

like the idea. You weren't going to tell me until it was *born*? Was I supposed to read about it in a newspaper, like last time?"

"I don't know." He too took a cigarette and lit it with shaking hands. "Coming to the house, Daisy. That was unforgivable."

"I didn't invite myself in. I was happy to stay outside."

"And let all the neighbours know you were there. In front of Virginia?"

"I've no quarrel with her. Poor thing. Pregnant!"

"I didn't know how to tell you. You can be so volatile."

"You're damn right, I'm volatile. Do you never wonder why I put up with you? You come to me whenever you feel like it. You share my flat, my bed, *use* me — "

"I don't use you," he hissed. "You want me as much as I want you."

"And what about her — your wife? Do you tell her you love her when you're doing it? Do you touch her like you touch me?"

"For God's sake!" He stubbed out

the cigarette again and paced the floor. "We can talk about this another time. Rationally."

"Not any more. This is it — the last of it."

"You don't mean that."

"Wait and see."

He looked at her helplessly. "You'll have to go. I don't know what I'm going to say to Virginia."

Daisy went to the door. "Try telling one of us the truth for a change."

★ ★ ★

She had believed afterwards that she never wanted to see him again. So convinced was she of this, that when Clem did come, one Sunday as she was checking the previous day's delivery of bolts of fabric, she felt exposed, off-balance.

He stood outside, his hands in his pockets, and did not speak at first when she opened the door.

"You'd better come inside."

He waited until she had finished her checking, sitting on the edge of her cutting table as he used to in the old days, watching her profile bent over the desk.

She had cut her hair since he had last seen her. It suited her, swinging forward and emphasising the elegant line of her neck. He ached as always to touch her.

"I didn't tell you about the baby because I didn't want to hurt you," he said after a while. "I can't leave Virginia. None of this is her fault, it's mine. And I won't ever leave her."

"I know. And I don't want you to." Daisy looked up. She had been wrong to think she had not missed him. "It doesn't matter any more."

★ ★ ★

It was perhaps the one time he had gone to her and she had not told him to go away.

For Clem, there was something infinitely poignant about the last time they made love. Could it be that she had already been planning her departure? As they lay in that state of pleasure where the mind and senses merge, she cried out as if with sadness, rather than joy.

For a while he was busy in London. He wrote to her at Christmas, but that was all; Daisy did not like cards and presents, never celebrated birthdays; she always said Christmas was overrated. He telephoned, and she said that she too was 'very busy', perhaps they could meet in the spring. She was vague, making no firm commitment.

He went to Leicester in March, and there was no evidence that the salon had ever been there. The windows were whitewashed; the sign *Maison Clem* had been replaced with one advertising a box company.

Clem stood for a long time, letting the significance of the changes sink in.

He made a few inquiries, and learned from the box company that she had been gone for several weeks, no one knew where; local people said she had always kept herself to herself, they did not know much about her. He contacted her suppliers and trade customers; but they too knew nothing, except that she had closed all the accounts in the space of a few weeks and gone away.

When he tracked down Maison Clem's chief assistant, Norah, working now at a nearby department store, she would tell him only that Mrs Carr had decided to move away.

"You must know something more about her," he persisted. "Someone has to know where she's gone."

Norah shook her head. He suspected she had been given her instructions to say nothing.

15

DAISY never let her love for a man, or conventions about marriage, duty and family get in the way of her purpose, Liz thought, watching the line of parents outside the school wave goodbye to their offspring. Daisy had never needed to consider someone else's ambitions, spread herself impossibly, lose part of her identity; she had stayed in control of her life. How enviable that seemed.

The coach was noisy. It was hard to read with the noise of the children singing, exclaiming, and crackling sweet and crisp packets. Reading became impossible once ten-year-old Toby Wyman in the seat behind decided to unleash all his comments and queries about the trip in her direction. How long until they arrived? Did she want a crisp? Did she teach French? Did she like frogs' legs? Would they have to eat frogs' legs in France?

"The holiday from hell," one of the teachers, Rosemary Harvey, had dubbed it, and by the time the coach had crossed the Channel, consumed acres of flat, beige-coloured French countryside, and reached the outskirts of Paris, Liz was wondering why on earth she had agreed to share the experience.

Don and his deputy Cliff shepherded the party from the coach to a barrack-like hotel; the children were compliant now, subdued by the journey, and disappointed in Paris, whose magic was hard to discover in the skyline of flats and office buildings north of the city. Liz too felt a sense of anti-climax, and she was in sympathy with Toby Wyman's disbelieving, "Is this what we came all this way for?"

★ ★ ★

Coming to her room, a single, because of the look of things, Don crept about like a lover in a French farce. They were tired, neither of them in the mood for sex, and Liz spoiled things by laughing when he stubbed his toe on the wall. For once he

456

did not see the funny side.

"Things will get better," Don promised the next morning.

They got worse.

Rain streamed from a grey sky as the coach took them into central Paris and tipped them out in the area of park behind Notre Dame. The children stayed close, wrapped in anoraks, hooded parcels on short legs, with anxious, inquiring faces wet with the rain.

They filed along the narrow pavement, under rows of dripping gargoyles with outstretched necks, and had almost reached the front of the Cathedral when a small voice near the back of the line gave out a plaintive request for the lavatory.

Don halted the crocodile of children, demanding, "Who else?", reminding them they had been told to go before leaving the hotel, displeased, but resigned to complications.

A scattering of tentative hands was raised.

"How useful it is to speak French," murmured Liz, as she gathered the incontinent ten — and eleven-year-olds

457

around her and turned back towards the park, feeling like a mother duck with a string of colourful ducklings behind her.

Liz stood under the chestnut trees with the queue of children and tried to imagine Daisy and Willow living in Paris, with Notre Dame as a familiar landmark, and knowing intimately the bridges and islands of the Seine.

The Rue des Petits Bois. Liz had looked it up on a street map. Why had Willow mentioned the café and street by name? A slip of the tongue? Or had she wanted her to go there, if only to bring back an account of what it was like now? Why did Willow put up such a front of hostility, and yet always seem to push her to find out more? What was it she had said — that she wished it could all have been different? But *what* would Willow have wanted to change? The nature of her friendship with Daisy? Daisy's relationship with Clem?

One of the children slipped her hand into Liz's and looked up at her. "Why is it raining?"

"So that it wasn't a waste of space in

your bag to bring your orange anorak," Liz said distantly.

"I miss my mum. And Miss Harvey was cross with me at breakfast."

"Well." Liz was at a loss for the right kind of consolation for a rain-sodden, homesick child. "I expect your mum's missing you too. But she'll be wanting you to have a good time. Best to make the most of it, don't you think?"

The girl stared at her with dark, thoughtful eyes. "I didn't want to come. Not really."

Liz bent to say with mock confidentiality, "I'll tell you a secret. Neither did I."

What am I doing here? she asked herself, looking up at the delicate flying buttresses and pinnacles and turrets of Notre Dame. God knows. But one thing's for sure, Daisy would never have found herself supervising a gang of schoolchildren in and out of a French lavatory.

★ ★ ★

459

It was dark inside the Cathedral, no sun lighting the rich reds and blues of the stained glass, and there was a strong smell of wet clothes. The child who had confessed to missing her mother clung to Liz's hand, glued to her since Liz's admission that she too was an unwilling member of the team. Others gathered around her, attracted by the novelty of Liz's non-teaching status, her impressively fluent communications in French when seeking directions, and by the rumours of her romantic link with Don.

"I feel like the Pied Piper," Liz murmured.

"Wrong town, wrong country."

Don was distracted by the sight of Toby Wyman tailing a posse of Japanese tourists, and left her, hurrying to haul the boy back in line.

It had stopped raining when they unwrapped their lunch-packs and sat outside the Cathedral, the children swinging their legs and chattering like monkeys on the benches. The seats were wet, but no one worried very much. Paris was beginning to work

460

its spell, thought Liz. The houses of the Left Bank looked elegant and quiet beyond the tracery of trees. She wanted to walk away from Don and Cliff and Rosemary and the crowd of noisy children, and yet there was something about the children that attracted her. They moved their whole bodies when they talked. They swayed, jiggled, gesticulated, were rarely still. She found herself smiling involuntarily. There was so much to make one smile: the clamour of young voices, the warmth of the sun, the wet blossom on the trees, the dignity of the buildings, the sense of being at ease.

The errant Toby, his chin in one hand as he surveyed the passing tides of tourists and the beggars and the traffic, was quick to ask questions, and to give answers when others posed questions. He was by turns solemn or smiling; his mouth was mobile, working even when he was silent, as if impatient to confide what was going on in his head. He was the type of child one would be happy to lay claim to — if she were ever to consider having children, which she was not, Liz reminded herself firmly.

"What next?" said Toby after they had finished lunch.

★ ★ ★

What next? The Beaubourg, with its street entertainers and a funfair of escalators; the metro, another playground, platforms and station names, skipping from train to train, a nightmare of head-counting; the Arc de Triomphe and the Eiffel Tower, 'better than Blackpool', and a cruise on a river boat with throbbing engines, past floodlit buildings and under bridges.

Liz lay exhausted that night, and when Don came to her room they slept until daybreak and the sun streamed in through the window.

"I've hardly spoken to you since we arrived," Don said, shifting his weight against her.

"Are we speaking now?" she said as he traced his hand down her body.

"It's a kind of communication. Isn't it?"

She linked her arms behind her head, and gave a sigh of pleasure. "Talk to me. I'm listening."

★ ★ ★

The sun shone on the sugar-fondant brilliance of the Sacré Coeur. More entertainment as they took the funicular railway in relays to the top of Montmartre, and Toby, attaching himself to Liz, told her about a film he had once seen, in which two men fought on the roof of a ski-lift hundreds of feet above a mountain ravine.

He walked beside her, one foot in the road, one on the kerb. "Are you really Sir's girlfriend?"

"Isn't that rather a personal question for a young man to be asking?"

"I suppose so."

"Let's talk about you instead. Are you enjoying being here? Do you like Paris?"

"I liked the Eiffel Tower, and the river boat."

"*Bateau mouche.*"

"Whatever."

"Anything else?"

"Oh," he shrugged. "Everything really."

"Me too," Liz said.

★ ★ ★

They had decided to take the children to the Louvre on their last day. When the staff met at breakfast to discuss the itinerary, Liz announced that they would not need her to translate once they were inside the museum.

Promising to be back by lunchtime, she left them, a party of adult and miniature explorers with their backpacks and colourful anoraks, queuing outside the glass pyramid entrance to the Louvre, the wind blowing spray from the fountains.

The sun, emerging from clouds, seemed to highlight Liz's isolation as she walked in the shade of lime and beech trees within the quadrangle of arcaded buildings that formed the Palais Royal Garden.

Did Daisy once walk here, pause by the pond, and feel at peace, cut off from the noise of the city by this very elegant garden?

Consulting her map, Liz entered the

464

quiet narrow streets beyond the arcades, and found the Rue des Petits Bois. She opened her camera. Willow would want photographs.

★ ★ ★

The *patronne* of the Bresil, neat, amiable and middle-aged, bustled about chatting loudly to the customers seated at the small tables in the basement restaurant.

Some of her comments were directed at Liz. Was she on holiday, staying long? Did she know Paris well?

Liz ordered a second coffee, waiting for a lull in trade and for the woman to pause close by, before addressing her in French.

A fashion house, here in the Rue des Petits Bois? The woman shook her head, turning down the corners of her mouth in a *moue*.

"The salon was called Maison Clem," Liz said.

"Perhaps my mother will know. My parents lived here before the war. My father has been dead a long time, but my mother will remember, she has seen many people come and go."

Pulling aside a curtain to a back room, the *patronne* spoke to someone at length, and after a moment an elderly woman emerged, dressed in black and pushing a comb into her thin white hair; she glanced at Liz with a nod of greeting.

"The couturière called herself Marguerite," said Liz. "Or perhaps you remember my friend, a model who worked at Maison Clem. She remembers your café. Her name was Willow."

The woman said in rapid French, "But of course I remember them."

Excitement filled Liz's mind, making her stumble over her words. "Was the fashion house near here?"

"Not in the Rue des Petits Bois, in the Faubourg St Honoré. But they lived here, and Marguerite worked here too when I was a child. She took rooms with us for several years. She was clever — alas, never among the very big names — but there were so many creative people in Paris at that time. They were good years, before the war."

"You really knew them?" Liz glanced round the restaurant in amazement.

466

"They *lived* here?"

"Upstairs. An apartment. Oh — all kinds of people came. It was a very exciting time for a young girl. You want to talk? You have time? I have some photographs. My daughter will look for them — "

"Is the couture house still there?" asked Liz, as the *patronne* slipped obediently into the back room and they sat at a table.

"Marguerite moved when the business expanded. It's all shops and offices now. She wrote from England after the war, and was going to return. But she never did. You know how it is, one loses touch — " She shrugged.

"She died," said Liz. "Soon after the war."

"Ah — I didn't know. How sad."

Accepting a tattered photograph album from her daughter's hands and placing it on the table in front of them, the woman opened it at random and began turning the pages.

"Here is my mother, who was then the patronne. And here is Marguerite — Mrs Carr."

467

Liz saw a brown and faded photograph of two women, one broad-hipped with heavy features, the other tall and well-built, but very elegant, her hair cut short and waved in a style typical of the twenties, unmistakably Daisy.

"That's what she called herself?" said Liz. "Mrs Carr?"

"Was it not her real name? We always thought she was a widow."

"She never married as far as I can tell."

The woman smiled and nodded, as if confirming something. "I was only a child when she came to us, but my mother would not have asked questions. Marguerite said she was a widow, and that is what everyone believed. She said her husband had been killed. A hunting accident before she came to France."

She turned back through the pages, revealing a sequence of faded photographs: groups of attractive, smiling men and women; a girl of ten or eleven looking shyly into the camera. "Myself," the old lady explained.

"And here is my mother once more." A photograph of a woman holding a baby.

"And Mrs Carr — la Marguerite."

Seated on a garden chair, in a hat and dark dress, Daisy too held the shawl-wrapped infant in her arms. She looked stern and uncomfortable, as if afraid she might drop it.

"Who was the baby?" Liz asked. "Your brother or sister?"

"No — " The woman touched the faded pictures tenderly. "No. That is Marguerite's child."

Liz stared again at the picture of Daisy. "But — " she said slowly. "I don't understand."

The woman did not seem to hear her, turning the pages to look at more old photographs. "I was eleven — the first time I saw or knew about such a thing as a baby being born. Don't I look proud to be holding her? There I am, Marie-Cécile, with the baby."

"*When* was she born?" Liz interrupted. "What year?"

"Soon after Marguerite came here. Let me think — 1921 it would be. I was delighted. A baby in the house. A little playmate. Ah — she was a sweet little thing. And when she grew older — " She turned the page. "She outshone even her mother. So pale. But strong. They were both strong, obstinate women."

"Her name." Liz looked at the photograph of a fair-haired, fashionable young girl of seventeen or eighteen, searching the eyes for the personality behind them. "What was the name of Marguerite's daughter?"

The woman looked at her curiously. "But you already told me. You said you knew her."

16

"MY name is Marie-Cécile. My mother has a café. Everyone knows it. You want to come? You are hungry?"

The girl was ten or perhaps a little older, and she had been walking up and down the paths of the public gardens for some minutes, watchful before approaching Daisy.

She spoke with the confidence of a saleswoman. "You want to sleep? You want a room?" The accent was difficult to understand, but they were the first words of English Daisy had heard since arriving in Paris that morning.

Suspicious of children blessed with such apparently artless guile, and having already walked a long way from the railway station, Daisy said, "You have rooms as well?"

"Of course."

"Is it far?"

The child was already heading towards

471

the street; picking up her suitcases, Daisy followed.

She tried to frame sentences to equip her for the necessary bargaining over a room and to relate the story she had concocted, but her body felt heavy, and her mind was dulled from the journey. Her French seemed to have reduced itself to the little she had learned long ago at the Poplars; phrases sang in her head, *Bonjour, au revoir, s'il vous plaît* . . .

"*Je suis enceinte.*"

No need to tell them that, they could see for themselves.

Her first reaction had been disbelief. "Impossible," she had told the doctor who examined her. "My husband and I have been married for six years. It was a doctor who told me I could never bear children."

"Well, he was wrong. I should say you are about four months pregnant. Congratulations."

Going about in a daze, refusing to believe the evidence at first, Daisy had begun to plan another abortion, realising only at the last minute that she could not go through with it again.

She might have told Clem, of course, and assured her child's future by extracting money from him. But the idea was fraught with complications, and it would have forced on her a dependency she did not want. The memory of the scene at his home and an image of the pregnant Virginia were still vivid in Daisy's mind. The fact that Clem would always put his wife and family first had persuaded her that the time had come to fulfil the ambition she had always held in reserve.

There had been a romantic kind of morality about facing the situation alone, an extremity about going to Paris, that had suited her mood. The sense of moral rightness still lingered, but the romance of the situation had not lasted. Circumstances meant that she had needed to wind up the business quickly. She had been scrupulous about paying the workforce and her suppliers, but she had been forced to abandon substantial sums of money owed by her customers.

Had she really believed she could start all over again, that she had enough ideas and skills to set up a new workshop in a foreign country, with no customers, a poor knowledge of the language, knowing next to nothing about Paris suppliers, and with a child to look after as well? It was all very well nursing a dream all those years, quite another turning it into reality.

Paris seemed no better, no worse than any other city she had encountered. Noise and dirt. Cars and horses. Endless streets of grey, towering buildings. And a cutting wind that ignored all promise of spring.

Daisy saw with relief that the girl was leading her only a few yards further to a building that looked clean and unpretentious. A sign above the door read in gilt letters, *Bresil*. A short flight of steps led down to the basement café.

★ ★ ★

"*Une tragédie*." Daisy embarked on her history in a mixture of halting French and English, with willing interpretation from the precocious Marie-Cécile.

"Your husband is dead?" exclaimed Marie-Cécile's mother in rapid French.

A large woman, with sympathetic, heavy Latin features, she threw up her hands in distress and sympathy, for Mme Bresil too was a widow; the war, she said, had created more widows than brides.

Daisy explained that her husband had been killed in a riding accident. "His family owned land, a big house in the country, a *château*. We both loved riding. But on this occasion — alas — I could not accompany him. Thank God. I did not know then about the child."

She and Mr Carr had intended living in France, after disappointments in England and disagreements with his family, she said. Before the war, her husband had always wanted to live in Paris. Now she had decided to make the move alone, and, because of heavy debts, about which she had known nothing when her husband was alive, she and her child must now live frugally.

How ready with their sympathy people were, if one hit the right note, thought Daisy. Subtly, she had depicted herself and Madame Bresil as fellow sufferers, hinting at the bitter-sweet pleasure they could share in the exchange of sad reminiscences in the days to come.

Mme Bresil could offer a couple of rooms at a reasonable rent; she said that Daisy might take her meals in the café with the other tenants — about half a dozen in all.

Daisy examined the rooms at the top of the house and said she thought they would suit her.

Brave women. She unpacked her suitcase, putting bundles of notes and her passport under the mattress. How many of us there are. She almost believed in her own widowhood. Clem might as well be dead to her. She had loved him, he had fathered her child, and now . . .

"*Fini!*" She snapped shut her suitcase and, lifting it on to the wardrobe, felt a twinge of discomfort under her ribs.

The attic was large and irregular, composed of several rooms, including the two Daisy and her child would occupy. The bedroom was furnished with an iron bedstead, a rug, a dresser and a wardrobe; the main room was provided with a fireplace, an ancient sofa with heavy feet and wooden arms, and nothing else. There was a bathroom with a tub in it two floors below, which Madame said Daisy might share with the other tenants, adding, with a trace of wistfulness, that she thought it would be very agreeable to have a widow and her child living in the house now that Marie-Cécile was growing up so quickly. Mme Bresil loved children. If only her own husband had lived longer there might have been many, many brothers and sisters to keep Marie-Cécile company. She had asked how long until the baby would be born, and Daisy, counting the weeks, remembered the sense of finality about the last time Clem came to her; already her life in Leicester seemed far away and unreal.

How long?

"The summer," she had told Mme Bresil. "My baby will be born in the summertime."

★ ★ ★

She was christened Willow.

Daisy told people afterwards that the name was inspired by the willow-cane laundry basket that served for the baby's cot; sometimes she said that the child was named after the pattern on the blue china bowl in which Mme Bresil first bathed her. Marie-Cécile said that Mrs Carr, taking one look at the child, had cried, "Poor little soul," and, because *saule*, in French, meant 'willow', Willow she had remained.

The birth exhausted Daisy, and overwhelmed her with the sheer terror of being alone with an experience over which, for once, she had no control. After the pain of the birth came low spirits and a sense of uncertainty, and as the days passed a growing despair about what she had done.

She wished the child would stop crying. What did it want from her? The crying tore at her emotions without mercy, hard to escape, impossible to ignore, setting her nerve ends jangling, so that she too wanted to scream.

Daisy remembered her mother nursing her babies with a passive resignation; she had made it seem so easy. Willow's tiny hands grabbed and pinched when she fed. Willow squalled and raged when she was hungry; her arms and legs thrashed

478

in protest when Daisy held her.

The realisation dawned slowly that this creature in her arms, with its screwed-up, grotesque little face, hostile blue eyes, and fuzz of hair, was not only relying on her for survival — it wanted to dominate her.

★ ★ ★

Turning her hand to a little dressmaking again before the child was born, Daisy had converted one half of her sitting room into an *atelier*, and the landing into an area where customers — mostly friends of Madame — might wait; she had used money from her store under the mattress, and bought rugs, painted everywhere white, covered the sofa with a Moorish tapestry and furnished the rooms with 'good' furniture, antique bits and pieces that Mme Bresil had helped her to choose.

Gathering ideas from the Bon Marché and Galeries Lafayette, copying dress designs from *Vogue* without compunction, altering a line or trim here or there, she ran up costumes for her customers, charging half as much as the originals. Now that the child was born, Daisy did not intend always to work from an attic above Mme Bresil's café. She envied the Paris couturiers their salons, knowing she understood couture as well as they did — she too knew the way a body moved, the way a fabric fell from the shoulder or hip; she understood instinctively how to cut a toile.

Persuading Mme Bresil to lease her more rooms in the attic, she let it be known that her ambitions covered more than executing a little dressmaking to pay the rent.

One thing Daisy was determined on: Willow would never slip into poverty, never go without the security of money, or lack material comforts as she had when she was a girl; Willow would grow up to be proud of her mother's work as a *modiste*.

This determination to make money and raise her daughter in comfort was translated by Daisy as love. And yet, when she looked at the child, there was no response in her that she could recognise as maternal attachment. She waited for the flood of feeling that would force from her a love for her child. Weeks and months passed, and Daisy felt nothing, neither warmth nor maternal serenity, only a deepening resentment that her daughter made such exhausting demands on her.

"I don't know how to handle her," Daisy confessed to Mme Bresil. She watched Marie-Cécile put Willow against her shoulder and soothe her by patting the baby's bottom, as she herself had done when Wilfred and Minnie were tiny. So, why did she now shrink from holding her own child?

"It will come. It's natural."

Mme Bresil smiled at Marie-Cécile, and was proud of her daughter, a natural little mother if ever there was one.

But maternal feelings did not come, and, for Daisy, there seemed nothing instinctive about the role in which she was trapped. The only thing that came naturally to her was work, creating garments; the only process that seemed fascinating was that of translating an idea from a sketch into a toile. Her imagination raced as she pictured the elegant Houses headed by the big names: Poiret and Worth, Lanvin, Chanel, and Paquin. One day, one day . . .

More and more, she allowed Madame to fuss over the baby, and to take her away when she cried, so that she might concentrate without distractions.

★ ★ ★

The vivacity of Paris bewitched Daisy in those early years after leaving England: the dizzy nightlife with its crooners and saxophones, and the syncopated rhythm of the Charleston; the lights of the city from Montmartre to Montparnasse; people dancing, talking, eating and drinking; the smell of French cigarettes as intellectuals argued for hours in the Deux Magots and the Café Flore of St-Germain-des-Près; and the *chic* of the Ritz and Maxims, the rarefied society around the Place Vendôme.

Mme Bresil's café was patronised by all kinds of society: French locals, Russian exiles, British and American ex-patriots, all of whom gossiped and discussed their favourite topics over the bar in the evenings. They talked a lot about the need to be in Paris in order to understand 'life'.

Daisy often joined Madame, chatted with the other tenants and customers, and helped out by serving wine and coffee. She told the story of her husband's broken fortunes, embroidering and altering her history to suit her audience: her father had been distantly related to the Duke of Westminster; she had learned couture from a governess, who had once been apprenticed at the House of Worth.

Those who knew Daisy as a *modiste* thought she was tough and splendid. Ignorant of her years working in Leicester, they admired her for embarking on a career. It was unusual for a woman in her circumstances, and from her 'background', to do such a thing, even in Paris, the centre of the *avant-garde*.

Daisy, in her turn, admired the arrogance of Parisian women, so different from English behaviour. Here women had an egotism that edged on insolence; and Paris *chic* had little to do with dressing appropriately, or knowing the correct procedure in society. She copied the best of what she observed, spent money on her own clothes, on dining in restaurants, and buying good wine, and flowers for her apartment. She gave the impression of knowing how to live well, and, because she was lively and outspoken and looked glamorous, she began to make friends among the wealthy.

* * *

It was some time after the discovery of the treasures of Tutankhamun's tomb, when the craze for all things Egyptian had infected the theatre, that Daisy went one evening with a party of friends to the Folies Bergère.

By nature indifferent to nurturing, Daisy in her thirties nevertheless looked maternal, and her clothes reflected her style: large, flowing, showy. She loved velvet and silk, embroidery and beads. She exuded a sensuality that attracted men to her side. Daisy enjoyed the company of men, liked being taken to dinner, going to the cinema, cabarets, and to jazz clubs that played American music and brought back memories of rare nights out with Clem; but she was sure that she would never again feel passion for a man, and she had vowed that she would never again fall prey to love.

As she watched the tableaux of dancing girls, and mock pharaohs and sphinxes at the Folies, ideas for a collection of garments incorporating lotus flowers and scarabs, in brilliant blues and greens, hummed in her mind.

On the way out, turning on the stairs, Daisy trod on the hem of her evening dress. An Englishman she recognised, whose social circle and hers often converged, caught her just as she was about to fall.

Athletic, a graceful dresser, and a sophisticate of Mephistophelean good looks, Alex Nash-Parkes had a reputation as a man about town and a lover of women; Daisy knew that he was intrigued by her solitary reputation, and that he viewed her as a challenge.

"Thank you." She felt the support of his hand on her elbow. "You did that very well."

"I have medals for it."

She glanced at the hand still holding

her arm, and waited for him to release her. "Yes, so I've heard."

"I understood you were always hard at work creating a fashion business, attracting rich American customers, and therefore impervious to gossip, Mrs Carr."

"All *modistes* listen to gossip. One never knows when it might come in useful."

"So, what else have you heard about me?" he said, clearly flattered, and with a smile lazily curving the dark line of his moustache.

The friends with Daisy began fussing about taxis as they reached the street. Ignoring Nash-Parkes's question, irritated by the confusion, Daisy decided she would walk. "It's such a warm evening. No — " She brushed off protests. "Of course I shall be perfectly safe walking alone."

"Would you let *me* walk with you?" said Alex. "Is it a long way?"

"Quite far." Daisy set off, careless as to whether he accompanied her or not.

"So — what have you heard about me?" he repeated, walking beside her with his hands in his pockets.

"That you're pretty fast. That you have a comfortable income. You are sexually experienced, and have expensive tastes in clothes and in women — and in the clothes you buy for your women."

He gave a pained exclamation of protest. "That is very blunt."

"If you don't like it, Mr Nash-Parkes, you don't have to walk with me."

"Alex. Please, call me Alex."

Daisy did not answer, she was glad to be out in the open and wished he would stop talking. He was personable, and entertaining, and, despite what she had said, she liked what she knew of him; but her mind was racing with ideas for her designs and she would have preferred to be alone.

"The Americans seem fond of you," he ventured. "My friend, Mrs Belmain, talks about you to everyone."

"I amuse her because I make elegant clothes as well as the French can. The Americans like me because I am not quite one of them, but when they're with me they don't have to talk French or struggle to understand what I'm saying.

People are lazy. Aren't you the same? I know I prefer talking English when I can."

"So, you don't mind talking to me?"

"Are you going to buy something for your mistress?"

"I don't have one at the moment."

"Then you're no use to me, Mr Nash-Parkes."

They walked for a while in silence. Daisy was used to the signs that preceded a seduction attempt, and she was sure that his goal was to seduce her, but he seemed unsure how to proceed with his campaign.

He settled for the rather feeble, "You're a fascinating woman, Mrs Carr — Marguerite."

She halted. "Why do you say that? Because you want to flatter me? Or because you hope, when you *do* bring your mistress to be clothed by Maison Clem, that you'll get better terms?"

"I don't think I shall recommend any woman to come to you at all, if you're going to reject all my attempts at normal conversation," he said irritably.

Daisy laughed at him slyly. "That's

better. Show yourself in your true colours."

"Don't you want me to recommend you as a couturière?"

"Of course I do. But for the right reasons. I don't want you to tell me I'm *fascinating*. I want you to admire my work."

Reaching the Rue Vivienne, Daisy walked more quickly, so that he had to hurry to keep up with her when they neared the solid outline of the Bourse.

"You know?" Daisy said, turning suddenly. "I have only recently begun to appreciate this city properly. I used to think Paris meant only the fashion houses, and later, that it was all that noisy, seedy exhilaration of the boulevards, or the Montmartre nightclubs, or the Folies. But this — " She halted suddenly. "This *quiet* on a summer evening amidst the intimacy of the buildings is what it's all about." She looked at him. "You don't understand what I'm talking about, do you? You like to live in Paris because of its glitter and charm."

"You enjoy fashionable society as well. You want to have rich, exotic clients, and a salon in the Rue de la Paix."

She shrugged, but did not contradict him, and they walked on until they reached the streets near the Palais Royal.

He stopped and lit a cigar. There was a velvety silence among the buildings, and the scent of cigar smoke drifted towards Daisy.

"Do you often walk alone at night?" he said.

"When I need to think. If I have a problem to work out."

"And you have a problem now?"

She turned to him, and saw that he was conceited enough to assume it might be connected with himself.

"I'm trying to translate the costumes I saw tonight into something I can use in the workroom."

"Ah — I see."

He was disappointed.

"People say you're very absorbed by your dressmaking. That you really do have ambitions about rivalling the big couturiers."

"Yes. I have. Is there anything wrong with that?"

"Life isn't all work."

"It is for me. I have a child to raise and educate. Life can be hard for a widow without means. My husband wasn't a careful man. He enjoyed a luxurious lifestyle, spending money, incurring debts."

"If you disapprove of people who spend money, why do you want to make clothes for the rich?"

"Because people who are *not* rich appreciate only the mediocre. It's all they can afford, so it's all they aspire to. I want people to come to me for style, regardless of cost, I want them to be excited by me."

"I am excited by you."

She turned to him and, seeing a look that she recognised, held out her hand in a gesture of dismissal.

"Thank you, Alex, for walking home with me."

"Shall I see you?" he called as she walked away.

"Come and buy something from me one day," Daisy called over her shoulder.

★ ★ ★

"I've heard Alex Nash-Parkes is madly in love with you," said one of Daisy's customers a few weeks later.

Daisy laughed. "It's news to me. I hardly know him."

"Apparently he talks of nothing else these days but your style and vitality and your *strong character*."

"Does he indeed?" Daisy smiled, but she was flattered.

"By *strong character*, I suppose he means he has not had any success in seducing you."

"Mrs Belmain, you are wicked." Daisy adjusted the drape of the bodice on her client and stepped back with an expression of satisfaction. So many of her customers disappointed her by being too skinny, with the tubular, androgenous look that was in vogue. Or else they were too heavy, with rolls of flesh on their upper arms and backs, or they wanted a dress that was conventional and 'reasonable in price'. How did one make such clients appear elegant? She was so limited by having to make reasonable clothes for a middle-class, often middle-aged clientele, when she wanted to experiment, to show everyone what she could do.

Mrs Belmain was different. Full-figured and yet chic, she was willing to experiment with Daisy's suggestions — here a bright jade and turquoise dress with Egyptian-inspired panels, abstract, jazzy and exciting. What was more, the American woman was spreading the word about Daisy's bright and exotic clothes to her friends.

"You could do worse than encourage Nash-Parkes," Mrs Belmain went on, lowering her voice. "He is worth — " and she named a sum of several thousand pounds a year. "Aren't you interested? He's very amusing. He could be very useful to you — he knows *tout Paris*."

★ ★ ★

Daisy was experimenting with a toile on a wooden dummy, draping the fabric on to the body and pinning the bodice, when Alex came to her workroom.

Checking her face and hair in the mirror, and hastily tidying the workroom, Daisy realised that Mrs Belmain had been performing the role of go-between for him.

"People usually make an appointment," she reprimanded from the doorway as he came up the final flight of stairs.

"I'm sorry. I had to see you."

"Are you here on business?"

"You said you wanted me to admire your work, and I realised that I couldn't do that unless I had seen rather more of it."

He stood with his hat in his hand, looking curiously shy.

"If you have something in mind, for one of your friends, she will have to make an appointment for a fitting."

He nodded. "But first I have to know that she will like what she sees."

Daisy led him into the *atelier*. Lit by cold north-facing windows, the toiles and finished garments hung on wooden mannequins, each with a polished round knob instead of a head.

She went back to moulding the toile on to the mannequin, adjusting the bodice, then pinning the sleeve.

"May I watch you work?"

"I start with a sketch," Daisy explained,

as if he had asked for a lecture as well as a demonstration. "But the best part is when I come to working with the toile, turning the original idea into an actual garment."

He did not answer, and she went on talking, needing to fill the silence. His visit was too close a reminder of other visits to her workroom years ago, stirring memories of Clem. It was disturbing to be alone with a man to whom she knew, if she was honest about her response to him, she was attracted.

"Once you understand the way a garment moulds to the body — the disposition of the weight, and the way a human body moves — then you can begin to experiment," she went on; but she sensed that he was watching her, rather than observing the way she pinned the toile. She became conscious of her appearance, dressed in the latest fashion, as always when she was working, because it was important to show clients how her garments should be worn; how could any *modiste* convince a client of a fit if she herself were wearing some old rag or sad little dress?

She wore her hair bobbed and shingled,

and an eau-de-nil V-necked dress made of chiffon silk, with a blouson top tied at the hip.

"You don't like collars," he said suddenly.

Instinctively, Daisy's hand touched her bare throat.

"Collars detract from the face and from the line and flow of a garment. The neck is one of the most beautiful parts of a woman's body," she added, remembering that it was Clem who had first told her so, as she turned the dummy to face him. "A well-turned neck is more aesthetically pleasing than anything. And, to enhance it, a dress should have simplicity."

"With a hint of richness."

"Oh, yes, there must be a richness of fabric and a sensuous quality — provocative even — but the style should be elegant, fluid. There are so many beautiful fabrics to work with, you know. Velvets, chiffon, georgette — "

"I'm sorry if I implied the other day that you were only interested in making money."

"Did you? I didn't notice."

496

"I can see now that you're in love with what you are doing."

"I love everything to do with the business. But you shouldn't romanticise too much about it. The money-making aspect of it is as important to me as the designing. And necessary. I was serious when I said I have to raise my child."

"Of course. Your daughter. How old is she?"

"Five."

"Where is she now?"

"Willow has started attending a school outside Paris, she comes home at the weekends." Daisy returned her attention to the garment, not wanting to talk too intimately about her child.

"Don't you miss her?"

"Not when I'm working. Willow would only be in the way, and she would get upset because she would want me to give her all my attention, and I don't find that possible. I don't want to talk about this. Tell me about your friend. When can she come for a fitting?"

"It's you. I want to buy an evening dress for you, and then I would like to take you out to dinner."

"You mean you want me to be your mistress."

"I am crazy for you, Marguerite. I've fallen in love with you."

Daisy's throat tightened as memories of Clem threatened to swamp her. Alex came close to her, and she fiddled again with the toile.

"No," she murmured. "I'm flattered, Alex. But, no."

"You can't really still be in love with your husband after all this time."

"He was very special."

He hesitated, with an air of beguiling uncertainty. "May I kiss you?"

She turned to him. Seeing the expression in his eyes, and feeling a response, she was afraid.

"No. I don't think so."

"What is it? Why won't you let yourself go? Work isn't everything. You need someone. Everyone needs somebody."

"You're wrong. I don't need a man to make my life worth living. But I should like to think we were friends."

"Very well." His tone became peevish, and she realised that he was not used to being rejected.

She was angry with herself after he had gone. Alex was wealthy, charming, and good company; but how could she, even for a moment, have compared him to Clem? Besides, she did not want to go through all that again.

* * *

The long summer meant that Willow was at home from school. Daisy did not find it easy working with a demanding child on the premises.

"I should never have been a mother," she told Mme Bresil. "I never was a serene, consoling kind of female, and there are other things in life besides children. I simply can't do what is expected of me."

Did that mean she was not a proper woman, or that she was a bad mother? Daisy regarded Willow's attachment to Marie-Cécile and Mme Bresil with feelings of guilt, blocking her ears when she needed to work so that she would not hear the child's chatter, or listen to her crying. Sometimes she wondered whether this guilt was not worse than the guilt she would have felt if she had simply gone through with another abortion?

"You should spend more of your time with her," protested Mme Bresil. "Marie-Cécile is almost grown up now, she is too old to be a playmate for her."

Was it possible to combine her dressmaking business with motherhood? Daisy told herself she could not discard her hopes and ambitions. She needed all her energies for her designs, for building up a clientele so that Willow would not starve, and so that she could send her to one of the good boarding schools recommended by her clients. How could she pay attention to her daughter, when she needed so much time for herself? She could not become like her own mother, a nobody, downtrodden, passive about everything except doing right by her children.

★ ★ ★

Willow had learned as she grew older to avoid her distant, often volatile and sarcastic mother. But there were moments, magic hours, when, though

500

she was tired, Daisy would curl up at the foot of her bed and tell her stories. And the stories Willow liked best were the ones about when her father was alive.

Willow knew that her father had been a very handsome man, wealthy and clever, and loved by everyone who knew him.

He and Maman had lived in a beautiful house somewhere in the English Midlands. The house was old and very large, with lots of rooms, tasteful furniture, and a number of servants. Outside, the gardens were full of flowers, with many, many varieties of scented roses. There were green paddocks too, and stables smelling of saddle-soap and leather where Papa had kept his horses, not only hunters, but race-horses, selected from Arab stock, which had won races on several occasions.

"Tell me their names," Willow would beg, burrowing into her pillows, seeing them all with their noble faces over the stable doors, taking sugar lumps from Papa's hand.

"Diamond," Daisy would begin. "Lucky Boy." Inventing and reciting the names easily, seeing them too, the horses at

Noonby, and the gardens full of flowers, and the acres of estate and farmland.

"And my favourite of them all," Daisy always finished. "Rosy Future, who won every race she ever ran."

She was Willow's favourite too. She loved to hear about her father's race-horses; she was always sad when they came to the part in the story where they all had to be sold after his death, because Papa had been cheated in business and had lost so much money. She had cried the first time Maman told her. But she never cried over the story of how Papa was killed. He was so brave and handsome in his riding jacket and knee breeches, riding Rosy Future out one autumn morning. Cantering home across the fields, he had reached the last gate and decided to set his horse at it and, superb horseman though he was, he had lost his balance as the horse landed awkwardly and his head hit a heavy stone.

"Rosy Future was brave too," said Willow. "Because she headed straight for home and brought help."

"Yes," agreed her mother. "Rosy

Future was brave, but it was all too late . . . ”

Daisy always finished abruptly at this point in the story, and for Willow the magic was over.

* * *

Daisy had leased rooms in a house in the Rue St Honoré and installed cutting tables and a team of cutters and seamstresses. With a sense of pure nostalgia she called the salon Maison Clem.

From time to time she saw Alex Nash-Parkes; whenever he was staying in Paris he would visit, and she went with him to restaurants, the theatre and the racetrack at Longchamps. Though he had settled for friendship with her, Daisy was aware that he was unhappy about it. Perhaps it was not satisfactory for either of them; but she did not pity him; if it was sex he wanted, she knew he would not go unconsoled.

Daisy had adapted unwillingly to the post-war changes in fashion, accepting cubism, futurism, modernism and all the other 'isms' that were in vogue, yet looking back with nostalgia to a time of narrow waists and corsets, of richness and romance. Among the big names in the fashion industry she admired very few: Coco Chanel because she had clawed her way to fame, though Daisy detested the uniformity of beige and her 'little black dress'. She respected Patou with his sense of dignity; Molyneux, who was dashing and debonair; and Madeleine Vionnet, whose clever bias cut everyone admired and imitated.

Daisy loved the bias cut and thought it profoundly elegant, copying it, and the mode for shorter skirts, but when hems rose to the knee she called a halt. Knees, she said, were ugly, vulgar. She compromised, extending a dress to the calf or ankle with panels and drapes, offering only a glimpse of stocking.

She adored intense colours: jade and cerise, acid yellow and eau-de-nil. She covered her dresses with beading, jewels and embroidery, and stuck to her insistence on the importance of the neckline. She became renowned for her collarless, richly decorated blouses and jackets, with V-shaped or wide low necks.

One season, she had a passion for pyjama suits and chiffon trousers; another, for skirts and jackets that reflected cubist art and Art Deco. But as the decade wore on, suspicious of new trends, Daisy was sometimes afraid that she was getting left behind, already *passé*. Was she getting old, losing her touch? In her heart she deplored the neglect of curves, and the loss of femininity inherent in the pencil-straight modern styles.

In the summer that Willow was nine and Daisy approaching forty, she employed more staff and leased a further workroom round the corner from the building in the Rue St Honoré, unaware that within a matter of months the Wall Street crash would deplete Paris of many of its American customers.

"If you need money, you only have to ask," Alex offered one day, after a series of poor seasons.

He leaned on the window-sill, looking down into the street, where the sound of traffic rose in distant, muffled tones. He looked fit and debonair and it was flattering to know that he was still interested in her.

"I could buy Maison Clem — you've never told me why you chose that name?"

"An admirer. It was a very long time ago."

"And you still retain some affection? How touching. Would you name something after me if I put some money into the business?" He turned to her and smiled his most wolfish smile.

"Don't you think I might be better off without your interference?"

"I would be an asset. I could help you get over this little hiccup."

"It's very kind of you, Alex, but I've managed very well on my own so far. I should like to keep it that way."

"Come away with me to the Riviera for the summer. Leave all this behind."

Daisy laughed, but she was pleased to have him around again; and he stayed in Paris for her summer collection; he was magnanimous, whipping up interest for her fashion show among his many acquaintances and filling the rooms with flowers for her — marguerites and lilies.

★ ★ ★

"Don't sway from side to side when you talk to people," Daisy murmured in Willow's ear. "You look coy and silly."

Willow stiffened her back to attention. She hated her mother for exposing her to the public gaze in a cerise dress tied with a green sash, her blonde hair cut in a solid fringe. She had been conscripted with one of the workroom assistants into showing guests to their seats. Clients were shown up to Daisy's salon via a hushed and padded lift and guided to their places on gilt chairs with red plush cushions. Women in furs blew kisses across the room to one another, scrutinised Daisy's collection with their heads tipped back, and made notes on their programmes as the models walked and pivoted in front of them.

Willow was aware that she did not fit into her mother's life now, any more than she had when she was tiny. She never knew where she was with a mother whose moods were mercurial, who could switch affection on or, more frequently, off when she was distracted by work, or ideas, or anything that interested her more.

Maman liked her to speak English, but it did not come naturally to her. "This is nice," Willow had said one day, touching a finished evening dress on a stand.

"Sound the 't — h'. Say 'This', not 'Zis'. And don't use the word nice," Daisy told Willow testily. "How I hate anything being called pretty or nice. If that's all you've got to say about it, don't say anything."

"But it *is* nice." Willow had caught the eye of one of the assistants, who winked at her.

The gesture of sympathy made her bolder than usual. "What should I say about it then?"

"Don't they teach you any decent English vocabulary at your school? Say something about the character of the dress, the style, its allure and elegance, but never that it is *nice*."

"I am bored. There is nothing to do," Willow had complained, wandering around the workrooms, picking up scraps of fabric and putting them down again, trying swatches of silk against her face in the mirrors.

"Then find something. Only boring people feel bored."

Willow had gone in search of allies at the Café Bresil; and Marie-Cécile, who was soon to be married, had taken her under her wing again; but Willow longed for her mother to take some notice of her.

She was so unhappy in the holidays, deprived of the friends she had made at her school in Normandy where she now boarded full time. Willow looked forward to the times at the end of the day, when, if she stayed awake for long enough, Maman would come home to the apartment at the top of the house above the café and carry on working. Daisy would make sketches until the early hours of the morning, playing gramophone records, like 'Always', and 'Bye Bye Blackbird', which Willow adored. Sometimes, if she was tired, or there was no pressing need to work, Daisy would notice that Willow's lamp was lit and sit on her bed and talk to her.

"Your father died a good death," she said one night, persuaded to talk about the house in England again, and suffering a wave of remorse, aware of her neglect. She had handed Willow a cup of chocolate and plumped up the pillows behind her.

"Papa wouldn't want us to be sad about the accident. He didn't like people to be sad, or miserable, or *bored*."

A rebuke because of her remarks in the workroom, thought Willow. Maman always had to spoil things by reminding her that she had behaved badly, or that she had said something silly, or done something that was clumsy and so had displeased her. But she had savoured the hot chocolate and felt with her toes under the chocolate, seeking reassurance from the scraps of sequined silk she had managed to steal from Maison Clem. Willow collected a strong *cache* every holiday: beads and sequins, to be strung together into necklaces for using as bribes among her friends when she returned to school, but most of all, for wearing when Maman was not looking.

Willow adored nice clothes.

She would love to have paraded at Maman's fashion show, gliding across the room just like the salon's models, elegant in eau-de-nil, or dramatic in black, instead of standing about in ghastly cerise, chosen for her by Maman. The only consolation about the whole event had been the arrival of Alex, who treated her as if she were ten years older than she really was, and who had told her as she showed him to a seat, that she looked 'heavenly' and had 'made his day'.

But Willow was aware that it was her mother who always completed any occasion for Alex. He adored her. All the men adored Maman; she could see it in the way they followed her about with their eyes.

In a waisted and flared chiffon floral print afternoon dress, Daisy looked very regal. Her collection celebrated the return of more curvaceous styles and the renaissance of romantic elegance, showing a wistful yearning in the use of fabrics such as velvet and filmy chiffons.

Everyone crowded round her when the show was over, wanting to be the first to congratulate her, and to do it more loudly than anyone else, talking with little nods of the head and gasping exclamations.

"*Un succès fou!*" "*Comme c'est magnifique.*" "Darling! You're so clever."

★ ★ ★

Daisy acknowledged the compliments with a tilt of her head.

Alex arrived by her side and took her arm, murmuring in her ear. "Marguerite, you are marvellous. Marry me. Tomorrow. Soon. I adore you."

Daisy saw that he was serious.

He moved away to talk to Mrs Belmain, and, weakening for a moment, Daisy considered the idea of marrying him.

She looked at the women in the salon, so good at looking well-groomed and at laughing in a charming manner. Their predictable conversation revolved around the latest social tittle-tattle, or comments about new books, films, and personalities — all of it secondhand. They made life wretched for their husbands, and would have done so for her too a few years ago, if she had been their little dressmaker in Leicester, and if she were the kind of woman to be easily intimidated.

Was this really what she had wanted and worked for all these years: the acclaim, and money to spend as she pleased? Sometimes, when she looked at her clients, Daisy was aware of a gnawing fear that she might become like them, was perhaps already like them, blowing air kisses, saying everything was 'too, too divine'.

Perhaps she should simply give in and become Alex's mistress, before it was too late and he no longer wanted her. There were times when she missed that side of a relationship with a man, and it was tempting to let his blandishments sway her; he was witty and stylish, and his money would be useful.

Alex took her out to dinner that evening and again he asked her to marry him.

"Darling, you know how much I would hate being married," she told him lightly. "I'm not in the slightest bit suited to domesticity. My whole life is devoted to clothes."

"I could give you all of that. You could spend money on every luxury you desired."

"I mean *my* clothes. I need to work."

"If you married me, you wouldn't need to do anything except look divine and be my wife."

"I mean, I *need* to — "

She realised he did not really understand. For all his offers of support, Alex did not really take her very seriously. But the temptation was there. Why not give in? She was over forty, growing tired of the struggle of commerce, and the hours that one had to put into the design and construction of every garment.

"You misjudged me when you once said I was only attracted to the Paris that glitters," Alex said. "Do you remember, when we were younger, you talked of what made Paris beautiful for you? The quiet intimacy of summer evenings? I have experienced heart-stopping moments too. The view from the Butte of Montmartre at night. The river, and the lights of the barges. The sudden deep tranquillity of an oasis of trees — "

"You sound as if you've only recently experienced them."

"It's true. I've done a lot of walking and thinking recently. Marguerite, what

514

is all the success in the world worth, if in the end that's all you have? I should know. My own personal life has been a failure."

"But not mine. I have my child."

The words rang hollow. He knew her too well; he was aware that when she thought of Willow it was with irritation, and that all too often the child returned her rare gestures of maternal affection with hostility and resentment.

"Marry me. For Willow's sake. Give the girl the stability she needs. She's fond of me. I could be a good father to her."

Daisy shook her head. She would not marry a man she did not really love, least of all for the reasons he suggested.

"I'm sorry, Alex, truly I am. I don't want a husband. I have never wanted marriage. For me it would be a trap. I've always felt that way about it."

"But you have *been* married," he said with a light laugh and a look of hurt puzzlement.

Daisy hesitated. For the first time in years she had forgotten her supposed widowhood.

She found herself stumbling over

words. "I mean — it *was* a trap."

"No. You said — you've *never* wanted marriage."

"Well, of course, when I was first married — "

He watched her, amazed at her confusion; he had never seen her anything but sure of herself.

"I've always thought you were happy in your marriage. Why was it a trap?"

"It's simply how I feel."

"You don't mean that at all. What is it?" Slowly, understanding dawned. "You never were — that's it, isn't it? Willow, poor kid, is a love-child."

"He was married already," Daisy said quietly. "I hardly ever saw him."

"Is he dead?"

"Not as far as I know."

"Was it the man you named the salon after?"

Frightened at revealing so much of herself, Daisy fell back on the security of lies. "No. Clem was a girlhood affair." She plucked a name out of the air. "I met — Leonard after the war."

"A married man who let you bring up his child all by yourself? Am I really so

516

objectionable that I couldn't make you as happy as he did?"

"I'm sorry, Alex. I'm very fond of you."

They could not finish the meal, and left the restaurant.

"What are you going to do?" Daisy tried to imagine the spread of the story among her friends and clients.

"I shan't talk. You needn't worry. I think too much about Willow to do anything to hurt her."

"I should never have told you."

"On the contrary, you should have trusted me ages ago. I thought, at least, we were close enough friends for that."

They walked on past the lighted windows of cafés and restaurants where people sat, laughing, talking, getting on with their lives. "I suppose that's all over now," Daisy said.

He did not answer, but she guessed she had lost him.

"Aren't you frightened?" Alex said when he left her.

"Of what?"

He gave her a twisted smile. "A lonely old age?"

"Alex won't be coming to see us again," Daisy told Willow the next day. "He asked me to marry him, and I turned him down."

"Why?"

Daisy regarded her daughter, pale, pretty and antagonistic. Now that she was older, with a look of Clem in her face, it was often hard to meet her eyes. Having spent years perfecting a story that would protect Willow, Daisy now searched her heart and saw that the stories had in fact been to protect herself; she had never really forgiven Willow for being born.

"I'll tell you something," she said, needing to redress the years of neglect. "Never marry a man you don't love." She thought for a moment. "And, if you do have the good fortune to find a man you love, don't be fool enough to let him go."

"Did you love Papa?"

"Yes."

"But he died," Willow said, looking puzzled.

"What?"

"You said, don't let him go. But that isn't how it was for you. My father died."

"Yes," Daisy said, and wondered if Clem ever thought of her these days. "That's true. He died."

17

LIZ was late getting back to the Louvre from the Café Bresil. A line of fractious children waited by the fountains with Cliff, Rosemary, and Don who was fuming because everyone was hungry.

"We've been out half an hour." He spoke with iron good humour.

"I'm sorry. I'm *really* sorry. You should have had your picnic without me."

"We said one o'clock," Don reminded her patiently, as if he were talking to one of the children with whom he was, beneath the composure, extremely annoyed. "We said we wouldn't eat until we reached the Tuileries Gardens. Once we start departing from the schedule we're going to be in a muddle, people getting lost, not knowing where they're supposed to be." He turned to the expedition party. "Right. In twos. Follow Miss Harvey and Mr Evans." He added under his breath, as the crocodile moved off after Rosemary and Cliff, "What the *hell* have you been doing?"

"Striking gold!"

Excited still, her mind reverberating from the shock of her discoveries, Liz was prepared to overlook his unbearably stuffy, headmasterly attitude.

"Listen, you won't believe this — " She paused for maximum effect. "*Willow* is *Daisy's* daughter."

To give him credit, for a moment he looked surprised.

"Isn't it amazing?" Liz said, as they brought up the rear of the school procession.

"Yes, isn't it? I just think you might have been more considerate about keeping to the time we all agreed."

"Don — I couldn't leave! I'd met someone who knew all about her. There's this gorgeous, very twenties little café where she lived. With Willow! Her daughter. I still can't believe it. I mean, I thought they were simply friends."

"Who was the father?"

She stared at him. "Clem, of course."

"Do you know that?"

"Do I — ?" She could not believe he

521

was being so stupid, nor so phlegmatic about it when questions crowded her own imagination in a hurried jumble. Had Clem known, for instance, about Willow being his daughter? Why was Willow so bitter and so cryptic about everything?

"For all we can tell, Daisy may have had a succession of lovers," Don said, more cheerful now as they neared the Tuileries and the children were running towards the benches.

"No. Clem was the big love of her life," insisted Liz. "Willow said as much. She never got over him."

"Well, Willow *would* say that if she wanted to build a romantic myth around fairly dodgy circumstances. She probably never knew which of her mother's lovers her father was."

"No. The dates fit too well. Willow was born soon after Daisy arrived in France. Lewis Brackenborough said that Daisy and Clem were lovers for ages before that; she must have run away to Paris when she found out she was expecting his child. She went without telling him."

"You don't *know* that." He seemed

determined to demolish the romance. "You're making assumptions on the basis of something his wife told their grandson years later. Daisy probably announced she was pregnant, and he simply wasn't interested."

"But Clem wasn't that sort of man."

He looked at her with mocking disbelief. Did she really imagine she knew anything about people whose lives were played out decades ago?

Feeling deflated, Liz went to eat her lunch on a bench with the children, preferring their unsophisticated conversation to Don's cynicism.

* * *

That evening, the children packed for the home journey and Rosemary and Cliff undertook nanny duty from the hotel bar; they were holding hands with their heads close together, as Don and Liz left them and took the metro into Paris.

"Did you know that was happening?" said Liz.

"Paris has that effect on people. Hadn't

you heard? Besides he's always been keen on her."

"I hadn't noticed a thing."

"You've been preoccupied," Don said grimly. "No more Daisy this evening. We are not spending all night at the Café Bresil."

"Come with me at least to the Rue St Honoré," Liz said. "I want to look at the couture house. It's not there any more, but I want to see the building and try to imagine how it was before the war; Daisy would have been at the height of her career."

★ ★ ★

The buildings on the street gave no clues as they walked, looking up at the blank, unrevealing upper storeys. How did one recognise an extinct fashion house nearly sixty years later?

Liz halted.

"Is this it?"

"I think so." She was nervous, wanting the atmosphere of the street to come up to her expectations, not because of Don — she did not care about losing face, only about spoiling her illusions.

There was a numbered door in the wall with a heavy iron grille over the panels. Liz pushed tentatively but it did not yield.

"Can you imagine it, the clients coming and going?"

"Quite frankly, no." Don saw only a series of shop windows and an anonymous building reaching up to the night sky.

"Daisy achieved her goal here."

Don indicated a nearby window displaying audio equipment. "There's authenticity for you."

"Well, of course things have changed," Liz snapped. "Other generations have taken over."

"You're disappointed. You thought you'd find ghosts."

"No." He had misunderstood completely. "I want to find evidence of *real* lives. Not ghosts. I want proof that Daisy Cornforth lived and breathed and amounted to more than an Edwardian girl in a provocative pose, encased in immobilising stays."

They walked away, towards the river

and along by the heavy grey mass of the Louvre.

"It means a lot to you, this search for Daisy, doesn't it?" said Don uncertainly.

"I thought I could identify with her. Now I'm not so sure."

"Hard to adjust to the idea of Daisy as a loving mother as well as a business woman?"

"Yes. I suppose so." All that day, Liz had been digesting the biggest reversal of all. "I don't know why I've been so surprised about her having a child. In those days women hadn't much choice about whether or not to have babies. If they had sex they ran the risk of getting pregnant."

"So what's the problem?"

"I thought she was an example of independent feminism, a dedicated career woman. Now I've got to admire her even more, because she managed to combine motherhood *and* a career. And she did it all alone and in a foreign country. That must have taken some courage."

"She looks a gutsy enough lady in her photo."

They crossed the river, leaning on

the rail of the Pont des Arts in the darkness.

"You don't like her, do you?" Liz said.

"Perhaps I'm jealous because she's occupied so much of your attention lately."

Liz lifted her face to his. "Silly."

They kissed, and were comfortable with one another again.

"Have I been taking you too much for granted this week?" Don said.

"A bit." Liz had seen a side to him, an I-am-in-charge, headmaster persona not previously encountered, and she was not sure that she liked it.

"I'm sorry. I *am* grateful. You've been great with the children. I know you didn't really want to come."

"I wouldn't have found things out about Daisy if I hadn't."

"Yes. I'm glad you found what you wanted."

But it wasn't what she had wanted at all, Liz thought. It was difficult to accept the new Daisy.

He folded his arm round her and she leaned her head on his shoulder. A *bateau mouche* approached with lights and music and the sounds of people enjoying themselves; its engine throbbed as it passed under the bridge, people waved at them, and they waved back.

Proper lovers would have been too absorbed in one another to notice the boat and its din, or the swell of water breaking in its wake, thought Liz. Were they in love? She looked at Don in the half light. They would *make* love when they returned to the hotel, and, in the weeks to come, when Don was back at school, and she in her office, putting the finishing touches to her book about the corset and its restrictive influence on women's lives, they would remember with nostalgia and a strong sense of romance the lights of the islands, the buildings on either side of the water, and the river boats reflected in the river.

The thing is, thought Liz as they walked on slowly towards the Left Bank, if Daisy could do it in the twenties — run a couture house, keep her individuality — with all the drawbacks of a hostile climate towards career women, why am I so afraid that motherhood would change me? If Daisy could bring up a child alone *and* have a career, why should I, with a supportive family, and a man beside me who desires nothing more than to be a loving husband and father, go in fear of being torn apart by conflicting demands? I have Don. Daisy had nobody.

"I've learned *something* at least from coming to Paris," she said, tucking her arm through his.

"About Daisy?"

"About me. I'm not so afraid of children as I thought I was."

"Could Toby Wyman have something to do with it?"

"He's partly responsible. For the first time, I've really seen children as people with minds that are interesting — fascinating." She felt Don's arm tighten under her hand.

"Does that mean you might be having a change of heart?"

"I don't know." Liz was suddenly afraid of shifting her ground too quickly.

"Eight hours on a coach with the little blighters will soon change it back again."

She squeezed his arm, grateful for his sense of caution.

"I love you, Liz. I want whatever you want."

"I know," she said guiltily.

★ ★ ★

The restaurants in the Latin quarter overflowed on to the pavements, and there was a festive atmosphere among the crowds that strolled from bistro to bistro and sat at the little tables. At a junction of streets a greasy-haired man with an accordion played for the tourists, while a girl in jeans and a T-shirt sang a French love song in a rich, throaty voice.

Don laughed at Liz's open-mouthed, smiling happiness.

"I love it," she said. "Everything. I wish we didn't have to go home tomorrow. Let's come back soon."

They found a vacant table and ordered wine and a *plat*, listening to the jostling conversations and distant music. Liz felt as if she were twenty-five and newly in love again. She drank red wine greedily and wondered how she could ever have taken life so seriously as to brood for

530

weeks and months about something as simple as being loved and loving someone back. She thought of Daisy, and felt sorry for her because of losing Clem; she felt sorry too for Clem's wife, because he had been in love with another woman; and for Willow, who was all alone, after knowing perfect happiness married to Albert.

"They were related," she said, thinking aloud. "Willow and Albert were related. She married her mother's cousin."

"There's no law against it." Don poured them both more wine.

"I just hadn't thought about it until now. Could that be why she didn't want to admit that Daisy was her mother? Some atavistic sense of taboo?"

"Liz — " He took her hand and stroked the fingers. "Do we have to talk about Daisy *all* the time? There are other, more important things right now."

She slurped the warm red wine, and the little candles on the red-checked tablecloths wavered and flattered people's eyes, and made their skin glow. She was beginning to feel as if she were in love with everyone: the singers on

531

the street corner churning out a flood of sentimentality, the waiters weaving in and out of the tables without knocking into them, the middle-aged couple on the next table eating stolidly through *choucroute* and *saucisses*.

"Why don't we stop pretending we're not sure about each other after all this time?"

"Is this another proposal?"

"Oh, what the hell if it is? Let's just do it," said Don. "We're in our thirties, not teenagers. We know what we're doing."

All the more reason for caution, thought Liz.

But the place and the mood and the atmosphere were seductive. Oh, what the hell, a more reckless side of her echoed. She raised her glass and grazed it against his knuckles.

"All right."

"You'll marry me."

She nodded, smiling. "If you like."

18

WAS it so impossible for men and women simply to be friends? The thought made Daisy wary of male company, so that her circle had become almost exclusively female.

Yet Willow hovered on the edge of womanhood with neither encouragement nor friendship from her mother, and when Daisy did pay attention to her, it was with a marked accent on criticism.

"My mother hates me," Willow would tell the women who worked at the salon, after Daisy had tossed a volley of biting sarcasm in her direction; she chattered in French to the models, and to the cutters and seamstresses when Daisy was not there. The women were sympathetic; Daisy was an autocratic employer; she was mean with wages, and could be as unpleasant to them as she was to Willow.

One of Daisy's workers, a Jewess, was

closer to her than any of the others; she had trained in England and learned there to cut and construct a toile; it was Sabine who, as Daisy's chief *vendeuse*, attended to the most important customers.

"Your mother does not hate you," she said to Willow one day. "Marguerite is jealous, and so am I, because you are young and beautiful, and, alas, your mother and I are growing older."

"Me — beautiful?" Willow smothered her mouth to prevent the ugly burst of laughter from escaping, and so proving she was vulgar. "Maman says I look like a giraffe."

"Your mother doesn't want you to become bigheaded," Sabine interrupted. "But we should not always listen so much to the ones who are closest to us. You, my darling Willow, are as graceful as your name suggests."

This unsolicited praise from a woman Willow had always admired, and who until now she had considered to be placed firmly in her mother's camp, had a profound effect on Willow's morale.

She had 'chic'? Assessing herself dispassionately, Willow saw large eyes, an unflattering, square-cut fringe of pale hair, and a figure that was perhaps, after all, more stylish than gauche if she were to throw back her shoulders and did not try to hide her breasts. It was as if Sabine had helped to free her from her crippling awe of her mother.

It was Sabine who, when Willow was fifteen, persuaded Daisy that she should model the house garments, saying that she ought to be usefully employed in the holidays, instead of wilting with boredom.

Showing the salon's outfits in public, Willow forgot to be self-conscious. She adored dresses with soft, wide shoulders, and long jackets encrusted with embroidery and beads that swung against her hips as she moved. She enjoyed putting on the detached insouciance of the mannequin, imitating the house's permanent models, Fleur and Lisette and Tipi; it made her feel strong and defiant. She enjoyed the quickly disguised expression of surprise and envy on Maman's face when she first saw her wearing a Maison Clem dress.

At fifteen, Willow was learning more than one kind of sophistication; she knew at school how to swear effectively, had learned to suck peppermints to disguise the smell of cigarettes, and she and her friends flirted with the men, with brown chests and muscled arms, who hauled the boats on the nearby canal, just enough for their own excitement, without giving anything of themselves away.

By the time she was sixteen, Willow had cut her hair in a more flattering style, and she began to attract the same attention the older models claimed from male buyers, the husbands and lovers of the clients who came to Maison Clem, and the playboys with time on their hands, who sent flowers and made ambiguous offers of protection. But Willow rejected them all, preferring the company of girls and boys of her own age when she was in Paris, discussing politics, art and love at the café tables, and blowing insolent smoke rings at passers-by.

Many young men fell for Willow's air of youthful sophistication, but there was one, a Jew called Philippe, whose animated conversation, long slow looks of adoration, and the touch of whose hands and furtive kisses she cared about more than the rest.

There was a growing unease in Paris; people were dividing into Right and Left, anti-communist, or those opposed to the totalitarianism of Fascism. Everyone seemed disillusioned with governments; and the older generation were afraid of another European war that might rival the carnage of 1914 – 18. People were beginning to worry too about Hitler's popularity in Germany; there was a fear for friends among one's circle who were Jewish — of whom there were several in the couture business and among the salon assistants and clients.

Did Maman not know that she should be encouraging Sabine to leave in case there was a war? Had she no idea what was going on? Nobody seemed to care, thought Willow. What did it matter to them that Europe was going rotten and people like Philippe and Sabine might soon be forced to leave the country? What did her mother care about Hitler or Fascism, so long as no one interfered with her precious Maison Clem?

★ ★ ★

Willow kept her unhappiness to herself when Philippe's family set sail for New York.

She watched Daisy and Sabine fussing about Maison Clem's next collection.

"I think that's divine, Sabine, dear," Daisy said, stepping back to admire the hang of an evening dress that revealed a lot of Fleur's back and bosom. "I wonder — don't you think we should alter this panel here, a tiny, tiny fraction, yes?"

Sabine made appreciative responses.

Willow spoke harshly, interrupting them. "I suppose you know there's going to be a war."

"There's no need to panic before it happens," Daisy said, glancing at her in surprise.

"What about Sabine? She should be getting out while she can, not worrying about your next collection."

Without warning, Sabine burst into tears. Her voice broken by sobs, she told Daisy she had already decided to leave France.

Willow watched her mother's dismay with an air of righteous satisfaction.

"*If* there's a war, Maman, you and I

could be interned."

Daisy knew Willow was right; she had seen the signs of change, along with everyone else; she had even begun to consider various plans for selling up, and had called in bills and begun transferring money to London. Alex had been to see her — though they had not spoken since the day she had rejected him; he had grown very bitter after learning the truth about her supposed widowhood; she had heard that he was drinking heavily, and that he went round calling her a 'sweatshop seamstress', which was not very chivalrous, Daisy had said, pretending it did not hurt; but he had kept her secret about Willow's father, and for that she had been grateful.

"Is this a friendly call?" Daisy had asked when he came to see her. "Or have you come to insult me?"

He had given her one of his familiar smiles as he bent to kiss her hand. "You know I have always been your friend."

He had wanted to know if she had thought of leaving, and Daisy had scoffed at the idea. Did it need Alex to tell her the time had come to close the dream down? Besides, what was there for her in England?

★ ★ ★

The state of tension in the air was almost tangible on the Sunday that war was declared; and yet Paris was quiet; there was little traffic on the streets, and most of the restaurants and shops were closed, including the Café Bresil.

Out in the street Daisy gathered news where she could. People talked of long lines of traffic leaving to go south, and the sight of soldiers in uniform around the area of Maison Clem was frightening rather than reassuring.

The week that followed was one of confusion: tailors and suppliers were being called up for the army; the seamstresses at the salon were nervous, swinging from fatalistic talk of bomb attacks to a jaunty confidence in the effectiveness of the Maginot Line.

Willow returned to the Café Bresil one evening to find Alex with her mother. Hearing voices, she moved quietly on the landing.

540

"I know people are leaving, and I understand why. Believe me, there are times when I feel scared as well — " Daisy said pouring Alex a drink.

"Do you have your papers to hand?"

"Yes, and Willow's too. But it's not that simple for me. There were good reasons why I came to Paris."

"You mean, because of your 'husband'," Alex said with heavy sarcasm.

Willow felt a leap of interest as she realised that Alex was talking about her father. But why was he talking about him in such a contemptuous way?

"I've never stopped caring about you, Marguerite," Alex went on. "You'll notice I've not married."

Daisy laughed. "That's not always a sign of a broken heart."

"You claimed it was in your own case."

"No, my heart was not broken, only bruised. And, anyway, these things are never one-sided."

She dropped her voice, and sounds indicated that Alex was about to leave. But Daisy's words, and Alex's tone — so scathing when he had said 'husband' — turned themselves over in Willow's mind.

What could her mother have meant about things not being one-sided? Something to do with her husband's debts? But did being burdened with debt constitute a broken, or even a bruised, heart? The more Willow thought about it, the less it made sense. She shrank from a third possibility: that her father, her lovely, handsome father had made her mother unhappy while he had been alive. Because of marital friction? Affairs? Could that be why Alex had said 'husband' in such a derogatory way?

★ ★ ★

Daisy had felt a strong impulse to let Alex take over. What a relief it would be, for the first time in her life, to fall back on masculine support and trust in his talent for organisation. She was beginning to tire of the years of managing alone. There were aspects of her life that seemed less attractive as she grew older. Now that she had achieved all she wanted, Daisy recognised more than ever the limitations of the day-to-day business of the salon; and when she looked ahead, the future was mixed up with fears about the fate of Europe, and the evidence of her own advancing middle age.

"Leave without us," she had said in the end. "Willow and I will take our chances with Mme Bresil." And when the autumn turned out to be a period of relative calm, the so-called 'phoney war', Daisy teased Alex because she had been proved right, and everyone else had overreacted.

He came to see her again that winter; too old for the call-up, he was working in London temporarily. In the spring, he returned to Paris, to work as an interpreter with one of the news agencies. But by then, tension was mounting again with rumours and speculation, and, this time, Daisy too was uneasy.

News of the disaster at Dunkirk, and a realisation that France was about to fall apart finally jerked her into action. When Alex rang on the last evening in May, to say he had a car and was ready to leave for Bordeaux, Daisy and Willow went with him.

★ ★ ★

Willow missed Paris: the cobbled streets, the cafés, and the intimacy of the city compared with London's grey sprawl. But she learned to adapt, finding in the company of fellow refugees in Chelsea and in the local pubs a parallel with her friends in Paris.

They lived at first in hotels, adjusting to a life of getting up late, pottering the streets to pick up their rations and a newspaper and cigarettes, and wandering about the antique and secondhand clothes shops looking for bargains to beat the government 'utility' scheme. Daisy seemed wary of making permanent plans; she had no friends except for Alex, no longer knew where she belonged; and she went about with an air of apprehension that seemed unconnected with the war.

Willow was aware that her mother and Alex had become occasional lovers. But Alex returned to France that August to help get people out, and Daisy and Willow were thrown on one another's company.

Daisy had begun to invent a romantic

kind of mythology about mothers and daughters, telling everyone about the escape from Paris, saying, "Of course — Willow and I have been through such a lot together."

She had taken a flat in Chelsea, bought a sewing machine, and began making clothes for people locally in defiance of 'utility', using secondhand fabrics — chiffon, velvets and raw silk. Willow sought work modelling clothes for various manufacturers.

After a while, Willow too began to believe that there was a new closeness between them, strengthened by the wartime mood of adversity, and — when the Blitz began — listening at night together for the sirens and the heavy drone of German bombers.

Daisy refused to go underground when there was a raid, saying, "To hell with the shelter." Instead, they put a record on the wind-up gramophone and danced to Louis Armstrong and Benny Goodman, or, if the bombs were close, they hid under the table and sang to keep up their spirits.

Perhaps in England she could at last

forget the loneliness of her childhood, thought Willow. She began to believe that her mother had always wanted to be close to her, but that it had not been possible because of Maison Clem. Maman had been forced to make sacrifices for the sake of their future; she had been a widow, burdened by debts incurred by a feckless and, she remembered the conversation with Alex, perhaps even an unfaithful husband.

★ ★ ★

"Daisy? Is it really Daisy Cornforth!"

A woman in a fur coat approached the mobile canteen at Victoria, where Daisy and Willow were serving tea. Her fair hair was a little coarser than in her youth, the features sharp-edged rather than fine-boned, but the woman was unmistakably Beatty Knighton.

If Beatty had once felt bitter towards her, there were no signs of hostility now. Daisy remembered the awful scene when they had parted at Noonby — Beatty's hysteria, Clem's indecision.

"It is, isn't it? I'd have recognised

you anywhere. Good Lord. I daren't count. It must be at least thirty years. Remember how we quarrelled over Clem Brackenborough?" Beatty laughed loudly, a middle-aged woman recalling her girlhood. "Well, this is marvellous. Tell me about yourself. What have you been doing all these years? I heard you had left Leicester."

"I've been living in Paris," Daisy told her, horribly conscious of Willow standing beside her.

"*Really*? How splendid! Working, of course? And married — are you married these days?"

Daisy turned to introduce Willow with her usual story about her widowhood.

"What frightful luck. My first was killed in the war. Our war, I mean, not this lot." Beatty beamed at Willow. "Absolutely charming. Very lovely, my dear. Mine are all boys. Grown up and joined up. I shall die of anxiety if this war lasts much longer."

"Do you still live in London?" Daisy said, beginning to feel faint and far too hot.

"I married a dear man who's working

for the War Ag Department. I'll give you my address. We must get together. The funny thing is, Clem works for the Ministry as well. You know he married? What idiots we were, Daisy." She paused to address Willow. "Your mother and I were rivals in love when we were very young and very silly. It took me a long time to forgive her though." She turned to Daisy again. "It was Clem who told me you had left Leicester."

Willow was listening with amused attention.

"I didn't know Clem knew much about it," Daisy said. It would only take a wrong phrase or word.

"Oh, I don't think he knew you'd left England.We were talking about the old times the other day. Henry knows Clem quite well, so of course it had come out that Clem and I had been pals. Clem's wife is *charming*. An exquisite dresser. You'd appreciate that, Daisy. Anyway, over dinner your name came up one way or another, and we laughed a bit about my storming off through the snow, and you saying some *terrible* things about having been *sleeping* with Clem, simply to shock his people. You shocked me too, I might add. What a *fuss* to make over a few kisses. Stricter times, eh, Daisy? And then Clem said, 'I haven't seen old Daisy for years, the last I heard, she'd upped and left Leicester for God knows where.'"

"Did he?" Daisy said weakly, beginning to feel as if she were trapped in a nightmare.

"I'll tell him I've seen you."

"I don't expect he'll want to be reminded about me again."

"Nonsense. He'll be pleased you've done so well for yourself. And *amazed* that you've produced such a heavenly daughter. He was convinced you would never have married — he said you weren't the marrying kind."

★ ★ ★

"What is it?" Willow said as they walked home. "You've been very quiet since we met that woman at Victoria. She said some pretty interesting stuff about you. Were you really such a rebel? And why

549

did she call you Cornforth? Was that your maiden name? And Daisy — short for Marguerite, I suppose? Though it does make you sound rather like a housemaid, Maman."

"We were once the best of friends. It was Beatty who helped me get started in couture."

"You weren't very friendly."

"Wasn't I?"

"You hardly said a word. It's almost as if you wished you hadn't seen her."

"Well," Daisy said lightly. "People change."

Beatty had become noisy, foolishly middle-aged. Did changes always have to be for the worse?

"Did you name Maison Clem after *him* — the man you quarrelled over?"

"Yes — but it was a silly, sentimental thing to do. I knew him such a long, long time ago." Not so much sentimental as dangerous, Daisy thought.

"I don't think it's silly at all." Willow found it rather endearing that her mother had a romantic past, and that she had called her salon after someone she knew and loved when she was a girl. If her father *had* been unfaithful, wouldn't her mother have clung to memories of a past lover in self-defence? "Why don't you want to talk about him?" she said teasingly. "I am quite old enough to understand these things, Maman. We are both women of the world."

"I told you. It's such a long time ago, it hardly seems worth remembering."

"I should think it was rather fun to remember one's youth."

"Do you always have to make me feel quite so old?"

* * *

Daisy did not recognise the stocky, middle-aged figure on the doorstep at first. It was snowing in the foggy darkness and fine drops of ice clung to his moustache.

"Clem?"

Her first thought was, thank God, Willow was at the cinema with one of her friends. Then she was aware that she felt hardly anything at all, except surprise, disappointment even, at how much he had changed.

"Beatty mentioned — I saw you, watched you this afternoon when you were on duty. I, er, flashed some papers, took the liberty of asking someone for your address."

"You've got a government job. Beatty told me."

"I tried to get an army posting, but they seem to think I'm a bit past it. Still. You never know. If this show goes on a bit longer."

"Let's hope not too long."

"No."

He smiled, and there was something in his eyes, a look that she remembered from long ago.

"I say, must we talk on the doorstep?" he said. "The blackout, and all that."

"Of course." Daisy was amazed at her sense of calm as she showed him up to the first-floor flat.

He handed her his coat and hat, taking in the luxury of antique furnishings and the pile of evening dresses and cloaks she had been unpicking on the table. He seemed agitated, gripped by a strong sense of occasion, in contrast to Daisy's own absence of emotion.

"I can't believe this is happening. After all this time."

"It might have been better not to come. Had you thought of that?" Daisy went to the sideboard and poured him a whisky.

"I've thought about it for days. Ever since Beatty told me she'd met you. But I had to see you, Daisy. I could never understand, you see — " He took the glass from her and twisted it in his hands. "I couldn't work out why you never said you were going away."

"I didn't want you to know."

"For some reason, I got it into my head that you must be in London somewhere. I spent ages looking. Absolutely ages." He smiled wryly. "That's how bad it had got."

"Oh, Clem. I am sorry." Daisy felt a very real remorse.

"It's not enough." He spoke quietly. "No — I'm afraid, even now, that's not good enough."

"There wouldn't have been any point in saying where I was. You had your family to think of."

"We might still have seen one another

from time to time. But, I suppose, what it comes down to is, you didn't want to."

"I'd had enough. It was different for you, there were other people."

He nodded, and took a swig of whisky. "Anyway. Water under the bridge."

How she had altered, Clem thought. He had been very frightened of the idea of seeing her again, terrified of reviving all the old feelings; but now he realised he had deliberately courted danger.

She was still graceful, with a smooth and fleshy opulence; to him she would always be beautiful, but she had lost the old magnetism, had put on weight and was showing signs of wear and tear.

"Beatty tells me you married," he said. "In France?"

"An Englishman." She could not look at him, afraid he would know by instinct that she was lying. "He died in an accident shortly before our daughter was born."

"Bea tells me she's very lovely. I was surprised you'd had a child. I mean, you always thought — " He broke off in embarrassment.

"My doctor said these things happen sometimes."

"You must be very proud of her."

"I am. Yes, I am. Willow has grown used to England, and to speaking English. In Paris we spoke French most of the time."

"Clever old Daisy."

"It took a while. It wasn't easy."

Daisy decided she too needed a drink, wanting the distraction of a glass in her hands.

"So, how old is she?" Clem said casually.

"Sixteen. She's just sixteen." The lie sounded brazen.

He nodded, and smiled politely. Daisy's daughter belonged to a part of her life he could not imagine; marriage and motherhood seemed alien to her; he found it hard to picture the Daisy he remembered with either a husband or a child.

He told her about his own family, showed her photographs from his wallet of Howard, who was in North Africa; Viola, in the Women's Royal Army Corps; and Hugo, still at school.

"Virginia knows everything," he said. "After you came to the house that time it was hard to keep anything from her. And after you left Leicester — " He snapped shut the wallet. "Let's just say, I was in a bit of a state. She's been a brick. I don't deserve her."

"I always imagined your wife saw me as the tart with whom you gratified the coarser aspects of your nature."

"Something like that; though, on the whole, she was remarkably understanding. We don't talk about it any more." He hesitated. "I'm very fond of her."

"Of course," Daisy said quickly, unable to prevent a stab of the old hurt. How easy it was for the wronged wife to snatch all the sympathy, particularly one who had behaved well and was 'understanding'.

"Will you tell her about coming here this evening?" she said brightly.

"No. I don't think so. It was very awkward even meeting Beatty again, having dinner with her and her husband, and reviving the row at Noonby as if it was an old joke. I don't want to upset her all over again. No. I just had to see you." He pulled a wry face and swallowed the last of his whisky. "You understand?"

"Wouldn't it have been better simply to have forgotten and let go?"

"Daisy — " His tone was reproachful, and he wore that boyish look of hurt that had always pulled at her emotions in the past. "Did I really mean so little to you?"

"One can't cling to the past." She avoided his eyes.

"There are no photos?" He glanced round the room again. "None of your daughter or husband?"

Daisy said that she did not go in for sentimental keepsakes, not even photographs.

"Still the same old Daisy."

She told him about the salon in Paris; about the people who had worked with her; and Alex, an old friend — "Well, lover," — deliberately exaggerating how long they had been together. She said she had not heard from Alex for several months and that if anything happened to him she probably would not stay in London; it would be easy enough to start up in business again somewhere; she had money — had transferred money from France before the war.

He stayed longer than she had intended; and as he left, Daisy was confronted by the worst scene she could have imagined.

Willow's face was pale with the cold as she met them in the downstairs hall, her skin translucent, and the melting snow spangled her hair under a large, burgundy-coloured beret. She wore a black wool coat, belted in the middle, high heels and nylons, and looked all of her twenty-one years as she glanced expectantly from one to the other.

"Hello. I'm Willow." She waited. "Maman — ?"

"This is a friend . . . " Daisy opened the door to the street at the same time as she introduced Clem.

"Ah — " Willow said with a knowing look when she heard his name. "*That* friend."

"Your mother has talked about me?" Clem said, glancing from one to the other.

"On the contrary. She's kept you a secret for years and years."

"You must be cold, Willow darling," Daisy said quickly. "Why don't you go upstairs?"

A silence fell after Willow had gone. They heard the upstairs door close.

"I'm sorry. She can be tactless and outspoken at times — "

"You said she was sixteen."

"She looks mature for her age — "

"Don't lie to me." Clem searched her expression, baffled. "I've always known when you were lying. Why?"

"I want you to go, Clem." Daisy shivered by the open door, her heart pounding violently. "Please. Just go."

"That's what you used to say, every damn time I visited. Go away, Clem. Don't come back again."

"And I meant it. *Please*, Clem. I never asked you to come today. I never did ask you to come."

"You used to want me though. We both remember that."

She tried to shut the door on him, but he wedged his foot in the gap like a determined salesman.

"What is it? Don't fob me off. What is it about her that you should want to lie about her age?" He studied her expression. "What is she — twenty? Twenty-one maybe?"

Realisation came.

"My God — of course. She even looks like Viola."

Clem shoved on the door and was beside her in the hall, slamming it shut behind him.

"Shush — oh, Clem, please, hush."

"How could you do that to me? Damn you, Daisy. How could you do that?"

"You had a wife and family."

"How much does she know?"

"She thinks her father's dead, that you and I knew one another years and years before she was born and never met again until tonight. And she mustn't suspect anything different."

"*Was* there a husband ever?"

"Yes."

"You're lying, even now. Why didn't you tell me that you were pregnant? After that first time — you know I would have helped you."

"She's grown up now. It doesn't matter any more."

His face was tense with anger. "After

all we were to one another. How can you say it doesn't matter?"

"I didn't need your help. Willow had me. I've given her everything she could want."

"Except the truth, that she's my child as well."

She opened the door again but he ignored it. "You've got to let me do something. Do you need money?"

"I told you — I have money."

"Daisy — she's my daughter."

"No, Clem. She's mine." Daisy moved to the door. "You've got to forget this. Forget you ever met me."

★ ★ ★

Daisy sat on the stairs, too weak to move, her heart thumping wildly. She had thought it was over, buried. It *was* buried, deep, deep. For God's sake, more than twenty-one years had passed.

★ ★ ★

Willow had joined the Land Army, and was posted on a farmhouse about twenty miles out of London; the houses all around were of tarred weatherboard, but High Farm had a look of faded prosperity. Willow decided she was going to be happy there.

She had been assigned to the dairy, to assist the resident staff. In the evenings, they took it in turns to cook for the other land girls, and for the gangs of outdoor workers, on a huge stove that poured out black smoke whenever the wind changed direction. "It's a nice house. You'd love it," Willow wrote to Daisy. "Roses round the door."

"I'm not in my dotage," her mother wrote back.

The War Agricultural Committee had commandeered much of the estate surrounding High Farm. Fields that had once held sheep and horses had gone under the plough. Hay meadows were taken over for growing turnips and potatoes. And, every so often, someone from the Ministry would arrive, sent to inspect what they were doing.

"Willow says you've been to the farm," said Daisy when she next saw Clem.

She had been surprised by how much

she had wanted to see him again, swayed by what? Memories? Or a sense that she owed him something for running away?

"An official visit," he reassured her. "I told you, Daisy, you can trust me."

There was an anti-climax about his knowing. All at once, the years of secrecy seemed such a waste. He had realised she was right, he said; for Willow's sake the truth was best left hidden. Could she have told him all those years ago? Daisy wondered, lulled into a sense of acceptance, as Willow wrote more often to say that Clem had visited her on the farm.

No revelations, no confessions. Clem kept his word.

* * *

Willow had grown fond of Maman's friend. He brought a present one day when he came to the farm, a bicycle strapped behind his car.

"How did you know the one I had in London was falling to bits? Maman must have been talking."

"One gets to hear these things."

He watched as she cycled up and down on the farm road ringing the bell.

"It's far too good." Willow came to a halt in front of him, and, on impulse, leaned across the handlebars and kissed him. "You're a darling man. Thank you."

He seemed touched, and embarrassed, and he said something about knowing how his own daughter would have felt if she had been forced to ride an old bone-shaker.

"She's my age, isn't she?"

"A year older."

"I sometimes wish I had brothers and sisters. I suppose, if my father had lived, life would have been very different."

"Perhaps," Clem said quietly.

"For a start, my mother would have had more time for me when I was little. I was always in the way. Other people took care of me. Did she tell you that she sent me away to school almost as soon as I could walk and talk?"

"Aren't you being a little unkind?"

"You don't know her very well," Willow called over her shoulder as she cycled away from him again. "You knew her once, I realise that, but she was probably extremely sweet and girlish then."

Clem laughed at the impossible image of Daisy radiating sweetness, but he sensed that Willow was not exaggerating the neglect.

Willow amended her assessment of Daisy as she halted in front of him, sending up a shower of dust. "I mean, she was probably different when she was young. Not so single-minded. She had no reason to be, had she? Even less so, when she married my father."

"I wouldn't know about that."

"Hasn't she told you? Papa was very wealthy. He bred horses. They lived in a house called Noonby Hall somewhere up north."

"I see," Clem said slowly.

"What is it? You seem sceptical. Or perhaps you *did* already know? There's something about my father, isn't there? Something Maman keeps quiet about."

"If I seem surprised, it's because I imagine your mother's life was far tougher than you say. I'm sure it's more worthy of admiration than you think."

"You mean, because of my father dying and going bankrupt?"

Clem pretended to examine the bike wheel. "I think there must have been other factors involved. There are things she has told me."

"But you're not going to divulge them. Did he have other women?" Willow added quickly.

"No." He straightened. "You were right the first time. I am not going to talk about it. And I thought you land girls had better things to do than stand around gossiping."

★ ★ ★

Alex had returned briefly to England. He looked tired and drawn and was, he said, going to Algiers with the Free French Army.

She could have been so much kinder to Alex in the past, Daisy reflected as he walked with her in the blackout. She felt a flood of gratitude for the many years he had been her friend.

"We have come a long way," she said as they reached the steps to her flat.

"Since dinner — or a long way from Paris?" he joked.

"I mean — from the Folies Bergère all those years ago."

"You remember?" He seemed moved that she should have recalled that first meeting, which for Alex was still suffused with memories of his need to have her. "You thought I was shallow, a womaniser."

"You were. You still are. I've watched you flirting with people, even in the restaurant tonight — "

"I have eyes only for you, Marguerite."

She laughed at him. "Alex — I'm over fifty." But she let herself be flattered all the same.

"Do you think age matters to me?" Alex said. "You're still beautiful. You still have style. You were born with that. No one can ever take it away from you."

"You don't know what you're talking about."

There had not been much style about Morton Street, Daisy thought. Men like Alex, Clem, and all the others of their class would never understand the legacy of poverty that had haunted her since those days. She could never tell Alex the truth about her background.

★ ★ ★

"Has anything happened while I've been gone?" Alex asked later that evening. "Apart from young Willow getting her hands blistered with hoeing potatoes."

Willow, who was home on leave for the weekend, spoke before Daisy could answer. "Yes, one of Maman's old admirers has turned up out of the blue."

Alex looked at Daisy quizzically. "A rival, eh?"

Daisy shook her head vigorously and said nothing.

★ ★ ★

"This fellow who's been coming to see you. Is it him?" Alex asked when they were alone. "Willow's father?"

"No," Daisy lied. "No, this one goes back much further."

"The one you were once so very fond of that you named the salon after him?"

He watched her from the settee as she padded about her flat, clearing away brandy glasses and coffee cups.

Daisy did not answer.

"Tell me about Willow's father. What was his name — Leonard? Does he live in London too?"

"I don't want to talk about him."

"That's what you always say when you can't face up to something."

"It was more than twenty years ago; it's time to forget."

"Is there any connection with this fellow Clem? They know one another? He'll want to get in touch? Is that what you're afraid of?"

Daisy looked at him, weary of the weight of so many lies and secrets, and aware that if she could trust anyone, it was Alex.

"Willow's father didn't know I had a child. I never told him. Oh, Alex — " She sat on the arm of a chair, suddenly, inconceivably ashamed. "I never even told him I was pregnant."

He stared at her.

"Was it wrong of me — cruel, not to tell him?"

"Who's to say? If he loved you, and you loved him — "

"Oh, yes, I did. I realise that now."

"Then I suppose it was."

"That's how it's always been with me. I was unkind — *am* unkind — to people." Daisy glanced up and, meeting his eyes, realised that she was about to be cruel to Alex too. It was finally over. He had performed the role of admirer beautifully, and she had enjoyed the fact that he was in love with her, but he never had been a threat to her peace of mind in the way Clem had.

"Alex, this man . . . this old admirer. He's made me realise I've been unfair to you. I think it's time — "

He did not let her finish the sentence. Stubbing out his cigarette, he gave her a wry smile. "Somehow, I thought this might happen."

"I can't explain."

"You don't have to. You called the salon after him. It must mean something." He stood up and reached for his coat and scarf. "Just tell me one thing, and look me in the eye when you answer."

Daisy looked at him obediently.

"Is he the one? Are Clem and Leonard one and the same?"

She laughed. "No, of course not. What an imaginative idea."

★ ★ ★

"Why don't we ever meet anyone from your family?" Willow asked as she prepared to return to High Farm.

Daisy had been working at some sketches for a private customer. Her glasses had slipped down her nose, and her hair was scraped into a bun, giving her the look of a plump, slightly comical academic. Shocked by the question — though she supposed she should not have been so surprised; the only wonder was that Willow had not asked her before — Daisy jerked up her head.

"I fell out with my family when I was young." She returned her attention to her sketching and avoided looking at Willow leaning against the table in her Land Army uniform.

"Why have you never said anything about them?"

571

"It's a long story. I don't want to go into it."

"What about my father's family? You fell out with them too. Did you quarrel with *everyone* you knew? And why do you never talk about Noonby any more? We could go there — well, why not? Don't you even want to know who's living there now?"

"A government department, I expect. You may not have noticed it, Willow, but there's a war on; this isn't the time for tripping off up north."

"But I must have grandparents, relations who would be thrilled to see us — "

"There's no point to all this," Daisy said. "In any case, as soon as the war is over we are going back to Paris."

"That could take years. Why are you being so silly? There's something you're not telling me, something to do with my father. Clem said — "

"What on earth has this got to do with Clem?" Daisy banged her hand on the table.

"He knows something. He said he thought there were other things, besides debts, that had made your life very difficult. I heard Alex talking about it once too. Was my father a philanderer?"

★ ★ ★

Furious, Daisy attacked Clem when he came to see her.

"I didn't know," he protested. "How was I to guess you had told her some story about living at Noonby and being a member of the upper ten?"

"Don't mock me, Clem. I won't have it."

"Why not royalty? Why stop at marrying the master of Noonby?"

"You asked me once. Remember?"

"And you turned me down." Clem took off his hat and coat and sat heavily at the table. "All right — why tell her stories? Why not the *truth*?"

"Because — we have lived with the story so long, I can't change it. She *wants* to believe that's how my life has been."

"No, Daisy. You wanted it to have been like that."

"Perhaps I did. Perhaps, after a while, I began to believe it really had happened that way. And when you consider what the truth was — Daisy Cornforth, mother of a bastard child — isn't that awful enough to want to keep it hidden? In love for years with a married man?"

"You never used to talk of love. Hardly ever, when we were together, did you tell me you loved me."

"I told you how much I hated you."

"Yes, you did. Often."

"It was true. I hated the way you robbed me of control and messed up my feelings."

"And now?"

"Now — " She looked at him helplessly. "Now, Clem, I wish it could all have been so very different."

He held out his hand in a gesture of conciliation, but she ignored it and, pouring herself a whisky, sat on the settee. After a while he sat beside her. "I'm sorry. I feel it too, you know. The way we *wasted* what happiness we might have had."

"Do you still go to Noonby?" she asked, feeling an unexpected affection for those years.

"Not much. Even with the air raids

574

Virginia has been happier staying in London, though she's desperate about the servant shortage. She's had to learn to cook."

"Poor thing."

"It's hard. One is simply not used to it. I never really understood, you know, what it must have been like for you, growing up with no luxuries at all."

"My family certainly never had to worry about the servant problem."

"Austen is at his wits' end at Noonby. Hardly any staff, and everywhere being ploughed up. Land that's never been touched before, now producing potatoes. But there's no arguing against it. By the way . . . I've been accepted by the army." He lit a cigarette. "A desk job. Still, it's better than nothing. But it may mean not being able to visit too often."

"Now you tell me," Daisy said.

"But when I *do* see you again, we are going to make the most of it, dinner, the theatre — "

They avoided talking about the war then, and fell back on reminiscences; remembering the time she had gatecrashed a Noonby party, the day her father

575

threw her out, and their tempestuous, but infrequent meetings in the years before she went to Paris.

Daisy poured herself another whisky. She offered Clem one, and he went to help her.

"Willow thinks you're after me again, hot with rejuvenated passion."

"What if I am?"

"What if you are?" she repeated, as if considering the idea carefully.

He took the bottle from her and placed it carefully on the sideboard before resting his hands on her waist. Spreading his fingers, he closed his eyes and shuddered.

"Someone walking over your grave?" Daisy said gently.

Clem shook his head. "I feel alive for the first time in years. May I kiss you?"

★ ★ ★

There was a bitter-sweet pleasure about sleeping with him again, an awareness of the years they had missed and the futility of having pursued such separate goals. They were shy undressing, afraid of disappointment, and of disappointing each other. How could they hope to recapture a passion that belonged to their youth? They came together as strangers, not intimate lovers.

And then, haunting recollections of touch and smell returned, familiar words and endearments came to their lips, and the years fell away; the power of memory was overwhelming.

"I never thought I could be so happy again," Clem said. "Do you remember — ?"

Daisy laughed. "I remember *everything*."

★ ★ ★

It was not fair, Daisy thought. It was so unfair that they had only now begun to talk honestly with one another and might perhaps have made up for lost time, and here he was joining the army again. Even in the past there had been so little time together.

Weeks went by, and Clem had not been in touch. Daisy grew impatient, and then angry; she began to wonder if he had, after all, been disappointed in her. She could not even write to him, because his wife would begin to suspect; but she could go to Hampstead, Daisy told herself. She could climb the hill as she had in the old days — not, as then, with jealous envy — but certainly in the hope of bumping into him.

She wanted, as much as anything, to feed her curiosity, Daisy admitted; she wanted to know how it all looked these days.

Little had changed. There were more shops, but the substantially built houses in leafy gardens where Clem lived were the same as she remembered. The memory of Clem, arm in arm with his wife, came back with a sharp intensity — Virginia heavily pregnant, Clem horribly embarrassed by the situation — and Daisy felt a brief pang of hurt as she looked up at the house.

Was it foolish of them to try to revive the past?

The curtains were half drawn, though it was early in the evening. If Virginia saw her — would she recognise her? Deliberately flirting with the danger of being seen, Daisy walked on towards the house, but her bravura deserted her when she saw that the front door had opened; there were signs of movement — someone about to leave.

Pulling her hat low over her eyes, she turned away and bent to tie her shoe, confident of going unrecognised if Virginia should pass her. Clem would assume she was there to make mischief of course, but if he was alone they would find an opportunity to talk, she would tease him out of any ill-humour, scold him for not finding time to see her.

A woman's high heels approached on the pavement; they halted as the figure drew level.

"Daisy?"

Daisy looked up and, straightening slowly, cursed the fates for bringing Beatty Knighton to Hampstead.

Beatty stood, her arms spread in a gesture of oddly despairing affection. She seemed to be at a loss for words. "Oh, Daisy — how did you know?"

"Know what? I was simply passing — " Daisy said.

"You mean — you *don't* know?"

579

Daisy watched with alarm, then a growing foreboding, as tears sprang to Beatty's eyes and her mouth crumpled.

"About poor Clem. Oh — poor Clem."

She had assumed Daisy was visiting Virginia, Beatty said. Virginia's friends had all rallied wonderfully . . . Clem had been in a car on official business . . .

An ice-cold fist closed round Daisy's heart. She took the news without moving, with no visible sign of emotion. Other people — sometimes one knew them — got bombed, crushed, buried by debris, but not Clem.

He had not stood a chance, Beatty said, drying her eyes and offering to walk with Daisy to a café where they could get a cup of tea; it must be a shock for her — remembering Clem and the times they had shared, all three of them had shared, in the past.

Daisy heard herself refuse. "Thank you for telling me," she said stiffly. "Please convey my condolences to his wife when you see her again — no, I won't intrude."

They made stilted, abortive conversation, recalling the old days at the Poplars; and all the while Daisy forced down her panic and horror at the images in her mind.

"If you want anything," Beatty said, drying her eyes. "Anything at all — "

Daisy shook her head. She had come so close to having all she had ever wanted.

★ ★ ★

Six months later, Willow sat in Alex's flat. There were feminine touches. Flowers. A lipstick on the mantelshelf beside a packet of Gauloises. If it meant he had found someone else, she was glad.

"May I talk to you?"

"That sounds very serious."

He poured her a gin and tonic.

"It is." She waited for him to sit down before saying, "What do you know about my father?"

"Your father?" Alex repeated warily. "What should I know? I never met him."

"I heard you and Maman talking once, while we were still living in Paris. She was saying something about my father, that something or other had not been one-sided."

"What a sneaky little girl you were, listening at key-holes."

"What did she mean?"

Alex looked at her and smiled, enigmatic but kindly. "I haven't the faintest idea."

"Maman has been very strange since Clem Brackenborough died. You remember — the man she used to be in love with?"

Willow had watched Daisy become harsher, shorter on compassion, and was puzzled by the change. Her mother had always been fairly ruthless; but it was as if Clem's death had left unexplained scars.

"I can't stand sentimentality," Daisy snapped when Willow tried to talk about him. "He was *my* friend. You hardly knew him."

It had been some months after Clem's death, and the war, at least in Europe, was over, when Willow had received a letter from Clem's solicitor.

"He's left me rather a lot of money," she told Alex stiffly.

"And you're wondering why."

"Wouldn't you?"

"He was very fond of your mother, I believe."

"That's what she says. But, you see, I've made enquiries, and I've discovered that the house she always told me about, where she said she lived in England, is where Clem Brackenborough lived — Noonby Hall."

"So that makes him your father?"

"I don't know what to think. She won't talk about it."

Daisy had denied everything. "He had grown very fond of you, Willow," she had begun unconvincingly.

"Not that fond. Why should your friend Clem leave money to me? And so *much* money. It says he left the bulk of his estate to his wife, five thousand pounds to each of his children — and the same amount to me. Why me, and not to you? Maman — tell me my imagination's running wild here."

Willow had watched the colour drain from Daisy's face. "I don't know what you're saying, darling. You're confused. I knew Clem years and years ago. I really don't want to discuss this any more."

"Look, Willow," Alex said gravely. "I'll be very frank with you. I do know that your parents weren't married — I found it out by accident. That's why Marguerite made up a story about her background. She probably chose Brackenborough's house at random, or because she had once been happy with him. Who's to say?"

"So, who *was* my father?"

Alex hesitated, and out of loyalty decided against further speculation involving someone — invented or not — called Leonard.

"I've no idea. But I do know that it wasn't Clem Brackenborough."

"*How* do you know?" Willow said childishly, her mouth trembling, unsure whether she wanted to believe him.

"Because I once asked her outright. Marguerite had no reason to lie to me."

19

"WHY didn't you tell me she was your mother?" Liz said gently.

"I don't know. I pushed her out of my mind for so long after marrying Albert. Habit at first, I suppose. I told myself I hated her. I was never *quite* sure, you see, about Clem. It wasn't until you told me that Lewis Brackenborough said the affair had gone on for years, that I knew for certain he was my father. She never admitted it. She told so many lies."

"I thought you were playing games with me."

"That as well. But it hurts, you know. It's not easy, remembering times when you were unhappy. You would think, fifty years on . . . but, there you are. The mind is full of surprises."

"Do you wish I hadn't found out the truth?"

"What's the use of wishing? You were determined from the start."

"You seemed to want me to know. You sent me to the Café Bresil."

"Marie-Cécile might not have been there any more. She and her husband could have sold after Madame Bresil died, or they might easily have been dead as well by now."

"But you took the chance. You *wanted* me to find out."

Willow made for one of the benches at the edge of the lawn. "I was getting tired of lies. *She* dealt in lies all her life."

"Does she really deserve to be hated so much?"

Liz was shaken by Willow's accusation that Daisy had been a bad mother. The label overturned her conclusion that Daisy had managed to combine successfully both her career and motherhood. Her thoughts turned to Don, and the decision she had come to; but she could not bring herself to tell Willow about their engagement, afraid of her look of scepticism.

Liz wished the engagement had not become public knowledge so quickly. "Did you have to tell Cliff and Rosemary?" she had said in disbelief when, smiling

586

and waving, having reunited the last of the children with their parents, she and Don had parted from the others outside the school. The festive, romantic atmosphere of the Left Bank of Paris had seemed impossibly remote twenty-four hours later, and she had felt hung over and exhausted.

"Didn't you want us to tell people?" Don was good at looking hurt.

"It's just — all that nudge-nudge business between Cliff and Rosemary."

"You snob," he laughed. "You don't want to believe Paris had the same effect on you as it had on them."

"They were like a couple of kids."

"Does it matter?"

"Mmm?"

"Does it matter what prompted us? It's the right decision, isn't it?"

"Of course," she had reassured him. "Yes, of course."

All the same, events were moving too quickly, throwing her into a panic. There was the need to make plans around the outcome of Don's interview in Norfolk, the possibility of giving up her university teaching, the prospect of telling friends, packing up at the Lodge. Above all, she would have to tell her family.

Willow sat on the bench, making room for Liz. "My mother resented me all through my childhood," she said. "I was a withdrawn, resilient child who thought unhappiness was endemic to my life."

"You must have cared about her once," Liz persisted.

"We were never so close as during the war. Certainly not afterwards." Willow was thoughtful, turning blades of grass with her foot. "If I had discovered Clem knew about me all the time we were in Paris and that he was ashamed of me, or if he had been the kind of father who had abandoned my mother for other women — I could perhaps have turned my hate on him. But I'm sure he had no idea I existed before the war."

"Don't you think she lied to protect you? In those days, illegitimacy was a much more difficult thing to live with."

Willow shook her head. "Daisy was ashamed of loving Clem. She saw it as a weakness. She wanted to believe the stories she told me instead: the brave widow who had risen above her husband's debts. She was ashamed of anything to do with her past in the end. She even looked down on her own parents."

"With reason, it seems. You told me her father was a cruel man."

"I never knew him. I only had her word for that."

"And Albert's. You must have believed him, or you wouldn't have told me."

"Why do you always defend her?" Willow said angrily.

"I still can't help admiring her."

Willow fell silent. Her own feelings about Daisy were as complicated now she was an old woman as they had been when she was a girl. She would never forgive her for the lies.

"Willow — how would you like to go to Noonby?" Liz said casually.

"Is this a spur-of-the-moment thing?"

"No. I thought I would get in touch with Lewis Brackenborough. I remember that you said you wanted to see Clem's portrait."

"I thought if I could see what Clem was like when she first met him," said Willow, thinking of the portrait. "Now that I've seen the photo of Daisy when *she* was young . . . " She tailed off, as if she had forgotten what she was saying.

But Liz understood; she too felt the need for romance, to create myths around known certainties — Daisy's photo, Clem's portrait — and to believe in them.

★ ★ ★

Don and Liz told her parents about their engagement at a family barbecue.

They were all there: Jennifer, Mark and the boys, and Peter and Prue — very heavily pregnant by now — and their children.

Ralph found a couple of bottles of champagne he had been saving for 'precisely such an occasion', and everyone said it was about time too, raising their glasses to Liz and Don, while the children went wild, whooping about on the lawn.

"So, when's it to be?" Mark said, his arm round Jennifer's shoulders.

She seemed detached from him, hunched, her fingers tense on the glass in her hand. "Don't rush them," she said unexpectedly. "They've only just managed to get this far."

Everyone laughed, because it sounded like a joke, but Jennifer remained unsmiling and after a few seconds she walked away to join the children.

"Oh, I don't think we shall wait too long," Don said, looking at Liz, his eyes raised to hers for confirmation. "Go for it, eh? We need to get a few things sorted out first, such as where we shall be living."

Liz tried to stem the little stabs of resentment at his casual use of the word 'we'. Disconnected phrases kept coming into her mind. *Follow your man. My husband and I.* He was hopeful of a second interview at Yarnest. She remembered that Lewis Brackenborough's wife had wanted a husband with a steady job, who would come home to a doting wife. It occurred to her that Don might have fitted the role perfectly — except, of course, that he was the wrong class; people like Don and herself moved in rather different social circles from the Brackenboroughs.

She walked round the garden sipping champagne, and went to join her father who was turning sausages on the barbecue.

"Happy?"

"Yes, of course."

"We shall be sorry to see you go so far away, but you know how fond we've grown of Don." Ralph handed her a plate and looked at her questioningly, giving her the opportunity to open up if that was what she wanted.

The rest of the family were being drawn to the source of food, except for Prue, who sat sprawled uncomfortably in a garden chair with her legs splayed, waiting with a frown of concentration for Peter to ferry a plate to her.

"I found out more about Daisy," Liz told Ralph. I met a woman who knew her. Daisy had an illegitimate child in the twenties, and — guess what — the father was Clem Brackenborough." She told him how Daisy had brought Willow up on her own in Paris. "I want to take her to Noonby," she added casually.

"Wouldn't it be better not to stir things any more than you have already?"

"Willow wants to see Clem's portrait.

She met him during the war, but he never let on he was her father. Neither did Daisy, though Willow guessed there was something she was not being told."

"What does Don say about all this?"

"Don?"

"Doesn't he think you should drop it now? If you're going to Norfolk — "

Liz looked at him in surprise and saw that he was serious; her father expected her to defer to Don's opinion. She felt a deep sense of disappointment in him.

Don was coming towards her with Ben and Josie in tow, Josie hanging on to his shirt cuff, staggering on unsteady legs.

Liz glanced at Prue, who had a glass and plate balanced on her bump and was listening, still with a frown of remote concentration, as Peter talked to Sally. Will that be me in a year or two's time? No champagne for me, thank you. No tea, no coffee, no stimulants because of baby. No conversation. Leave that to Don, he is the one with the opinions.

Shaking herself out of her peculiar mood, Liz spread her arms so that Josie, leaving the anchor of Don's sleeve, could run to her.

"Clever girl," Liz murmured, sweeping her up into the air. The child laughed with pleasure at her achievement.

Putting her down, Liz saw that Mark and her parents were gathered round Prue's chair. Her sister was struggling to her feet.

Peter, already running towards the house, shouted, "I'll phone the hospital, tell them we're on our way."

"I'm fine," Prue was saying. "There's plenty of time." She grimaced with the discomfort of a contraction.

* * *

They sat around the garden after Prue and Peter had gone, waiting for news from the hospital and entertaining the children.

"There's something essentially female about Prue," Don said as they drove home later, after Peter had rung to say that Prue had given birth to a girl. "Look how magnificent she was about the whole thing. How serenely she carried it off."

"Is that a particularly female trait, doing things with serenity?"

594

Don glanced at her in surprise. "You've been very scratchy today. Is something wrong?"

If there was, Liz did not want to identify it.

"I guess I felt uneasy about Jennifer and Mark. Has it got so bad between them they can't even put on an act in public any more?"

"You're afraid we might go the same way?"

"You're hardly a womaniser, like Mark," Liz said. Wasn't the truth more that she feared a future that would mirror the lives of Prue and Peter?

"You're nothing like your sisters, either, so stop brooding," Don said, and paused. "Why don't you go and see Willow again next week? You're going to have to prepare her for the possibility that you won't be able to visit her regularly if we leave Somerset."

Liz hesitated. She had not told him yet about her plan to take Willow to Noonby Hall, but she did so now, explaining about Willow's need to see the portrait of Clem when he was a young man. "I think it means a lot to her."

Don was uneasy with the suggestion, but he was also reluctant to sound obstructive. "It's up to you. If you think it's a good idea."

★ ★ ★

Was *any* of this a good idea? thought Liz, staring into the muddy darkness beyond the tube train window. Her attention flicked to the map of the Northern line as she reached each station, checking the number of stops before Hampstead. And was the habit of lying catching?

Perhaps, in some mysterious — and, of course, totally improbable — way, Daisy had taken her over since her visit to Paris. She was no longer responsible for her own actions. What other explanation could there be for telling Don she was going to see her publisher, when she had no intention of going anywhere near Moira today while she was in London.

"This young man — Lewis," Willow had said. "Is he anything like his grandfather?"

"Not really. Well — perhaps a little."

"Why do you want me to go to Noonby?"

Liz had looked at her in surprise, realising that she did not know. To reconcile Willow and Daisy?

"I suppose I feel responsible because I started all this by showing you Daisy's picture. If I hadn't come to see you — "

"I'm glad you did." Willow's gaze had been steady, unclouded by age or confusion. "You remember that. I'm glad you did."

Liz still had not told Willow about her and Don's engagement.

She worried about her ambivalence now that the decision had been made, but wasn't it Lewis who had told her that men and women needed one another?

Walking to the lift, jostled by people pushing through the doors from behind, Liz tried to consult the address on the piece of paper in her pocket.

Lewis had sounded surprised over the phone when she had said she wanted to see him. "I'm in London next week. Can we meet somewhere there?" he had said. "Better still — why don't you come to the house. Did I tell you that I live in my grandmother's Hampstead cottage?"

No, he certainly had not, thought Liz. There was something startling in the revelation that Lewis occupied the same territory as Clem and Virginia — where Daisy had once 'behaved outrageously'. Wasn't that how Lewis had put it?

Liz emerged from the tube station into brilliant sunshine and with the roar of traffic bursting on her ears. It was impossible to imagine either Clem or Daisy in such a setting. Despite the dark red tiles and Art Nouveau decoration, the station echoed modern, graceless London; there was no aura of more leisured times, and, climbing the hill, the antique shops and restaurants had little sense of history either.

Liz left the main street, entering the lanes and squares leading off it, and the atmosphere pitched at once into a more alluring silence: no sound but the click of her shoes on the pavement, the distant muted hum of cars and taxis, someone whistling in a side alley.

Liz paused to count the house numbers, and turning a corner saw the house where Clem had lived — mellow bricks, bay windows, far too grand to be called a 'cottage', especially when she thought of the Lodge; yet perhaps not quite a mansion. A sense of the past invaded her in a momentous tide of awareness: Daisy had been there, had perhaps stood on that very corner.

Had Daisy too been intimidated, suddenly, by a sense of being out of her depth?

Why *am* I doing this? Liz asked herself as she mounted the flight of steps to the front door — and the question had nothing to do with taking Willow to Noonby.

Was she still trying to get in touch with Daisy in some way, or — Liz tried to be honest with herself — had she begun to build a romantic image around Lewis, as well as falling for Clem, his ancestor.

He answered the doorbell almost at once.

"Liz — how lovely to see you."

He showed her into a sitting room at the back of the house, overlooking a lawn and a garden with flowering shrubs, brick paths, and a high brick wall against which a white climbing rose was in flower.

"This sounds intriguing," he said, after he had offered her coffee and made polite inquiries about her journey. "You said you had something to tell me."

"I didn't feel I could say it over the phone."

Not something as important as the fact that Willow had suddenly become his responsibility as much as hers. Clem's daughter: closer to the Brackenboroughs than Liz's wife-of-a-grandfather's-cousin who turned out to be a half-cousin, or perhaps it was a second cousin-twice-removed — she had given up trying to work out the permutations of her own connection with Willow.

She told him about her discoveries in Paris. "So — Willow is your aunt," she finished. "And by a quirk of fate, I suppose that means you and I are related as well."

Lewis was quiet for several seconds.

"Have I shocked you?" Liz said. "I wasn't sure how you would take it."

Perhaps it really was *not* good news to be told that she and he were linked by his grandfather's illegitimate child; after all, Lewis's family was moneyed, aristocratic, and hers was still only two generations away from Morton Street.

"Not shocked. No. I'm glad you took the trouble to come and tell me in person."

"I have to admit, I was anxious to see where you lived, when you said this was Clem's house. I mean, you said Daisy had once been here and created a scene."

"I think that was the point when my grandmother found out about them. I suppose Daisy meant her to — or she would never have come to the house."

"Perhaps she couldn't help herself," suggested Liz.

"Yes. I believe in fate, up to a point."

"Do you think Virginia knew about Willow? Clem left Willow money in his will."

"If she knew, or even if she only guessed, she kept it to herself." He smiled. "Well, Liz. You've brought quite a surprise with you. I wasn't expecting this."

"There's more."

Liz explained quickly about wanting to take Willow to see Clem's portrait

601

at Noonby. "I'd like you to be there as well. I need someone with me who will understand what it's like for her to be confronted with her past. I know it's a lot to ask — "

"No," he interrupted. "I'm flattered. No, truly. And I ought to meet her — would *like* to meet her," he corrected. He glanced at his watch. "You must be hungry. How about some lunch?"

* * *

They went to one of the little restaurants in the main street. Lewis was charming and attentive, and Liz felt pampered. Comparisons with Don were, she realised, odious, but they became more compulsive as she watched him turn to the waiter and order from the menu.

"How was Paris?" Lewis said, as they ate.

Liz talked about the Café Bresil, and the children, and Toby Wyman, and — because she was beginning to enjoy herself rather more than she ought to in his company and needed to bring herself back to earth — she told him, "Actually, while we were in Paris Don and I became engaged."

Lewis's gaze met hers briefly, then flicked away. "Well — that's the place to do it if you're going to."

"Yes," said Liz. "That's what everyone tells me." And she felt lessened in his eyes, the sort of person who liked Venice for its gondolas, and Paris for its reputation among lovers.

She drank the white wine, pretending not to care what he thought about her, and told him about Don's hopes of a headship in Norfolk and the inevitability of moving if he got the job.

"It must be wonderful, living in Clem's house," she added as they waited for coffee. And that too now sounded foolish, the sort of thing said by someone who liked 'historic' houses and theme parks.

"I'm thinking of a more permanent break with my life in London," Lewis said. "Changes are a bit of a wrench though, after getting used to a certain way of life. I'm sure you feel it too about going to Norfolk. Breaking with fixed habits, old friends." He looked at her.

"This house has too many associations for me."

"Of course," said Liz. "Your marriage."

"I rushed into it rather. Not like you and your fiancé. We were very young and hardly knew one another."

He told her a little about it, how he had met his wife through family friends, how everyone had approved.

"Nanny always told me to marry someone who came from a good family and whom my mother spoke well of," he said with a wry smile. "That was Amanda."

They returned to the house.

"There's something I haven't told you — should have told you," he said, suddenly awkward with her. "There's a child. That is — I mean, I have a child. I don't see much of him. The courts aren't very sympathetic about fathers wanting custody. He lives abroad with his mother."

"There's no reason why you should have told me at all," said Liz.

"No. But I wanted you to know. And, if we're going to be collaborating about Willow and the portrait — " He paused.

604

"Come and see my grandfather's study. It's the one room in the house that hasn't been altered very much. My grandmother never liked going in there. For her too there were 'associations'."

★ ★ ★

They were met by a smell of old books and leather furniture and even, faintly, tobacco, though Liz was sure that Lewis did not smoke. There was a leather sofa with hollowed cushions, much worn at the corners, an old-fashioned gramophone in a rosewood cabinet, and a wall lined with books behind glass doors. In the window overlooking the street stood a huge, immovable desk.

"That was Clem's too," said Lewis, going to the window and opening it a fraction.

"It's fantastic. Like a time capsule. You'll have to decide what to do with the furniture if you move away. Was the gramophone his too?"

"Oh, I think so. There are some records somewhere." He rummaged in the bottom drawer of the desk and pulled out a pile of seventy-eights.

Liz sat on the sofa. "Where will you go?"

"To Noonby," he answered, sorting through the records. "I shall come to some arrangement with the Trust. We've already had discussions."

He lifted the lid of the gramophone and wound the handle, then put on a scratchy version of the 'Twelfth Street Rag'.

He sat on the desk, watching her, and Liz felt vulnerable, because he had his back to the window and his expression was in shadow.

"What about you?" he said. "Are you looking forward to the possibility of living in Norfolk? It will be grim in winter after Somerset."

"I'll soon get used to it," Liz said defensively.

"I suppose one can write just about anywhere. It would be marvellous for photographs. How's the book?"

"I'm on the final chapters," Liz said, "All about the death of the corset equalling female emancipation, and women now being able to choose whatever they want to do with their lives."

"You don't sound too sure."

"I don't think choices are that much easier for women. I did once. Now — you're right, I'm not so sure."

"Any particular reason?"

"Don wants children. I know he does."

"And you don't?"

"I don't think so. What about my work? What if I had a child and didn't want to work any more? That would be terrible. On the other hand, women are supposed to have this deep need for motherhood, and I haven't got it. I mean, I'd be hopeless."

"Why choose corsets as a subject?" he said, watching her closely.

"I was interested in textiles, and fashions. And then — it seemed a fit metaphor for the way women's lives have been restricted for generations. Emancipation from corsets seemed to represent an escape from all the old ideas about how women should behave. Only — I'm not sure any more. Perhaps there *is* no escape in the end."

"There are expectations laid on men too, you know."

"Of course there are. But that's not something that preoccupies me."

"Because men didn't wear corsets?"

"Oh, in some eras they did. But one of the most interesting aspects of the corset for me is the fact that it told lies about what women really were like."

"Do you mean in terms of blubber — or are you still talking in metaphors?"

"Both," Liz said seriously. "What secret ambitions lay underneath all those conventional, conforming exteriors?"

"You make it sound as if women had been waiting to burst out and conquer the world."

"I think it's true."

"Aren't you forgetting that many women were achievers despite their corsets? And what about the less worthy or symbolic aspect of it all? Didn't corsets serve to conceal a whole load more — what about sex, all those heaving bosoms, all that sensuality laced in?"

Liz remembered Don lacing her into the Victorian corset — but she did not want to think of Don here. There was something more compelling in letting the atmosphere of the room take her over, hearing the gramophone with its urgent syncopated ragtime, and enjoying the novelty of Lewis challenging her thesis.

"Perhaps you are ignoring the erotic aspect of your subject," Lewis suggested. "Does sex frighten you?"

"No, of course it doesn't frighten me. I've covered eroticism in the book — "

"But have you really thought about it?"

"What is this — the Inquisition?"

"I'm sorry." He smiled suddenly and went to the gramophone, turning the record over. "I expect you have these arguments with your fiancé all the time."

"Don't," said Liz. "I can't stand that word."

He looked at her in surprise.

"*Fiancé*," Liz explained. "It's almost as bad as *engaged*."

"Don't use them then."

"No." She pulled a rueful face. "I don't know why I object so strongly."

"Perhaps you're thinking you shouldn't have done it."

"I didn't tell him I was coming today.

He's sick of hearing about Daisy and Clem."

He wound up the gramophone again. "Was that the only reason?"

Liz did not answer.

"I should have told you about my son," he said, in a way that seemed to have no connection with Liz's own confession.

"That's hardly the same sort of thing in terms of being dishonest."

"It is. You see, I *deliberately* did not tell you." He hesitated. "I found you — find you — very attractive, and I thought it might put you off."

Caught off her guard, Liz drew her breath in with a gasp.

"You know what I'm talking about, don't you?" he said. "I mean, you feel it too?"

"Oh, yes," Liz said in as rational a voice as she could manage. "Of course, it's only because of them — Clem and Daisy. You even look a bit like Clem — and I've developed a crush on his portrait. I'm nothing like Daisy, mind you. I should have brought her picture to show you. It would have destroyed any illusions you might have had about me."

They were silent.

"I don't want you to get the wrong idea," Lewis said, sitting beside her. "I mean — I'm not looking for complications in my life."

"Nor am I," Liz assured him, and reminded herself that her great-grandfather had dug Noonby's gardens and her great-grandmother had waited on its bedrooms. "After all — this isn't complicated. It's to do with *them* — Clem and Daisy. And, anyway, I'm engaged to Don."

He covered her lips gently with his fingers. "You weren't going to use that word — "

Liz knew he was going to kiss her, and she wanted him to; every ounce of her ached to be touched by him.

He smoothed back her hair from her face with a tender gesture. "Perhaps we should view this afternoon as a kind of time slip. What would they have done in this situation?"

The leather cushions were softened with age; they smelled deliciously of times past, were broad and welcoming — an exquisite place to make love, thought Liz, in the study where Clem had once worked and thought of Daisy.

"You know what they would have done." Liz's voice had thickened and her body trembled with tension.

Daisy had behaved outrageously, she remembered as Lewis kissed her.

* * *

He had been remarkably adroit in producing a condom, Liz remembered. No commitments. No silly vowing of eternal love. She ducked her head and retrieved her tights from the floor.

Lewis offered her the use of the bathroom and clean towels. She stood after showering, facing the washbasin with its old-fashioned taps and green copper stains on the porcelain. An experiment? A test? She did not know whether they had failed it, or passed. Daisy had got pregnant, she remembered. But modern women were too clever for that, too clever to fall in love with someone who was unsuitable, or to mess up their lives in any way because of a one-off fling. Modern women were in control, knew how to juggle their needs around all aspects of their existence — creative, cerebral or carnal.

Had Clem stood here and shaved in front of the mirror? Liz wondered. Had he padded about in slippers and a dressing gown, dreaming of Daisy? Thankful for no commitments. Was that how it had been for them too?

Liz felt a chill of disappointment. It was time she stopped this, she told herself, dressing again before she went downstairs. Don was right about one thing. She had become obsessed with Daisy's story — to the point of neurosis if it meant she could have sex with Clem's grandson in the name of a romantic experiment. She made herself think of Lewis's wife, and tried to picture all the other women who might have stood in Clem's bathroom. Why had she done it — because the idea of a romantic adventure had been temporarily more attractive than facing up to real life and making things work?

Lewis was friendly but distant, his kiss almost brotherly as he offered her tea.

They talked about dates when he would be at Noonby, Liz's plans for driving Willow to the Midlands, everything except about what had happened less than an hour before on Clem's sofa. As she passed the study door on her way out, Liz began to doubt whether it had happened at all.

★ ★ ★

"Now then," Willow said, noting Liz's moody silence as she watched people drift at the edges of Meadowfields' lawns. The grass was dotted with daisies and it needed mowing.

"Let's go, shall we? When? At the weekend?"

"You think so?" Liz felt a pulse of nervousness at the thought of having to face Lewis again.

"While I'm in the mood. Don't wait for me to change my mind. You can help me decide what clothes to take with me. And I'll need to get my hair done," Willow said, as they walked towards the house. "Daisy taught me all about style. You'd never have guessed she'd been brought up as she had. She knew all about the best fabrics, good food, furniture. Alex had something to do with that. Did I tell you about him — ?"

* * *

"She is so excited," Liz said to Don. "It's as if the promise of going to Noonby has taken years off her. She was chatting away about various people from the past. It's as if she's free to talk about Daisy normally at last."

"So, you think it's all been worthwhile?" said Don, watching her pack.

"It will be. After Noonby."

"And what if it's too much for her?"

"Don — she's not delicate."

She wished she did not have to justify what she was doing. Why couldn't he see that the trip to the Midlands was what Willow needed?

"Come with us," she said on impulse, and immediately regretted the suggestion, imagining the meeting with Lewis. He had been distant on the phone, very correct. Liz had concentrated on talking about Willow, glad they could ignore what had happened in Clem's study, yet amazed too at his coolness; she could only suppose that he was practised at it.

Was she too becoming practised at lying? It had been surprisingly easy pretending to Don that she had been to see Moira in London, inventing conversations, non-existent quibbles about the book.

"I can't go to the Midlands *this* weekend," he said pointedly; and Liz realised that she had committed the unforgivable; she had forgotten that he had been called back to Yarnest for a further interview.

"I'm sorry — your final interview. I forgot."

"I thought I'd stay over the whole weekend. I sort of hoped you'd be coming with me, and that we could look at houses."

His attempt to look unruffled failed, and Liz felt horribly guilty.

"Willow's so keen to go to Noonby straight away. How can I disappoint her?"

"You can't. Of course not. We can

look at houses another weekend."

"Will you see Pamela while you're in Norfolk?" Liz said lightly.

To her surprise, his colour deepened.

"I noticed she sent you a postcard." Going through the post at the Lodge one morning, Liz had found the card with his former girlfriend's neat handwriting and signature. "It was good to see you and to get your letter . . . Pam." A cartoon of Bugs Bunny had filled the front. A shared joke?

"We bumped into one another." He laughed to show how coincidental it had been. "She's back home, got a job in Norwich."

Liz nodded. It was, of course, perfectly innocent, whereas she . . .

"I'll ring after the interview," he said before he left that Friday. "Or you can catch me at Poll and Bill's."

She gave him Noonby's telephone number.

* * *

Liz set off for Meadowfields early after lunch, wanting to reach the Midlands,

617

settle Willow into their hotel, and make sure she was rested before the ordeal of Noonby. It was going to be an ordeal in more senses than one, Liz realised, however much she persuaded herself that meeting Lewis again would be fine, and all she had to do was concentrate on Willow.

It occurred to Liz that she was relying on Lewis to make the visit a success, and reminded herself that this visit was her responsibility. If it went wrong, she was the one to blame.

Willow had been waiting in the lounge, keeping a watchful eye on her suitcase by the wall; she was alert to Liz's mood as she helped her into the car.

"Nervous?"

"Not if you're not," Liz said, giving her arm a squeeze.

"Have a nice time, dear." The nursing sister turned to Liz, "I do think a little holiday does them a world of good. Takes them out of themselves."

"Silly bitch," Willow said, as Liz got in beside her and started the engine. She waved regally from the window, "I told her I was going to see my father.

She said, "I'm sure your father must be in his grave by now, dear," as if I were half-witted. How did she know my father was not stuck in some twilight home waiting for his telegram from the Queen, or with it already framed on the mantelpiece?"

"She didn't think. That's all," Liz said patiently.

"Some people have nothing to think with."

Liz hoped it was not one of Willow's days for doing battle. She imagined rows with the hotel staff, a personality clash with Lewis tomorrow, a disastrous time at Noonby.

But Willow was in a good mood by the time they reached the motorway. Wearing a green costume, with a fox fur collar that Liz suspected was real, she sat with her feet neatly crossed, clutching an expensive leather bag on her lap. She was in a conversational frame of mind, and conducted a running criticism of the other drivers along the road.

"How's the book?" she said after a while.

"Just tidying up the loose ends."

She had found a sense of security, a return to normality in getting on with the text, but Lewis's challenge that she had avoided the erotic aspects of her subject had echoed in her mind, subtly forcing her to re-examine the conclusions she had planned.

"How's your young man by the way?" asked Willow.

Liz's attention jerked at the question. She told her about Don's second interview. Breaking it gently, she let Willow know that she had said she would marry him.

"You mean, if he gets the job you'll be leaving for Norfolk?"

"I suppose we will."

Willow did not pursue the subject. She began humming to herself softly, a tune that sounded vaguely French, and Liz, remembering the Left Bank of Paris, found herself telling Willow how she had been carried away by the idea of Daisy managing to run a home life with a child as well as a demanding business, and how seductive had been the mood of that last evening in Paris before she and Don returned home.

Glancing at her shrewdly, Willow turned her attention to the traffic. "Look at that!" she said, as a driver passed them at speed and cut in closely. "Maniac!"

"Did you ever drive, Willow?" Liz asked.

"Only a bike," Willow said, remembering the bicycle Clem had bought her one Christmas during the war. "Daisy drove though. She learned in an Austin Seven. She drove with great confidence, very erratically and very fast."

Her voice tailed off, and Liz was aware of an absence of bitterness; but when she turned her head, she saw that Willow's expression was sombre. Of course — Daisy had died in a car accident. Was she remembering? It was something they had not yet talked about.

"Albert drove," Willow said after a while. "He had several cars over the years," she continued as if talking to herself.

She paused. "I haven't told you all of it. You know that?"

Liz tightened her grip on the wheel. Why had she assumed she knew all there was to Daisy's story.

"Do you *want* to tell me?"

"I'm not sure."

Willow was silent for a while. "Did I ever say how I met Albert?"

20

WILLOW had been living in a modern, simply furnished apartment building in North London after the end of the war. Her mother's life was one of clutter, and Willow had wanted a change: clean lines, white walls, spaces to be filled with things of her own choosing or else left empty.

Her mother was learning to drive, there had been a car parked outside the flat one day when Willow went to see her. "It's mine," Daisy said. "I thought it would be useful to have a little runabout." She talked vaguely these days of going back to Paris, and said that she had written to Mme Bresil, but she made no move towards leaving, and seemed content with a small regular clientele in London.

The journey north was uplifting after London's landscape of skeleton buildings, bomb-sites and dust blowing about everywhere. The railway passed fields and farmsteads, clusters of villages that seemed to have been untouched by the war, and woods tinted red and gold in the sun.

The area around Leicester had not been hit as badly as some, Kirby Langton hardly at all. Beatty — the only person Willow could think of who might talk to her freely — had been happy to chat about her youth in Kirby Langton, and to reminisce about Clem.

"He was such a beautiful man when he was younger," she had said. "Your mother and I were both in love with him."

Willow had listened as the woman chattered on about the old days, how her mother had been young and cheeky, and had gatecrashed a party at Noonby Hall. Willow's imagination had leaped. All that talk about a wealthy background — and Maman had actually been a corsetmaker?

She had not told Daisy about going to the Midlands in search of her family. She and Daisy had little to say to one another any more. It was the shabby secrecy of her mother's life that hurt the most, Willow realised. The fact that she had hidden the truth from her with stories.

Beatty had given her the name of the street Daisy's family had lived in, but had not known the house number.

Morton Street remained unscathed by the bombing. The houses here opened directly on to the pavements, with no front gardens, and there were children playing in the street; a group of them had fastened a rope round one of the lampposts and they were using it as a crude swing, shouting to one another with shrill voices. Willow tried to imagine Daisy growing up there, living in one of the dingy houses, and going to work each day in a factory. She walked uneasily towards the children, conscious of being in alien country.

"Nobody round here called Cornforth, not so far as I know," said one of the boys, chewing gum at the side of his mouth in imitation of some American film idol.

"There was an old lady used to live at number thirty," volunteered one of the older children. "But she's dead now."

"Was she called Cornforth?"

"I think so. She was Mrs White's sister."

Deciding that this information was better than nothing, Willow followed the house numbers to number thirty.

There were net curtains at the front window and the step was marked with a chalked edge. A black saloon car parked by the kerb seemed out of keeping with its surroundings.

The door to the house opened at the same time as Willow raised her hand to the knocker, revealing a man in a striped suit and a raincoat who smiled at her and raised his hat.

"There's a sight for sore eyes for a man on his way out with a flea in his ear."

"I beg your pardon?"

"I guess you know what it's like."

Willow stared at him, feeling bewildered. He was good-looking, in a tough, flashy kind of way, with an overt attraction that reminded her of the men she had once practised flirting with at her finishing school in France.

"You *are* the district visitor?" he said.

"No."

"Not from the Council, come to see Mrs White?"

"I don't even know who Mrs White is."

"She's in a cranky mood." He grinned. "Told me to get out and not come back and mind not to tread on the step as I go." He looked down at his feet. "She's very house proud."

"I see."

"Who are you then?"

"My name is Willow. Willow Carr."

"From?"

"It's complicated." Willow hesitated. "I'm looking for my relatives who used to live in Morton Street. But, if Mrs White is cross, as you say, she may not want to talk to me."

"It's a strong possibility." He looked at her speculatively. "Will I do instead?"

"Do you live here?" Willow's glance fell on the car.

"Used to do twenty years ago. I come back regularly to see my mother."

"Mrs White."

He nodded.

"My mother's name was Daisy Cornforth," Willow said.

He stared at her, shocked out of his air of self-confident worldliness. "You don't say?"

"You knew her?"

He held out his hand. "I'm her cousin Albert."

★ ★ ★

They drove to a café in Kirby Langton's High Street and sat at a table in the window. She watched him fetch two cups of tea from the counter; he was, she guessed, around forty.

He sat opposite her, looking at her without speaking at first.

"I'm a bit stunned," Albert said. "Where has your mother been all these years?"

She told him briefly about their life in Paris.

"Are you French?"

"Sort of."

"I thought so. You've got the accent." He leaned back in his chair. "Fancy you popping up like that, Daisy's daughter. She's become a bit of a family myth. To be honest, I hardly remember her. Fancy her living all that time in Paris. I ought to be asking you all sorts of questions, I suppose, but it's hard to know where to start. You probably know a fair bit about us already."

"No." Willow said. "My mother has told me nothing at all about her family."

"You mean she's ashamed to?" He laughed, then saw Willow's puzzled expression. "You don't know? Her father once threw her out of the house, said she wasn't fit to live in Morton Street. Well, Willow — Miss Carr — I wish John Cornforth could have lived to see you, that's all. That would have given him something to think about."

"My grandfather is dead?"

He nodded. "Your grandmother too. My Auntie Letty. She just about brought me up when I was little."

"Were there others? Did my mother have brothers and sisters?"

"There was Wilfred, he turned religious; and Minnie, she's doing all right for herself in London. They don't keep in touch. Sidney was the youngest, killed in North Africa."

"I'm sorry."

Clem's son had been in North Africa too, thought Willow. She would like to tell this nice, easygoing stranger about Clem.

"Sidney was the only one who stayed close," said Albert. "His wife was killed in an air raid with their little girl. I was in Egypt when I heard about it. Sidney's wife and my wife were friends."

"I'm sorry," Willow heard herself saying again, but, though she tried hard, she could not feel that any of these people — aunts, uncles, cousins — had anything to do with her own life.

"Daisy never knew her youngest brother," Albert continued. "She left home before Sidney was born. The bomb dropped smack on the house where his wife was with their young baby. The tramlines outside were thrown right up into the air."

"And your wife?" Willow asked cautiously.

"She ran off with a Yank. We're divorced."

She recoiled in shock. "But that's terrible."

"You're dead right, it was terrible."

"Don't you care?"

"Of course I bloody care. She took our son with her." He lit a cigarette and offered her one. "How old are you?"

"Twenty-five."

"Are you married?"

"No."

"How did you spend your war?"

She told him about the work at High Farm. "I'm living in London again now. My mother's talking about going back to France and starting up her fashion business again."

"Will you go with her?"

"Back to Paris? I don't know." Reluctant to talk about the rift between them, Willow limited herself to, "My mother and I don't get on very well."

"Does she approve of this — you coming back here?"

"She doesn't know. There are some parts of her life she wants to forget."

"Don't we all?"

★ ★ ★

He drove her around Kirby Langton, showing her the places Daisy would have

631

known, and the factory where she once worked.

"Take me to Noonby Hall," Willow said on impulse. "Please. I've heard about it. I would so much like to see it."

He glanced at her curiously, but said nothing as they drove out of town.

Leaving the car, Willow was overwhelmed by a sense of recognition. It was the dream of her childhood: the acres of estate, the house with a clock tower in the middle, the stables, fields and gardens.

A group of people was gathered at the front of the house. A car started up in the distance and voices drifted on the autumn air. In a moment, the vehicle would drive towards her. And yet, thought Willow, the people here were all wrong; they were called Brackenborough, not Carr; if they knew about her at all it would be as that other beneficiary of Clem's will; had they too speculated on the reasons, decided not to dig too deeply?

The car sped on towards her and, panicking, Willow turned back to where

Albert waited, parked by the grass verge.

"Let's go."

They drove away from Noonby and into Kirby Langton again. Albert glanced at her from time to time, but still said nothing.

"Letty went downhill pretty badly after Daisy left home," he ventured after a while. "It just about broke her heart. That — and all the talk."

"Talk?"

Suddenly embarrassed, he did not answer; but she sensed he had said it deliberately.

He began talking then about Daisy's parents, how they had met as servants. Pulling the car into the kerb, he said, "Why did you want to go to Noonby?"

She looked at him, feeling instinctively that she could trust him, and that he was warm and sympathetic. Willow told him everything she knew, and all she had thought she knew, and when she had finished it was growing dark.

"It was public knowledge that something had happened between her and Brackenborough. I remember all the talk when I was a child," Albert said.

"But Maman insists that it happened years before I was born. Could their affair have lasted all that time, do you think?"

"Could be. Nobody knew where she went after she left Kirby."

"She never married," Willow said. "If she and Clem were in love when they were young, why didn't they marry?"

"A Brackenborough marrying a Cornforth?" He started the car again. "Hardly the thing. Bad form."

* * *

Daisy lay on the settee in a fuchsia silk dressing gown with a flowered turban covering her hair; one foot was raised on a cushion in a balletic pose, one hand caressed the pile of the carpet.

"So, you met young Albert. My God, he must be forty now. Did he drag out the dirty family washing for you?"

Recognising that Daisy had been drinking, Willow went to the cocktail cabinet and closed the door. Since she had moved out, her mother had descended into bouts of self-pity that

634

seemed increasingly laced with alcohol.

"Albert told me what he knew about you and Clem."

"He didn't know anything. He was only a child at the time."

"*Could* you have married Clem?"

"Clem was a Brackenborough. I was the woman who made his sister's clothes. He gave in to family pressures."

"He wasn't like that," Willow said contemptuously. Her mother was cold-hearted, a liar, incapable of loving anyone deeply.

"It's true. You didn't know him."

"Thanks to you," Willow said bitterly. "If it had been left to you, I would never even have known about Morton Street."

"You wouldn't *want* to have known. You, my girl, are an ungrateful wretch. I pulled myself out of Morton Street by my own efforts. I didn't need Clem or anyone else. If you had seen what it was like, growing up in a back street, sharing a bed with my little sister, hating my father." Daisy went to the cocktail cabinet and, pushing Willow aside, poured herself a gin, though her head ached from drinking most of the afternoon. "I suppose Albert's told you a pack of lies."

"He wants to meet you."

"The little boy with his arse out of his pants who was always hanging round our house? Never."

"He remembers you more kindly. He's a nice man. I'm sure your mother was a nice woman."

"Nice? Nice — what do you know?" Daisy said bitterly.

"About families? Very little. I never had one. I was always away at boarding school."

"I sent you away for your own good. I worked hard, so that you wouldn't have to live the way I had done. I *had* to work. Not slaving in a factory — but I had to do something worthwhile, make something of myself for both our sakes. For you security. For me dignity, being true to myself."

Willow clapped her hands sardonically. "A good performance, Maman. *Toujours fidèle à toi-même.*"

★ ★ ★

636

Albert wrote a few days later to say he had been in touch with Wilfred and Minnie. He enclosed their replies.

"I thought it only fair to be honest with you."

"I'm sorry. It must have been disappointing for you," he said later, speaking on the telephone. "Maybe it's as well not to pursue it if they genuinely feel they don't want to see you. They remember what it was like better than I do . . . If you feel like coming north again, I'd be pleased to show you around. There's some very pretty country round here. Of course, if you'd rather not, I understand — "

★ ★ ★

He took her over the company where he worked as a partner in a three-man enterprise; advertising was the thing to be in these days, he said with conviction, raising his voice above the noise of the printing press.

He collected his hat, and they walked out to his car.

"Where shall we go?"

637

Suddenly, Willow found herself less interested in touring the places connected with her mother's childhood than in the fact that he was pleased to show her around.

"Anywhere. Let's simply drive, and then walk."

Almost from the beginning, Willow found herself falling in love. There was no one she would rather spend time with, walking the country lanes and footpaths around Leicester and Kirby Langton; no one she had ever found so easy to talk to.

She did not know if Albert felt the same, until, parting from her at the station one weekend that winter, he said, caressing her arm, "I think I should come to London and see Daisy. This is getting serious for me. How about getting married?"

★ ★ ★

Daisy was dressed to go out, in a blue costume cut longer than had been fashionable for a while, with a waisted jacket, her own design. A little curved hat rested on one of the chairs beside a pair of gloves and a clutch bag. The room was cluttered as always, with tapestried cushions on the sofa, and tumblers, books, and ashtrays full of cigarette ends littering the table.

"You're thinking of what?"

"Getting married."

"But he's a relative!"

"Hardly at all. He's your cousin, not mine."

"He's too old. You hardly know him."

"He doesn't seem at all old to me. I love him. We're going to get married, and he wants to come here to see you, and tell you to your face."

"You must be mad. You think I brought you up for this, to have you throw away everything I've ever done for you?"

Daisy was close to hysteria. Albert was a no-hoper, a child she remembered in hand-me-down clothes. How could Willow even contemplate becoming part of the world she had tried so hard to escape? All her efforts to raise herself had come full circle back to Morton Street? The irony was too dreadful.

"He's a business man, Maman. He's made something of his life, exactly as you did — "

"How dare you! How dare you compare Maison Clem with anything Albert White might have achieved!"

A thought struck her. "He's forty. Why isn't he married already?"

"He's divorced."

"A divorcé!"

Daisy was having nothing to do with the situation. She 'forbade' the relationship. Pretending to herself that it would go away, she reached for a cigarette and took a long time over the small actions involved in lighting up. She blew out a cloud of smoke. "You are coming with me to Paris. We always knew we would go back to Paris after the war was over."

"I'm going to marry Albert," Willow told her patiently. "You've got to accept the idea."

"Paris is where I've always felt we belonged," Daisy continued, ignoring her. "And now that some of the restrictions have been lifted — "

"I wish you'd stop this. As far as I'm concerned, Maison Clem is over and done with."

"Don't be disrespectful." Frowning, Daisy puffed at her cigarette. "If there's one thing I always had from you and the other girls, it was respect."

"That was then, Maman."

"Maison Clem will be a name again when I get back to Paris. I have written to Mme Bresil. Everything is still as it was. We only have to open. People will remember. Alex always said, if there's one thing you do well, Marguerite — "

"You've done nothing well," Willow said in exasperation. "You've made a disaster out of your entire life."

The words were unkind, and untrue, Daisy told herself. But they came back to her after Willow had gone, and she went to the cocktail cabinet and poured herself the gin she needed.

"If there's one thing you do well, Marguerite," Alex had said. What was it? What did she do well? Dear Alex. He had been in love with her. She should have married him, and then none of the rest of it would have happened.

641

Clem wouldn't have come looking for her. Willow wouldn't have turned into an ungrateful daughter.

Daisy glanced up and caught a glimpse of herself in the mirror on the wall opposite — a woman of a certain age. She was putting on weight, she acknowledged, smoothing her hands over her waist; she needed a firmer corset. A deep sense of panic swept over her. Was it all too late? Was there anything left for her in Paris these days?

She sat on the sofa, too depressed now to go out. She heard laughter in the street from the young people who lived in the flats opposite.

How she envied the young. It was all very well wearing make-up to cover the lines, and corsets to hold back excess flesh, but how she envied Willow for being twenty-five.

Was she *really* going to marry Albert White? Daisy shuddered, remembering her mother with her arms to the elbows in the kitchen sink. That would be Willow's life from now on.

And yet, what if Albert really had

achieved something? How much worse, in a way, that would be. She had been the one who had ambition, the one with the ideas and the imagination to escape. Albert, her mother, Minnie — even Wilfred — belonged, and should have stayed, where she had left them, in Morton Street.

★ ★ ★

"She is so selfish," Willow said. "She knows I'm worried about her. All this talk about going back to Paris is simply to make me worry about her even more. I really don't know if she's capable of setting up Maison Clem again."

"What can you do? If she won't accept what's happening — "

"She's got to," Willow said miserably. "I have to make her."

At last, tired of the battles, Willow left London and went to live in Leicester.

"I don't know why I didn't break free properly before," she told Albert. "I seem to have been under her spell for so long. That's how she affects people, one becomes a part of Maman's plans."

643

She found herself a flat close to Albert's office, and joined the company, typing letters, and learning the various stages of the printing processes.

"She'll come round," Albert kept telling Willow. "Give her a little time, then we'll go and see her and talk to her about the wedding."

Willow knew he was wrong. Maman was not like that, she did not forgive opposition.

★ ★ ★

Daisy was working when Willow went to London in the spring to see her. The table was covered with sheets of paper, sketches and scrawled notes, the obligatory glass of gin and packet of cigarettes close to hand.

"You're designing again?" Willow said in surprise, picking up one of the drawings. The style was that of her mother's youth, with tight waists and curves.

"Don't touch anything." Daisy began counting sheets, gathering them into a pile.

644

"But that's marvellous. I'm so pleased."

"Why? Because it makes you feel less guilty?"

Willow sighed. "No, Maman. I want you to be happy."

Daisy did not answer, frowning as if she had mislaid something, holding the sketches against her breast. She was dressed in a pair of blue slacks and a silk blouse, her hair looked as if it needed washing.

"Are you well?" Willow said.

"I haven't been."

"You should have let me know. You have my telephone number."

"What use will the telephone be when I'm in Paris and you're in Leicester? Are you going to come flying across the Channel every time I feel unwell?"

Willow placed an envelope on the table. "Here's your invitation."

"I'm too busy for parties."

"I mean, an invitation to our wedding."

Daisy gripped the table for support. "He's only after what he can get, you know." She would not look at the card. "He's only after the money Clem left you."

645

"I don't think so. I'm investing it in his company."

"Are you crazy?" Daisy threw her a look of pitying scorn.

★ ★ ★

How she disliked sherry — it gave her heartburn — but she was out of gin and needed something to blot out thoughts of Willow and Albert, and everything else she didn't want to think about, until only the good times slid through her mind. Clem sitting on the workroom table while she sewed. She could imagine it if she half closed her eyes. The hum of the sewing machine, the rattle of the treadle, she could almost summon up the smell of oil and of the new fabrics. It had been such a pleasure to be working in those days.

She poured herself another glass of the sherry, sweet and sickly, and sat at the table, a blank sheet of sketching paper in front of her, but she did not pick up her pen.

Why was Willow so difficult? There had been a time, during the war, when they had enjoyed being together. She needed her again now, to help her run Maison Clem. It was so lonely with no one at all: Clem gone, Sabine in America, Alex talking now of marrying some French woman he had met in Algiers. There was only Beatty left, offering a friendship she did not want.

Going to the window, Daisy cradled the glass in her hands. Rain was falling into the foggy stillness. The night Clem came looking for her it had been snowing, she remembered. A middle-aged man, no longer the lovely boy she had adored. The snowflakes had clung to his face and had melted there, and he had shown her photographs of his children.

She pressed her head to the glass and could hear someone whistling in the street.

Doubts came to mind about the course her life had taken. Had it all been so worthwhile? Her work was all she knew, she told herself, all she had ever wanted. Once she got back to Paris and started designing seriously again, everything would fall into its proper place.

The whistling was louder somewhere below her on the pavement. Had someone come to see her? Daisy opened the window and leaned out. A man pushing a hand trolley trudged through the rain from block to block, delivering newspapers.

He looked up, seeing the light from the window and her figure silhouetted against it.

"You all right, dear?" he shouted.

"Yes. Quite all right," Daisy said with dignity. She closed the window and pulled the curtains across it.

"Dear!" she repeated contemptuously. As if she were already an old woman.

Sitting at the table, she looked through the drawings she had done that day. They were exciting. There was a thrill in taking off in a new direction. She had been out of the fashion scene for far too long, and had hated the 'utility' fashions during the war. But at last there was a feeling of being part of it all again, because her era was back, exciting, feminine, provocative: people were returning to an elegance and sophistication that everyone thought had vanished long ago.

Dior's 'New Look' was in all the fashion journals: skirts flaring round the calves, cinched-in corseted waists, and yards and yards of material. Women wanted romance again after so much austerity.

Daisy began drawing, pushing her finished sketches around the table, allocating them different positions and discarding some altogether. From time to time she refilled her glass from the sherry bottle, until she began to feel very drunk, a signal to call it a day and undress for bed.

She could hear a car pulling up outside. Someone tooted a horn, and Daisy's thoughts flew at once to the Poplars, remembering Clem coming to fetch her and Beatty for the races. Oh, she thought with pleasure. Some of it had been such fun.

The car horn sounded more insistently, and going unsteadily to the window Daisy opened the curtains.

The car was parked in the street; its occupants called out to her, laughing. "Come on. You're late."

"I'm coming," Daisy murmured. "But

I need to know who you are."

If she was going to the trouble of dressing for a party, she must be sure it was worth the effort. She had an invitation, she remembered, and searched for Willow's envelope among her papers. She found it and returned to the window.

The catch was hard to move, heavy and obstinate under her hands. Swinging the window open with a jerk she leaned out, trying to identify the people around the vehicle.

The driver had not left his seat. She could see the end of his cigarette glowing in the darkness, and one gloved hand gripping the steering wheel. His companions called out again:

"We'll have to go without you if you don't get a move on."

The driver climbed out now, and stood in the road, his hands thrust deep into the pockets of his coat. Clem? Daisy grasped at the window handle for support, feeling the darkness pull her towards the scene below. She tried to call out again, did not want them to leave without her, before she could attract their attention.

Leaning further from the window, not

noticing the young couple leave the building opposite, Daisy grew giddy as the rain wet her face. "Clem? Is that you?"

The young couple moved into the lamplight and started to cross the street, and with a cry of alarm Daisy felt the window catch slip from her hand. She saw the lights of the car, the world turning upside down and the driver's face lifted towards her, his expression frozen in a half-smile.

21

"**Y**OU said she was killed in a car accident."

"I lied." Willow sat very upright, staring ahead through the windscreen. "Like mother, like daughter. A half lie, anyway."

"But why?"

"I suppose — because it sounded better."

They drove in silence for a while.

"I began to think that she had done it on purpose, to make me feel guilty, to stop me getting married. Oh, all sorts of ideas went through my mind."

"Do you really think it could have been suicide?"

"She had been drinking. I know she was depressed. Maman always did something dramatic when she couldn't get her own way. I hated her then, more than I'd ever hated her before. After a while, I blocked it out altogether. I convinced myself none of it had ever happened. No Daisy, no Clem. Albert was all that existed for me from then on. We never discussed it."

"Until I arrived with her photograph."

"She had cut my father out of my life. I did the same with her. Daisy became what she had always wanted to be: Marguerite, Paris couturière, a minor fashion legend."

"Where is she buried?"

"In Kirby Langton churchyard. It's funny really. If you or anyone else in the family had gone there, you would have found the grave quite easily, next to Letty and John Cornforth's grave. Her name is on the stone. 'Daisy Cornforth'. At the time, I felt a perverse pleasure in seeing her brought back to her roots."

"How do you feel about her now?"

Willow glanced at Liz sideways. "I'm glad she died when she did. She could never have tolerated going through what I am now, growing old, getting more feeble. In her case, getting fatter and more cantankerous."

"So — you've forgiven her?" Liz said cautiously.

Willow did not answer, becoming vague again.

"How much farther is it? Aren't we nearly there?"

★ ★ ★

The gates to Noonby stood wide open to the public. Coaches and cars were parked in the distance, the sun glinting off metal roofs lined up in rows. Liz pulled into the lay-by and turned to Willow, who had clutched involuntarily at her arm.

"We don't have to do this, if you don't want to," Liz reassured her.

Willow shook her head. "No. Drive on."

"You'll like Lewis. He's — " Liz had been going to say, "Not at all like Don," but realised this was more than a touch disloyal and changed it to, "He's very nice."

She thought of her phone call to Don the previous evening, and his jubilation because he had, as they expected, got the job at Yarnest; she recalled more clearly her poor effort to sound pleased. He

654

had noticed, and the conversation had become strained.

Liz put the car into gear.

"I was just . . . " Willow began, and tailed off; and Liz assumed she had forgotten what she was going to say. But, seeing the frontage of Noonby loom closer, Willow was remembering the last time she had been there, the moment of panic, the need to escape because she did not belong. "I suppose we only feel happy with ourselves when we have faced up to things."

"That sounds very profound."

"True though." Willow hummed softly to give herself courage. "This Lewis — my nephew. Will he make a lot of fuss?"

"No, he's not that sort of person."

Liz parked the car among the others to the side of the house. "I told you. He's very nice."

★ ★ ★

She had forgotten quite how nice, until he appeared as they waited for him at the pay desk. He was wearing a pullover

655

and cords, smiling as he came down the main stairs to meet them.

"Is that him?" Giving her a meaningful nudge in the ribs, Willow said, "You ought to marry him."

"What?" Liz was startled.

"Marry him. He fits. He's the one. Take my word for it."

"I'm marrying Don," Liz hissed under her breath, hoping none of the desk staff had heard, and that Willow would have the discretion to keep her thoughts to herself once Lewis himself came within earshot.

He walked towards them. "Hello," he said, still smiling. He was nervous, thought Liz, because of Willow — or did he too find it difficult to dismiss the memory of Clem's sofa?

"You must be Clem's daughter."

Liz flashed him a look of congratulation. He had hit exactly the right note. No mention of Daisy. This visit was about Willow and Clem.

"And how are you, Liz?" His eyes held the merest hint of a question as to whether she was relaxed about everything.

"She talks about you all the time," said Willow, and, to Liz's horror, trod heavily on her toe and gave her another nudge. "You made quite an impression, young man."

Lewis pretended not to notice. "Where shall we start? The family portrait gallery, do you think?"

"Oh yes," said Willow. "But let's save Clem until last." She beamed at him, suddenly flirtatious. "We'll keep the best to the end."

Tourists glanced at them as they climbed the stairs, assuming that Willow, in her fur-collared costume and hat, clinging to Lewis's arm, was some visiting celebrity.

They passed from portrait to portrait, Lewis explaining the history of each family member as he had done months ago with Liz. From time to time he glanced round to see if she was following. He threw her a smile, which Liz returned self-consciously, watching him from her position as Willow's minder when he moved on. She was reminded again of how alien his background was: the country house setting, the privileged world of money and birth and sense of leisured history.

"And this is Clem when he was a boy," Lewis said, halting in front of the painting of a child on a pony.

"It could be me at that age," Willow said. "I had that look, sullen, awkward. I didn't like having my photograph taken."

She turned to the painting of Clem in his forties. "That's how I remember him. He bought me a bicycle, you know, during the war. He was very kind, but never told me he was my father. He should have said." She turned to Lewis with an air of childlike trust. "Don't you think so?"

Liz glanced at Willow anxiously, recognising a vagueness, a disorientation in her manner. Over the next months or years, would such moments of uncertainty creep closer? What if Willow's mental state was already more fragile than she had supposed, and coming to Noonby proved to be too much for her?

"I guess Clem did what he thought was best," Lewis answered gently.

"Best for Daisy, you mean. She had him under her thumb. Everyone always did exactly what she wanted."

"Would you like to see the other painting now?"

Willow nodded. She walked carefully, holding Lewis's arm, as if the ability to put one foot in front of the other might at any moment elude her. They proceeded to Lewis's photography room and, closing the door, turned to face the portrait of Clem as a young man.

Watching for Willow's reaction, Liz was aware that Lewis did the same, resting a hand on her arm as if sharing the responsibility.

Willow said nothing for a while, then, "It's good. You can tell he must really have looked like that."

She did not move.

"Well — " she added, turning away at last, with a sniff of resignation rather than emotion. "You can see why it all happened, can't you? He was very good-looking."

Liz released a sigh of relief. It was going to be all right.

Willow walked about the room, touching things and looking out of the window. She turned to Liz.

"You asked me if I'd forgiven her. I suppose I have. I suppose she did the best she was capable of."

"Isn't that all anyone can hope for?" asked Lewis.

In theory she could go home now, thought Liz, aware of a strong sense of anti-climax. Nothing left but to take Willow back to Meadowfields, put away Daisy's picture in a drawer, and finish the book. What were the lessons to be learned? Don't make mistakes? Don't deliberately, perversely, make the wrong choices?

Moving away from Lewis and Willow, Liz noticed a stack of mounted photographs on the table.

"May I — ?"

He nodded.

To her surprise, they were nearly all shots of the rose garden where she had taken some pictures at Easter.

"Are these recent?"

"I wanted to do a series, showing the garden in different seasons. The last of them will be under snow."

"It doesn't snow these days like it used to," commented Willow. "You should have been around in the forties."

"We should," agreed Lewis. "We might have met Daisy and Clem for ourselves, instead of having to imagine how it all was."

Liz was not listening. Lewis's photographs threw a tension over what ought to have been the conclusion of her quest. Why had he chosen to photograph the rose garden where, according to his grandmother, Clem had kissed Daisy, and then given in to family pressure?

A clock struck downstairs. It was four-thirty. Noonby's visitors had begun leaving.

"You don't have to go straight away, do you?" Lewis said. "Stay for tea. We'll have it in the rose garden."

"The rose garden?" Liz said uneasily. She felt trapped, but told herself she was being totally irrational.

"That sounds a splendid idea," Willow beamed at them. "Lead the way."

They sat on a bench, munching scones and drinking tea, and the sun bore down on them, heating the red brick of the high walls.

"Shall we go for a walk?" Lewis stood

and looked at Liz, indicating the gravel paths.

Moving slowly, waving to Willow as they reached the far corner of the garden and looking back to where she sat in the sunshine, Liz told Lewis how Daisy had died, falling from a window after a bout of drinking.

"If it was suicide — it was quite some revenge on her daughter for not doing as she wanted," he commented.

"We'll never know for sure. We're still left with a mystery, aren't we?" Liz said, feeling that the story needed a conclusion.

He ignored the comment, as if his thoughts were suddenly taken up with something else.

"Norfolk is closer than Somerset," he said. "Will you bring your fiancé — sorry. You don't like the word. Will you bring your lover — to see Noonby when you're settled?"

"Perhaps not." The thought of Don coming here now seemed inappropriate.

"I like Willow," Lewis said. "I can see why you've grown fond of her. I'm sure I shall too."

"The truth is — " Liz began. She looked at him, and confessed in sudden anguish, "I don't think I can do it. How can I abandon her?"

"But if you're getting married — "

Liz began to pace the gravel path. "I feel so confused."

He hesitated. "Liz, I hope I haven't clouded the issue for you. What happened between us . . . "

"It's not you," Liz assured him quickly. "Though that has something to do with it, of course. The thing is, this whole business about Daisy has got to me. It's as if she and Clem and Willow have been trying to tell me something."

"Not to get married?"

"Yes — no. I don't know. Daisy didn't marry Clem, and look at the mess she made of things."

"People can mess up their lives in all sorts of ways."

"Oh, I'm good at that. I always have been," she said earnestly. "I can tell you, because you understand about not wanting commitment. That's probably how I should live really. I should stay independent and single. I'm not cut out for relationships. I sort of drift into things, and then I panic. What if I never get it right?"

"What does Willow say?"

Liz looked at him and remembered exactly what Willow had said.

"Willow tells me that if it's the right thing to do, I will know. She and Albert knew almost straight away, but that's simply luck. I mean, it happened to work out for them. It didn't for you and your wife. And I don't know if it will for me. Do you think Daisy and Clem realised they had found one another in the beginning? If they did, why didn't they marry?"

"Circumstances, class, all sorts of things got in the way for them."

"No, it wasn't only that. They got it wrong. People get things wrong."

She looked at him. He seemed to be waiting.

"Oh, why are the most important decisions in our lives so *difficult*?"

"Are they?" he said. "It seems to me you've made a decision already."

★ ★ ★

664

Liz rang Don that evening.

"I'm staying on for a few days. Willow likes it so much here." She hesitated. "She's talking of finding a residential home in the area, somewhere similar to Meadowfields, and I've said I might help her to look."

"But that's ridiculous," said Don. "How long will you be?"

"I don't know."

"I thought we could celebrate about the job — Liz, that's a crazy idea about Willow."

"Lewis thinks he could keep an eye on her. After all, he's her nephew, and he's going to be spending more time at Noonby. He's really taken to her, and she to him. Besides, if I'm going to live in Norfolk, I would only be a couple of hours or so away."

"But why should Willow want to move to the Midlands?"

"She would be near to Clem and Daisy. Daisy is buried in Kirby Langton. I'm going to see the grave tomorrow. I had this lovely idea — "

She heard his exclamation of disbelief. There were sounds in the background, music, and people laughing, as if there was a party going on.

"I thought I might plant a pot of marguerites on her grave," Liz continued. "It would be a nice kind of finishing touch."

"You are so impractical, Liz. You want to spend your entire life making sentimental gestures, instead of facing up to what matters. Doesn't it even occur to you that I might want you here."

"It sounds as if you're celebrating well enough without me."

"Aunt Poll asked a few people round."

Liz heard bursts of laughter. A thought occurred to her. "Is Pam there as well?"

His antagonism vanished. "Poll asked her. What could I do?"

"Why didn't you say?"

"I didn't want you to get the wrong idea."

"But I wouldn't — " Liz began."

"At least Pam is pleased about my getting the headship. She thinks it's a good career move. She's *interested*."

"Don — I have to go. I don't know what to say. I don't think I know about anything any more."

666

"We'd better talk about all this when you're back."

She nodded into the phone, feeling miserable. "Yes — all right. When I'm back."

★ ★ ★

"Have you finished that book?" Lewis asked as he drove towards the cemetery.

"Not yet." Liz pulled a rueful face at him in the driving mirror. "Still too many loose ends."

"Time you got them sorted out," chimed in Willow from the front seat.

"By the way — I brought this to show you at last," Liz remembered, pulling the photo of Daisy from her bag and handing it to Lewis. She added to Willow, "I thought you might like to have it."

"No. You keep it." Willow glanced at the picture, and then looked out of the window.

"We can be sure of one thing, anyway," Liz said. "Daisy would certainly have been anti-corsets when she was older."

"But she wasn't. She loved all that, the 'waspy' waist and tight little bodices," said Willow. "She wore corsets all her life."

"She was a masochist?" said Liz in dismay.

Willow looked round with a meaningful glance at Liz. "Aren't we all?"

"That is so unfair," said Liz, dwelling on the idea of Daisy subscribing to the tyranny of a corset. How could Daisy, a career woman, a rebel, a feminist in everything but name, have clung to such outmoded thinking?

"Perhaps she was a romantic," suggested Lewis.

"There's nothing very romantic about corsets."

"No?"

He gave her a look as he handed back the photograph.

* * *

Liz walked in through the gates of the cemetery with Lewis carrying a pot of marguerites. At the last minute, Willow had said she thought she would wait in the car, she had done enough digging about in her past of late.

They found the grave and that of Daisy's parents alongside it. Liz halted. What was she doing? What had she come for — to mourn? Or out of curiosity? What right did she have to investigate and speculate on other people's lives?

Liz took the marguerites from Lewis and stooped to find a place for them near the headstone with its simple inscription:

Daisy Cornforth, 1890 – 1947

"It seems so sad."

"She must have had plenty of good times as well as bad," Lewis said.

"But I can't help thinking that she could have been happier if she had done things differently."

"I think they both had the happiness that was allotted to them."

"Does the same go for everyone?"

"Oh — I think so."

She stood looking down at the flowers swaying on their stems in the light breeze. "You said you believed I had made a decision."

"And?"

"You were right."

"So, you're not going to Norfolk?"

"No. I'm not."

He smiled. "Good. I'm glad. Down with marriage and commitment."

They walked among the graves, reading the inscriptions. The sun was warm on their backs, and the bees droned among the flowers.

Liz remembered what Don had said about her wanting to spend her life being sentimental. But Don seemed far away right now, and was getting more distant with every hour she spent with Lewis and Willow.

"If there's nothing romantic about corsets," said Lewis, "how is it that Daisy's photo set you off on this trail?"

"It was her eyes — her expression."

"Don't you think it was the whole thing, the look, the period, her confidence in knowing that she was provocative, and to hell with everyone?"

"No," Liz protested. "The corset symbolised all the feminine conventions she escaped from."

"But Daisy kept — *enjoyed* her corsets."

"I know," Liz said, feeling exasperated. Why had Daisy not finished with her?

Why was she still overturning her assumptions. "I don't know what to do about the book," she said after a while. "I'm going to have to rethink some of my ideas."

"To do with female emancipation?"

She looked at him. "Yes."

They were silent, contemplative.

"Shall we go?" Lewis said suddenly.

Walking ahead along the path, a sense of recklessness made Liz swing round, and she caught the expression in Lewis's eyes before he could disguise it.

"I should have been sorry not to see you again," he admitted.

"Me too." She was aware that even those brief words had said too much.

"What are you thinking?"

Liz was remembering what Willow had said about Lewis, "He fits. He's the one." Last night, Willow had taken one look at her after her phone call to Don, and said, "I told you. Take my word for it." Here we go again, Liz told herself. Another disaster?

"Too private?" Lewis suggested.

"Oh, I think so. For now."

They walked back to the car, where

Willow was looking in her hand mirror, putting on lipstick, making a wide 'O' with her mouth.

THE END

FATAL RING OF LIGHT
Helen Eastwood

Katy's brother was supposed to have died in 1897 but a scrawled note in his handwriting showed July 1899. What had happened to him in those two years? Katy was determined to help him.

NIGHT ACTION
Alan Evans

Captain David Brent sails at dead of night to the German occupied Normandy town of St. Jean on a mission which will stretch loyalty and ingenuity to its limits, and beyond.

A MURDER TOO MANY
Elizabeth Ferrars

Many, including the murdered man's widow, believed the wrong man had been convicted. The further murder of a key witness in the earlier case convinced Basnett that the seemingly unrelated deaths were linked.

THE WILDERNESS WALK
Sheila Bishop

Stifling unpleasant memories of a misbegotten romance in Cleave with Lord Francis Aubrey, Lavinia goes on holiday there with her sister. The two women are thrust into a romantic intrigue involving none other than Lord Francis.

THE RELUCTANT GUEST
Rosalind Brett

Ann Calvert went to spend a month on a South African farm with Theo Borland and his sister. They both proved to be different from her first idea of them, and there was Storr Peterson — the most disturbing man she had ever met.

ONE ENCHANTED SUMMER
Anne Tedlock Brooks

A tale of mystery and romance and a girl who found both during one enchanted summer.

CLOUD OVER MALVERTON
Nancy Buckingham

Dulcie soon realises that something is seriously wrong at Malverton, and when violence strikes she is horrified to find herself under suspicion of murder.

AFTER THOUGHTS
Max Bygraves

The Cockney entertainer tells stories of his East End childhood, of his RAF days, and his post-war showbusiness successes and friendships with fellow comedians.

MOONLIGHT AND MARCH ROSES
D. Y. Cameron

Lynn's search to trace a missing girl takes her to Spain, where she meets Clive Hendon. While untangling the situation, she untangles her emotions and decides on her own future.

NURSE ALICE IN LOVE
Theresa Charles

Accepting the post of nurse to little Fernie Sherrod, Alice Everton could not guess at the romance, suspense and danger which lay ahead at the Sherrod's isolated estate.

POIROT INVESTIGATES
Agatha Christie

Two things bind these eleven stories together — the brilliance and uncanny skill of the diminutive Belgian detective, and the stupidity of his Watson-like partner, Captain Hastings.

LET LOOSE THE TIGERS
Josephine Cox

Queenie promised to find the long-lost son of the frail, elderly murderess, Hannah Jason. But her enquiries threatened to unlock the cage where crucial secrets had long been held captive.

THE TWILIGHT MAN
Frank Gruber

Jim Rand lives alone in the California desert awaiting death. Into his hermit existence comes a teenage girl who blows both his past and his brief future wide open.

DOG IN THE DARK
Gerald Hammond

Jim Cunningham breeds and trains gun dogs, and his antagonism towards the devotees of show spaniels earns him many enemies. So when one of them is found murdered, the police are on his doorstep within hours.

THE RED KNIGHT
Geoffrey Moxon

When he finds himself a pawn on the chessboard of international espionage with his family in constant danger, Guy Trent becomes embroiled in moves and countermoves which may mean life or death for Western scientists.

TIGER TIGER
Frank Ryan

A young man involved in drugs is found murdered. This is the first event which will draw Detective Inspector Sandy Woodings into a whirlpool of murder and deceit.

CAROLINE MINUSCULE
Andrew Taylor

Caroline Minuscule, a medieval script, is the first clue to the whereabouts of a cache of diamonds. The search becomes a deadly kind of fairy story in which several murders have an other-worldly quality.

LONG CHAIN OF DEATH
Sarah Wolf

During the Second World War four American teenagers from the same town join the Army together. Forty-two years later, the son of one of the soldiers realises that someone is systematically wiping out the families of the four men.

THE LISTERDALE MYSTERY
Agatha Christie

Twelve short stories ranging from the light-hearted to the macabre, diverse mysteries ingeniously and plausibly contrived and convincingly unravelled.

TO BE LOVED
Lynne Collins

Andrew married the woman he had always loved despite the knowledge that Sarah married him for reasons of her own. So much heartache could have been avoided if only he had known how vital it was to be loved.

ACCUSED NURSE
Jane Converse

Paula found herself accused of a crime which could cost her her job, her nurse's reputation, and even the man she loved, unless the truth came to light.

BUTTERFLY MONTANE
Dorothy Cork

Parma had come to New Guinea to marry Alec Rivers, but she found him completely disinterested and that overbearing Pierce Adams getting entirely the wrong idea about her.

HONOURABLE FRIENDS
Janet Daley

Priscilla Burford is happily married when she meets Junior Environment Minister Alistair Thurston. Inevitably, sexual obsession and political necessity collide.

WANDERING MINSTRELS
Mary Delorme

Stella Wade's career as a concert pianist might have been ruined by the rudeness of a famous conductor, so it seemed to her agent and benefactor. Even Sir Nicholas fails to see the possibilities when John Tallis falls deeply in love with Stella.

CHATEAU OF FLOWERS
Margaret Rome

Alain, Comte de Treville needed a wife to look after him, and Fleur went into marriage on a business basis only, hoping that eventually he would come to trust and care for her.

CRISS-CROSS
Alan Scholefield

As her ex-husband had succeeded in kidnapping their young daughter once, Jane was determined to take her safely back to England. But all too soon Jane is caught up in a new web of intrigue.

DEAD BY MORNING
Dorothy Simpson

Leo Martindale's body was discovered outside the gates of his ancestral home. Is it, as Inspector Thanet begins to suspect, murder?